I0818064

Heretic Behaviour

THE SECRETS OF DEMONS

E.C. GLYNN

EARTH & EMBODY PUBLISHING HOUSE

Paperback: ISBN-13:978-1-7636764-0-4

Hardback: ISBN: 978-1-7636764-1-1

ebook: 978-1-7636764-2-8

This book is dedicated to all those who feared to examine their religion too deeply – but did anyway.

To honour the bravest parts of myself.

And to my mum.

Contents

Prologue

It takes no special talent to kill a human, the High Priest Abbott mused as he watched the woman thrashing before him. *No special training or ceremony required. Any hard object swung fast enough will often do the trick...*

He stared with disgust at the struggling woman's thin black horns that were beginning to protrude from her long mass of blonde hair.

Yes, he thought. *Death is a simple thing to accomplish where humans are concerned. Demons on the other hand...*

"To die with such pageantry," he told her solemnly, "is proof your death really means something. Consider it an honour many are not afforded."

Anger and hate flashed across her pale face as she looked up at him and opened her mouth. For a moment, Abbott thought she might speak, but instead, she screamed.

He'd heard many screams in his time. Screams for mercy, screams of pain, of fear...but this scream, the High Priest Abbott instantly knew, was different.

It nearly blew out his ear drums.

The force of it opened the heavy wooden doors of the Grand Cathedral and rattled the stained-glass windows in their sockets. His spies later reported that it had defied the laws of sound completely and had spilled out onto the winter streets of Jeralusah, travelling right over the outer walls of the small Holy City.

Good. Let them all know.

Despite the unnatural power of her cry, and the pain it caused him, Abbott refused to lower the censer to block his ears, and he was pleased to see that none of the elite warrior priests who held her, his jesu, flinched either. Instead, two of them pulled the noisy demon to her feet and began to haul her forward into the main hall of the Grand Cathedral. They braced for her resistance and were not disappointed. As soon as she stood, she stopped screaming and began to thrash violently in their arms, fighting against their grip and the choking clouds of sedative incense that Abbott determinedly swirled. Despite her efforts, the jesu bore up well and continued to drag her forward.

They were professionals, and this was not their first time.

The demon's blue eyes flashed up at Abbott in helpless fury again. He noted that her horns were starting to retract into her head, and she did not scream again.

Perhaps she cannot. Perhaps her abominable power was all used up in that single moment of desperation. How pathetic.

Despite the cool winter air, her naked torso glistened as streams of sweat poured down her lithe body, and her long blonde hair clung in thick, knotted clumps to the back of her neck.

Beautiful.

The word rose unbidden in the High Priest's mind as he drew his eyes away from her and surveyed the entire sacred ceremony, the Sacrament of Contrition.

Nearly two hundred priests and acolytes who served the Church of Midas stood at attention in lines that spanned down either side of the Grand Cathedral. They hummed a low, hypnotic droll, with their heads bowed and palms pressed firmly together in reverence.

The stained-glass murals on the towering windows above them caught the winter morning sun on its entry into the hall and turned its cool light into sharp rainbow streams. The glass depicted images of Midas emerging triumphantly from the depths of the ocean and presenting himself as the One True God to the cowering folk of Artor, a pivotal moment in the Church's fresh history.

Beautiful, it was all so beautiful.

Abbott watched as his jesu pulled the demon closer to her death. The sedative smoke was finally starting to take effect, and she stumbled now, looking disorientated. He shifted his gaze from her to the God-King, who was greedily eyeing the scene, like a stalking crocodile, from upon his throne of glass and sand.

Midas seemed to sense the High Priest's gaze and glanced over at Abbott, who swiftly forced his focus back on the ceremony at hand, maintaining the rhythmic swinging of his censer and preparing for the ritual lines he would soon deliver. It was always considered improper to stare too directly at the Divine, but today, of all days, it seemed particularly voyeuristic.

"With this smoke and herb," he intoned, "I cleanse thee, demon, so that thou may be a fitting offering for our Almighty God-King. We earnestly pray that he may forgive this sinful and blasphemous world. That his wrath and anger may be appeased, and that he will look upon us for yet another season, with his Divine mercy."

The jesu had dragged the demon close enough to Midas for him to touch her now.

She had been forced to her knees again and now knelt with a face frozen in fearful intensity. The expression somehow made her simultaneously beautiful and ugly to the High Priest, and he considered it thoughtfully. The fear was very good, he conceded, but he saw considerably more fear in the eyes of the jesu who held her.

That, he mused silently, *is even better.*

The demon was one of ten sacrifices being provided by the nation of Artor to the God-King for the winter season. It was a requirement of his rule that kept even the most devout fearful and wary of a misstep.

Abbot moved behind the demon. He signalled for the humming in the Grand Cathedral to stop. Two hundred priests obeyed instantly, as if he had pinched the sound from their throats. The low droll was replaced by an eerie, heavy silence that fell over the ceremony like a smothering hand. It was a strained absence of sound, more akin to the silence of a drowning man than the peaceful silence of a sleeping baby, the kind of silence that could only be made in the moment when two hundred priests paused, waiting for their God to perform a miracle.

Midas removed his gloves and extended his palm towards the demon. His eyes unfocused the moment that he pressed a thick thumb into the centre of her forehead and his power struck the woman.

Abbott marvelled for the millionth time how incredible it was to watch someone's body transform, and how beautiful the Golden Sand looked as it glinted in the highlights of the sun on its journey to the ground.

The Heretical Behaviours

Selling One's Soul to Obtain Demon Powers.

The God-King alone holds the rights to supernatural powers and abilities. It is forbidden to accept the Devil's contract and sell one's soul to Viah in exchange for powers.

Dancing, Revelry, Festivals or Celebrations.

The nation remains in an age of contrition. This must be observed by all citizens at all times until the Divine Mercy and Forgiveness of the God-King is decreed.

Using the God-King's Name in Vain.

His name is sacred and powerful. Flippant or ill-considered use is forbidden.

Misuse of the God-King's Golden Sand.

All that is created by the God-King's holy power remains an extension of his divinity. Any use of his Golden Sand must be approved by the God-King himself. It is expressly forbidden to use it in any form of trade or financial transaction.

Idolatry.

All gods worshipped before the arrival of the Almighty God-King were false gods. Worship of any but the One True God-King is forbidden.

Disrespecting the Church.

The Church is the Arm of the God-King. It implements his will. Its authority and personnel must be respected at all times.

Harbouring a Heretic.

Any person found to be harbouring one who is known to have committed a Heretical Behaviour will be considered to be colluding in that transgression and punished.

Misconstruing Dark Age History.

It is forbidden to fondly reminisce or misconstrue the Dark Ages, especially if committed with intent to cause disruption to the rightful ascension of the God-King and his Church.

No Clemency

Three Months Later.

While Mila held her breath, she prayed that the other prisoners were all letting the smoke fill their lungs.

An acolyte was walking slowly down the line, fumigating each of the chained ikarei with the incense emitting from the large handful of herbs he held upon a brass pewter plate. Mila knew the distinctive peppery aroma of mintlock, a sedative used to dull the mind and senses. She wondered if any of the other sacrifices also knew this. She hoped they did not and were all breathing deeply.

Sedation wasn't a particularly kind thing to wish upon her fellow prisoners, but the situation was dire, and if she was going to survive this, she needed them all to stop feeling their fear so damn loudly.

Please, she silently begged them. *I need to be able to think.*

For days now, the other ikarei had been unintentionally broadcasting their emotions so intensely that Mila's power had been overwhelmed. She had been able to focus on little else, and it didn't help that she was also suffering intense withdrawal headaches from lack of access to an entirely different plant, rubane. She'd grown too used to smoking the weed and living for years in the peaceful silence of its dulling properties. Without access to it over the past four days, it felt as though her power was now spewing out from her body in an enormous, unruly wave, catching and dragging in every energetic signal in its vicinity...every plant's cry for water, every insect's determined march, every thought and reaction of any human within a hundred-foot radius. That included the deep well of hysteria and fear that her fellow prisoners had been energetically digging in their captivity.

With the mintlock incense now thick in the air, the pulsing, horrific emotions in the room were finally quelling. Mila kept her breaths small and shallow, her face turned away from the cloud of incense. Slowly, the fog in her mind began to lift. She could finally think for herself again, could finally comprehend her situation with clarity.

It was not good.

In the next few minutes, she and the other ikarei would be led out into the Grand Cathedral to kneel before the God-King, and soon after that, she'd experience exactly what it felt like to transform from her mortal body into a glowing pile of Golden Sand.

If she was going to escape this fate, she had to do something now.

She analysed the golden metal bindings that held her wrists to the collar of the man who stood before her in line. They were solid, and her arms were numb after having been clipped to the back of his neck for days. She knew she was now awkwardly dragging his head backwards, but she no longer had the strength left to try to hold them out at an angle that didn't pull at him, let alone muster the strength to somehow break the solid gold chains themselves. The one small blessing of her situation was that she was last in the row of prisoners, so there was no one behind her similarly dragging her own neck back.

After determining that physical force wasn't an option for escape, she mentally gathered the ragged edges of her scattered and disobedient power and forced it to focus on conducting a sweep of the energies within the stiflingly hot room. Like a snake flicking its tongue to taste the air, Mila let her smooth, black horns grow slightly outwards from her scalp. She didn't technically *need* them extended to use her power, but doing so helped greatly in achieving specificity, and right now, as she hunted for any nuance in sentiment or attitude that might be useful to her, specificity might be the thing that could save her.

She tried not to let it touch the other prisoners. She already knew too well exactly how they felt, and they were equally as helpless as she was. Their despair did nothing but suck at her like a delicious black mire, beckoning her to join them, to dive in and lose herself again.

No. She wrenched her power away and continued to scan for all other life in the room. There were six guards and four warrior priests, jesu they were called, escorting the chained line of sacrificial ikarei, and two guards outside the door. She ran her power over each of them, looking for anything in their energy that might help: a drop of mercy, of impatience with their work, of pride...anything at all that she could maybe, somehow, exploit to escape.

Nothing.

The dark, pulsing energy of the holy jesu who guarded them pressed gratingly against her mind, and if the guards weren't utter zealots themselves, then they were simply too full of fear to be useful. Fearful guards were as useless to her as the hot fear radiating out from the group of imprisoned ikarei she stood amongst. The intermingled energies of the room reminded her nauseatingly of the dynamic she'd once sensed between the workers and animals waiting in line at an abattoir.

She retracted the small horns back into her head and whimpered quietly when the headache returned with full force. The situation was hopeless. Perhaps she was better off sniffing the mintlock. At least then maybe she wouldn't be in pain before her death.

The heavy wooden door behind her suddenly banged open, and two more robed jesu entered the dark room. They moved towards her, inspecting her face, and Mila fought to ensure that her gaze appeared unfocused and hazy, as though she'd taken a full hit of the mintlock. It would do no harm for them to think she was dazed and docile.

There was more movement from behind her, and she started a little when the High Priest himself passed by. His shadow crossed her as he moved towards the front of the line.

"The moment has come," he intoned calmly, reciting the official damnation by heart as he walked. "By committing the First Heretical Behaviour, you have sinned in the eyes of the Church and the eyes of our Great God-King Midas."

As he spoke, the jesu unclipped her hands from the neck of the man in front. Mila gasped in pain as they dropped heavily in front of her, and blood began to rush back into the sorry limbs. Her hands remained bound, but at least they were finally pointing back towards the ground.

"Such a sin demands punishment, and our Divine Lord demands the seasonal sacrifice of ten heretics quarterly to appease his wrath. Thus, with your demonic nature revealed, your punishment has been determined by the Church, and I pronounce it now."

The two jesu were working their way up the line, unshackling the other ikarei one by one.

"You are to be immediately sacrificed at the hand of our God-King, to ensure both that justice is served and to enable our humble nation to demonstrate our enduring contrition and obedience for yet another season."

The hold of the mintlock was strong, and no one in the line moved at his proclamation, but still, a collective moan of fear and despair flowed through the group, and Mila could not help but be affected by it. She tried desperately to retain her sense of self, to remain energetically sovereign, but resisting the strength of the emotion around her was like trying to hold onto a handful of salt amidst a torrent of water.

The jesu had now reached the front of the line. They swiftly unshackled the young man who stood there. In unison, they took him by the shoulders and led him out of the small wing and out of sight, through the mosaic archway to where Mila assumed the main hall of the Grand Cathedral awaited. He stumbled along with them obediently.

She knew the moment the man reached his destination, because a deep rumbling noise suddenly filtered down the hallway and into the wing where she and the others waited. True terror contaminated her when it dawned on her that the sound was not a distant horn, but the slow, deep, tolling chant of hundreds of priests and acolytes as they observed the Sacrament. The baritone hum of their voices echoed throughout the entire cathedral, a deep and expressionless drone that merged somehow with the smoke and the dark and the overwhelming stench of despair.

"Please."

She heard the young man's sharp voice suddenly cut through the dull hum, begging.

"Please!"

Mila knew there would be no clemency.

A fresh wave of fear washed through the waiting prisoners as his pleas quickly turned into wordless scream after scream. They echoed into each other, unrelenting, ceaseless, until the moment that his voice was abruptly, sickeningly, cut off.

Mila desperately tried to retain her sense of calm amidst the tide of panic swiftly rising around her. Despite the fact she'd avoided the full force of the initial dose, the residual essence of the mintlock still hung in the air and was making the sensitivity of her power worse, dampening any ability she still retained to block out the anguish of her fellow prisoners.

She had to do something.

She desperately flung her power out again and this time, as it rounded the outskirts of the room, she found something new.

Previously, she'd felt the energies of two guards positioned outside the door but...no longer. There was a noticeable lack of human energy in the spaces those two bodies had once occupied. They were gone.

She did not think, did not breathe, did not pause to question her next move. The other guards and jesu in the room were momentarily facing towards the archway, their attention drawn in the opposite direction by the young man's screams. This opportunity might never come again.

Mila took three steps backwards, slid the door open a crack with her fingertips, slipped through it and ran.

Run.

The tunnel was beautiful but Mila barely acknowledged the green and blue stained-glass that spidered out across the curved roof in all directions. She turned to the left and ran, not knowing where she was going but praying she'd stumble across an empty room, or even just a dark corner to hide in. She was weakened from days of imprisonment and knew that, despite the athleticism she'd cultivated by living in the rainforest, right now she wouldn't outlast a chase. Her only hope was to hide and perhaps slink to safety when the focus of the search went elsewhere.

Her feet pounded along the dark grey stones, and she held her bound wrists to her chest awkwardly as she ran. The sunlight glimmering in from the stained-glass above her created blotted streams of aquamarine that pooled down from the roof onto the floor, and she stumbled swiftly through this haze of colour, a tiny brown leaf tumbling in whirling floodwaters of light. She extended her horns as she ran, throwing her power out before her in the hope of giving herself even one second of warning before she barrelled into anyone.

Unbelievably, it seemed that there was no soul in front of her. Behind her, however, angry shouts suddenly rang out, and she heard a heavy door slam, followed by the sounds of running feet.

They were after her.

Her adrenaline surged and she pushed on until she came to the first deviation in the hallway, a narrow, winding staircase that was built into the left-hand wall. It went both up and down.

In the split second she had to make the decision, she chose down. She hurtled down the stairs, not worrying about falling and breaking her neck. A broken neck would be a blessing compared to the fate that awaited her if they caught her. She left the light of the beautiful tunnel behind her and descended into the darkness below.

It took her eyes a moment to adjust when she hit the stone floor. She blinked rapidly as she stumbled forward, throwing her bound hands out blindly and praying there was nothing in her way that she could run into.

Up ahead, she saw a tiny sliver of light. She stumbled towards it. Perhaps it was a window or door in the distance? But as she drew closer, she realised it was a simple oil lantern that had been left atop a large cement block.

Not a cement block, she realised in horror. A grave.

She was in a crypt.

A chill gripped her spine and she made to return to the stairs but had barely taken a single step when she bumped directly into the chest of the owner of the lamp. The unexpected collision threw her off balance and with her hands still bound, she was unable to steady herself. As she began to topple over, strong hands reached out to grab her and helped her regain her balance.

The owner of the lamp was a striking man with blond curls, a broad jaw and a powerful energy that barrelled into her without hesitation. She briefly wondered how she hadn't sensed his presence when she entered this place. While his face was taut and stern, his grip on her arms was gentle, and despite the fact his green eyes were rimmed red, as though he'd been crying, she could still feel the strong energy of his intrigue washing over her.

"You're not a priest," he accused softly, his voice smooth as a river stone, his eyes scanning over her bound hands with interest, "Or a jesu. Who are you?"

She did not reply and tried to pull away from him, but he did not let her go. He opened his mouth to speak again but was interrupted by sounds of her pursuers coming down the staircase and into the crypt.

Moving on instinct more than thought, Mila tried once more to pull away from the man, and this time he let her go. She ducked down and hid behind the gravestone, her heart thudding so loudly that she thought her chest may well rip at the seams.

"Who goes there? What's going on?" the blond man with the lantern called out in the direction of the stairwell, his tone now far more authoritative.

The footsteps abruptly halted.

"We're hunting a demon who has escaped the Sacrament," a jesu voice called out from the gloom. "A female. We mean no disrespect, but have you seen –"

Without warning the blond-haired man exploded with rage. "Disrespect? Do you even know the *meaning* of the word? This is a private family crypt. It is forbidden, on pain of death, for any not of the bloodline to enter." His words echoed throughout the cold, hard space. "And yet you storm in here, during my time of mourning, and all but accuse me of harbouring a demon? Of heretic behaviour? Get out!" He spat the words at them.

Crouched behind the grave and feeling as though she were made of stone herself, Mila heard the pursuers leave. She dared not rise, even when she felt sure they'd left. Eventually, she heard the lone footsteps of the blond man approaching her. His shadow crossed her face, and she shivered with fear as she met his eyes. They were no longer rimmed red. They gleamed.

"A demon," he said with a small tilt of his head. "Well, well, well."

Mila shivered under his scrutiny, waiting for the blow to fall. The man's concentration broke and his head suddenly snapped up as the echo of more voices in the hallway tumbled down into the crypt.

"You'd better get moving," he said. "Someone of a higher rank will surely come down here and won't be so easily deterred from conducting a more thorough search."

Mila blinked. "You're letting me go?" she asked, confused.

"I'm not." He said sternly, holding up a finger to correct her then slowly lowering it. "I'm just...not detaining you either. Not yet anyway." As he spoke, a slow drawl of a grin began to spread across his face, as if he'd just realised that today he'd been gifted the good fortune of observing a very entertaining hunt.

And she, the hare.

"Besides," he said. "They don't need my help to detain you, if the commotion above is anything to go by."

She agreed, nodding fervently and backing away from him, not quite daring to turn away from the unusual man until she was well out of arm's reach. "Thank you."

He raised his brows and grinned at her in the candlelight. "Good luck," he said in a soft, sing-song tone.

When Mila reached the staircase, she tried to calm her racing heart and took a moment to consider her next move.

The sounds of tens of jesu running around in the tunnel, barking orders and clanging their armour was nearly deafening.

There were so many of them. She'd never be able to outrun them. Her only option was to try outsmart them.

So, when she detected a brief break of movement in the tunnel above her, she made her move. She ascended the stairs, passing by the ground floor completely, hoping the jesu would stay in the tunnel and assume she was searching for a way out. It was not much of a bluff, but her options were limited. If she could find somewhere further up to hide until nightfall, that could save her.

She leapt up the steps three at a time, but when she reached the top landing, she realised with dread that the decision had been a poor one. The stairway did not lead to another level. It led only to a single, beautifully carved wooden door. And beyond that door, Mila's powers informed her, there was only one small room...and it was already occupied.

Occupied by a being whose energy dominated the space like a thunderclap.

The sheer volume of it stopped Mila dead in her tracks. Cruelty, impatience, a desire to be seen. She'd never come across someone who projected so much and so loudly. There was something childlike in the concoction, like the energies you'd expect from a toddler about to torment a frog.

Entering the room was not a good option. Descending the stairs again and trying the tunnel was a certain death sentence. She could hear the jesu swarming below her like angry ants of a disrupted nest. Mila prayed she could just hide here on the landing and never have to open that door, never have to be the frog, but when she heard voices at the bottom of the stairwell she realised that her attempt at a ruse had been foiled by the sheer numbers of those after her. They had enough to split ranks and send someone up the stairs, as well as press ahead into the tunnel. They were coming, and in about two seconds, Mila would be discovered.

A yell from below told her they'd seen her.

There was no other option.

She pushed open the door, burst into the room, and blinked heavily in the blinding gold light that accosted her eyes. When she registered where she was, she blanched in horror.

It was a viewing platform, an ornate suite with a balcony that looked down over the Grand Cathedral and onto the Sacrament in progress below. The echoing chants of the priests and acolytes rose up around her in a deafening mist, filling her ears and dominating the air. Her stomach plummeted in dismay.

She was right back where she started.

Cruelty and Chaos

The escape attempt had been for naught.

The pursuing jesu were moments away from reaching the room. Would they toss her over the balcony when they caught her? If so, she'd land on the immaculately tiled floor below, probably right before the God-King. Would he still accept a sacrifice with a broken neck?

One of the jesu finally reached the doorway. He was panting, but he didn't immediately reach for Mila. Instead, he looked over her shoulder and spoke with deep concern etched into his face.

"Princess, forgive me."

Mila turned and registered the other occupants in the room for the first time.

The powerfully loud energy came from a striking woman, who sat atop a high-backed, golden chair.

Mila had never seen anything or anyone like her before.

She was tall and dark. Her dominating frame emphasised by the sleek black fabric that wrapped tightly around her body. It whirled in thick swaths around her long arms and legs, reaching all the way down to her wrists and ankles. Sewn into the fabric were the skins of hundreds of golden snakes, and she toyed with a tiny live one between her long, manicured fingers. Her black hair hung in thick, tight curls down around her neck, and delicate, gold feathers had been woven through small braids that hung from her temples. Her skin was as immaculate and sheer as a dark mirror, and Mila judged that she couldn't have seen more than twenty-five summers or so. Her lips were painted with a strong, metallic blue, and two streaks of golden paint adorned her sharp cheekbones.

This must be the God-King's daughter – Princess Jezebel – but she didn't look like a princess. She looked like a goddess.

"Well," Jezebel said, raising a perfectly arched eyebrow and looking Mila up and down slowly, dark eyes lingering on the thin, black horns that were still protruding a few inches above Mila's scalp. "This afternoon is already panning out to be far more entertaining than I expected. Someone...explain." She flittered her fingers in the air commandingly.

Beside her a tall, muscular man with cropped hair and a bare chest stood poised to attack. He did not look remotely amused. Instead, his sword was drawn and his deep brown eyes narrowed as he surveyed the scene and the intruder. To the other side of the princess was a serving woman, who might as well have been invisible beside the physical and energetic pull of her mistress.

"Someone explain," the princess said again in a low, deadly tone, as though unaccustomed to repeating herself.

Despite the heat of the room, Mila shivered.

"I...she's a..." The unfortunate jesu behind Mila spluttered on his words, unable to believe that, of all the people in this building responsible for the demon's escape, he somehow had the poor fortune of being the one to report it to Jezebel. "She's a d-demon. Meant to be below with the others. My sincere, sincere apologies for the disturbance. I'll take her with me now."

"Wait!" The order was sharp, and the princess rose from her chair, gliding towards Mila like a panther moving through shadows.

Mila felt her body automatically freeze as the woman approached. Her nose was assaulted by the wave of perfume, dark spice with notes of vanilla on top. It was gorgeous and sultry and overwhelming but was nothing compared to the actual wearer. Even if Mila had wanted to look away from her, she couldn't. She was too beautiful, and her energy was too dominating.

Eventually, she stood right before Mila and inspected her, her deep brown eyes scanning from bottom to top. Her lip twitched with disgust as she surveyed the dirty, olive, cotton shorts that covered Mila's slim legs, and the cream crocheted top that hung over her small breasts. They lingered on the many golden piercings in Mila's nose and ears but lit up when they reached her horns again. She even reached out to touch one, and when her graceful hand stroked it, Mila's legs nearly bucked from the sharp, electric sensation that ran through her. Jezebel's smile truly brightened at that response and her eyes gleamed. Finally, she fixated on Mila's long, straight brown hair, and when she noted the length, her eyebrows raised again with interest.

Nothing about Mila's appearance was unusual for a Highlander, except the length of her hair. Due to the constant humidity, Highlander women usually cut theirs short to allow any precious breeze to access their necks, but Mila hadn't moved there until she was fourteen. She'd spent her childhood amongst the devout and hardworking plains people of Prious, and in Prious, the women wore their hair long.

Despite the pain the memories of her past life caused her, Mila had never been able to bring herself to sever that connection to her childhood. Keeping her hair long and healthy in the forest had been a mammoth effort, but the knowledge she'd cultivated of rainforest fruits and their nourishing properties had helped. Usually, she wore it tied up and out of the way, but her grass hair tie had broken on the journey here, so now it hung loose, draping down to her ankles. It had never been cut before and was shiny, healthy and rich.

"Your hair," Jezebel said, and before Mila could open her mouth to reply, she snapped her fingers, and the guard approached. "I want it," Jezebel said simply, cocking her head slightly to the side.

Without hesitation, the guard seized Mila's hair, and in one swift movement of his dagger, he sliced it clean away from her head.

The immediate disappearance of the weight that had been silently present for all her life was as shocking as a bucket of ice water being thrown over her. She gasped for air, her bound hands instinctively reaching for her head.

No one in the room acknowledged her response. Instead, the maidservant hurriedly stepped forward and held a mirror up for the princess, who held Mila's hair up in a bunch to her scalp.

The princess tucked her braid to the side, studying her reflection for a moment before shrugging. "Upon further consideration...I don't think it's quite the right shade for me."

In three quick steps, she strode to the small gold brazier that quietly burned in the corner and abruptly tossed the heavy cut-off hair into it.

It was consumed by the flames in all of two seconds, the balcony swiftly filling with the acrid scent of burning hair.

Mila stared dumbly at the brazier, and then at the woman, in disbelief, trying to fight down her outrage and make sense of what had just occurred.

Princess Jezebel stared back with barely masked delight, waiting for the response, the reaction, a flinch...anything she could latch onto in order to extend this fun game she'd just begun. The malicious energy pulsed from her with renewed intensity, and Mila suddenly recognised the danger the princess truly presented. Despite the fact she was probably minutes away from being sacrificed, the immediate threat to her life was suddenly this woman who stood directly in front of her.

And yet.

She could not bring herself to drag her eyes to the ground in submission. If Jezebel was going to kill her here and now, she wouldn't cower. She was suddenly overwhelmed with fury and frustration that she'd spent her entire life hiding and cowering. If this was to be her last stand, she might as well stand strong.

So, she stared back at Jezebel, unyielding in her gaze, and felt the woman's excited energy rise in response, as though she were relishing in the novelty of coming across someone who was not yet quite broken.

Those perfect lips curled into a cool smile. "You *are* interesting. What's your power?"

The question took Mila by surprise. She wasn't expecting this silent battle of wills to turn into a conversation. She'd been expecting death.

"I can sense energy," she said tersely.

"What do you mean energy?" Jezebel demanded.

"Emotions, intentions, state of being... Whatever is the driving force of living things in my vicinity."

"Is that so? And what is *my* energy?" she said with a leer.

In that moment, Jezebel reminded Mila of a bored rainforest monkey she'd once seen. One that had pushed a rival's vulnerable babe off a branch for the sake of its own entertainment.

Mila considered her answer for a second and then answered truthfully.

"Cruelty and chaos."

Jezebel said nothing for a long few minutes, taken aback by the candid answer and the courage of the giver. Mila continued to hold her gaze, still unable to look away, although she became dimly aware of the sound of footsteps and more people coming up the stairs. Another guard, two jesu, and even the High Priest Abbott now appeared in the doorway.

"Seize her," the High Priest ordered, his tone panicked.

The jesu moved towards Mila.

"Stop!" Jezebel ordered curtly, and when the jesu did not immediately halt, she whirled on them in fury, stomping her foot like a petulant child. "Did you not hear my command?" she bellowed.

The movement towards Mila stopped, but Mila sensed an air of uncertainty to their obedience. Who was truly in charge here?

"Princess?" The High Priest looked faintly annoyed, but he was not about to disobey the daughter of his God-King on the very afternoon they were holding a sacrament to appease his wrath.

"Unbind her hands." The princess pointed to Mila. "This one is now mine. I will take her as my new pet."

Mila baulked silently at her words.

The High Priest was less restrained. "Highness..." He struggled for a moment to try to articulate his complaint whilst remaining respectful. "She is an intended sacrifice, a demon. If you take her, we'll be one short for this season."

Jezebel seemed to consider this, then she turned towards Mila. "What do you think, demon? Should you be sacrificed today? Or do you think you and your power can sufficiently entertain me for a few months until the next Sacrament?"

Mila did not know how to respond, but Jezebel seemed to be expecting her to speak. Eventually, she simply said, “I wish to live.”

“Excellent.” Jezebel clapped her hands delightedly, a childlike energy seizing her. “Abbott, tell my father that I’ve taken one for myself. He can’t have this one yet. I’ve got plans for her, and I intend to extract every last sliver of entertainment from her this spring.” She suddenly giggled. "How quaint. A spring pet".

“Princess Jezebel... Forgive me, but... I – ”

Mila was amazed that he seemed still prepared to argue with her. So did the princess.

“Am I not half Divine?” She interrupted him with a stony, warning glare, her energy shifting from childish excitement to murderous intensity in an instant. “Do you not worship my family line? Obey me.”

Jezebel’s personal guard also chose that moment to step forward, his presence shadowing Jezebel’s back and reinforcing her command. The High Priest glanced at him and then took a deep breath to steady himself in what was clearly a humbling and difficult effort. Finally, he seemed able to remember his place. He sucked his lips tightly into his mouth as if to stop them opening of their own accord, then nodded to one of the jesu, who strode forward and roughly unlocked the cuffs on Mila’s wrists.

Jezebel did not spare anyone else on the balcony a second glance. She seized Mila’s arm and dug her long nails into it, pulling her along as they left the room and descended the stairs.

“This is going to be fun,” she said with confidence as they strode swiftly out of the cathedral, followed closely by the huge guard and the handmaid.

Mila was far less certain.

The Princess Jezebel

Princess Jezebel strode with the speed and determination of a woman possessed. She all but dragged Mila behind her into a carriage that carried them a little distance away from the Grand Cathedral to a far smaller, but still ornate, tall, white building. Mila soon realised this must be the princess's own personal apartments.

Together, they marched up the winding, white-tiled staircase and did not stop until they reached the very top and entered an opulent bedchamber.

Thick, towering, sandstone walls rose to meet the roof that, like the tunnel in the cathedral, was a stained-glass mosaic. This one was a rainbow of colours, interrupted only by five dark, exposed wooden beams that spanned the width of the room. Huge windows had been carved into the stone walls, each a various-sized crescent, except for the one in the middle, which was perfectly circular. Mila stared at the design for a moment before realising she was looking at carvings that depicted the waxing and waning phases of the moon.

The centre window was large enough to fit two plush, red seats inside it, and Mila could see a tiny, black-wire fence balcony jutting out on the other side. Each of the other windows were lit from beneath with small, elaborately twisted jars that expelled a soft golden glow. On closer inspection, Mila realised with horror that the jars were filled with Midas's sand. She swiftly averted her attention away from them, praying she would not feel the death energy that she knew they held.

The western side of the room was dominated by an intricately painted wooden wardrobe that spanned the entire length of the wall. It was accompanied by a number of freestanding mirrors and dressing curtains that were made up of all manner of materials, such as feathers and woven reeds and giraffe skins.

On the eastern wall lay an enormous, black, four-poster bed. It was adorned with spider-web thin fabric that draped from the supporting beams of the ceiling and trailed down, across the mound of pillows that lay on and around it. Each was a different colour and stitched with an assortment of tessellating patterns, desert flowers and hypnotic swirls. The entire room was an explosion of colours, textures and shapes. It was gorgeous and awful at the same time.

Mila finally stopped gawking and turned back to Jezebel, who had dismissed all attendants save the one guard. Now alone, she drew Mila towards the bed and then proceeded to undress in front of both Mila and the guard without ceremony.

Mila's instinct to breathe completely abandoned her at the sight of Jezebel's perfect naked body.

"Men have been so... *unsatisfying* recently," the princess said as she peeled off the last of the gorgeous black fabric from her skin and discarded it in a pile on the floor. "And I'm getting quite sick of having them killed for finding their moment of pleasure before I find mine."

She sighed and tilted her head gently, exposing her neck in a display that, for the briefest of moments, was the perfect portrayal of heartfelt consideration.

Then she suddenly snapped back to a more exacting stance. “It’s a selfishness I cannot abide. I’m the daughter of the God-King. If I can’t even have good sex, then I shudder to think what the other women of Artor endure.” She tittered a little at her own joke and then looked over Mila’s shoulder and spoke directly to the guard.

“And as always, Jahan, you’re free to watch, but do not interrupt,” she said in a voice that had abruptly changed again, this time from the whinging girlish tone to one that was deep and sultry and mocking.

“Highness,” was all the guard replied, his face impassive. His energy matched his words, stoic and professional.

“Unfortunately – ” she turned back to Mila and sighed theatrically, “ – he’s handsome, but he's also boring. If I wasn’t so certain he’d be equally as boring in bed, I’d have tried him on years ago.”

Mila could tell that she enjoyed talking about the guard as though he were simply an object that she could choose to use on a whim. Perhaps, to her, he was. Perhaps now Mila was too.

That realisation unsettled her even more.

Jezebel’s dark eyes were hard, shiny beetles as they studied her, and Mila’s stomach plummeted at her next words.

“I’ve been with women before too. However, against my better judgement and much to my own misfortune, I always seem to be drawn back to men. Have you been with women before?”

Mila answered honestly, although it drew bile to her mouth to do so. “Yes.” A brief flash of memory threatened to interrupt but Mila pushed the images away. Now would be a dangerous time to indulge in nostalgia and she wanted the taint of this situation nowhere near those memories. She needed to focus on the moment if she wanted to survive this encounter.

"Excellent." Jezebel's eyes flashed with glee. "Perhaps you'll be skilled enough to keep my attention for longer than a single tumble. And if you truly can feel my energy with your power, then I expect you to use it and read my desires. I don't want to have to tell you what I want. I just want you to do it." She clapped her hands in delight, thrilled by the cleverness of her idea and her certainty that she'd determined exactly how Mila's powers worked. "This has potential to be extremely entertaining. Let's begin."

With the confidence of a woman who had never been rejected or denied a thing in her life, she reached for Mila's hand and forced it upon her left breast. "Here, tell me what you feel."

Mila closed her eyes and tried to block out the pounding of her own heart, the near overwhelming adrenaline and panic, the feel of Jezebel's cold skin and sharp nails on her hand. Her power whirled around the room uselessly and aimlessly. It wasn't going to work as Jezebel thought it would. Mila couldn't read minds with her power. She had no idea how she would do this thing the princess expected her to do.

Certain that she was going to be sent back to Abbott within the hour, she felt utterly helpless and overpowered, a tiny bird in a cyclone.

Stop, she told herself. *Stay calm. Breathe. Think. Focus.*

She pushed the constant pangs of her searing rubane headache away and took a deep breath in and out. She forced herself to extend her thin, black horns the full few inches that they could grow and urged them to enable the full sensitivity of her power.

You can do this. Just like you used to help those other women.

Years ago, before the effort of chasing rubane's blocking effect had taken over her life, she'd been an accomplished midwife. She'd helped women in the village to deliver by secretly sensing their baby's energy beneath their skin as she'd worked with them, her horns hidden beneath a hat.

Surely, she could use her power in a similar way now? She just had to try to remain calm.

She focused her full attention and power on the woman before her and breathed deeply again. She urged her power to go in.

There.

She could see Jezebel's energy more clearly now that she was calmer, and it truly was chaotic: purple and black, swirling like an angry tempest within her. Mila probed further in, looking for more, looking for the answer that would save her.

There. The key to surviving the night.

Boredom.

Above all things, Jezebel was too powerful for her own good and so bored with it all. She was a woman who had spent a lifetime getting exactly what she wanted without any effort or risk on her part. No one denied her. No one chastised or surprised her. Jezebel might not even know it herself, but Mila's power sensed that she craved the unexpected, the game, the risk.

Mila considered this new information carefully and then trusted her life to the skill of her power, risking it all with her next words.

"I am a demon," she hissed into Jezebel's ear. "Spawn of Mud and worms. I am soulless, evil. I have no morals or qualms. From this distance, I could *easily* kill you, and there's nothing you or your guard could do to stop me." She drew a short breath before delivering the final blow. "But I'd be satisfied tonight with hearing you scream."

She was rewarded instantly by the deep, primal pulse of energy that emanated from within Jezebel's core. When Mila opened her eyes, she noted the slightly feral excitement peeking out from behind Jezebel's brown eyes.

Emboldened, Mila straightened her shoulders and did exactly what Jezebel's silent energy was begging her to do.

She did not break eye contact when she stepped forward and invaded Jezebel's space. She reached up and grabbed a fistful of the woman's thick hair, roughly forcing her head up, as she moved in lockstep with her, back towards the bed.

Out of the corner of her eye, Mila saw the guard move to protect his princess, but he was stayed by a small flick of Jezebel's hand.

She understood what Mila was doing and was allowing it to happen. For the first time in Jezebel's life, someone was wresting control from her, demanding space and forcing her to yield it, and from the yearning look on her face, Mila knew that, at least for tonight, this was exactly what the princess had been craving.

* * *

Hours later, Mila lay listening to the soft, slow breaths that barely punctuated the night. She looked over at Jezebel, who now lay fast asleep beside her atop the terracotta silk sheets, limbs flung out in abandon. Her dark skin caught and held the first silver ripples of the rising moon in a way that made her seem almost more painting than human. She was beautiful, made more so now to Mila by the easy contentment and peace radiating from her.

In fact, Mila registered with sudden surprise, other than the horrible death pulse that emanated from the small jars of Midas's sand, the energy of every being inside the room was peaceful, and this had not been the case for a single moment in the days since Mila had first arrived in Jeralusah. The absence of human stress or fear was as welcome to her as cold water is to a burn.

Unfortunately, her head still throbbed and she was beginning to feel a nauseating ache in her stomach from the continual lack of rubane. She fought to ignore it and, instead, considered her new situation.

She had transitioned from a condemned religious sacrifice to the nearly bald plaything of the God-King's daughter within an extraordinarily short amount of time. She wondered what this would mean for her tomorrow.

Was the evening's submission simply an itch the princess had desperately needed scratched? Would Mila be sent back to Midas when the sun rose? She had no way of knowing but had done her best tonight to use her power in a way she'd never done before and ensure the value of her life in the princess's eyes.

She'd discovered that, with skin contact, her power was far less likely to dilute itself throughout the room, and she could more easily read the princess's energy accurately, tailoring her touch to meet the internal, silent demands of the other woman.

It had worked. And now, for the first time since her capture, Mila felt a glimmer of hope – knowing that her powers could intimately provide Jezebel with an experience that just might be unique and satisfying enough to save her own life.

In a sudden flash of inspiration, Mila let her horns grow again and reached her hand out to gently touch the princess's extended index finger. She sent her power running through that physical bond into the woman, curious to know if she could glean anything else that might be of use. Something that might only be apparent now in this moment of vulnerability, something that was usually hidden within the ever-whirling tempest of Jezebel's conscious mind.

Sleeping Jezebel's main energetic projection was that of peace and contentedness, but Mila pushed her power beneath the surface layer of Jezebel's psyche and searched through the sea of energies she found there in a way she'd never done before, a way she hadn't quite known was possible.

What was causing the peace? Surely, there was more here than the mere happiness of a pleasurable physical release?

She was surrounded by the colours and textures of Jezebel's inner self, and carefully, not wanting to rouse the woman, she mentally sifted through them until she found one she could put a name to.

Seen. Jezebel had finally felt seen.

Like wriggling backwards out of a foxhole, Mila slowly extracted her power and drew it back into herself, feeling her horns slide back beneath her skin like a sword into a sheath.

How curious that Princess Jezebel could have all the power, control and wealth of the world, and yet the thing that brought her true peace was the experience of someone actually truly seeing her, even if it was only for a glimmer of a moment.

A bubble of hope began to form in Mila as she considered that seeing Jezebel's authentic energy was exactly what her power made her capable of doing. Overuse of rubane may have weakened the control she'd once had over it, but skin-to-skin contact still seemed to be an effective way to hone it. Mila had faith that the control would return if she stayed alive long enough. And if she could just keep Jezebel in a perpetual state of peace and happiness, then perhaps this new situation might be survivable.

Or at the very least, it might allow her to survive long enough to find some way to escape before the season turned.

Overwhelmed by the small wave of relief that accompanied this realisation, Mila allowed herself a long exhale, and then turned her attention towards the guard, who still stood watch. She allowed her horns to grow slightly longer as she sent her power out towards him, practising her control and certain he wouldn't be able to see them from where he stood.

He had not moved from his post since the halting flick of Jezebel's wrist. As Mila studied him, she wondered what he'd thought of the whole affair. Mila's unruly power flittered from him and began to scan aimlessly around the room, catching the calm of the many plants that hung from the boudoir and the sleeping waves of the birds on the windowsill before it finally found the guard again and settled on him. She felt nothing hostile emanating from him. By all accounts, the guard was currently contributing to the feeling of peace inside the room. The glimpses she could see of his energy were characterised only by professionalism and a small ounce of fatigue. It had evidently been a long day for him too, and he seemed happy it was nearly over.

As if he recognised that her thoughts had now turned to him, or perhaps because he had, indeed, somehow seen her horns grow and suspected himself to be the subject of her analysis, he broke from his position and approached the bed.

"Come," he said quietly when he was close, not wanting to wake Jezebel. "I'll have the maids clothe and feed you and show you to a nearby room you can claim. I suspect the princess will want to have you close by in the morning."

"Thank you," she replied, grateful for the small kindness on a day that had been filled with nothing else but fear and abuse.

She slipped from the bed and tried to follow him but stumbled. The guard's arm found her and wrapped around her middle before she could hit the floor. She gripped him gratefully as she found her feet again.

"Thank you," she murmured, but was too exhausted to read him more deeply. Too exhausted in that moment to contemplate seeking an opportunity to escape. Too exhausted even to be ashamed of her nakedness in his arms.

Just then, the idea of sleep, in a bed away from this room and this turbulent woman, was as irresistible to her as the shoreline is to a wave. When she saw the plain white sheets of a bed in a spare servant's room before her, she crashed headlong into them without hesitation.

Trial by Cat

On the day Mila had been betrayed, she'd been surprised and hurt, but never seriously concerned that the mob would actually expose her as a demon.

Despite the plethora of theories that abounded, there was only one true test that could correctly identify a demon, and it was unlikely that the villagers who came for her knew it. Some of the false tests were unpleasant, but none of them were dangerous. Most had been invented and spread by ikarei themselves, such as making a small cut to the arm to prove that one's blood ran red, rather than blue. Or plucking a hair from one's head and proving that it was mundane and would not turn into a hell-worm when it hit the ground.

On the day they came for her, she'd been more fearful of the mob's fervour than anything they might subject her to by way of a test. She tried to diffuse their energy with her demure stance and lack of theatrics. She'd learned long ago that, with this particular sect of society, there was no real way to win against them, and the occasional chance to score was only achieved by startling them with unexpected dignity.

"Look at 'er," she had heard one man jeer, "'olding herself like she were some kinda princess. I swear I've seen 'er 'orns before. She lies with the worms!"

"Now, now," a calmer male voice interceded. "All we have is rumours, Brennan. Wait until the test is conducted before tainting her with such a brush."

Mila detected the reluctant '*hrrumph*' behind her and tried to suppress a small smile. She did actually quite like the gentle and industrious worms that determinedly worked magic in her garden beds, but she knew that those were not the worms of the afterlife that the speaker had been referring to. The worms of the Rot.

An icy blade of true fear struck her when she caught a glimpse of the priest waiting for her at the testing area. This wasn't the first time in her life that she'd been approached by a group of humans demanding proof of her humanity, but this was the first time that group had included a priest, and that was very bad news.

Fully ordained priests were an unusual sight in the rainforest Highlands. Usually, the unrelenting humidity, the difficult terrain, and the isolation of the small villages deterred all but the most determined of acolytes to venture out to mission and spread the Church of Midas.

Acolytes were dangerous to ikarei in the way that an errant spark is dangerous to a fireplace, capable of causing problems, but usually containable. They led weekly Church sermons and tried to enforce the observance of the Heretical Behaviours within their small, allotted villages. They usually travelled too frequently to truly identify someone who did not quite fit into their community.

Priests, on the other hand, were as dangerous as a wildfire in a dry field. Priests did not conduct paltry sermons in backwater towns. They arrived only when requested by an acolyte, and they had the authority to test and condemn demons.

If a priest had come all the way here from Jeralusah for Mila, then she had no doubt that whoever had betrayed her had raised a very compelling case.

Probably Oberon.

She pushed the name away. Speculation wouldn't help her survive what was coming next.

The priest eyed her coolly as she was brought forward, but he said nothing. His firm, handsome face was neutral and calm, and he was dressed well. His grey travel robes had evidently only recently been donned, as they were clean and dry – a rarity for clothes in these parts. A thick, brown leather belt was cinched neatly around his flat stomach, and from this hung his instruments of prayer, along with a tiny, waterproofed leather book that contained the Holy Text of the Heretical Behaviours.

Once Mila had been deposited by the mob into the centre of the rocky circle, the priest turned his back to her and walked to his cart, returning with a black wooden cage swinging gently from his hand. Mila's heart sank as she caught a glimpse of white fur poking out between the wooden slats and she knew at that moment that her time had come.

It was happening. The true test. Trial by Cat.

The priest placed the cage down outside of the circle and went back to his cart again, this time returning with three large, thin, white crystal circles. He entered the circle where Mila stood and laid all three out on the ground, leaving some distance between each of them.

Once he was satisfied with the placement of the circles, he looked at Mila and said, "Choose one to stand upon. Once you have made your decision, do not move. If you fail the test, you will be arrested as a demon, and you will be sacrificed at the upcoming Sacrament of Contrition as a heretic. If you move at all or attempt to disrupt or injure the cat, then the test will be halted, your guilt as a demon will be assumed, and you will be flogged for committing the Sixth Behaviour prior to your sacrifice. Do you understand?"

Mila's mind sifted through her recollection of the behaviours and remembered the Sixth, *Disrespecting the Church of Midas*.

She nodded.

"I need to verbally hear you confirm."

"I under –" she choked on the words with her dry throat and coughed a little to clear it.

The crowd jeered.

"I understand."

"If you are innocent, I implore you, stand still and this will be over momentarily."

As he spoke, he relayed no compassion. Mila didn't waste any energy trying to wring sympathy from him somehow. Instead, she inspected each crystal circle and then chose the second one to stand on, nodding to the priest to indicate that she had chosen and that she would not move.

Once the priest was satisfied with her positioning, he bent forward and lifted the lid to the box. A haughty white feline leapt out joyfully, winding its fluffy tail around the bottom hem of the priest's robe before moving to the open space where the crystal circles lay.

Just like that, the test had begun.

The priest spoke to the now silent crowd as the cat moved towards the crystal circle on Mila's left.

"Trial by Cat is simple in its design," he explained. "Testing Cats are specifically bred for their affectionate nature and are trained to stand upon each of the three white circles. If this woman is not a demon, the cat will wind itself around her legs, meowing and pawing at her for treats or pats. But if she is a demon, it will not even know she is there –

for these cats are pure, selected by the Divine himself, and cannot see those without a soul."

Mila watched with her heart in her mouth as the animal strode boldly up to the first circle on her left. It sniffed at the edge, hopeful to find a treat. When it found none, it stepped up onto the crystal, turned, sat, and looked back expectantly at the priest, who leaned forward and rewarded him with a small portion of dried jerky.

The crowd politely clapped, and the cat chewed deliberately before proceeding with purpose towards the next white crystal circle – the one Mila was standing on.

Despite the warning she'd been given, she couldn't help but try to shuffle her feet as the cat approached her, to try make any kind of noise to alert the cat to her presence. But it was clear that the Testing Cats were also specifically selected for their deafness, as its tiny ears yielded not the smallest flicker of movement.

However, her actions had not escaped the attention of the priest, who, for the first time since she'd been seized by the villagers, allowed an inch of emotion to cross his young face. It was the look a snake gives a mouse in the moment it decides to eat it.

To her surprise, though, he said nothing. In hindsight, she realised that he'd known in that moment that she was about to be exposed by the cat as a demon, and he had determined that this would be a far richer and more satisfying outcome for both himself and the crowd than simply stopping the test because she'd shuffled her feet.

He was a showman, this priest, and a clever one.

The beautiful, white cat unfaltering sniffed at the edge of Mila's circle for treats, and when it found none again, it attempted to step onto the crystal, making absolutely no effort to avoid walking directly into Mila's left shin.

At the sudden, unexpected contact, the cat shrieked and hissed in fear, its back arching towards the sky, soft tail now angular and tense. It scarpered back to the priest and leapt into his arms, fearful and unnerved by the invisible brick wall it had struck.

The crowd cheered, the priest's eyes gleamed, and Mila's heart sank. The test's objective had been met.

The Unpleasantness

Jezebel's screech of rage pierced through the otherwise calm morning, and Mila heard the echo, audible despite the thick walls of her suite. A moment later, a burly, buzz-haired guard burst into her room and roughly seized her, dragging her from her bed before she'd even had time to dress. Even if she hadn't still been suffering horrendous pangs from the rubane withdrawals, the manner of her entry back into Jezebel's room would have been painful. The brute all but dragged her up the stairs and tossed her roughly onto the floor, where she landed firmly at the feet of a small crowd of serving staff. They stood huddled together like scared chickens, waiting for a fox's judgement. Mila felt waves of streaming tension flowing from the group, but after she blinked for a moment and orientated herself, she swiftly realised that the tension was not for her.

The guard who had been kind to Mila the previous evening now knelt in the centre of the circle of people. His shirt was ripped, and his bare chest was half visible through the torn linen. His face was downturned, but Mila could still see him bleeding from three long lines across his cheek. Scratches, she realised, from Jezebel's strike. Despite the hubbub, he seemed calm, and his body remained motionless, but when Mila gently let her horns extend a little, she could feel his fear pulsing out quickly in time with his heartbeat.

"You took it upon yourself?" Jezebel's tone was stiff and cold. "To remove something I own from my possession, without my knowledge?"

Her face was red with rage, but Mila also sensed glee emanating from her. She was clearly relishing this, a welcome opportunity to reinforce her power and ensure that even those closest and most loyal to her knew, without a shadow of a doubt, that they would be punished if they put a foot wrong.

"I believe that's defined as theft, Jahan!" Her voice now became hysterical. "Have you been stealing from me all these years? Removing anything else you saw fit to part from me?"

"No, Highness, never," Jahan replied instantly, contritely.

"Never?" Jezebel lambasted. "Well, you did last night! How am I to believe anything you have to say about the matter? How am I to ever trust you again?"

Jahan had no reply to this, or perhaps realised that a reply was futile. Mila realised with shock that Jezebel was equating his gesture of simple human kindness – a bed and room to herself – as the equivalent of robbery. As though Jahan had removed jewels from the room without asking Jezebel's permission.

Mila felt what little hope had bubbled in her chest the night before dissolve. This woman was truly mad.

"Nothing to say?" Jezebel crowed. "Well, then... " Her tone returned to its earlier calm with chilling swiftness, "The punishment for thievery is usually the loss of a hand." She let that statement linger in the warm morning air for a moment before continuing on. "However, you've been loyal enough for many years. We've known each other since we were children. That bond does not mean nothing to me. Would you like to keep your hand?"

"Highness..." Jahan's reply was barely audible.

"Louder!" Jezebel demanded.

"Yes, Highness."

"Beg me, Jahan. Beg me for your hand."

Jahan did not hesitate, as though he'd seen enough of Jezebel's punishments over the years to know that she only responded to utter subservience, and for him to hold onto any sense of pride was futile.

"I beg of you, Princess, daughter of the Almighty God-King Midas, powerful, beautiful and magnificent." His voice was low and quiet. Mila heard true contrition laced in every word. "Please, forgive your servant for his transgression. It shall never be repeated. The lessons learned today shall be applied henceforth through every step of any future service I am graced to bestow upon your person. I remain your most devoted servant. Please, allow me to keep my hand."

Jezebel let the silence fester for a long moment, then spoke. "I will be gracious this time." She paused and considered her next words. "You may keep your hand, and you may even remain in my retinue as one of my guards, although you will no longer be permitted to be my Guard of the Body."

His shoulders did not relax an inch at the sentence, as though he knew this outcome was too good to be true and was waiting for the true blow to fall.

He was not wrong.

Jezebel luxuriated in the tension before continuing in a somewhat lecturing tone. "I suspect this transgression was influenced, not through a sincere desire to steal for me, but by what you took to be a situation where a pretty, young woman needed care. You are wrong.

You forgot for a moment, I suspect, that she is a demon. She has committed the First Heretical Behaviour. A reminder to all," she raised her voice and cast her gaze about the audience, "this means she *sold her soul to obtain demonic powers.* She is a heretic. She is a living evil, and treating her as anything other than that sets a dangerous precedent on how to treat her while she remains in my service." She turned her attention directly back to Jahan. "Her unsuspecting appearance and meek demeanour fooled you into believing she is one of us. She is not."

Jezebel let that statement simmer, marinating in the attention of her captive audience. "Now that I've schooled you on one of the behaviours, it's your turn. Remind me, Jahan, what is the Sixth Heretical Behaviour?"

Jahan did not hesitate, as though he'd been born reciting the Holy Text. "The Sixth Heretical Behaviour is any display of disrespect towards the Church of Midas."

"And would you concede that your lapse of judgement about the demon straddles that line of heresy? Flirts with it, perhaps?"

Jahan remained silent. Everyone in the room knew what Jezebel was doing. The Sixth Heretical Behaviour was a famous catch-all for any sin. Anything could be considered an act of disrespect towards the Church in the right context.

"Let your eyes never deceive you again," Jezebel announced finally. "And you will lose one of them for this transgression."

The shock of this judgement landed on Mila like a blow to the face.

She imagined that a braver, more fearless version of herself would have stepped forward to argue against the monstrous punishment. To defend the man's actions. To roar in Jezebel's face that, demon or not, she was a living being and that the guard had been the only example of human decency she'd experienced since she'd arrived at the Holy City.

But she did not. To her great shame, she found that she could do nothing but watch.

Jezebel narrowed her eyes at Jahan in disdain, and two other guards stepped forward to escort the proud, trembling man away to receive his punishment.

Later, Mila tried to tell herself that she'd done nothing because she could sense the futility of any rebellion in that moment, but the darker and more cowardly truth was that she had simply been too frightened. Scared bone deep.

Whatever understanding she had hoped to foster between herself and Jezebel was shattered. The woman viewed Mila as property, nothing more, and had ordered the blinding of a kind man who, by all accounts, was a childhood companion, simply because he'd dared to treat Mila otherwise. It was the most evil act she'd ever beheld.

When Jahan disappeared from the doorway, Jezebel turned to Mila with a sickly, sweet smile, and the fear cemented deeper.

"And now that this unpleasantness has been dealt with, I'm ready for a repeat performance of last night's efforts. Come." She clicked her fingers, and Mila somehow found the strength to take a step forward, knowing that if she had any chance of surviving another few minutes here, there could be no shadow of doubt that she was anything but an obedient slave.

And, she told herself, she would keep up this pretence for however long it took for her to figure out a way to escape.

The Dress and the Collar

It was only a little later that morning when Jezebel and two guards escorted Mila into a carriage outside. Once in, they left the high, black walls of the palace and went into the whitewashed city of Jeralusah. The city was remarkably clean, but felt uncomfortably so, in the way a child's room is clean after they hurriedly sweep their toys under the bed. The streets were pristine, with evidence of the daily morning rinsing now rising from the cobblestones in a glistening mist, but many windows remained shuttered, and for a city in the peak of its midmorning bustle, it seemed awfully quiet.

The few people moving about on the streets were striding with purpose, not dallying to mingle in the new sweet, spring sunshine. They bowed respectfully when Jezebel's carriage passed, but averted their eyes, and collectively, their energy seemed to exude frustration with the interruption, rather than excitement at seeing their princess.

Mila surmised that Jezebel must venture out often, and her presence was probably more of an inconvenience for the city folk than a novelty.

When they stopped out in front of a seamstress's shop, Jezebel gestured to the guards to haul Mila out of the carriage, saying nothing by way of explanation until they met the demure, young seamstress. The plump woman would not look directly at Jezebel, and visibly shrank back from Mila when she saw her horns.

Jezebel delighted in her reaction. "Yes. Now capture whatever it is you are feeling in a dress, Lorelai. I want all who see her to revile, desire, pity and fear her, in a single moment. And, most of all, I want them to know that I own her."

"Of course," the trembling woman said quickly, but Mila also felt her energy rise at the idea of the interesting challenge. There must be a reason that this seamstress was Jezebel's one of choice.

* * *

It was late into the afternoon when the outfit was finally finished. Lorelai had long overcome her fear and aversion of Mila. She now looked over the new attire she'd created with pride.

Mila was exhausted. She hadn't eaten in nearly three days, and the symptoms from the rubane withdrawals were now hitting her like a flu, causing her to tremble and ache as she'd stood for hours under Lorelai's administrations. Jezebel either hadn't noticed or didn't care.

"It's perfect!" She clapped as Lorelai stepped back for the final time. The princess had supervised the entire project from a deep green ottoman in the corner, barking out suggestions and corrections as Lorelai worked.

"And her hair?" the seamstress asked, inspecting Mila with a critical eye. "Are you happy with how it is, or do you wish it styled somehow?"

"Leave it," Jezebel replied. "It's not important to me that she's pretty. It's important that she makes an impact."

The outfit achieved exactly that.

In the mirror, Mila could see that the floor-length, sweeping black dress was designed to appear unfinished in parts, making it difficult to tell if she was wearing something magnificent or tattered rags. For the bodice, she'd been stuffed into a corset that laced up the front rather than the back. The crisscrossed lace tie had been deliberately left loose enough so that Mila's skin was exposed all the way from the top of her breastbone to the top of her pubic bone. If she'd had more of a bust, it would have been utterly scandalous. From her hips downward, the fabric of the dress was a mix of black layers and green velvet strands that had been clipped and hung in awkward places to look like strands of algae and riverweed. This, together with her short, brutally cut hair stabbing out awkwardly from her head made her unrecognisable. She truly looked like a creature that had crawled out of a swamp, a demon of the Muds.

Terrifying and seductive all at once.

Thankfully, she'd been permitted to keep the small gold hoops in her ears and nose. She stared hungrily at these in her reflection, trying to use the familiarity of them to find her old self.

Home, they reminded her, and for a moment she was enveloped by a crushing wave of sadness and despair. *Would she ever see it again? Did Cari know what had happened to her? Was it Cari who had betrayed her?*

Summoning her inner strength, she shoved the thought away. Letting that pain in would not help keep her alive today. She needed to focus. The small brown eyes that stared back from her reflection were hollow and pinched with stress and fatigue but remained determined.

There came a knock on the seamstress's door and another guard entered. He walked straight to Jezebel and presented her with something Mila could not see, but she clearly felt the princess's second-hand delight.

Jezebel turned to Mila and held out the item. It was a golden collar and matching lead.

Mila shrank back from them in horror as Jezebel approached. The guard was anticipating this and moved to block the exit.

Mila could do nothing but clench her eyes shut in misery as Jezebel leaned forward and clasped the golden collar tight around Mila's neck, clipping it together and locking it securely.

"Made from the melted gold of all those who've failed me," Jezebel whispered in Mila's ear.

As she drew back, Mila shuddered in horror but filled with morbid curiosity, she turned back towards the mirror. Unwilling to look, but unable not to.

The golden collar stood out brightly against her tanned skin and her dark new apparel. The long lead held in Jezebel's tight grip seemed to twinkle in the candlelight. The energy of the thing was like a perpetual death knell. Sheer sadness and pain made into an object that was now latched permanently to Mila's throat. Her knees trembled under its force.

"How do you like it?" Jezebel asked.

"I'm in agony," Mila croaked back, tears in her eyes.

"Good."

When they left the seamstress's townhouse, Jezebel surveyed Mila's new attire and expression of anguish with pleasure. She clutched the lead tightly, as though feeling even more possessive now that her new pet looked so fine. It occurred to Mila then that, with this lead now around her neck, the likelihood of her slipping away in the night and escaping had all but vanished. This thought made her chest ache, and she was nearly overcome by the impulse to burst into sobs and throw herself into the path of one of the many oncoming carriages rumbling up and down the busy street.

Her soul couldn't bear this.

As if she knew her thoughts, Jezebel smiled as stepped into the carriage, yanking on the lead as she did which caused Mila to stumble up the steps behind her.

When they were seated, Jezebel let out a sigh of pleasure and knocked on the roof of the cabin to signal to the driver that they were ready to return.

"What a fabulous day," she said out loud to herself. "I don't know why I didn't think of doing this earlier. I'm having so much fun. Oh! And we'll definitely be taking a trip to Lady Picory's house soon," she said. "Show that arrogant woman that she's not half as interesting as she thinks she is."

While the thought of being paraded around in this attire by Jezebel made Mila feel even more physically ill, knowing that she would be out of the palace again tomorrow shook her a little out of her depressed stupor.

It's just a lead, she silently reminded herself. *It's not a cage. All Jezebel has to do is put it down and leave me unattended in a room for one minute. Perhaps even within reach of a dinner knife. That's all I would need.*

That tiny adjustment of perspective provided just enough hope. Mila felt the cloud of despair recede slightly, and it became a little easier to breathe again.

The sun was starting to set as the carriage returned them to the palace. As they entered the thick, black cast-iron gates, Mila made an effort to stare out the window and learn as much about her surroundings as possible. It was hard not to be distracted by the sheer beauty of it all. As the carriage trundled past the many grand buildings that lay within the palace estate, Mila took in the sight of hundreds of gold lanterns that paired beautifully with the deep orange glow of the dusk sky. Together, they lit the road up brilliantly and heralded the way to the Grand Cathedral, which now lay immediately before the carriage. Its four, tall sandstone spires and enormous stained-glass windows made it impossible to miss. It had powerful lights shining at its base, which illuminated it right up to the top of its tips of gold. Mila found herself thinking that, if she didn't hate the structure so much, it would have taken her breath away.

Around it, Mila could see a few smaller, but equally breathtaking buildings. She wished she knew what each one was used for or who lived in them, but Jezebel did not offer an explanation, nor did she seem inclined to even acknowledge Mila's curious stares. The only noise Mila heard in the carriage now was the omnipresent cicada symphony from outside that had commenced the moment the sun dipped below the high black walls.

The carriage continued to rumble quickly along the cobbled road, moving away from the buildings and now through a small forest of fruit trees, decorative gardens, and occasionally passing a beautiful sculpture or fountain. Once, it passed over a bridge made entirely of stone and glass. The water in the hand-cut stream below was illuminated by glowing stones, and the blue light shining back up through the glass bridge floor was one of the most spectacular things Mila had ever seen. She wondered how many commoners had ever been allowed to see any of this.

The palace was separated from the rest of the city of Jeralusah by a round, slick, towering wall of obsidian. Guard posts manned by jesu were dotted along the wall at even intervals. The palace was simultaneously a place of worship, a home to the elite, and a fortress.

Finally, just as true night fell, they arrived at Jezebel's private apartments, which sat on the western boundary of the property.

Dinner was waiting for the princess when they arrived, and she did not hesitate, descending on the plate with a hearty appetite after issuing a brisk order to Mila to sit on a cushion by her feet.

Despite the large table, Jezebel ate alone. Mila assumed that Midas must have a similar living arrangement on the other side of the property. She wondered for the first time what their relationship was like. Did Midas ever join his daughter for meals? Did Jezebel ever invite him?

She also wondered, with increasing urgency, if she would be fed at all.

Jezebel also seemed to be considering this exact question, eyeing Mila at her feet with great pleasure as she sucked the rich skin off a chicken bone.

"It's been a big day for you today. You must be hungry."

Mila hadn't risked saying much all day, but at this point, silence seemed the wrong choice.

"Yes, mistress," she said softly, bowing her head in the picture of submission. Internally, she frantically scanned the princess with her power for any inclination of what she might expect next.

It didn't help. Now, satiated with food, the energy radiating from Jezebel was a thick, toxic mix of callous boredom and arousal.

"Well, if you're hungry – " the princess spread her legs, leaned back and raised an eyebrow.

Mila complied.

Meeting Midas

With all the controversy, curiosity must have got the better of the God-King. Word soon arrived at Jezebel's apartments that Midas was demanding an inspection of the demon who had been plucked from his Sacrament of Contrition in a manner so outraging to his High Priest.

Mila had been expecting this, and she tried to mentally prepare herself to be calm and poised for the presentation, but when the day came, even Jezebel had woken differently. Mila had sensed a heightened level of stress emanating from the woman, which could not be assuaged with sex. Even the princess was afraid of her father, and that morning, she was nursing a sliver of doubt about what he would make of her reckless decision to keep Mila as her pet.

When they entered the main hall of the God-King's Grand Cathedral, Mila's breath was swept from her body by the sight of it and its accompanying rush of death energy.

The vast expanse of space was lined with glass columns on either side that formed a wide aisle. Each of them was at least ten metres high, about a metre in diameter, and filled to the brim with the heavy sand made of pure gold particles. Particles that had once been living creatures.

Mila's mind struggled to grasp the enormity of the graveyard she was walking through. She knew that when Midas had first appeared from the sea and announced himself to the nation of Artor, he'd been challenged by humans and demons alike, and eventually, there had been a war. She'd also been taught that Midas had stood as one man, one God, alone against an entire Artorian battalion. In an enormous display of his strength and power, he'd proceeded to individually disintegrate every single arrow, net, horse, stone, sword and eventually soldier, as they'd come at him, turning them all into an insignificant pile of Golden Sand. She'd always assumed that the tale had been exaggerated. Now that she saw the amount of sand that made up the wide, glass columns that lined the Grand Cathedral, she wasn't so sure.

Regardless of whether the story was a parable or not, it remained undeniable that none could walk in this hall without being reminded of Midas's enormous power, and his unquenchable demand for Artor's subjugation. In fact, the very order was inscribed into the northern-facing wall of the cathedral as an eternal reminder.

"Provide ten sacrifices to me, by the end of the season, every season, as demonstration of your contrition. Or I will destroy you and all you hold dear."

It was a mammoth effort to retain her impassive mask as she shadowed the princess through the hall. The High Priest Abbott was also present, his heeled boots echoing in the hall as he walked one step behind Mila, her noisy, scowling shadow.

It was a relief when they finally arrived at the far end of the hall and she was permitted to kneel and drop her head to the floor. A blessing that she no longer had to look at the pillars of death or feel Abbott's gaze upon her back.

"Well, daughter?" The God-King's voice was deep and rich, reverberating through Mila despite the distance she stood from the high-backed throne.

Filled with both fear and curiosity, she risked a tiny peek up at him. He'd been anticipating it and, to her horror, met her gaze with his own, one full of white fire.

She ducked her head again swiftly, inwardly cursing her reckless gesture. It had, however, given her a tiny snippet of context for what was about to befall her.

Midas was enormous, taller than the largest man Mila had ever seen. He was not especially handsome or youthful, and his face was dominated by huge, hawkish, dark eyebrows that were narrowed in a perpetual sneer. His nose was crooked and angular, as though it had been broken in his youth – but were gods ever really young, and who would have ever struck one?

The questions sprung unwillingly into Mila's mind, but she had no time to dwell on them. Midas awaited her.

His tanned skin ran deep, with lines that sat entrenched through the middle hollow of his cheeks, nearly down to his chin. Despite his weathered face, his body was in impeccable condition. He sat shirtless, save for a gold shoulder panel, which hugged his thick neck and shallowly covered both shoulders. Aside from this and a belted warrior skirt, he was naked. His huge, corded arms and wide expanse of chest were on display for all to see, meticulously presented as if sculpted from stone. Except for his hands, of course, she corrected her assessment. Today, as always, he wore his protective, sacred, red gloves. The only items in the world that did not disintegrate at his touch.

"I hear you robbed me of a sacrifice this season." He continued to address Jezebel. "Abbott is most distressed."

He himself didn't sound too distressed. Curious, perhaps. Maybe even slightly amused at his daughter's antics and his High Priest's response, but he was also clearly expecting an explanation.

"Father." Jezebel performed a deep bow. "It is merely a small delay. She will be sacrificed at the next Sacrament. I am merely indulging myself...temporarily."

"I see."

There was a long pause, and when Jezebel realised that neither his approval nor disapproval was incoming, she pressed on. "Mila's unique demon power, combined with her desire to avoid death, is keeping me entertained, and you know how much I have struggled with boredom, Father."

"Oh?" the God-King rumbled, his interest piqued. "And what is her power?"

"She can sense the energy of living things."

There was another long pause, then, "Bring her to me."

Mila heard Jezebel huff in surprise. This demand was apparently completely unexpected, and Jezebel was hesitating, fearing that Midas would use the moment to destroy Mila before Jezebel was finished with her.

Mila felt the petulant energy flow from Jezebel as she considered disobeying for half a second, before she finally submitted and pulled Mila forward by the neck, placing the lead in the God-King's gloved hand.

Now that she was this close to him, Mila began to tremble in earnest. She'd been around demons with strong powers before, but Midas was a god and he could kill with an effortless touch.

No demon had powers like that. As a rule, demon powers, whilst all different, couldn't transform the world around them, and certainly couldn't kill. They were as harmless to others as the whispers of ants were to a sleeping lion.

Mila was so close to him that she could smell him. A scented oil covered his skin and accentuated the harsh lines of his muscles. Its smoky, plum smell made her feel nauseous. Three white, fluffy cats wound around his feet, oblivious to Mila's closeness. She felt a pressure beneath her chin as Midas gripped her with his red-gloved hand and forced her face up, so that her eyes looked directly into his.

"Well, demon?" Menace and the promise of death laced through every word. "What is my energy?" he growled.

Mila was frozen. She tried to read him, but her powers seemed numbed and muted. Despite her pride, she began to cry with fear. She was so frightened, terrified that he would whip off his glove and disintegrate her within the next second.

"I do not know," she choked out. "I cannot sense you."

And it was the truth. She felt nothing at his touch, as though he were invisible to her power.

He considered her answer for half a second and then spoke. "That is because I am not a living thing," he said softly, releasing her face so abruptly that she fell back a step. "*I am immortal!*" he roared to no one and everyone, but most especially himself.

"Praise be," Jezebel intoned, fully cowed now, showing no ounce of defiance.

"Praise be," the High Priest Abbott repeated dutifully.

"I am not entirely opposed to the idea of demon pets entertaining my aristocracy before their sacrifice," Midas said, appearing mollified by their subjugation. "Especially if it amuses you, daughter."

Jezebel blinked. It was clear she hadn't been expecting the conversation to take this turn, and Mila knew she certainly had no plans to share the outrage and attention she was receiving with others in her circle.

"Your Eminence," the High Priest Abbott spoke for the first time. His voice was flat with barely masked outrage.

Of all the priests who served Midas, Abbott was the one known by name throughout Artor. Even Mila knew of his reputation, despite the self-imposed isolation of her previous life. She'd heard a number of disturbing stories about his devotion. How, in his youth, he'd once reportedly lit his own feet on fire to demonstrate the strength of his conviction. These stories were not only good for bards to regale to sweaty listeners in the airy drinking gardens of the Highlands, but they were extremely effective when it came to exporting and enforcing the rule of the Church across the vast nation in rapid form. Despite the fact Abbott was now an old, thin man who lived off self-flagellation and gratuitous displays of routine starvation, the reputation stalked him like a shadow.

"I warn," Abbott continued, "that to allow the perpetration of such an anomaly within the very walls of your palace may lead to your subjects being tempted into sacrilegious...attachments to these creatures." He turned to Jezebel and his gnarled voice turned sermon-esque. "Never forget, Highness, that while they may present to us like humans, it is not their true form. They are fallen. They are humans who have sold their souls to obtain the slightest whiff of power. I wonder if you'd enjoy the close proximity of such a creature if you could see its true form – a black and shapeless form of energy. A being who has deep capacity and unrelenting desire for deception and destruction. A demon's earthly power may have some uses and bring small pleasures and conveniences, but they are to be viewed as nothing more than a sinful temptation. They are, at their core, rotten beings – ”

Jezebel was nodding in fervent agreement with him, but to Mila's surprise, Midas chose to interrupt, seemingly annoyed that the priest had chosen this moment to rant and dampen a rare moment of his daughter's enjoyment.

“I remind you, High Priest, that there is no hierarchy among the behaviours. The First is equally as toxic and corrosive as the Eight, no more, no less. It would do well for the humans in Artor to remember that. Especially as the demon population begins to dwindle but my need for the Sacrament of Contrition remains ever present.”

“Your Eminence,” Abbott conceded immediately, scraping his forehead to the floor. Mila resisted the urge to read his energy. trying to keep her focus purely on Jezebel. But she was very curious to know what he truly felt about the rebuke, even as he said, “It shall be the subject of this week's sermon. A timely reminder.”

Jezebel looked jubilant, and Mila felt from her the flow of great satisfaction, reassured that her actions straddled the border of theologically acceptable.

Interesting, Mila observed, *this dynamic between Jezebel and the High Priest.* But even more interesting was another little tidbit Mila had learned during the exchange. She'd never known that the God-King viewed all Eight Heretical Behaviours as equally unforgivable. How curious to learn that the Second, ‘public displays of joy or group celebrations’, was as worthy of the same punishment as the First, ‘selling one's soul to obtain demon powers’.

Mila studied the hard face of the High Priest Abbott carefully and realised then that the nation-wide persecution of ikarei was almost entirely a construct of the Church alone.

Midas might demand sacrifices, but Abbott was the one, through his sermons and lessons and preaching, who had caused the Church to turn the people of Artor so specifically against them.

Why? she wondered, and tentatively reached her power out to read him, but all it took was a yank from Jezebel's hand upon the lead to bring her power back where it was most required. No time to pull the thread on that mystery, at least, not while she had this abominable Princess to entertain.

She dutifully followed the princess as they left the priest and the God-King behind them in the Grand Cathedral.

As they departed, Mila observed with interest that Jezebel could not keep the smirk from her face, and her energy was still exuberant, as if scoring such a victory over the High Priest was something she'd long desired.

Lady Picory's Party

Navigating Jezebel's ever fluctuating emotional state to earn herself food became Mila's sole purpose as the days passed. In the evenings, she would lie awake long after Jezebel had fallen asleep, and try distract herself from the pain of her stomach eating itself by pondering the mystery of Abbott's deliberate persecution of her kind.

Was he simply scared of ikarei? Or was something more sinister at play?

There were no answers readily available, and Mila's opportunities to read the High Priest were limited. Jezebel hated him and avoided him whenever she could, choosing instead to socialise outside the palace wherever possible.

One such morning, Jezebel announced with glee that they would be visiting Picory Manor. Mila could barely rouse herself to be curious about the destination. She could not tell if it was the horrid leash's aura, the starvation, or the rubane withdrawals causing her to feel lightheaded. Probably a combination of all three.

Breakfast had not been offered.

Conversely, Jezebel's mood could not have been more bright. Mila sensed great excitement and anticipation radiating from her as they drew closer to the manor, and she wondered what exactly the princess had in store for her that day and who they'd be meeting.

"Eliza Picory," Jezebel said, as though answering Mila's unspoken question. "She and Meredith, who you'll also meet at some point, are part of the new nobility." She saw Mila's questioning gaze and rolled her eyes. "God, you are truly a heathen, aren't you? The new nobility is what we call the wives whose husbands were among the first to lay down their weapons and swear obedience to my father. They were richly rewarded for their loyalty and now all own titles and manors in the land that lies within a day's carriage ride around Jeralusah. You'll need to understand all of this if you're to be of proper use to me, demon."

"Yes, mistress," Mila agreed with a fervent nod and silently noted the manor they approached with awe. If this was the type of reward available for recognising Midas's ascension as God-King, then it was little surprise that the war had been short-lived.

Especially when the opposing option had been death.

The carriage came to a halt at the large wooden doors of the manor, and Jezebel accepted a footman's hand as she descended. She pulled Mila behind her and did not pause even for a moment to allow her to gain her footing on the small step. Only her agility from a lifetime living amongst trees saved Mila from a painful fall onto the sharp gravelled courtyard.

The doors to the manor opened slowly, and Mila followed Jezebel inside to the greeting room, where they were made to wait a surprisingly long time before their host appeared. Finally, the door pushed open, and a tall woman with curly brown hair and a dancer's gait waltzed in. Mila's power was drawn to her involuntarily and she wrestled with it, trying to draw it back onto Jezebel.

"Princess! Welcome. I wasn't expecting you to grace us with your presence today."

Lady Eliza Picory's welcome seemed so sincere and warm that Mila was surprised to feel the undertone of resentment and dislike directed towards the princess. The look of horror she cast in Mila's direction, however, was entirely undisguised, and Jezebel laughed loudly when she saw it.

"I had to show you my newest pet, Eliza. A *demon*. I know," she said gleefully to the shocked silence. "Now come, let us go to the sitting room, and I'll show you how she can entertain you too."

For a horrifying moment, Mila wondered if Jezebel really intended to share her around for the sexual gratification of her social circle, but that thought was interrupted when she felt Lady Picory's own sharp waves of energetic discomfort at the idea.

The woman was a master actor, and without Mila's powers, she wouldn't have noticed the flood of concern that suddenly enveloped Lady Picory at Jezebel's suggestion. But she continued to smile broadly as she said, "Fabulous. Now I'll just warn you that there are already a few of the girls upstairs. I do hope it's alright to show her off to a few others as well?"

"Of course!" Jezebel was delighted by the idea of a larger audience.

However, once they ascended the grand golden staircase and pushed open the double barrel doors to the sitting room, the abrupt silence that met them on their arrival made it quickly apparent that Lady Picory had understated the social event she was hosting. She had, in fact, been throwing quite the party, one that had almost certainly included dancing, joy and celebration. A truly heretical, secret gathering of elites.

And it was clear that Jezebel had absolutely *not* been invited.

Mila wasn't sure if the absence of the invitation had been because Jezebel was the daughter of the God-King, or simply because she wasn't liked, but either way, the snub was obvious. She could feel Jezebel's outrage and humiliation sizzling from her as the princess found herself standing in the centre of a silent room, filled with people who didn't want her there.

Mila paused behind Jezebel, using the woman as a shield against the size of the crowd, but their energies came barrelling towards her anyway. She shrank her horns reflexively to minimise the impact, but the action just drew attention to them and made things worse. A number of distressed gasps emitted from those who had witnessed it.

Fear, horror, curiosity.

She was unsure which of those energies were directed at her and which at Jezebel, but either way, it didn't matter. They hit her all at once, bombarding and overwhelming her senses, forcing her to physically gasp for air to steady herself. She fought for control of her power, and finally, with great effort, she managed to draw it mostly back into herself, blocking out the frenzied energies of the fifty or so people in the room and leaving just a small beam that linked her to Jezebel alone.

Jezebel's energy was mixed. Her humiliation and outrage had dulled as she comprehended what she'd interrupted and was steadily being replaced by anger and pride. She was determined not to let the occupants of the room know that she was upset. Showing indifference was the only way she could save face in this situation, something Lady Picory understood perfectly. She tried to help, breaking the uncomfortable silence with a carefully worded explanation.

"Apologies, Princess. I believed you to be quite busy with our Holy God-King following the Sacrament of Contrition and expected that you wouldn't want to be bothered by such a small gathering. It's really been nothing more than just an...embarrassing demonstration of gross opulence."

There was a titter of nervous laughter from the other women and men in the room.

Jezebel gave a close-lipped smile in response. "Yes, you're right. I have been busy. In fact, I barely have time to grace you all with my presence today. But I was passing through and thought I might pop by and show you all my new conquest. My demon pet."

She stepped aside, fully exposing Mila in her new, horrifying garb, for all the party to gawk at.

"A *demon*?!"

"I *knew* I saw horns."

"How has this been permitted?"

It seemed an age passed before the room had their fill of staring, and Jezebel was more than happy to stand in silence and stare them all down until they did. Finally, the tension lifted, and general chatter slowly resumed.

Jezebel accepted a drink from Lady Picory and allowed herself to be escorted to a magnificent chair next to one of the far windows. There sat eight or so women. Jezebel's friends, Mila assumed, or at least, women she expected to indulge her.

Once Jezebel was seated amongst them, she ordered a server to bring over a bowl and some bread. She was swiftly obeyed.

When the items arrived, the princess placed them on the floor at Mila's feet and gestured to them. "Eat."

Hungry but wary, Mila knelt slowly and leaned towards the bowl.

When the tips of her fingers touched the rim, Jezebel rapped out a sharp, "No! No hands. From the floor will suit you just fine."

It was humiliating, but Mila was starving, and in this situation, pride was a dead currency. Food was food.

So, she knelt and ate the bread with her mouth alone, like a puppy by its master's feet.

"Her power," Jezebel's voice sounded from above her, "is the ability to sense your energy."

"That's the power she chose?" The woman who spoke had a lilt of a laugh to her voice. "Ahh. I'm sorry, Princess. I can't help but laugh when I hear of the powers demons accept in exchange for their souls. They could not be more useless, more ridiculous."

"Well, that's half the evil of Viah on display there, isn't it? Entrapping children in their dreams with the promise of great powers," someone else said.

"Entrapping the weak," Jezebel corrected. "Remember, we're all subjected to Viah's temptation in our sleep as children. We – " she gestured to the group around her, " – were among those devout enough to resist."

Mila felt an air of superiority settling over the group.

The woman who'd mocked Mila's power sat with a white cat nestled sleepily in her lap. She reminded Mila vaguely of a peacock: tall, and slim enough that her clavicle was all but poking free of her skin. She was older than all the other women by at least two decades, and wore a shimmering, ocean-green dress, her gold hair piled high in an updo, which pulled the skin on her forehead taut.

"She certainly has an...earthy quality to her," she said.

The observation was a barbed critique, especially considering how much effort Jezebel had put into dressing Mila in a manner that could be described as anything but "earthy".

Jezebel let the comment roll off her as she reclined further into the chair and gestured to a maid holding an enormous, feathered fan to commence cooling her.

"Judge her all you like, Meredith." She turned to the wider group. "You'll all come to hate her soon enough." She could barely conceal her delight. "My demon can sense your energy," she repeated. "And for those of you too thick to figure out what that means yet, it means that anything you once thought to hold secret from me will be secret no longer."

Mila didn't know who tried to hide their horror more, her or the ladies of the room. Jezebel ploughed on, totally aware and completely delighted by the reaction to this information.

"Demon," she ordered, "read Eliza's energy."

She evidently had not forgiven the host for not inviting her to the party.

Obediently, Mila turned to face Lady Picory and reached her hand out towards her, to help direct her unpredictable power. The wall of hostile energy radiating from the woman hit Mila like a charging horse.

"She would kill me if she had the chance," Mila responded honestly, trying to appear bland and disinterested in this news. Jezebel was dangerous, but she also did not want a woman like Eliza Picory as an enemy.

"Don't appreciate my little reader, Eliza?" Jezebel laughed again. "I wonder what you think you have to hide from me."

"I hide nothing, Princess," the woman harrumphed. "She is a demon. I merely believe she should have been sacrificed with the rest for both her sin and for our nation's repentance. The world would be a safer place without her kind."

"As would we all from your ambitions." Jezebel sneered, and Lady Picory pursed her lips.

Mila tried to draw her power away from Lady Picory and return her attention to the bread that still lay before her. Her power did not obey. It flew from her weak mental grasp and scattered throughout the room again, reading everything in the vicinity, overwhelming and meaningless to her in its sheer volume: *lust, anger, hunger, delight, human, human, mouse in the wall, plants hanging from the ceiling, thirsty, anxious, human, human, ikarei, human, human –*

Mila sat bolt upright.

Ikarei energy? There was another ikarei in here somewhere?

Forgetting the bread entirely, Mila wrestled for control of her power, trying to scan the room more deliberately, wishing that she could hone it more accurately and with less effort.

It was useless.

There was another ikarei in here somewhere. She knew it, but maddeningly, she simply wasn't powerful enough to identify who it was. Not without touching each and every person in the room, and that was never going to happen.

It was beyond frustrating.

With resignation, she allowed herself to be distracted from this startling discovery by the new topic being discussed by the ladies.

"There must be something done about them. Their voices grow stronger in Traders Bay every week, and soon it will spread, as these things always seem to do."

"It's straight up blasphemy, it is. Who do they think they are to know better than the Church?"

"I know better than the Church," Jezebel chimed in haughtily.

That caused a slight hiccup in the flow of conversation, but the woman named Meredith smoothed it over swiftly. "Of course you do, Highness. You're half Divine. But these dissidents... Where do they even come from? Who are *they?* It's sheer arrogance."

"It's a phase," another woman huffed dismissively, wanting to return to gossip rather than politics.

"It's a threat," Meredith corrected. "I'm telling you, Cedrik gets multiple reports these days of small crowds gathering to hear them speak."

"Speak about what, exactly?"

"I dare not repeat specifics here," Meredith wisely said. "Safe to say, it's critical of the Church. Especially the High Priest."

Mila was surprised to see Jezebel snort at that. "Is that it? Well, take it from me, the High Priest could do with a little critiquing now and again. Hardly worth troubling our afternoon over, Meredith. Now, who is next for my demon's scrutiny?"

As the conversation around her continued, it quickly became evident that, while the princess was enjoying the scandal she'd created by bringing a demon into the room, there were more people than just Lady Eliza Picory who could not reconcile her actions with their beliefs. Mila's presence caused an undercurrent of tension to Jezebel's social circle in a way that the princess had not expected, nor did she understand.

Mila, however, understood it perfectly.

When Mila had been a human child, she'd been counted amongst the most devout. Living in a hardworking town in the region of Prious, she'd dutifully gone to Church with her family, and she'd obeyed Church law with fervour and excitement. She loved being recognised and praised by her community as "such a good girl". It had all been so easy to do, and the alternative was so frightening that she couldn't imagine living or being any other way.

Even though she'd been young, she still remembered the way the priest had described, in excruciating detail, the Rotting Muds of the afterlife that awaited all nonbelievers and heretics. Fear of that fate had been paralysing, and the mental image of a place where Viah, the great Worm of Death, stewed in the filth of the Rot, devouring the souls of the fallen, frequently gave her nightmares.

That fear had been reinforced weekly, through a variety of mechanisms. She remembered for years of her youth, she'd been separated from her parents every Worship Day. While the adults had attended lessons run by the priest, the children played with toys in a back room under supervision of an acolyte. The toys available to her were figurines of Midas, the jesu, and a warped, horrendous-looking creature that Mila was told was a demon. The only acceptable game to play was the one where the demons were vanquished.

She also remembered story time, where one of the attending acolytes read fables to the gathered children. Fables that centred around the story of Viah, the devil who dwelt on his throne of grot and bile, and plotted ways to tempt young humans while they slept, to convince them to sell him their souls.

The message was always clear: *be prepared, strengthen your mind and resolve against this threat now, for when he comes for you in your sleep, the strong will prevail and the weak will fall.*

As she'd grown a little older, she'd been permitted to attend the sermons with the adults, and she'd witnessed firsthand the way these teachings had crippled meaningful connections outside of close-knit family groups. Her parents were forever mistrustful and wary of those who seemingly had reason to be happy, always whispering that the neighbour who'd recently given birth, or become betrothed, must be secretly dancing and feasting in their homes. They were also unable to show hospitality or compassion for any outside their tiny, exclusive selection of trusted friends. Mila distinctly remembered her father turning away an old travelling woman during a truly ferocious storm, out of fear that he may unknowingly harbour a heretic inside his house.

This was the key issue that Jezebel's circle had with her decision.

The enforcement of the Heretical Behaviours had waged a quiet war on the centuries of culture and tradition that had existed within the many diverse regions of Artor. There were many older folk still alive to whom the 'Dark Ages' were more than a cautionary tale, but a life they remembered and enjoyed.

So, to them, their princess's apparent disregard of the punishment given to heretics was a slap in the face to the sacrifices they'd made to ensure they were following Church law.

On the other hand, Jezebel was Midas's daughter. She was guaranteed a place in Aluah, the heavenly afterlife, regardless of her actions, and as such, she would never truly experience the questioning, the betraying insecurity that almost all others felt about the fate of their immortal soul at one point or another in their life.

Mila remembered clearly the dawning horror she'd felt on that morning fourteen years ago when she'd awoken with horns poking a few inches through her hairline. She had no recollection of the dream where she'd agreed to a devilish pact with Viah, but the horns were evidence that it had happened and that she'd failed the test. Somehow, despite her years of devotion, she had been tempted and tricked, and for reasons she could not discern, her sleeping mind had agreed to become his demon. At thirteen she'd condemned herself to an afterlife of torture and misery in the Rot. She probably would have tried to end her own life that very day out of shame if she hadn't suddenly become so fearful of what would happen to her after she died.

Mila shook that memory, and the aftermath of that morning, from her mind. It would not be helpful today, or any day, to remember what had transpired next.

* * *

Ultimately, citing a busy schedule, Jezebel did not stay long at the party, and everyone, for their own reasons, was grateful. When back in the carriage and jostling along the road again, Mila waited for Jezebel to make good on her threat and demand to know about the true energy and feelings of the so-called friends within her social circle. She wondered if there was ever a pleasant way to tell someone they were universally disliked. She wondered if Jezebel would lash out at her in pain and punish Mila for their feelings towards her. She wondered if she'd be able to plausibly lie.

To her surprise, the question never came, and when she next routinely ran her power over Jezebel, she realised that the reason for the lack of intrigue was simple. Jezebel already knew, and as much as she pretended it didn't affect her, it did.

They arrived back at Jezebel's apartments and, once inside, Jezebel ordered a beautiful stained-glass bath to be drawn and a book of uncouth poems to be brought to her, ordering Mila to read aloud while she bathed.

Mila was surprised by the choice, but as she sat on the cold black tiles, with the bathtub warm against her back, she found herself trying not to laugh as she read, despite the mood of the day that had transpired.

"There once was a girl from Artor
Was a teacher, but also a whore
She did sums on the side
Whilst riding astride
She's efficient, but also she's poor."

Jezebel did not hold back, laughing freely. With interest, Mila felt the tight clutch of humiliation and hurt that Jezebel had been wrapped in slowly loosening with her laughter.

"There once was a boy from the plains
Big breeches but lacking some brains
Any girl he would wed
Would take him to her bed
For a night, and a sheet full of stains."

Jezebel laughed again and then, to Mila's surprise, began to construct her own.

"There once was a girl from the west
Who had a large, singular breast
Just one, not the two
Lopsided, askew..."

"It was hard to find quite the right vest?" Mila didn't know what boldness possessed her in that moment to say anything or where the line even came from, but it worked.

Jezebel snorted in amusement. "That's a good one. Let's try another."

"There once was a girl from Artor,
Had an arse that was big as a boar..."

"Big as a boar?" Mila challenged cautiously. "That doesn't make any sense!"

"You do better then!"

Mila couldn't believe that she was actually enjoying this exchange. She wracked her brain for a moment and then began,

"There once was a girl from Artor,
Her name was Eliza Picor
She had tiny red lumps
On her breasts and her rump
They were permanent, itchy and sore."

Jezebel's full-bellied laughter echoed throughout the entire apartment.

They went on like this until, eventually, Jezebel called for a servant to bring two large plates of food. The smell of sesame-roasted root vegetables served alongside small, hot balls of spiced mince and cabbage filled the air, and Mila looked agonisingly over at Jezebel who smiled and inclined her head in concession.

Mila ate properly, for the first time in days.

The Test

Two weeks later, Mila woke and sensed two very important things had changed. The first was that something was very different about Jezebel's mood. She was nervous and subdued and wouldn't respond when Mila inquired why. It worried her, and Mila knew she needed to figure out the reason quickly.

She couldn't blame it on Worship Day. That was tomorrow, and even though Jezebel resented sitting in the Grand Cathedral for hours, listening to Abbott drone on, she'd never been nervous about attending the weekly sermon.

Could it be the weather? Mila wondered. The spring was pressing on and these specific weeks in the season were known as The Build-Up, easily identifiable by the near-constant, oppressive humidity that never allowed a storm to bring relief. It was uncomfortable to do much of anything during these weeks. Perhaps that was contributing to Jezebel's mood? But no. Why should that make her nervous? If anything, the weather had created more stability and routine to Jezebel's days. An early morning walk around the palace gardens before the crippling humidity struck, a nap in the heat of the afternoon, and then socialising during the evening after the intense wall of humidity built like clockwork just before sundown. No storm though. Stormweek would come later in the season, right before summer.

No. None of these were satisfactory reasons for Jezebel's nervous mood, and Mila's ignorance made her stressed.

The second important thing she realised, was that she'd finally awoken without the searing burn of pain behind her eyes.

Her body had finally adjusted to the lack of rubane and was no longer punishing her for its absence.

Sweet, blessed relief – finally.

In fact, over the past week, she felt as though she were being rewarded in more ways than one for her patience. She'd steadily gained more control over her power and was now able to sense Jezebel and her surroundings with far less effort. On top of this, Jezebel now seemed to have grown accustomed to Mila's dutiful, quiet, constant presence. The result was a few lapses in her security, including letting the lead fall to the ground during her most recent dinner. Mila knew that as she gained the woman's favour and trust, lapses like this would happen more and more often. All she needed to do was wait for one she could exploit.

Mila had anticipated most of these changes happening eventually, but what she could not have predicted was Jezebel's growing enjoyment of Mila's company. Since composing limericks in the bathroom, Jezebel now spoke to Mila directly and even occasionally explained things when Mila asked questions. She never asked Mila for her opinion, and regular meals were still not guaranteed, but the lack of food seemed to stem more from Jezebel's short attention span, rather than a malicious desire to starve her new pet. In fact, Mila noticed a curious instance of Jezebel glancing across at her whenever the princess was being funny or clever, as though, now that she'd acknowledged that Mila was intelligent, she wanted to be acknowledged as such in return. Mila's small rebellion came in the way she made a point of never giving Jezebel such recognition, not unless she was ordered to do so. It was the one semblance of autonomy she still retained, and she was determined not to relinquish it easily.

* * *

The mystery of Jezebel's nervous mood prevailed as they headed out on their scheduled morning walk, and although Mila was determined to figure out the cause, she couldn't help but be distracted by the beauty of the gardens. The sudden absence of her rubane headache made her feel as though she was able to truly see and appreciate them for the first time.

The use of the word 'garden' to describe the horticultural marvel that Midas's gardeners had managed to create over a mere forty years was an insult. It was enormous, and the vast area was divided into segments that represented every single specimen of flora that could be found across the vast and diverse regions of Artor. Along the eastern side, where they walked today, Mila discovered with delight that it had been planted with the rich, tropical flora that dominated large swaths of her home in the rainforest Highlands.

Around them, stood the towering, hundred-year-old bayan trees that had been carefully uprooted from their original homes and now lined the marble pathway. Despite the heat, the thick branches and unusual roots of the huge trees managed to create a cool walkway with their shadows. The sight of them made her powerfully homesick, and for a brief moment, Mila couldn't help but reminisce about her own beautiful cottage.

It sat nestled between a sister-pair of huge bayan trees that, over time, had come to grow around, and seemingly embrace, the small, sweet cottage. The thick roots, which grew downwards from the lowest hanging branches on the trees, acted as pillars that protected her house from the elements and also created small alcoves where she'd been able to clamber up and sit to meditate in the mornings before the cooler air submitted to the humidity.

Inside was largely bare of any furniture that she had not painstakingly created herself from the foraged wood of fallen trees. Her windowsills were overrun with small plants, which had simple energies. Mila could easily sense their needs with little drain on her body, and she'd delighted in giving them what they needed in order to grow to their full potential – be it more or less sunlight, or more or less water. Her attentiveness had been rewarded by being bathed daily in their content and pragmatic energy.

Her cottage lacked the usual human smells of babies, chewing tobacco and rubbish. Instead, it smelled primarily of smoke, herbs and sweet florals. The rubane she'd smoked daily had an earthy, nutty aroma that complemented the concoction, but the pretty weed itself grew prolifically around the outside stones, turning red, yellow and pink as the seasons changed. It was beautiful. She missed it desperately.

With a semblance of hope, she considered looking for it in these gardens. It was a Highland native plant, after all, so if it would be anywhere in the palace, it would be in this area. But it was a weed, so perhaps it hadn't made the cut.

Her visualisation was broken by Jezebel's sharp "Well? Isn't that funny?"

"It is," Mila agreed smoothly, although she had no idea what had been said. She brought her attention back to the princess. The golden lead to her collar continued to dangle loosely between Jezebel's fingers, and the new Guard of the Body followed, always a few paces behind, holding himself taut as a drawn bow, ready to intervene if his princess's demon decided to turn on her. Mila sensed his never-ending nervousness for the tenth time that day and sighed. Attacking Jezebel in that moment was the furthest thing from her mind, and the guard's anxiety was ruining the otherwise unusually peaceful morning.

"I need to relieve myself," Jezebel abruptly announced, and Mila's stomach tightened as she watched the princess tie the end of the lead to a nearby bench before walking off in the direction of the garden lavatory.

The guard seemed as confused as Mila. He hesitated for half a second before finally deciding to follow the princess. Despite the questionable wisdom of leaving a demon alone in the garden, his duty was to protect Jezebel at all times.

Mila was alone.

Her breathing tripled in pace. This had never happened before. Was now the moment she'd been waiting for? It seemed too good to be true.

Incredulously, Mila watched the princess and the guard depart. As soon as their figures were out of sight, she turned and inspected the knot. It was loose and performative. Mila could have yanked on the loop half-heartedly and it would have come undone.

It set off alarm bells in her head. Something about this wasn't right.

Mila closed her eyes and sent her power out into the garden, pushing past the immediate energy of the dense surrounding vegetation and exploring deeper amongst it.

There.

A human...no, two humans. Courtiers spying on her, waiting to see what she'd do.

Well, at least the cause of Jezebel's mood was now revealed. This had been a test, and a timely reminder that Jezebel might be spoiled, cruel and vain, but she was certainly not stupid, and it would be dangerous to assume that she did not suspect Mila of plotting to escape.

So, instead of tugging at the knot, Mila sighed and made a show of sitting comfortably on the bench to wait like an obedient pet, fanning herself as the surrounding din of crickets denied her even a moment of peace and quiet.

Patience had always been her strong suit, and she knew that earning Jezebel's trust now would be invaluable for her future plans. And she had time, she still had two months.

Jezebel and the guard returned. She tried to keep her face neutral, but Mila was so well tuned to her now that the princess could not disguise the energy of joy and relief that rose when she saw Mila waiting dutifully for her return.

"Good girl," Jezebel said happily, and the condescending phrase suddenly triggered in Mila an old memory.

"Mila is such a good girl." They had all said about her. Her family, her village, the acolyte... She'd loved the praise, lived for it. But none of it had mattered on the morning she'd awoken as a thirteen-year-old and found that she could suddenly grow horns and feel the energy of the household. Mila was momentarily awash with memories – the way her sister had screamed and how her mother's face had turned ashen grey. The way her father had smashed things, and for the first time in her life, Mila had been afraid of him, afraid he might convince himself that he could somehow beat the taint out of her...

Push it away.

Mila shut her mind down and forced the memories out of her head. Jezebel was looking at her expectantly, and Mila knew that she would not be able to keep the pain off her face if she allowed herself to remember that morning in more detail.

"Highness?" She forced herself to look up innocently, acting as though she was confused by Jezebel's praise, as though an escape attempt hadn't even crossed her mind.

Jezebel said nothing more but glowed happily at the response and turned to continue down the garden path.

Mila had passed the test.

The Artor Trading Company

The following day, Jezebel informed Mila that they would be attending a dinner in the city that evening. She also mentioned offhandedly that Jahan, the former Guard of the Body, would be joining their entourage. Mila felt a thrill of excitement at the news.

She knew she'd earned Jezebel's trust now, and this event, more than any other she'd attended with Jezebel thus far, seemed most likely to yield a potential opportunity to escape.

Knowing that Jahan was to be the guard in attendance was possibly another bonus. He'd already shown himself to be sympathetic towards her once. Perhaps he could be persuaded to help her again. Perhaps, she fantasised, he was so resentful of Jezebel that he might even join her in her escape.

With this thought in mind, Mila could hardly wait to see him and gauge his energy, and the day seemed to crawl. When the evening finally arrived and Jahan arrived at Jezebel's apartments, Mila looked up at him with hope and pleasure, but Jahan's energy was anything but reciprocal. Her optimism swiftly came crashing down.

Jahan's energy was pure professionalism once more, despite the gaping, bloody hole in his face that was now slightly healed, but still unmissable and grotesque. Jezebel had prohibited him from covering the wound tonight, with even a cotton patch.

"This," she informed him with glee as the carriage departed the palace grounds, "is to reinforce to all gawkers the repercussions of disappointing me tonight or treating the demon too kindly."

There were a lot of gawkers around tonight.

The purpose of the dinner was to honour and welcome a new board member to the Artor Trading Company, a powerful corporation that Jezebel was heavily invested in. She explained it to Mila in the carriage, prattling excitedly about her stake in the evening.

"The Artor Trading Company deals almost exclusively in the procurement of luxuries and exotics, and they have an extensive network of contacts that span the most remote corners of the globe. They also have a private army of guards that is larger than the Church's own private Corps of Guards. And I'm the official Patron of the entire enterprise!"

Mila had heard the name before. The Artor Trading Company was infamous for many reasons. Not least of which were the lack of qualms they had about dabbling in the human slave trade. She remembered once meeting an envoy of the company in her remote home village of Brome, and he had severely frightened her.

The tall, angular man had arrived in explorer's leathers and with a sharp, manicured beard that looked heavy and awkward in contrast to the bare-faced Highlander men. He had claimed to be searching for rare mushrooms and had proposed generous employment terms if someone in the village would consent to be his collector and purveyor.

Mila had feigned ignorance of the Company's existence, but even she remembered how hard it had been to say no to the man. The money he'd offered had been good, but his demeanour, coupled with the five guards at his side, had silently implied that they hadn't travelled this far to leave empty-handed. They would ensure that they found something – or someone – to sell if the mushrooms weren't available.

Mila was not surprised to learn that Jezebel was a heavy player in such an organisation.

While the dinner tonight might have officially been in honour of a new shareholder, Jezebel made it no secret that she considered herself to be the true guest of honour, and she ensured that she timed their arrival at the dinner perfectly to command the full room's attention.

Heralding her approach were six young footmen, intentionally dressed by Jezebel in striking, but ridiculous, long grey sacks that hung from their shoulders to their knees. Their faces and hands were hidden by white masks and gloves. She also ensured that she was flanked on one side by Mila in her dark swamp-creature gown with her horns out at full extension, and on her other side stood tall Jahan, with his disfigured face.

Jezebel herself had gone to excessive lengths for her evening's attire. She'd spent two hours having her entire nude body painted by artists with tiny gold dots of varying sizes and patterns, over which she'd laid a thin, spider-silk sheer dress that hid nothing.

In this risqué attire, and flanked by Mila and Jahan, her entrance could not be ignored, and she was not disappointed.

A hush fell over the dining room as the footmen parted like water to allow Jezebel to mince through and wordlessly present herself.

She stood for a long while in the doorway, allowing all inside to glimpse *all* of her, and then, with a light tug on Mila's lead, she strutted over to a seat at the head of the table. She had to fight to keep a nonchalant expression on her face but was unable to completely hide her glee.

Mila and Jahan stood behind her, and Mila braced for impact as the energies of everyone in the room came rushing towards them. She was not disappointed.

"I pride myself on being unpredictable," a male voice from across the table called out. "But even I have never dreamed up anything like this...What in fates are we looking at, Princess?" Mila followed the sound of the voice, and it took her a moment to place why the speaker seemed familiar. Then it struck her.

The man from the crypt. The man with the green eyes who hadn't betrayed her. Who was he, and what was he doing here?

Outside of the crypt, she was now able to see him properly. He had a very handsomely cut face, with dark brows, a broad jaw, and the light shadow of wild stubble around his lips and chin. She hadn't noticed back in the crypt that his blond hair was so long that most of it was pulled back and secured behind his head in a bun, with some unruly golden waves refusing to be captured in this manner and bounding forward from his forehead and down his face. They framed his lovely eyes beautifully. She noted also, with interest, that he had a tiny, gold circular earring in one lobe. Very unusual for anyone to have such a piercing outside of the Highlands, let alone a man.

Something about it endeared him to her.

He was impeccably attired. His Company dinner jacket sat draped across the back of his chair, revealing a posh, fitted, dark grey waistcoat that clung to his broad chest. The loose, white shirt billowing underneath lent some softness to the otherwise harsh lines, and a thick, dark blue Ascot tie complemented the golden complexion of skin that had clearly spent a lot of time under the sun. He was unmistakably a sea-faring man and while his attire looked so tidy and expensive that he could easily be accepted at a glance as a ship's captain. On closer inspection of his roguish demeanour, one could be forgiven for jumping instead to the title of 'pirate'.

Mila watched the man languidly place his elbows on the white tablecloth and crack a knuckle as he leaned forward. He surveyed Mila, and as he did so, what little relief she might have felt at seeing a familiar face soon vanished. There was nothing in his expression or in the eager lean of his shoulders that revealed any recognition or sympathy for her situation. She tried to reach out with her power to read him, but frustratingly, found that she couldn't and wasn't sure why. Her ability to channel and hone her power had come so far in the past month. This should have been easy enough to do, and yet tonight, from him, she felt...nothing. Just a vague shadow energy that indicated something alive was sitting in his seat.

Thankfully, she didn't need her powers to read his body language, and what she saw she disliked. He held himself in a loose, rolling manner, as though he meant to appear jovial and nonchalant but he couldn't quite hide his intensity. She was reminded of a cobra poised to strike.

"Oh, these?" Jezebel replied, throwing a hand in the air with exaggerated flippancy. "Merely my pet demon and a server who made the mistake of treating her as though she were human." She moved on from the explanation swiftly, as though the enormous news she'd just shared was little more than an afterthought, certainly not worth more of an explanation. "Congratulations on your new appointment, Christopher," Jezebel continued, "Although I am terribly sorry to hear about what happened to Martin. And I regret your father couldn't join us tonight. Is he well?"

So, this is Christopher Culis.

Mila had now attended enough social events with Jezebel for the name to mean something to her.

Christopher Culis was the great-grand-nephew of the Artor Trading Company's original founder, and tonight, he was taking over as the company's second largest shareholder following his older brother's untimely demise, which, although tragic, had not been wholly unexpected.

For the past eight generations, the eldest sons of the Culis family had all found cruel and unusual ways to die in their thirty-fifth year of life. The family had always insisted that the phenomenon was the result of a curse obtained by a sea-faring ancestor. Many social observers, however, would state that the only true curse in the family was the gene of unbridled ambition that ran through the bloodline.

Cursed or not, this exact fate had recently fallen upon Christopher's eldest brother, Martin, who had fallen from his horse four months earlier, leaving Christopher as the second most powerful man in the company and the newly instated heir to the Culis fortune. Mila assumed this was who he'd been mourning when she found him in the crypt; however, with the way he carried himself tonight, as though his new status were a physical crown perched upon his head, it made her wonder if she'd imagined his red-rimmed eyes that day.

With effort, she pulled her gaze away from him and looked around the room at the other shareholders, who all kept their faces carefully neutral as they surveyed her. It was as though they didn't know how to react to her presence and didn't want to risk displeasing their fickle princess by revealing the wrong emotion. So, despite spotting a few fleeting shadows of fear and intrigue, Mila noted with interest that they all decided to follow Jezebel's lead and ignore Mila's presence entirely.

Christopher Culis was the exception. He stared openly and hungrily at her.

"You effortlessly show us, once again, the difference between princess and mere mortal," he flattered Jezebel, refusing to be distracted by her questions about his family. "But going so far as to take a demon as a pet is unheard of. How has the Church permitted this to occur?"

"The real question here, Christopher, is who do you think has more authority?" Jezebel chirped back delightedly. "Your Princess or the Church?"

With that challenge left floating in the air, she took her seat and signalled to the string quartet in the corner to start playing. This seemed to be the cue for the room to resume its chatter, but Mila sensed that the private conversations didn't stray far off the topic at hand.

Until there was another entrance.

The front door opened again, and this time, it was the Lady Eliza Picory who stepped through with her young handmaid.

Lady Picory surveyed the room with a horrified look that betrayed that, whatever she'd expected from this invitation, it certainly hadn't been the sight she saw before her now. She nervously shrank when she saw the formal Artor Trading Company dinner jackets worn by the other attendees and looked downright ill when she saw Jezebel and her footmen, specifically what the latter were wearing.

Jezebel's cackle told Mila immediately that she was about to witness retribution for the hurt Lady Picory had caused the princess all those weeks ago. The woman had evidently been sent an outfit by Jezebel to wear as a gift, but here she was, dressed exactly as one of Jezebel's attendants, in a long, shapeless, grey smock and white gloves.

“Who is...is that Eliza Picory?” an older man at the table exclaimed, peering over his glasses. “Dressed as a server? What are you doing, woman?”

“I...” Lady Picory’s face was now beet-red as she realised she was standing before the most powerful men in the country, men who frequently competed with her husband for access to rare goods and services, dressed as Jezebel’s servant.

Jezebel could not wipe the smile from her face as she pointed to the door. “The kitchens are that way, Eliza. I’m sure the entrées are nearly ready to be brought up.”

To her credit, Eliza gathered what little of her pride she could, and held her head high as she turned heel and headed to the kitchen.

What else could she have done? Publicly disobey the princess? Jezebel laughed again, and the sound was joined by the laugh of Christopher Culis from across the table.

“Well now, *that* was entertaining,” he said, and the hearty words could be heard clearly from the other end of the room. Mila felt Jezebel’s energy beam in response to his solidarity.

“Jahan.” Jezebel snapped her fingers and the handsome, disfigured ex-guard stepped forward and refilled her goblet, which she quickly drained, extending it immediately out to him for more.

Mila watched this with interest. Jezebel liked to drink most nights, but not recklessly like this. Something about this dinner was different for the woman, and Mila was beginning to suspect it had something to do with the presence of Christopher Culis.

Excellent.

If Jezebel was distracted and drunk enough then escape might truly be an option tonight. Mila’s blood thrummed with adrenaline as she scanned the room’s doors and windows and identified the servers’ entry. That would be the best route out of this building. Servants would be the least likely to prevent her if she slipped down that passage. And even if she was confronted, she could say she'd been sent on an errand for the princess. These were not the serving staff of the princess's palace apartments. No one here knew of the tight control Jezebel usually wielded over Mila. It might just work if she could hold her nerve for long enough.

She breathed deeply with excitement at the thought of this prospect, but then forced herself to turn her attention back to the conversation at hand. If she behaved at all suspiciously tonight, Jezebel would surely notice. Until the moment of her breakaway, her behaviour needed to be as routine as possible.

"I can barely restrain myself, Princess," she heard Christopher Culis call across the table again. His words came out as a laugh, but there was an edge to it. He was clearly a man accustomed to getting his way, and he wanted more answers about the demon situation than he'd received so far. "Do not hold me in suspense a moment longer. Tell me, are demon pets a new commodity?"

Jezebel considered her reply carefully. Mila knew that she hadn't liked the idea her father had briefly suggested, of enabling those in the aristocracy, such as Eliza, to have their pick of demons for entertainment. She enjoyed the notoriety and the exclusivity of having the only one. However, Mila also sensed that there was something about Culis's attention and approval that Jezebel deeply desired, and she was not ready for him to lose this intense interest in her just yet.

"I am considering it," she said eventually, haughtily. "My exposure to demons is more than most, and I have found that, despite their inherently evil and vile nature, many of them have harmless, and in some cases even useful, abilities. My demon here, for example, can read energies." Again, she decided to use the opportunity to threaten the room. "She will report to me after this dinner exactly who among you can be trusted... and who harbours poisonous intent against me. So be warned, do not say anything at this table with a half-truth stuck in your throat."

Mila noted with interest that, once again, the room shifted as the men tried to consciously change their energy towards the princess – without quite knowing how to do so. She felt with fascination the way they tried to reshape their fear and disdain for the woman into thoughts of appreciation for her beauty and strength.

All except one. Culis.

With burning curiosity, Mila sought answers from him again, forcibly pushing away the energetic hum of the rest of the room to try to focus just on him, and again she was thwarted. While she could sense him in the room as a living being, the specifics of his energy were blurred and unreadable, with a muffled, hazy quality to it, despite her best efforts. It was inexplicable, and infuriating.

He saw her staring, and although he misunderstood the reason for the frown on her face, he correctly assumed what she was trying to do and smiled in response, a cool challenge written in his eyes. "No need to worry about me, little demon. I'm happy to tell the princess exactly what I think of her, and she knows that."

Beside her, Mila felt Jezebel flush with both outrage and desire, which heightened as the sleek man rose from his chair and approached hers. He knelt beside her and leaned forward with a familiarity Mila had not expected to see. There was clearly a history between these two.

"Hello again, Princess," he said in a low voice and with a wry smile.

"What do you want, Christopher?" Jezebel said with playful wariness.

"Only to see your beauty up close."

"Flatterer," she accused. "And...liar."

"Guilty," he agreed with a laugh, then leaned even closer. "You know exactly why I'm here, because you know exactly what you've done to me by bringing this thing here." He gestured in Mila's direction. "This is how a spider reels in a fly, placing the web right over the most interesting flower in the meadow."

"You're saying I'm a spider, Christopher?"

"I'm saying," he gestured to himself with flamboyant self-deprecation. "I'm a predictable, mercantile fool, who will be miserable all night – at my own dinner party, nonetheless – unless you have mercy and toss me the smallest morsel of an answer to my questions."

Mila listened to the conversation, incredulous that he was able to take such a tone with the princess. She'd never heard anyone speak with her like this, but it seemed to be working. Jezebel sighed, as if this was all very boring, but Mila could feel her enjoyment resonating strongly.

"I'll be brief," Culis spoke softly, and only to Jezebel, as if they were co-conspirators. "I believed your Divine father to be the sole...consumer of these creatures. What would happen if these new pets turned out to be valuable and people were... reluctant to sacrifice them?"

Jezebel nodded slowly at his words, luxuriating in his close presence. "A valid point. I'll admit I have not discussed the specifics with him directly. But he did mention vague support for the concept of demons as pets when I presented this one to him. I imagine that, if it could somehow be assured that each demon would be sacrificed eventually, he would be amenable to the idea. It's the High Priest Abbott who would have a conniption."

"I think both you and I would enjoy watching that."

"What do you mean?" Jezebel asked.

"Well..." Culis was slightly more cautious now, pausing briefly before replying. "That question you posed to the room earlier, about who is more powerful, you or the Church? Well, let me answer it with one of my own – why is that even a question we consider at all? You are the God-King's daughter. Who in the Church has the gall to challenge your authority... ever?"

"Abbott," Jezebel hissed, almost to herself, but Culis leaned into it, his lips close to hers as he whispered.

"And wouldn't you relish the opportunity to wipe that question from Abbott's mouth?"

And wouldn't you love to ride on her coattails as she does? The thought came to Mila swiftly, and to her surprise, Culis looked over sharply at her, as though he'd somehow heard it.

"What's this one's name?" he drew back slightly from Jezebel, motioning towards Mila with his head.

"It's..." Jezebel stopped in her tracks, realising without embarrassment that she had never thought to ask. "I have no idea," she laughed.

Culis looked at Mila expectantly, waiting for her to share it, but unless Jezebel ordered her to, Mila resolved that she would not, and Jezebel did not seem inclined to humanise her demon an inch more than she had to. So, Mila said nothing and just stared back at him, waiting to see what would happen next.

Eventually, Culis conceded defeat on the question of her name, but continued to address Mila. "And you can sense energies. Very intriguing. Does that mean you can sense the difference between humans and demons too?"

What a good question. Smart man. Dangerous man.

"It does."

Not even Jezebel missed the way his eyes lit up at her response. "If you're trying to figure out a way to use my demon for your own purposes, then I'd stop," she said with a tight laugh. "I don't like to share."

"I do love a challenge, Princess. You know this."

"It's a challenge I'm afraid you'll lose."

"I'm not sure I've ever felt afraid." He playfully raised an eyebrow. "What's it feel like?"

Jezebel giggled, and Mila sensed the blood pounding in the princess's body. Jezebel opened her mouth to reply, but at that exact moment, the servers arrived from the kitchen, Eliza included, bearing the entrée, a rich, wild mushroom and rustic garlic soup, and Culis was forced to return to his seat on the other side of the table.

In his absence, the discussion at Jezebel's side turned to other matters, to new islands discovered on a recent voyage that were inhabited by a tribe that seemed to consist entirely of women. Although Jezebel was distracted by the new topic and ridiculing a red-faced Eliza whenever the opportunity presented itself, Mila could tell that something had changed. A seed, something to do with proving something to Abbott, had been planted in her mind.

The Display

As the night wore on, Jezebel continued to drink heavily, and Mila sensed a hard edge take over the princess. She considered the snippets of information she'd picked up about the woman over the past few weeks and tonight, slowly, the bigger picture of Jezebel's life started to reveal itself.

Jezebel was in her own quiet struggle with the Church, specifically with the High Priest Abbott, for relevance and power. Unfortunately for her, the Church as a national institution had far greater ability to impact the lives of citizens than Jezebel did. Despite the mythology that surrounded Jezebel's existence, her only true influence amongst the population was as an icon in seasonal fashion. In some circles within Artor, this held great weight, but in others, it did not, and in the evening's current company, she had very little to offer in tales of adventures or near misses with pirates. Tonight, those stories were social currency.

In this room, amongst these people, Jezebel's insecurity that she was nothing more than a sideline distraction, rather than a true political power, began to flare, and what happened next to Mila and Jahan, Mila realised later, was all part of that insecurity.

"Jahan, I'm...I'm inclined to have my dessert before my main meal. Fetch it for me from the kitchens. And I could use a footrest, demon," she demanded of Mila.

For a moment, Mila's heart jumped into her throat, thinking that she might be sent away from the room to fetch the object, but when Jezebel made no move to unclip her from the lead, Mila realised what she meant. She acquiesced, kneeling before Jezebel and allowing her to place her feet upon Mila's shoulder blades.

When Jahan returned, Jezebel realised that her little display with her attendants had attracted the attention of the room again. She smiled, determined to hold it for as long as possible.

"Jahan," she said, her tone cool, "put your tray down and move over there. Take a spare chair with you." She gestured to a large window that had a slightly raised floor protruding from it like a small stage. The man obeyed and placed his chair on the platform.

"Demon," she leaned down to unclip Mila's collar from the lead with a small laugh, "join him, but take this bowl."

Mila's stomach dropped as she found her feet again. She was finally free from the lead, but she was acutely aware of the attention. The buzzing hunger for entertainment that hung about the room felt as dangerous as finding herself standing inside an angry wasps' nest. All eyes were on her as she was handed a bowl that held small, sweet grapes in it.

Something about the pageantry of the directions and Jezebel's cruel energy pulsing throughout the room made her survival instincts kick in.

Now was not the time for escape.

She moved over obediently to where Jahan stood and waited for further direction.

"Now, Jahan," Jezebel called from her seat, directing them as if she were an orchestral conductor, "sit down, and demon, I want you to sit on his lap, and feed him grapes."

Jahan did not hesitate. His face was a mask of composure as he sat in the chair and looked blandly up at Mila, radiating his resignation to whatever was about to happen. Mila slowly, agonisingly, turned to face him.

The whole room paused in their meal, watching in amusement. As she stood over Jahan, Mila considered for a moment refusing the command, weighing the cost of her defiance. The answer to that question was the gaping hole where Jahan's eye had once been, and eventually, her fear of Jezebel's retribution won out. She finally placed her legs over Jahan, straddling his lap as commanded.

Someone from the table gave a drunken, appreciative whistle.

"Wonderful." Jezebel clapped, her hard eyes shining. "Poor Jahan's been working so hard recently, and with only one eye too. He deserves a little rest and attention, I think."

"Don't we all?" another man of the company called out, and Mila shivered in fear.

She raised a grape to Jahan's mouth. Haltingly, he parted his lips for her, and she placed it in. They did not speak, but as he chewed and swallowed, he watched her cautiously. He made no move to touch her – hands remaining as though rooted to the sides of the chair – and she lifted another grape.

His lack of movement caught Jezebel's attention.

"You have a beautiful creature on your lap, Jahan," she crowed. "I know she's a demon, but if you don't at least touch her, I'm going to think you're unappreciative of my goodwill."

Jahan's hands left their place and moved to Mila's sides.

"I'm sorry," he said softly as he placed them against her waist and moved them slowly up and down her body.

"Whatever we have to do to survive," was all she dared whisper back in response, placing another grape in his mouth.

Together, they breathed slowly in and out, enduring this moment as a single unit, wondering if the next order from Jezebel would demand more.

Jahan's hands were not exploratory upon her body. They maintained a repeated, predictable pattern, as though he were a man petting a cat for comfort rather than a man groping a woman for the pleasure of a voyeuristic audience. Mila found the sensation of the weight and warmth of them almost comforting.

Jezebel grew disgruntled with the obvious lack of fire between the two of them, as if she'd somehow expected them to passionately fall into one another's arms for her entertainment on a whim.

"He needs a little more encouragement, I think, demon. Kiss him."

Mila reminded herself that public humiliation was just a tactic of the vulgar. Kissing Jahan for Jezebel's amusement did not diminish her unless she let it. She could still move, breathe, smell, see...and so long as she was still able to do all those things, she would survive, she could escape one day.

She repeated that mantra over and over as she leaned forward and placed a hand to the unharmed side of his handsome face before kissing him. It was a chaste kiss, no more than a placement of her soft lips upon his, but the close connection meant she was swamped momentarily by his energy. It was calm and stoic, Jahan accepting the moment for what it was and taking strength from her strength. For the first time in her life, Mila found an energy that exactly matched hers, and it was the most reassuring sensation she'd ever experienced.

It felt as though they were both helping the other cling to a rock in a turbulent ocean.

The solidarity after weeks of isolation caused her so much joy that she couldn't help herself. Almost as a reflex, she leaned into his energy, and by doing so, she involuntarily deepened the kiss, turning her head slightly to take in more of him. His hands tightened around her waist in response, and from behind her, she heard another wolf whistle.

"That's more like it." Jezebel's gratified energy hit Mila from behind, waking her from the spell of the safe space Jahan had offered.

She drew back from him, clear-eyed but a little flustered. "I'm sorry." It was her turn to whisper now.

He nodded. "Whatever we have to do to survive," he repeated her words back to her.

"You know, Princess," a man said from behind them. "If you like this sort of entertainment, I have some slaves especially trained for this. Perhaps we could schedule another visit soon, and I'll bring them along."

"Mmm, that does sound interesting. Demon, fetch me some more wine, then come rub Vastifan's feet as he elaborates further."

Obediently, Mila rose, grateful that her role in the spectacle seemed to be over for now, but also mournful for the sudden distance she now had to put between herself and Jahan. His calm energy and close heat had felt protective. Its absence made her feel cast adrift again.

She moved over to where the old man, Vastifan, held out a clean-ish foot for her to rub with a very satisfied smile on his face. She took it without hesitating, hoping that her continued compliance would distract Jezebel from clipping her back onto the lead. And it worked. She remained free to move around the room, but unfortunately, not free from Jezebel's hawk-like attention.

Jezebel forced Mila to dance for the men during dessert and wield demonstrations of her power like a fortune teller during the rounds of port. Most of the room's occupants found the entire thing delightful, Culis watched it all intensely, and Jahan stood impassively behind Jezebel's chair, burning with feelings of sympathy.

Mila repeated her mantra to herself.

It doesn't diminish you unless you let it. Survive and you can escape.

With this playing in circles inside her head, she kept her emotions in check and simply continued to do what she needed to do to survive the evening.

* * *

Once the dessert had been cleared, Culis again approached Jezebel's seat and knelt beside her, placing his face close to hers. The two spoke conspiratorially, with bemused smiles on their faces, and not even Mila could make out what they were saying. Jezebel was leaning in, lips pursed and cleavage bursting. Culis was less intoxicated but playing a game he knew well. He leaned in, close enough to blow a soft kiss of breath against her jugular, and Jezebel's eyes rolled back, anticipating the lips that never came.

Infuriated, she abruptly stood from the table and took his hand, pulling him from the room and out onto the small balcony at the side.

Mila coolly glanced around the room to see who else had noticed their departure.

No one.

This was the moment. It would never come again.

Her heart pounded as she slowly reached for the dirty napkins on the table, acting as though she were assisting the servers in clearing them. Dirty napkins in hand, she walked slowly in the direction of the servers' door, wondering if any eyes in the room were following her.

They were not. The dinner guests were all engrossed in their own private conversations.

Mila continued to pace towards the servers' door. She was five steps away, four steps, three...

Clink.

A noise by her ear made her jump, and she spun to see Jahan by her side. For a moment, she wondered with elation if he was coming with her, but then she saw the golden lead in his hand, the end of which was now securely reattached to her collar, and her stomach plummeted.

Jahan said nothing, but his eyes and energy told her that he'd seen everything and knew exactly what she was trying to do. She wondered if he'd tell Jezebel. She had the sick thought that perhaps tomorrow morning, she would find herself also blinded. She began to tremble in fear as she followed him back to the place beside Jezebel's empty chair.

"I'm sorry," she whispered to him.

"Clearing the napkins is a servers' role, not yours," he said coldly, then, almost as an afterthought he added, "I didn't think *'whatever it takes to survive'* meant signing my death warrant."

She realised then that he believed Jezebel would have punished him in retaliation if Mila had escaped, and perhaps he was right. She hadn't thought of that.

"I'm sorry," she said again and then dared the next words. "Come with me. While we still have this chance. Let's leave this place."

Mila felt her words strike a strange chord within the man. His energy shifted to one of intense fear, and also shame, as if he was ashamed that a demon could believe him so easily swayed away from his beliefs and his prestigious role. He did not deign to reply to her question, and Mila turned from him in misery.

Thwarted. And she'd been so close.

It didn't seem real. She couldn't believe that this opportunity had been taken from her so abruptly. Jahan would surely report her escape attempt to Jezebel, and her life wouldn't be worth living. She couldn't give up now. She had to do something tonight, had to change something about her situation *now*.

In a moment of inspired desperation, she stuck her foot out just as Eliza in her serving role was backing away from the table, causing the poor woman to trip. A crystal goblet she'd been carrying spun in the air before striking the corner of the table. It smashed into several large, jagged pieces.

Mila dropped to her knees, wincing with pain as she hit the floor, but ensuring that her dress covered a large piece of glass.

"I'm so sorry," she said loudly and made a show of helping Eliza and other servers collect each piece of visible glass on the floor before her.

As she stood, she tried to discretely palm the piece of glass that had been hidden beneath her dress, and perhaps Jahan would have caught her in the act if Jezebel hadn't returned from the balcony at that moment, looking dishevelled and deeply unhappy. The sound of a smashed glass wouldn't have been enough to break her preoccupation with Culis, but it had served as a sufficient enough excuse for him to extract himself from her, and she was very unimpressed.

The princess now moved to where Jahan and Mila stood and snatched Mila's lead back into her hand. Her energy was roiling and raging with hurt and fury, as though she couldn't believe she'd been abandoned so easily. She shot Mila a daggered, accusatory glance as she then, without ceremony or need to excuse herself, stormed out of the hall and back to the carriage. She dragged Mila painfully by the neck all the way back to her apartments and into bed.

* * *

The sex was demanding and angry.

For once, Mila was not in control, but simply a vessel for Jezebel to unleash her pain and hurt. At the end, Mila found herself holding the furious, desolate and heavily intoxicated woman, who sobbed large, salty tears into her collarbone.

"Ignored and rejected...after everything I've done for him," she cried. "Nobody loves me unless they can use me."

Mila made soothing noises and held her as she trembled, rocking her as a mother gently rocks a distraught child.

It became clear then that the ordeal Jezebel had put her and Jahan through tonight had been, in some warped way, all about impressing Culis. But it had backfired. It hadn't made him more impressed with Jezebel. It had simply made him more curious about Mila.

Mila couldn't help but feel a modicum of pity seep through for the woman.

The life Jezebel had here in Jeralusah was opulent, but not a good one. She was lonely most of the time and continually hurt by those around her. Her mother had died soon after her birth and she'd been raised by simpering servants. She didn't know how to interact with others to achieve what she wanted and so resorted to childish petulance and irrationality to maintain people's attention.

Mila knew that, deep down, she just wanted what anyone wanted: to be loved unconditionally, to have friends who noticed her needs and enjoyed her company. She wanted to be admired and respected, by colleagues and lovers, but instead, she was merely tolerated – and she knew it.

Her status was her curse. Who would Jezebel have been if she hadn't been the daughter of the God-King?

Thankfully, it wasn't long before Jezebel's hiccups turned into a snore, and Mila detangled herself from the mess of arms and legs, moving obediently, under the watchful eye of the Guard of the Body, back to her dog mattress at the foot of Jezebel's bed. There, she subtly retrieved the small shard of glass that she'd tossed under the bed as they'd entered the room. She lay on her side with her back to the guard, pretending to fall asleep as she quickly tore a tiny hole in the fabric underside and tucked the glass shard safely inside.

She then let out a deep breath, trying to expel the stress of the evening from her body.

She was alive. She'd survived. And now, she thought with a grim smile, picturing the shard safely tucked beneath her, she was comforted by the knowledge that if she really needed to, she could slit Jezebel's throat.

Surviving Jezebel

The next day, Mila waited with a despairing pit in her stomach for Jahan to tell Jezebel about the escape attempt. But for some reason, it never came. Perhaps he also noticed Jezebel's new dislike for Mila in the week that followed the Artor Trading Company dinner party and realised that it hardly mattered whether he said anything or not. Whatever Christopher Culis had said about Mila to Jezebel had been enough to light a fire of jealousy in the princess, and although Mila tried her best, nothing she did could extinguish it. The unique camaraderie Jezebel had accepted from Mila in the days before the dinner were gone, and now she could barely look at her. When she did, it was with a sneer, usually coupled with an insult.

The countdown to the next Sacrament ticked on, and despite Mila's vigilance, another opportunity for escape did not readily present itself. For two full weeks, Jezebel refused to take Mila with her to any social engagements and ensured that Mila was securely tied up and under guard whenever she was left alone. Mila never thought that she'd miss being paraded around as a spectacle, but she knew she needed to be outside the palace walls to make any break for freedom worthwhile. Inside the walls, the best chance she had to escape was to try befriend some of the serving staff, or even a guard, to help her, but she was cautious in her attempts, lest someone report her to Jezebel. Her meagre efforts yielded no results. The staff were either too devout, or too scared of Jezebel to entertain the idea of engaging with Mila in any kind of dialogue, let alone anything meaningful. So, for days on end, Mila found herself alone, tied to the bedpost in Jezebel's magnificent parlour, with nothing to do and no one to talk to.

Mila was used to silence. She'd lived such an isolated life in the Highlands, venturing only briefly into the nearest town, Bori, for supplies she could not find herself. She ventured further only when a woman in childbirth specifically asked for her presence. Her name was whispered in those circles as someone to call upon only in the most dire of circumstances.

That was how she'd met Cari. Cari with the longest legs and the thickest mane of red hair Mila had ever seen. Cari with the stern husband, Oberon, who had sneered when Cari asked to meet with friends or have her own pursuits away from their two children, but who'd cried when he thought their third might not be delivered safely.

He had hunted Mila down, demanding her name from another nursing mother Mila had recently helped, and had practically dragged Mila through the forest to attend the birth.

What he couldn't have anticipated was the connection that would grow between the two women in the months afterwards. The friendship and trust that had eventually turned into desire.

On those long days that Jezebel left her alone, Mila finally had time to dwell on her memories of Cari.

What would she have thought of Mila's disappearance? She would have certainly heard about the trial by now. News like that travelled fast and wide. Would she be feeling betrayed?

Mila had never told Cari outright that she was a demon, but she'd always assumed that Cari had figured it out by herself. Had she been the one to betray her?

Surely not.

But perhaps an offhand comment to Oberon had sparked his intrigue, and Mila wouldn't put it past the stern husband to file a complaint with the local acolyte. Despite the fact Mila had known that he'd been growing suspicious of an affair, she'd found it too hard to leave. It was too heartbreaking to relinquish the sliver of acceptance that Cari's companionship brought her. Too hard to accept a lifetime of loneliness again.

Look where that got you.

In some ways, recognising the reason behind her reckless addiction to Cari made her understand Jezebel better. Jezebel, although constantly surrounded by people, was also alone in this world. Mila had been the one person who could truly 'see' her, and now, thanks to Culis's interference, Jezebel now felt threatened by her.

Mila sighed and wracked her brain. She needed Jezebel to trust her again. But how...?

And then it hit her.

Jezebel was jealous because she believed that Culis was more interested in Mila than in her. But what if Mila emphasised her interest in someone else? Would that help deflect from Culis's attention? It might be enough to iterate to Jezebel that Mila was loyal to her and didn't want to play into Culis's game.

It was a risk, and it could backfire dramatically, but at this rate, Mila was going to spend the next month and a half tied to a bedpost, alone, with no chance of escape. So, without any other better options revealing themselves, she knew she had to try.

Jezebel returned home later that evening, and Mila ran her power over her, reading her energy. It was much the same as it always was after a social event – drained, lonely and hurt.

Mila tried to act happy to see her, but Jezebel brushed it away as she flopped onto the bed.

"I've had enough of sycophants today, demon. Come undress me, but keep your false happiness far away."

"Mistress," Mila said dutifully, bowing her head and moving to sit beside the princess, unlacing the ribbons that had been elegantly crisscrossed around her large bust.

"Fates, that's better." Jezebel moaned in relief as the cool air hit her naked, sweaty skin. Stormweek was close now, and even though night had fallen, the air was still hot. The weather was a constant reminder to Mila that her time was nearly up. If she was going to do something to save herself, it had to be now.

"Mistress, I wondered if I might ask you a question?"

Jezebel's eyebrows flew so high they were nearly lost in her hairline. Mila rarely spoke when she was not being directly asked a question – let alone initiating.

"You might try," she said slowly, obviously trying to decide whether she was intrigued or offended by the petulance. "And see what happens."

Mila noted the threat and gulped but forced herself to push on anyway. "I was wondering if...if your guard, the one I kissed at the dinner a few weeks ago... Well, I was wondering if he's...if he's been asking after me?"

Mila didn't need to act embarrassed or feign a blush. She was mortified that these words had even come out of her mouth, that, in these circumstances, she could be thought of as a silly, lovesick little girl. But she also needed to shock Jezebel and give her something other than Culis's words to focus on.

It worked.

Jezebel sat up from the bed and stared for a long while at Mila, before a slow, predatory smile began to work its way across her mouth.

"You know you are to be sacrificed at the end of this season, demon, and yet, of all the things you could ask me, you want to know if a man likes you?"

"I...I..." Mila stuttered. "I'm sorry. I know it's not appropriate. I've just had a lot of time to think since that dinner, and that kiss was..." She let the silence act as words for her.

Jezebel threw back her head and laughed, true amusement flooding through her. "Jahan is one of the most devout members of the household. His mother was a fisherwoman at the Village of Truth. She was among the first humans to follow the word of my father, and now, somehow, he's gone and got a demon infatuated with him. Oh, he'll be mortified. This is wonderful." She clapped her hands in glee. "No, he hasn't been asking after you. But now that you mention it, why shouldn't he? You're beautiful." She said the last a little begrudgingly. Then added, "Ahh, I can't wait to see how this all unfolds." She lay back on her bed, hands clasped over her heart, emanating pure glee. "Oh my. You do really know how to make me happy. A new project is exactly what I need. We'll start tomorrow."

"Start?" Mila asked in confusion.

"Yes." Jezebel gave no more information than that, but Mila knew that the idea of allowing Jahan to forge feelings for Mila, then breaking his heart when she was sacrificed, was Jezebel's idea of ultimate entertainment.

It was a monstrous plan, but it had broken Jezebel's ire towards her when nothing else had, and that was step one of the great escape plan accomplished.

"Lovesick"

"Lovesick, I tell you," Jezebel crowed to her small audience in the sitting room of Lady Dumbrell's manor. "Just look at her."

Mila let the embarrassment she felt show, and it was read incorrectly by all in the room.

"Oh, how depraved!" another woman said with delight. "Whatever shall you do with such a creature?"

"Well, there's really only two options," Jezebel said with mock seriousness. "Lock her away until the next Sacrament, which is only a few weeks away now. Or...give her a chance to experience love for the first time in her life. Who knows...maybe the secret to turning a demon back into a human is true love's kiss!"

The group tittered like excited birds, and Mila fought not to roll her eyes. At least she was out of the palace walls again for the day. In the coming weeks, she would have to take any opportunity she could to seize her freedom. Even if it meant accosting Jezebel herself.

But for now, she enjoyed being back in Jezebel's good graces, and she wondered what Jahan would make of all this once it reached his ears.

She did not have to wonder for long.

Jezebel had arranged for him to arrive at the manor soon after tea was served, a decadent spread of soft cheese on lavendile-infused biscuits, with ripe fruits and berries on the side to cleanse the palate between each bite. When Jahan arrived, he was escorted to the sitting room by Lady Dumbrell's staff. He stood in the doorway looking very confused and concerned. His short, warrior's haircut was fresh, his dark blue shirt neatly pressed and buttoned to his neck, and he was wearing dark brown pants that had a trace of golden thread glinting through them. Evidently, someone had ordered him to dress in his best, and Mila could not have been more mortified to see him looking so handsome. She deliberately ignored the very real flutter she felt in her stomach at the sight of him

"Jahan!" Jezebel's joyous voice trilled. "How lovely of you to come join us. Please. Come sit. No, not there. Beside the demon will do. Yes."

Jahan walked with the caution of a man who could smell a trap. He slowly lowered himself onto the seat beside Mila and looked around the room, still trying to predict what might happen next and having no luck.

"Jahan, I'd like you to ask the demon three questions about herself, so that we all might get to know her a little better." Jezebel's smile could not have been broader.

Unsurprisingly, Jahan was taken aback by this command, but he did as he was ordered. He cleared his throat and turned to look Mila in the eye. "Uhh... Where were you born?"

"I grew up just outside the city of Wallatsford, in the region of Prious. My family were barley and oat farmers."

"I see..."

Mila could both feel and see his anxiety and confusion as he tried to think of another question. Why was he being asked to do this? What was the right or wrong question to ask? Why did this demon keep crossing his path and putting him in such devastatingly precarious situations?

"What do you like most about Jeralusah?" he asked.

"Oooh!" Lady Dumbrell interjected with rapt fascination. "That's a good one!"

Jezebel shushed her and looked at Mila for her response, her eyes beady and bright.

"I like... I *love* the palace gardens. They're beautiful. I've never seen such a marvel. The way the glass and light have been designed to play off one another, and the way it has all been weaved into nature. It...it brings me a lot of peace."

Mila loathed opening up in this way, especially in front of Jezebel, but she also knew that, in order for her ruse to be believed, she had to behave as though she were sincerely trying to share a part of herself with the man, to offer him something he might be drawn to. And in this, it seemed that she'd struck true.

Jahan nodded thoughtfully at her answer and then said, "That is also my favourite part of the city. I love spending time in the gardens."

"So much in common!" Lady Dumbrell whispered loudly. The older woman, Meredith, could not hide her smile as Jezebel smacked Lady Dumbrell to silence her.

"Another question, Jahan," she ordered.

"What have you enjoyed most in your time spent alongside our princess?"

He was giving her an opening here, a chance to flatter Jezebel and put them both in her good graces. Mila knew that her next words would utterly shock him, but that they might also give him some idea of what was going on.

"I most enjoyed the...the night at the dinner party. With you."

"With me?" he said, flustered.

"When we...kissed."

Again, Mila blushed, and Jahan's jaw dropped. He studied her face intently, perhaps looking for signs of madness. Around them, the ladies whooped and clapped in childlike pleasure. Entertained beyond measure at her boldness, and his discomfort.

"Well, go on, Jahan," Jezebel demanded. "Put her out of her misery. Kiss her again!"

Confused and unhappy, Jahan dared not disobey. He tipped his head forward and gently lifted Mila's chin to allow his lips to meet hers. The kiss was chaste and short, but his lips were soft. He smelled like soap and faintly of lemon.

When he pulled away, he found the opportunity to discretely whisper, "I can't help you."

You already have, Mila thought to herself, but there was no other opportunity for her to explain anything. Every interaction between them was scrutinised and delighted over by Jezebel and her group.

"Okay, your turn, demon. Three questions for the handsome Jahan. Well, perhaps slightly less handsome these days."

"If I were to cook you a meal, what would you most enjoy eating?" Mila asked.

Jahan's energy turned from wary to furious when it dawned on him that Mila was a willing participant in whatever scheme this was. Beneath that fury, Mila sensed his fear, and it matched her own. It wouldn't take much of a misstep for this situation to spiral out of hand, not with a creature such as Jezebel acting as the conductor. But for now, thankfully, she seemed content to watch Mila's awkward attempts to flirt and Jahan's horror as he tried to navigate himself through the unprecedented situation he found himself in.

That evening, Mila fell to her pallet, exhausted from all the attention and playacting, but sure it had been worth it. If doing this continued to open up opportunities for her to be outside the palace walls, it would be worth it. And, she considered with a tiny smile just before she fell asleep, it certainly wasn't *hard* to pretend to be infatuated with Jahan.

His own Brand of Chaos

Summer was now only a month away. Despite the Church's ban on public celebrations, the people of Artor had found other ways to generate the buzz of excitement for a new season. A dramatic shift in costumes and food was tradition, with an emphasis made on the consumption of light, cold meals, eaten often, and in smaller portions throughout the day. Spring clothes made of sheer and flouncy fabrics were slowly being stored away, and summer garb was gradually donned. Jezebel led the trends and made sure she was seen often in the city wearing newly made outfits. This year, her choice emphasised feathers and flowing, braided strands of silk that blew aside in the breeze and enabled airflow as opposed to modesty. Others soon followed suit, and for those who could not afford the extravagance of such materials, it was common to see skirts and halter tops of dried grass worn instead.

The incoming summer also saw a change to the usual residents of the palace grounds, as nobles moved about the country. During the year, they took turns living at the palace, trying to curry favour with Midas and the High Priest.

One such addition, on a hot spring morning, was catastrophic to Mila's plans.

Lady Meredith was sipping iced tea on the balcony with Jezebel, Mila sitting dutifully at their feet, when Christopher Culis's carriage unexpectedly arrived in the courtyard. The three women watched from above as the swaggering man stepped out from the cab, all sun-kissed and wind-swept, and looked up, calling out to Meredith, whose role for the Church included managing the Palace's visiting noble accommodations.

"Lady Meredith, I was told I might find you in such esteemed company. I'm after accommodation and you're apparently the person I need to speak to about it."

"What are you doing here, Captain Culis?" Jezebel called down haughtily, clearly happy to see him but unwilling to let him know. "Aren't you meant to still be at sea?"

Culis squinted up at them and grinned. "There's the real reason I'm here, and then there's the reason that's less grounded in truth, but far more entertaining. Which would you prefer to hear, Princess?"

Jezebel laughed. Culis's eyes never left hers as he spoke, even as Meredith allocated him to a residence that was located just a short walk away from Jezebel's own private suites.

"That will suit my purposes nicely. Thank you."

He gave them a brief, two fingered salute as he alighted back into his carriage and departed in the direction of his new apartment.

Jezebel turned to Meredith with sparkling eyes.

"What do we think he's here for?" she whispered in breathless delight.

The answer was made apparent within the hour by the arrival of a bouquet of jewels. They were the colours of the rainbow and had been cleverly stemmed as though they were flowers, tied with a gold bow and an accompanying card from Culis.

He was here to woo Jezebel.

At least, that was the official word. But from what Mila observed over the next few days, it seemed that he was rather more intent on simply creating his own brand of chaos. Scuppering all of Mila's hard work to regain her footing with the princess.

Christopher Culis seemed to enjoy his days doing little else but gallivanting around the palace grounds, provoking and flirting with Jezebel, whilst eyeing Mila up as though she were sumptuous meat at a banquet. For a time, Jezebel was mollified by her belief in Mila's infatuation with Jahan, but even she could not ignore the way Culis pointedly stared at Mila, and it began to sour her towards Mila once again.

Mila could have killed him.

His unexplained, silent obsession with her was ruining everything, and on top of this, she still couldn't read his energy and had no idea why he seemed to be immune. She remembered that'd she'd been able to read his energy in the crypt and she couldn't work out what was different between that interaction and these prolonged visits. Even so, it didn't take demon powers to be able to see that he knew exactly what he was doing, even if no one else could figure it out. They were all pawns in this game he was playing.

He toyed with Jezebel, whose fickle and childish nature was encouraged by the drip-fed attention that the dangerous man gave her. He'd court her over dinner one night but ignore her over the following drink. Invite her to play bowls with him one day, then snub her reciprocal invitation the next. He was maddening to her, and Mila watched on with wary fascination.

Everyone knew that Jezebel could easily tire of him, and if she was seriously displeased, there was a real possibility he could find himself kneeling in front of her father, awaiting the Midas touch. Yet it was his seemingly blatant disregard of such a fate, and his confidence in his winning charisma, that made him irresistible to the princess.

Despite the way it interfered with her plan, even Mila caught herself occasionally admiring the man's self-assurance. But it did interfere, and there were no more flirtatious soirees arranged by Jezebel to give her and Jahan time together. In fact, she now hardly saw the man, and Jezebel seemed to have forgotten all about the idea that had so delighted her just one week earlier.

Appealing to Christopher Culis and devising ways to entrap him in her social snares was Jezebel's new obsession, and removing Mila from the equation was an obvious step to achieving her goal.

***

In the days just before the season finally turned, as the next Sacrament of Contrition was rearing its head, Mila slaved for Jezebel tirelessly. She watched on with exhaustion as, no matter how she tried to please her, Jezebel's interest in conversation or interactions with her faded. On the first day of Stormweek, as the rains finally broke from the sky and brought sweet relief from the humidity, Mila knew that her time was up.

On the night before the sacrifice, Mila was not chained to her usual mat at the foot of the bed. Instead, she was chained to the golden foot of the heavy, stained-glass bathtub in Jezebel's ensuite, as though Jezebel knew that Mila had been thinking about the glass shard that was still tucked away under the mattress and had been trying to summon the courage to use it.

Foiled.

Removed from her cushion, Mila didn't even have the option of using the hidden glass shard on herself, to choose the time and manner of her own death that evening.

Hopelessness rose up inside and engulfed her mind like a dark mud.

This was it. She'd lost. She was going to die.

The night passed too quickly, and when the grey notes of dawn began to breech the sky, Mila felt clammy and cold with stress.

Jezebel said nothing to her when she woke, caught between a mix of somewhat enjoying Mila's panic and being preoccupied with the decision about what to wear for the day.

Mila was grateful that she finally didn't have to care, and angry that she still had to watch.

This was to be her last morning alive ever. The last time she'd ever see the sun poking through green fronds, the last time she'd ever hear morning birds chirping. And instead of enjoying any of that, she was being forced to watch Jezebel preen. She could not have hated her more.

It didn't seem real. Nothing seemed real.

Midmorning, an unexpected invitation arrived from Culis, with an offer to escort Jezebel to the Sacrament. Jezebel had responded with such delight that he may as well have asked her to marry him. This also prompted a complete overhaul of her outfit and a morning of spinning joyfully around the apartment.

Mila watched on from her corner in the bathroom, feeling numb, her body leaden and slow in its movements. Eventually, Jezebel settled on a swath of layered, golden peacock feathers that hung from a golden circlet about her neck and fell to her knees. It offered tantalising glimpses when she moved, though never fully revealed the promised land beneath.

When Culis met them at the door of Jezebel's apartments, his attention was laser focused upon the princess, appraising her with an eye that appeared to critique rather than drink her in. She giggled nervously under his gaze and swooshed the feathers as she turned one way, then the other, showcasing herself.

"Immaculate," Culis couldn't help but concede, but his facial expression remained tauntingly neutral, and even in her growing state of panic, Mila could sense frustration from Jezebel.

This was unsatisfactory. She stormed over to where Mila sat despondently and snatched the lead up. "Come."

During the carriage ride from Jezebel's apartments to the Grand Cathedral, Culis switched with distracting frequency between being enraptured by her and acting as though he were downright bored. In response, Jezebel's energy fluctuated violently between ecstasy and rage.

Mila tried to ignore them both. She didn't have to pretend to care about Jezebel's romantic entanglements any longer. She was about to die and was determined to drink in as much nature and experience as she possibly could in these remaining hours. It annoyed her that she could not block Culis's suave tone and honeyed words from her ears.

She briefly wondered whether to use these final moments in their company to expose his game for what it was and wreak the same havoc on his life that he'd wreaked on hers. She considered it for a long moment, but then realised it was highly unlikely that Jezebel would care. She had never once asked Mila for a read on Culis's intentions towards her, she was too wrapped up in his spell. And moreover, Mila realised, she *wanted* to be bespelled. Culis treated her unlike any other courtier or suitor. He wasn't afraid of her, and that was intoxicating to

Jezebel. So much so that she was comfortable with her own delusion of what she meant to the man.

It would have been fascinating to watch if Mila wasn't more preoccupied with her impending death.

When they finally arrived at the Grand Cathedral, they both fell silent as they passed under the great archway. Culis took a step back, following the princess's lead as she made her way up a flight of stairs and into her private viewing balcony. The cold, angry energy of the dead pulsed out from the thick golden pillars, and despite the renewed control she'd managed to find over her power in the past few months, it still hit Mila in much the same way as a physical blow. She tottered slightly, reeling from the impact, and to her surprise, rather than feeling the pressure of the collar yanking her forward, her stumble was supported by a large, warm hand at the small of her back.

"Alright there, little demon?" Culis whispered, his breath blowing the hair at her ear.

She did not acknowledge him. Could not.

I am about to die, I am about to die. That thought repeated over and over in her head. There was no room for anything else.

As they entered the balcony, Mila felt an intense sense of déjà vu. The brazier remained lit in the corner. She wondered briefly if this was the first time it had been lit since the last Sacrament. Would she find the ashes of her hair in there still, or had it been cleaned out since then?

Three chairs had been laid out in the small space, two in front and one behind. The scant contents of Mila's stomach curdled when Jezebel gestured that Mila, rather than Culis, would sit beside her in the seat of honour. If the reason wasn't immediately obvious, then Jezebel's delighted, predatory energy soon gave it away.

From this seat, Mila would have an unobstructed view of the Grand Cathedral floor, of every sacrifice.

“You are slated for sacrifice today, demon." Jezebel announced theatrically. "But! I do not pretend that I have not enjoyed your company this past season. And so, I have decided that you will have one last chance to earn your survival."

Mila's stomach flipped. Jezebel continued. "You will watch the sacrifice with me, and the only expression I want to see on your face is joy and relief for the mercy that I extend to you. If I see a flicker of anything else, I’ll consider you ungrateful and send you down to join them, understand?”

The depths of Jezebel’s depravity struck her then like a scorpion’s tail. Light-headedness swept over her as the full bleak truth of her situation was finally unveiled.

Jezebel fully intended to sacrifice Mila today. She knew this, and Mila knew this. But she was pretending to offer Mila a chance to save herself, and the cost of it was watching the deaths of all the other demons first.

It was beyond cruel, and she realised in that heartbeat that she’d been wrong about Jezebel ever having any kind of regard for her. The months of her hard work to earn the princess’s trust, to make her laugh, to hold her while she cried...meant nothing. Mila was nothing to her, had never been anything other than an unusual form of entertainment.

Mila couldn’t breathe. Couldn’t think. It couldn’t be happening like this. She couldn’t sit here and watch the deaths of her people without being distressed. She’d rather die than try.

She felt the panic rising in her chest. Her breathing became ragged, and she could feel it emitting loudly from her mouth like a panting, injured animal.

The Sacrament was about to begin. It was all happening too fast.

"I'd fix that breathing immediately," Jezebel tutted as she pulled the lead and forced Mila down onto the chair. "Not starting out well."

The priests and acolytes who lined the walls below began humming low and hypnotically. The incense was already thick in the air, making Mila's eyes water as she blinked dumbly at Jezebel, fighting for control of herself, fighting to breathe against the dizzying wave of horror and disbelief. Jezebel stared back, the wicked curve of her beautiful mouth unyielding, and the energy of her amusement shrouded in cruelty.

For a moment, Mila considered what few options remained to her, and seriously contemplated attempting to strangle Jezebel. Perhaps wrestling her off the balcony, as a final act of defiance.

But before her brain committed to this decision, an unexpected arm reached between them and broke the spell of her panic.

It was Culis's arm, and he was turning Jezebel's face towards his, in what was the most intimate touch he had ever shown her. Jezebel was immediately transfixed, and her viperous energy drew away from Mila, transforming into openness and wonder for the man.

"Princess." His voice was like rough velvet. "My feet are in dire need of a wash. I don't suppose your pet could assist me?"

"Oh...but of course she can," Jezebel acquiesced immediately. The promise of earning Culis's favour seemed to instantly wipe away all desire to play this tantalising game she'd planned for Mila.

"Shall I get a washcloth, sir?" Mila whispered to him, uncertain how her mouth was even forming words right now.

Behind her, she could hear the heavy curtain of the waiting wings draw open. The chanting of the priests stopped, allowing the High Priest Abbott to recite the official damnation. Mila heard a low groan as an ikarei, a young woman by the sounds of it, was led into the hall. It took all of her self-control to keep her eyes fixed on Christopher Culis's face, and his beautiful, cold green ones did not leave hers either.

"Too late now for a cloth, I think. The ceremony has begun." His grin was playful, but his eyes remained calculating. "Your tongue will suffice."

Jezebel's delighted giggle was accompanied by the background sound of clinking chains. The sacrifice was led forward and down the hall, her terrified, hysterical energy pulsed like a thick, syrupy wave at Mila, threatening to drag her down into her torment. She fought against it, fought to remain present in her own body.

She knelt, still staring at Culis, who continued to boldly meet her eyes. That infuriated her. She refused to be the one who looked away first. There was something inside her now that was burning, a fury that she could not dampen, and he knew it, was watching it. A spectator.

He slipped off his sandals and made a pointed gesture down with his eyebrows. "Well?"

She was finally forced to look down.

His feet were clean and had been adorned with a scented oil that was vaguely reminiscent of rosemayne. There was a thick silver ring around one of his thin toes.

Mila dutifully, angrily, dipped her head and began to lick.

The moment her tongue touched his skin, she was struck by Culis's evasive energy.

Ah, she realised. This was the answer. She could only read him through physical touch. How bizarre.

She flung her power into him, reading everything she could, searching for any indication that he was going to save her, have sympathy for her. His response boiled through her like a hot pot of water.

Power, control, manipulation.

There was no salvation to be found here. He was focused entirely on Jezebel, deliberately ignoring Mila.

She heard Jezebel gasp with glee at the same time she heard the cries of the sacrifice, now being forced to her knees and presented to the God-King.

The priests continued to hum, low and rhythmically, and her own heart hammered in her chest with hatred and fury for them all.

But, in that moment, most especially for Jezebel and Christopher Culis.

As she licked obediently, she heard the woman below sob in fear. As her sob was abruptly cut off, Mila fought back a choke of vomit.

Just like that, the woman's life had been ended by the touch of the God-King's hand. Interestingly, she also felt Culis's energy waver in distaste, and his foot twitched under her administrations. He didn't like witnessing this either.

She heard the clink of another set of chains being hauled forward now. No accompanying sounds of protest or fear. Perhaps this ikarei had seen how useless it was to struggle. Perhaps they were petrified and unable to make a sound.

"Come visit me tonight," Mila heard Jezebel say to Culis from above. It was the first time she'd been brave enough to command it of him so directly.

"Of course," Culis replied without hesitation. "I thought you'd never ask."

Mila sensed a bubble of joy rise within Jezebel, a deep energy of satisfaction.

Culis then added something unexpected. "I'd like the demon present as well."

Mila's stomach clenched, and Jezebel's energy instantly shifted into suspicion and stress.

"Why?"

"It'll be more fun with an audience," Culis said easily, not rising to her tension.

Mila could feel both longing and outrage pulsing from Jezebel. She wanted Culis desperately, but her jealousy was hard to overcome.

From her contact with his foot, Mila sensed that Culis knew this, but that he didn't care. She felt him smile above her in response to Jezebel's displeasure.

"Trust me. There's something about having an audience that adds...*more* to the experience."

"I think the idea sounds quite fun," Jezebel said with a pout, "but can't it be anyone else? I promised Abbott she'd be sacrificed today."

Mila's whole body went cold, and she tensed in anger at those words.

"Precisely," Culis continued. "There's no one else in your staff I'd invite into the parlour with us. No one else is as easily disposable afterwards."

Begrudgingly, Jezebel saw the logic to this and agreed. Culis rewarded her for it with a kiss on the neck, then placed one foot on Mila's back, which had been rising slowly as she'd listened to their conversation in horror. He forced her back down to attend to his other foot, and the contact pulsed his energy through her again.

To Mila's surprise, it was not full of lust or desire, despite the conversation that had just occurred. Instead, it was now an energy of cold pragmatism. Whatever his plan for the evening, there was more in this for him than just sex.

Mila was grateful, at least, that she was facing the floor, so no one could see her tears of rage and humiliation. She warred bitterly for control of herself, forcing the tears back, so that, when the Sacrament finished and Culis finally permitted her to rise, her face was nothing but the epitome of calm neutrality.

She made sure to glare at him, desperate to wordlessly impart to him that, while he might do everything in his power to shock and humiliate her, ultimately, he could not touch her inner strength.

Culis met her gaze with cool interest, and then, as Jezebel rose to leave, he leaned forward and softly whispered to Mila, "You're welcome, little demon."

She pondered his words as she was pulled away by the golden collar, and as she caught a glimpse of his grimly satisfied expression, it dawned on her that, despicable as his actions had been today, he'd just saved her life.

Jahan

In anticipation for her unexpected evening soiree with Christopher Culis, the remainder of Jezebel's day was chaotic. There were a number of eclectic and extravagant requirements that the princess declared to be *essential* to ensure the success of the night ahead. Procuring these over the course of the afternoon left Mila no space to dwell too fiercely on the fate she had narrowly avoided, and Culis's role.

To ensure everything was ready in time, Jezebel made the unexpected decision to relinquish control of Mila's lead to Jahan for the afternoon.

"I need you to be able to move around and oversee the necessary preparations while I'm being sewn into my new dress," she ordered, as she handed the hateful golden lead to the guard.

Jahan was absolutely astonished, but not entirely unhappy, to see Mila still alive.

"You know what I like," Jezebel said with a dismissive wave. "Make sure it is all perfect."

Perhaps it shouldn't have surprised Mila that Jezebel expected her to fall easily back into her role of the docile pet. But she did, and for now, Mila was happy to play along if it kept her alive for another day.

Together, Jahan and Mila left Jezebel's boudoir and quickly made their way down the winding staircase to the ground floor.

"You're alive," he said incredulously as soon as they were out of earshot of the princess. The words burst from him as though he'd been waiting months to talk freely with her, and perhaps he had.

"I am," Mila agreed grimly. "And I can sense that you're not as upset about it as many others in the palace are."

"I'm just glad you didn't die and leave me wondering what the hell you've been playing at this past week. Leave me out of your schemes." His voice was cold and hard. He was angry with her.

"I'm sorry to have involved you," she said sincerely. She decided then to educate him on her plan. "I needed Jezebel to believe that I had developed an infatuation with you. It was the only thing I could think of that would save me from the jealousy Culis evoked in her at the dinner party."

"Oh." Jahan eyed her critically, as if weighing this reasoning, then snorted in derision. "That man wreaks havoc wherever he goes."

"Generally, I would agree with you, but I think he may have deliberately saved my life today."

Jahan raised an eyebrow. "Really? That's interesting if its true. Perhaps the princess does have legitimate reason to be jealous of you." He mulled this over for a moment, then said, "Right. Where are we going first?"

"The main greenhouse," Mila replied, and then returned to the topic at hand as they walked in that direction. "I'm sorry that you seem to be inescapably tied into my fate in this place. I'm grateful for the kindness you showed me on that first night, and I'm truly sorry for what it cost you. I don't want you ever to suffer on my behalf again."

Jahan was not ready to accept the apology. "If you were truly sorry, you would leave me out of this new game."

"I can't stop now," Mila said sadly. "The wheels are already in motion. I'm sorry, but there was no one else I could have meaningfully pretended to have these feelings for. I've had no real interactions with her other staff. I know it's a lot to ask, and you have no reason to help me but...if you could just...play along for a while, it might help me survive the summer months. Jezebel wants to foster a romance between us. The idea is entertaining to her."

"Everything is a risk when it comes to entertaining the princess."

It wasn't an outright no, but it certainly wasn't a yes either. His energy gave her no clue as to what he would decide, but one thing was clear, he was not happy about being put in this position.

Mila decided to try another angle. "You don't seem to despise me, at least, not as deeply as others in this city do."

"Most of them have been misguided into believing that committing the First Behaviour is worse than committing any of the others," he said curtly. "But I have been around the palace since I was a young boy, and I have heard the God-King's teachings on the matter firsthand. I know that I have no more reason to hate you for your decision to commit the First than I should hate a teenage boy who blasphemes, or an old woman who reminisces about her childhood. It's all heretic behaviour, and for the God-King alone to judge and punish. If he wanted you sacrificed today, you would have been."

Mila realised he was right. Regardless of the game currently being played between Culis, Jezebel and Abbott, if the God-King had demanded her sacrifice today, she would have been handed over without hesitation. Why hadn't he?

"That's...that's not what the Church teaches," Mila challenged quietly as they reached the tall, white, domed greenhouse.

They paused the conversation for a moment as she directed the head gardener to cut one hundred branches of the longest and greenest ivy from the garden, to decorate the princess's enormous room, floor to ceiling. With Jahan looming over her shoulder, she was obeyed without hesitation.

When the gardener rushed away, she turned back to Jahan. "The Church teaches that demons are more evil than humans, that we challenge the authority of the God-King when we accept our powers. That's why we are hunted down and sacrificed at the Sacrament of Contrition. Artor *wants* to be rid of us."

"Yes, well, over the years, the Church has taken to picking and choosing the elements of the Holy Text they follow and enforce upon the population," Jahan said. "It suits them to have demons as a common enemy. It means the Church remains favourably viewed amongst humans, who are kept safe from being sacrificed, and it keeps them in power. It's all politics."

Mila was stunned to hear such a critique from him. These words were blasphemy, a direct contravention of the Sixth Heretical Behaviour – speaking ill of the Church.

"Does this mean... Are you saying that you don't believe... what the Church says about demons – "

Jahan cut her off abruptly. "Do not misunderstand me. The teachings of Midas are clear. To accept supernatural powers from Viah and become a demon is unacceptable to him. You are a heretic, and you're bound for the Rotting Muds of the afterlife for your decision. But it does not mean that your kind should be persecuted while humans who sin are left unpunished."

"That is...quite a progressive view on the Holy Text," Mila said in astonishment.

"It's actually far more fundamentalist." He corrected, and Mila was afforded some time to mull this revelation over when the gardener returned and handed the vines to her.

She took them gratefully and then informed Jahan their next errand would require a visit to the servants' quarters, located in the city. A carriage was swiftly arranged, and as they rode beyond the palace walls and into Jeralusah, Mila was reminded of the conversation she'd overheard at Lady Picory's manor.

"So, what you're saying," she said slowly, "is that you follow the word of Midas, not of the Church. You view them as separate authorities."

"Precisely," he agreed. He seemed pleased that she'd figured it out, and his open energy indicated that he was now enjoying the conversation.

"Are you a dissident?" she asked curiously. "I've heard there is a movement of such progressive ideas happening around Traders Bay. Do your ideas belong in such a group?"

"No," he said firmly. "Despite my unique views, I have no desire to topple the Church or challenge Abbott. Not while the God-King tolerates them."

"And so how did you come to form these views?" She'd never met anyone quite like him.

"My mother," he said, glowing with quiet pride. "She was a fisherwoman in the Village of Truth."

Mila recognised the name from the conversation with Jezebel.

"She was one of the first to recognise the God-King's divinity," he continued, "and she left her life by the sea to follow him. Until she died, she was amongst his most devoted followers and attended all of the original Twelve Sermons, scribing them into texts that she eventually presented to the Church for posterity."

"I've never heard of additional Holy Texts. I thought there was only the one."

"Of course you haven't," Jahan said with a grim smile. "The Church doesn't want their existence known. It's far easier for them to simply distil the contents of these sermons down into eight Heretical Behaviours and give those to the population to follow. Can you imagine the chaos that would ensue if they gave every man and woman the opportunity to interpret complex religious texts and determine their own meaning from it?" His tone was dripping with sarcasm.

"You disagree," Mila observed.

"I believe in the right of all people to hear the God-King's word directly. Humans are fallible. The Church is well intentioned, but fallible. I believe it's wrong to keep secret the sermons of the God-King that my mother scribed."

They arrived then at the quarter of the city where Jezebel's servants lived, and the two of them abandoned the conversation to rouse all the handmaids, even the ones who were off duty for the day.

Once everyone was dressed, Mila directed a few of the maids to run and purchase a hundred of the tallest, slowest burning, elaborately carved, beeswax candles they could find. Others were to procure two live peacocks and take them directly to Jezebel's chamber. The remainder she tasked with descending on the market to acquire every exotic aphrodisiac they could find: foods, perfumes, feathers, anything and everything. Again, despite a general air of disbelief that she was still alive, she was obeyed promptly and without question. She'd been seen catering to the princess's every whim for long enough now that her word carried authority on the matter of the princess's desires, and Jahan towering at her side helped to enforce the urgency.

With the required items procured and en route to Jezebel's suites, Mila and Jahan headed back to the palace.

"Well, I've come to know far more about you on this little jaunt than I could ever have hoped to learn from the poor line of questioning I gave you a week ago," Mila said with a small smile.

Jahan groaned at the memory, but smiled in return. "Now don't *actually* become infatuated with me, demon," he joked, and she laughed, grateful for the humour. It was the first laugh she'd shared with another in months, and it felt like a healing balm placed over her tired and stressed soul.

"My name is Mila," she said, saying her name out loud for the first time since she'd arrived in Jeralusah. It felt good to hear it. "And don't worry," she replied. "I have little energy for engaging in anything other than staying alive at the moment, and it remains to be seen what Culis and Jezebel's plans are for me tonight."

"Mmm," Jahan hummed. "Culis is bad news. If he risked both Jezebel's and Abbott's wrath to keep you alive today, then he has some plan for you. Don't take heart from that. I wouldn't trust him to be any more merciful or painless than either of them."

"Believe me, I know," she agreed.

"All of the Culis family is bad. His brother Martin was apparently the best of the bunch, but Christopher is renowned for being just like his father, a two-faced, lying, greedy scumbag."

"Well, that he probably is," Mila agreed. "But I still have to try to ensure he is pleased in Jezebel's chambers tonight. Do you know what kind of drink he prefers?"

Jahan snorted. "Probably the blood of infants."

Mila laughed again, feeling lighter than she had felt in...weeks, despite her impending fear.

"Thank you," she said as the carriage pulled up at the front of the apartments and Jahan escorted her back up the stairs. "You're the only soul here who has ever treated me with a degree of dignity. It means more to me than you could possibly ever know."

"Hush now," he said softly as they entered the top level.

Mila obediently fell silent, knowing that for Jezebel to hear Mila conversing with him in such a manner was not akin to the flirtation she expected of them.

They entered the room, and Jahan departed as soon as he'd handed her lead back to the princess.

Afterwards, Mila reflected on the conversation and realised cautiously that it had caused some hope to form again within her. Jahan had revealed himself to be, possibly, the one person who would not seek to punish her or find reasons to hasten her sacrifice – and he hadn't been afraid to let her know it. He was the closest thing she had to a friend in this place, and if she was to continue surviving day-by-day, she needed all the friends she could get.

In the Boudoir

The heat of the day was defeated by another summer storm. Cooling winds and dark clouds roiled through a deep, magenta sky and Jezebel paced anxiously back and forth across the black and white tiles of her boudoir. She was anxious, and determined that nothing could go wrong tonight. Her dress was a shade that matched the dusk sky. Magenta velvet feathers trailed from her shoulder to the floor, with a long gap that curved up her left leg and exposed her skin all the way to the hip, before crossing her belly and hugging the curve of her right breast. Mila marvelled at the seamstress's talent and what she'd been able to create under such conditions. The dress moved with the beautiful woman's body, never peeling away or revealing more than it was designed to, and yet the design itself was artfully revealing.

By contrast, Jezebel had decided Mila should wear a hessian sack. Without a handmaid's assistance, Mila placed the sack over her head and tried not to notice the smell of potato, or the tiny bugs that still lived inside the rough fabric. She couldn't have cared less how she looked, but it frightened her that Jezebel seemed to care. The jealousy that lurked inside her was never far away, and she was certainly suspicious that Culis's visit to her chambers had only eventuated because of something to do with Mila.

Mila knew there was truth to her fear.

The man had gone out of his way to save her from execution, and also made an effort to ensure she understood that this had been his intention. Why? Did he simply want sex? Sex with a demon? Was it as simple as that? Something told her otherwise. She hadn't sensed any lust from him that morning when she'd been licking his foot. His energy had all been extremely calculated.

No, Culis had some other plan afoot that involved her, and it made her very nervous.

A sharp rap at the door announced his presence, and Jezebel released a long, deep breath. She glanced swiftly around the room, conducting a final inspection before nodding in approval to her handmaid to open the door.

Right before the door swung open, she glanced at Mila. Almost as an afterthought, she hissed, "Down."

Mila dropped to all fours immediately, understanding that to have Jezebel feeling threatened by her right now was very dangerous for her life expectancy.

When Christopher Culis entered the boudoir, with his hair combed neatly into a bun and his white shirt unbuttoned down to the top of his chest, the scene before him was staged to perfection. The breathtaking Jezebel was posed in the wide, round windowsill, adorned in her magnificent dress. She was lit to perfection by candles, mirrors, and jars of Golden Sand that cleverly diffused the light and made her seem more curvaceous, and somewhat otherworldly all at the same time. Two dead peacocks lay at her feet, and the golden lead trailed from her wrist to the neck of her pet demon, whose head was bowed as she knelt on all fours, clad in a hessian sack. It was the perfect portrait of power and subservience.

"Well, well," Culis murmured as he surveyed the scene and approached them. "You never disappoint, Jezebel." He raised a hand to her face and stroked it before kissing her deeply.

Jezebel instantly dropped Mila's lead, her hands flying up into his hair, and Mila seized the opportunity to scuttle away, back to her designated mat, hoping to avoid either monster's attention.

The night that followed was intense, but Mila noted that Culis refused to fully give in to the princess's demands. Jezebel tried to initiate sex several times, but he always evaded deftly. He teased her, brought her to the brink of climax, but continually refused to put her over the edge. Despite her best attempts to resist reading Jezebel's energy, Mila couldn't help but feel the princess's frustration and lust broadcasting loudly though the room. For a few blinding seconds at one point, Mila was overcome by Jezebel's desire for the man – an alien energy to her own. It was terrifying and confusing and made her feel hot in her own skin.

Eventually, the princess became enraged, but also seemed unwilling to unleash her frustration wholly, as though fearful Culis would view it as a childish tantrum and would be even more unlikely to satisfy her in his displeasure. She was aware enough to know he was playing some sort of game, and she tried to have patience with it, rather than take it to heart. It was the most self-restraint Mila had ever sensed coming from the woman, and it made her realise that Culis was more than just a conquest to Jezebel. She truly felt something for him, or at least, wanted him to feel something for her.

It was such a convoluted situation that, despite Culis's earlier insistence that Mila be present for the occasion, both seemed to forget she was in the room. Mila had never been more grateful to be invisible.

She watched them cautiously out of the corner of her eye, frightened that the power of her gaze could draw their attention, but still compelled to watch the silent politics play out. After over an hour of insufferable torture, she watched as Culis lent over the bed and pulled a phallic object carved from jade from the pocket of the waistcoat he'd discarded on the floor. He returned to where Jezebel lay and pressed it between her legs enabling her to reach her peak and tumble over the edge into climax. Finally.

Afterwards, they both lay back, seemingly exhausted and content to let sleep take them, but Mila knew Jezebel hadn't expected any of this. She'd expected sex and then for Culis to leave her quarters soon after. The fact that he was staying, curled around her with an unexpected amount of tenderness, was disarming. Mila sensed her confusion, but also her delight. Jezebel embraced the moment, sighing contentedly and quickly falling deeply asleep.

Mila soon followed suit, grateful to be alive another day longer than she'd ever thought she'd be.

* * *

Mila was awakened deep in the night by Culis rousing from the bed and moving quickly towards her. His long blond hair had fallen askew from the bun and was hanging over his face in a shaggy and dishevelled manner. Sleep ringed his eyes, but nevertheless, he had a determined air. He moved towards her with such speed and purpose that, for a moment, Mila thought he was coming to kill her.

When he reached her, though, he knelt down and addressed her softly. "Hello, little demon." His tired eyes had a glimmer to them. "I've been waiting a long time for the opportunity to speak to you alone."

It all became obvious then.

This entire evening with Jezebel had been orchestrated simply to have this conversation with her.

Mila tried to calm her racing heart while he waited for her to respond. He stared her dead in the eye, entirely un-self-conscious of the fact he was completely naked.

Mila couldn't help but stare back at him. He had a traveller's body, one made up of lean, sinewy muscle and a broad chest, carved by the practicalities of lifting heavy cargo from one ship to another. There were a few scars across his body that also stood out in the moonlight, the largest being a jagged pink line across his upper thigh that looked only recently healed. His gold earring was caught in the newly escaped curls that tousled down the nape of his neck and glinted cheekily out at her in the candlelight. He was tall, but he did not need height to dominate a room. His energy and presence did it well enough for him.

When it became obvious that Mila was not going to speak, Culis said, "I cannot risk Jezebel waking and seeing us conversing in such a manner, so for both our sakes, it's best that you answer my questions quickly and without subterfuge. I want to know about your power. Tell me exactly how it works."

Of all the things, she'd expected him to say in that moment, this was not it.

"I can sense the energy of living things," she replied softly.

"You misunderstand. I mean, how exactly do demon powers work? Explain the specifics to me. I assume your horns have something to do with it?"

"Why should I tell you?" she demanded, suddenly suspicious, concerned that this information might have repercussions for other besides herself.

"Because your situation here is utterly unique and it has intrigued me."

"So far, capturing your intrigue has not been in my best interest."

He didn't seem offended. "My intrigue saved your life today," he said, "and you may yet find it continues to do so, especially if you can prove yourself useful to me."

"What do you mean?"

"This – " he gestured around them, " – is obviously not an ideal situation for you. You've lost your freedom. You serve at the whim of a – " he glanced back over at Jezebel's sleeping form, " – and, well...the threat of your inevitable sacrifice draws ever closer every day."

"Yes, thank you. You've summed it up quite succinctly." Mila kept her tone low and cutting.

Culis smirked. "Nice to see there's still a spark buried in there somewhere."

She pursed her lips and did not respond, sensing a trap.

He let the silence linger for a moment, studying her. Then he said, almost gently, "While I know this isn't ideal, the alternative is your death – and you haven't chosen that. You're fighting to live, I can see that. I respect that."

"Make your point," Mila demanded, unwilling to play into his game.

"Fine," Culis snapped, his act of sympathy extinguishing like a blown candle. "Here's what I want. I want to buy you from Jezebel. I want you to willingly serve me instead."

"Wha – Why would I do that?" she demanded, her heart hammering painfully in her chest at his words.

"Because your time here is nearly done," he said softly, and for a moment, a sliver of a moment, she thought she caught a true glimpse of the kindness and sympathy she'd seen in the face of the man she'd met in the crypt all those months ago, although, without touching him, she had no way to know if it was genuine.

"You want to *save* me?" she asked incredulously.

His mask snapped back on. "I want to *use* you, your power," he corrected. "And I can't do that if you're dead."

"What would serving you entail?" she asked softly.

"A vast number of things," he said. "Now is clearly not the time or place for detail." He threw a wary glance back over in Jezebel's direction again.

Mila didn't know what to say. She was stunned into silence at the proposition.

"This is obviously unexpected," he said. "So, I'll leave you now to think on it. It is your choice. Make sure you think it through thoroughly. I don't want you if you're going to be uncooperative. Come willingly or not at all." He waited for her faint nod before continuing. "The one last thing I'll say is this. You've no doubt realised by now that I am not a particularly good or kind man. I am not a moral person, and I have no qualms about doing what needs to be done to get my own way. But if you can trust one thing about me it is that I like to make money, and I look out for the interests of those who help me acquire more money. If you agree to work with me, I will use you to help make me obscenely rich. What I will not do is use you as Jezebel has done. You may not like all the things I require from you, but you will never be forced to be my personal plaything, or anyone else's, for that matter. That much I promise you."

He held her gaze intently as he spoke, as though imploring her to believe him, and it occurred to her that if he didn't know she couldn't read his energy, then surely he would not be trying to lie now.

"Or, alternatively," he said, "you can remain here, under the yoke of Jezebel's insanity until the next Sacrament and you find yourself kneeling before the incoming thumb of the God-King. I'll leave you to mull it over."

With that, he nodded abruptly, stood up, and silently donned a robe before slipping out the door.

Mila watched him leave, and when she was able to breathe again and properly consider his proposal, she began to tremble.

No Choice

When Jezebel woke, her chaotic and fickle nature grated on Mila more than ever before. In fact, she seemed worse than usual, incensed, no doubt, by Culis's art in dodging actual sex with her.

Either to distract herself, or for some other unknown impulse, she decided to dangle one of her handmaids out the second-storey window that morning, only finally hauling her in when the woman was somehow able to turn her screams of fear into screams of praise and adoration.

Mila drew again on the inner stoicism that had kept her alive up until now and managed to watch this scene impassively, despite the way her insides were boiling with her own petrified fear.

Culis might not even need to win her over with the moral nature of his pitch. The promise of being saved from such immediate proximity to Jezebel's chaos might be incentive enough.

The rakish man in question met them in the gardens on the way to Worship Day prayers and bowed low, his soft blond curls blowing a little over his face as he stood in the shade of a blossom tree, attempting to mitigate the midmorning heat.

When they approached him, Jezebel delightedly linked her arm into his offered one, and as he escorted her, Mila looked for anything in his actions, anything that might indicate something other than utmost attentiveness towards the princess. She found none. It was as if the conversation he'd had with Mila the night before had never occurred, and this unnerved her more than ever. He was so genuinely engrossed in his playacting, and was so unreadable to her power that, had she not known otherwise, she would have assumed he was being entirely genuine.

It made Mila recoil from him and question if life would truly be better under such a master. The man was as sly and untrustworthy as a hungry fox.

When their trio reached the front of Jezebel's private garden chapel, the two of them tied Mila up outside and walked in, kneeling together at a pew and commencing their obligatory weekly service. The chapel was made entirely from glass bricks that contained the Golden Sand of Midas's vanquished and was encased almost wholly within the purple flowers of the surrounding wisteria trees, making it possible to walk past and completely miss it if you didn't already know it was there. It was only visited by Jezebel and her chosen few, created expressly for her.

One of the High Priest's chosen ran the private service for Jezebel and Culis today, and despite being left out in the blazing summer sun without a patch of shade to shield her, Mila was overwhelmingly relieved that she was not permitted inside the chapel. She had no desire to be even one inch closer to that sand, subjected to yet another parroting of damnation.

Instead, she used the time to do her own form of worship, reaching out to the calm, steadying energy of the nearby tree. As she mentally explored its systems, its cool, underground roots welcomed her mind in and granted her a sensation of reprieve from the heat.

Suddenly, she felt at home, and for the first time since her capture, she allowed herself to feel truly emotional about her homesickness, her fear, and her longing for the life she had led before. Her chest seized with hot, unshed tears, and her mouth ached with the effort of restraining a sob.

The pressure of trying to survive here was killing her in its own way. The spark within, which usually burned hot and vibrant inside her, seemed faint and depleted. She barely felt present in her own body at all. Despite still receiving very little food, today she'd found herself unable to eat when food was offered. It was as if by continually forcing herself to find that internal, stoic place to exist in, she'd completely managed to disassociate from herself. Now, through the simple generosity of some cool tree roots, she'd been reminded of what she once had been.

There were no good options available to her, only monsters, but it was in that moment she knew she would accept Christopher Culis's offer.

With the decision made, she surrendered to calm and let her mind sink deeper, to utterly fixate on the cool offering of those roots and the feelings of hope and life they offered her. She was so engrossed in her meditation that she did not notice when the chapel service ended.

Jezebel delighted in thwarting Mila's powers during moments when it was apparent her concentration was elsewhere. She did so now, breaking Mila's peace with a hearty yank of the lead, choking Mila and injuring her throat. The pain stung fiercely, and Mila coughed, but made sure to contain her flash of anger, always the sign of defiance Jezebel hunted for.

Culis stood behind Jezebel, watching on, his arms folded and a small smile in his eyes.

"I said attend me, demon," Jezebel spat at Mila, who scrambled to obey. The princess was always worse to her after the weekly service. She held out her arms, displaying great sweat patches running through the fine fabric. "I am uncomfortable. Dress me in another gown."

"Princess." Mila scraped her forehead along the ground in a demonstration of complete subjugation, then held up the second gown. It was customary in this heat for Mila to carry a second gown for Jezebel, who was required to look immaculate at all times. The spare was a navy blue, floor-length wrap that Mila had picked out for her that morning. The material was largely sheer, and things such as shapely silhouettes would not be able to be ignored.

Jezebel's face lit up happily as Mila held up the garment. She stripped off the old one immediately in the garden, completely unashamed. Once wrapped up again, with the new gauzy fabric hugging her figure and the tiny, embroidered birds doing very little for her modesty, she turned back to Culis, who had politely averted his eyes during the change.

Mila and Jezebel both secretly watched his face as he appraised the new attire. It remained neutral, unaffected by the new display of skin, denying Jezebel the very response she was desperate for. She turned away with a poorly disguised huff.

Culis's eyes slid briefly over to Mila's, and when it was possible to do so undetected, he wryly raised an eyebrow.

An answer, she realised. He wanted to know her answer.

She drew a small breath and gave a barely perceptible nod, just once.

Fast as a spring-loaded trap, Culis turned back to Jezebel and dialled up the dotage. “You realise that this new attire is entirely inappropriate for a Worship Day.” He paired his words with a seductive chuckle and a hand that ran down the small of her back and over the curve of her backside. “How am I supposed to mediate on the priest’s message today with this kind of distraction before me?”

“I had little say in the matter!” Jezebel protested in delight. “The demon’s inappropriate selection has forced me to put you in such a position.”

“Regardless,” he scolded softly, “you’d better proceed directly to your bedchambers and don something less...”

“Less...?” she prompted with a sickly smile.

“Less likely to have me destroyed if your father were to read my mind today.”

Jezebel laughed, and Culis continued. “It’s true. He’d see the gaze in my eyes and suspect me of worshipping *you*, instead of him.” He turned her towards him and kissed her deeply, then whispered, “Indeed, when it comes to being on my knees, I know which form of worship I’d prefer.”

Mila fought to repress her bile, but Jezebel glowed in delight and began to tug him towards her chambers.

“Shall we remove the offending outfit then? You can help me select a more appropriate attire?” She was nearly breathless, her eyes bright with lustful fever.

“Before we do.” He drew her back to him. “I have a point of business I need to put to you.”

“Business? On a Worship Day? Surely that’s too droll, even for you.”

“Sell me the demon,” he said with a quiet smile and playful air.

The playful, bantering atmosphere between them disappeared as Jezebel sobered up from her love haze almost immediately. "What? No. Why?" Suspicion and jealous energy now dominated her entire body. Her glance towards Mila was an arrow of death.

Mila shivered and tried her best to also look shocked by Culis's proposal. If this deal did not eventuate, the only thing that would keep her from immediate execution was if Jezebel did not suspect that the two of them had conspired behind her back.

"I want her because *you* want her," he said plainly, not backing down, but trying to lighten the situation with his tone.

Jezebel's brow furrowed. "I don't understand."

"Let me explain." He took her hands in his, then twirled her in his arms before continuing. "You are the beloved daughter of our vengeful and all-powerful God-King. You could be bored of me within a day and exile me to the furthest reaches of the land at a whim. You could order anything from me – of anyone – and it would be done. Your power knows no limits." He drew her close and kissed her forehead. "Even now," he whispered, "we both know you could just order me to your bed, and I would comply. But, so far, you've refrained from doing so, because of a truth we both know."

"Which is?"

"That it's worth more to you, and the sex will be better for us both, if I come to your bed willingly." He took a deep breath and ran his fingers over the front of the gauze wrap, finding the gap in the fabric and slipping his hand inside while he continued to speak softly. "Now, Princess, I am a proud man. My second religion is status, followed closely by that of power. I worship them because these are both inescapable, unavoidable, omnipresent facets that permeate all aspects of life, especially good sex. Anyone who tries to tell you that sex is about anything other than power is a fool."

Mila could sense Jezebel's lust rising. Her eyes clouded over as he continued to run his fingers over her body, allowing them to move lower and lower, below her navel.

"Now when it comes to you and me?" he continued in a drawl, "you will always hold both power and status over me. There can be no tussle for dominion, no uncertainty between us in this regard. And this poses something of a dilemma for me... because the way I see it, unless we can both be temporarily deceived of this fact, then our sex will never be anything more than mediocre."

At this, he withdrew his hand, and Jezebel raised an eyebrow and bit down on a wry smile.

Culis ploughed forward. "It's true," he insisted, "and I have no intention of being mediocre in any facet of my life. If you cannot relinquish an inch of power to me, then you will soon tire of me and cast me off, as you have every other suitor who has ever come to your bed. I have no desire for that to occur. I wish to be in your inner arc for as long as conceivably possible."

He let this statement linger for just one breath longer than usual before saying, in a somewhat softer tone, "You are, at once, the most beautiful and powerful woman in this entire nation. I want both of these things close to me for professional and...personal reasons." The bold statement hung between them, then he slowly raised a hand to her face. "That's why I want the demon. Not because I want *her*, but because I want you to submit to me. Inconvenience yourself for me." He spoke now in a low whisper and ran a finger along her cheek. "Do something you *don't* want to do for once. Give up a prized possession...and take the risk that the consequence may be a relationship that runs deeper and more potent than any you've ever experienced before."

Mila watched the entire exchange with a held breath, gobsmacked at his words and the spell he'd weaved in their delivery.

And Jezebel? The princess never stood a chance. If Culis was a snake, Jezebel was a hypnotised rabbit.

By the time the afternoon heat descended, the contract had been drawn, the payment exchanged, and Culis had disappeared for hours into the silken folds of the princess's bedchamber.

Saved by the Baird

Much to Jezebel's ire, once Culis had formally acquired Mila, he made plans to return to his home the following day. Mila braced herself as she witnessed the moment when Jezebel realised he'd never actually intended to stay with her in her apartment, even though he'd heavily inferred that he would during the negotiations.

The ensuing tantrum was devastating to a number of priceless statues. Mila suspected that if Culis's contract had not stipulated that she be delivered to him unharmed and alive, Jezebel would have found a way to ensure an unfortunate accident occurred in the few hours Mila remained with her.

Her restraint failed entirely when Culis's black carriage, pulled by two beautiful charcoal horses, arrived in the courtyard below to collect Mila. At the sight of the somewhat lordly escort, it dawned on Jezebel that the outcome she'd assumed this contract would precipitate was not occurring. Somehow it was Mila, not her, who was going to go live with Culis, and she was about to be left all alone.

"This," she hissed, "is unacceptable. He cannot send for you in this carriage, as though you were some honoured guest."

Mila kept her head down and tried to look as unoffensive as she could. Her moment to escape the princess was so close she could nearly taste it, but she had to survive this last hurdle. Now that the time had come, Jezebel seemed about to renege on the deal.

"Tell me." Jezebel suddenly whirled on Mila. "Does he love me? Does he desire me at all, or am I a pawn to him?"

"I...I don't know," Mila replied truthfully. "I cannot decipher his energy."

"Liar!" Jezebel bellowed and punched Mila straight in the face.

A shooting, red pain flew through Mila's nose. She stumbled but maintained her footing.

Jezebel raised her fist again, and Mila covered her face.

"Princess." A deep voice at the doorway held enough authority that Jezebel checked her next blow and turned to see who it was.

A very tall, burly man with long, red hair and a thick, red beard stood in the doorway. He wore the Artor Trading Company sigil on his breast pocket and tiny gold glasses perched precariously upon his large, hooked nose.

"I've come to collect Master Culis's property."

Mila sensed Jezebel's rage temper at his use of the word 'property', as though it mollified her to meet someone who viewed Mila's status correctly.

"Get her out of my sight." She all but threw the lead at him and shoved Mila away. "I'm sick of my quarters being tainted with such vermin."

Mila did not hesitate. She stumbled quickly towards her saviour, and when she reached him, saw with surprise that behind him, hiding out of Jezebel's sight in the hallway, was Jahan.

The burly, red-haired man didn't hesitate. He took Mila's lead in his hand, bowed swiftly to the princess, and then departed. Mila and Jahan followed.

"You were right," the man said to Jahan when they reached the bottom floor. "I probably arrived just in time. Thanks."

Mila looked sharply at Jahan, who nodded quietly at her. He'd been looking out for her, she realised. He'd known the danger she'd been in and somehow made sure Culis's man reached her before Jezebel's wrath was fully realised. That sort of protection was the last thing she'd expected from anyone in this household.

She turned to him before she entered the carriage, tears in her eyes. "Thank you," she said softly, not daring to say more.

"Good luck," he replied with pursed lips. His energy was unhappy. Was he sad to see her leave?

She didn't have time to dwell on it. She had to get out of Jezebel's reach as soon as possible. Mila stepped into the carriage with the giant man, and they departed, although she did not breathe freely until the black obsidian walls of the palace had passed well out of sight.

"It'll be a few hours before we arrive at Culis Manor," he said. "It lies on the outskirts of the Jeralusah regional boundary."

This was comforting. It seemed to Mila like this was a far enough distance from the palace to have fair warning about Jezebel's approach if she ever decided to visit.

Her companion suddenly leaned forward and wordlessly unlocked her collar. His energy was calm and pragmatic. There was no sympathy in him, only a sliver of curiosity.

"Don't try to escape. It won't work," he said softly and then mercifully turned aside and lost himself in a weathered paperback.

The free air circling around her neck, and the sudden lack of Jezebel's constant looming threat, made Mila feel as though she'd been dunked in ice water. She shivered as the reality of the change hit her, and then, blessedly, realised she was allowed to rest now.

Truly rest.

And so she closed her eyes and slept.

* * *

She was woken by the man tapping her shoulder.

"We're here," he said as they entered the property.

He helped her down from the carriage and led her through a back door into a kitchen and through to a small, private room. Mila was too bleary to take in many details of the house, and the man seemed to understand.

"Rest here," he said. "No one will come in or disturb you today. If you need food, the kitchen is just there, and the cook will feed you. If you need anything else, ask for Baird and I will come. Understand?"

She nodded, grateful, exhausted. She fumbled her way over to the bed and fell asleep before Baird had even left the room.

Culis Manor

On the first morning Mila awakened in Culis Manor, she almost didn't recognise herself. It was the first time she could remember that she hadn't been awakened by Jezebel's rampant lust or terrifying moods. She lay quietly in bed and allowed herself to luxuriate for a moment in the peacefulness of her surroundings and the utter novelty of being alone. Her room was a simple stone turret, located on the ground floor, and annexed to the kitchen. It had a small, arched window seat with a white cushion that looked out over the kitchen gardens. There were birds outside. The bed was a flat, hard pallet that hung suspended by heavy chains from the ceiling and swayed gently when she lay in it. The mattress was soft, the linen clean. She could see sunlight curling past the glass and hear the muted bustling of the morning's breakfast being prepared on the other side of the door. Fresh bread and some kind of stewed, spiced fruit by the smell of it. Her stomach grumbled, and Mila realised she might have an appetite again.

She had also been provided an option of clothes. Three modest shift dresses hung from a tiny wardrobe in the corner: blue, green and yellow. Their irregular fading was the only indicator that they weren't new; otherwise, they were clean and well-fitting. She stripped herself gratefully from the swamp-creature gown and donned the simple blue one slowly. She closed her eyes with a deep inhale and exhale before turning to the simple mirror in the corner and opening them.

It was the first time she'd seen her reflection since the seamstress's townhouse, and she was worried about what she'd find.

It wasn't as bad as it could have been. All the essential parts of her were still intact. Long limbs, small nose, almond eyes, all still present and functioning. The gold rings in her ears rung out merrily, easily seen without her long hair to hide them.

But she was skeletal, and something, a spark, was missing in her eyes. She felt like she was looking at a ghost. She turned away.

She was nervous about what the rest of the day would bring, and what Culis's expectations of her would be, but so far, this was a vast improvement from her previous situation.

The reception she received from the household staff when she left the safety of her small room was similar to what she'd experienced from the staff at Jezebel's apartments: fear and curiosity. It was highly likely that the kitchen staff had never seen a demon before, and by the looks they gave her, it seemed they half expected her to burst into flame and destroy the place on a whim.

Shakily, a serving girl held out a plate with a few thick slices of buttered bread and a little bowl filled with cinnamon-stewed apple. Mila smiled warmly at her and took it gratefully.

After she dipped the first bit of bread into the pot and placed it into her mouth, it abruptly became a battle to mind her manners and not scarf the rest of it down. She hadn't realised how hungry and depleted she was until that moment. Incredibly conscious that she was being stared at by the entirety of the kitchen staff, she did her best to eat with as much civility as possible, and then proceeded to wash her face and hair in the sweet water provided to her in a jug and bowl by another maid.

After breakfast, she went out into the kitchen gardens and wiggled her bare feet in the soil.

It was amazing, the feel of the cool earth against her bare skin. It connected her back to herself more fully than even the full night's sleep had done.

She opened her eyes and surveyed the garden, scanning for any greenery that looked familiar.

And there it was, in the corner, growing weakly against a stone, a small tuft of rubane.

Mila ran towards the tiny red leaves and swiftly plucked them from the rich soil. There wasn't enough of it to even cover her palm, but it was something. She fought the urge to crush it and inhale the scent of the oil directly. It would work, but smoking it would be more effective...

No! She reined in the thought before it could mature. The withdrawals she'd endured for weeks from this weed had been bad. She was now free from its hold for the first time in years. She knew the control over her power that she'd now spent three months honing was worth hanging onto, essential even, for her survival here.

But still...tempting. She turned it over in her palm and carried it back to her room as though it were a small, precious child. She placed it in her windowsill to dry, sighing with happiness. Something about having access to even a small amount of rubane put her even more at ease in this space.

She contemplated staying in the small, quiet room for the rest of the day and pretending the world didn't exist for a while longer, but eventually, she realised it would come find her anyway, so she may as well be on the front foot.

With that, she left the room, and the rubane, and went to find the man who had purchased her.

Her plan was thwarted when it quickly became apparent that Culis was not in the manor. The staff she came upon all seemed too afraid of her to talk, so she assumed he must be out on business. For a moment, it felt odd and empty to not see Jahan amongst the ranks of household staff. She hadn't realised how accustomed she'd grown to seeing him out of the corner of her eye most days.

Rather than returning to the small bedroom to wait for Culis to come get her, Mila decided to explore every nook of his house while she seemingly still had the freedom to do so. She wasn't sure how this arrangement was going to play out once he returned, but she'd be a fool not to make the most of the relative freedom she had at the moment.

The staff avoided her as she passed them, and although she recognised no one, she was not stopped or questioned about her movements around the house, not even when she was headed towards Culis's private rooms. She wondered what he had said to them about her before her arrival – if anything. She wondered if Baird would get in trouble for letting her wander like this. After three months behaving as Jezebel's shadow, it felt wrong to now have so much freedom.

The decor of the house was curious. In the hallways and rooms that one would commonly expect visitors to be received by a host, everything was rather bland. These spaces lacked any distinctive character and were not dissimilar to the decor in the other houses of nobility she'd seen during Jezebel's social visits.

However, other parts of the manor, including the private rooms, and even the servants' hallways, were a different story. They were full of...clutter. Dark green hallways were lined floor to ceiling with plants, shells, stones, statues, artwork, trinkets, valuables, rubbish...everything that Culis had evidently collected during a lifetime of travels that he hadn't deemed worth selling for a profit but still, evidently, appreciated.

Mila ran her fingers gently over some of them. The carved mud figure of a pregnant goddess, a primitive sword with the handle broken, a charcoal sketch of two people, who may or may not have been Culis and a chieftain standing arm in arm.

Fascinating. She'd always thought of him as a man motivated by nothing but greed, but here was proof of something else, proof he was someone who valued items that objectively had no value.

This knowledge made her feel far more calm about the decision she'd made to enter his world.

That is, until she entered the last, windowless room.

The room's energy swamped her like a tidal wave, nearly bowling her over.

Death.

Mila stood in the doorway, gasping in agony, silently drowning in the thick, syrupy darkness for three full heartbeats before she was finally capable of stepping back and slamming the door.

The images burned into her retinas. A large wooden table stood in the middle of the room, an altar, she realised, caked with dried, brown blood. All around it were different shaped knives. Some of them clean, some of them lying in disarray from recent use. Threatening black symbols had been scrawled onto the whitewashed stone walls, black paint dripping down like blood onto the floor. There were mummified animals splayed out across sticks and hanging from the ceiling. A number of human skulls sat piled in the dark corner.

It was beyond horrifying.

Was this a form of private worship Culis secretly conducted? Was this why he wanted her here? To hold her across that table and cut her throat as some kind of sick offering to Viah?

Panic flooded her, and she turned and ran. She had to get out of here, and she had to leave while she still could. Nothing was holding her here. Yet.

I have to get out, I have to get out.

She found a small side servants' door that led into the sweet, hot summer air of the outside world, and pushed her way out of the suffocating hallway, stumbling into the open sunlight. From there, she ran towards the tree line in the distance.

But after only a few steps, she had enough presence of mind to realise she wouldn't get far that way. She was exhausted, her body too depleted from her captivity at the palace.

Instead, she whirled and ran to a large structure nearby, hoping to find somewhere that was simply away from the manor, somewhere she might hide, regain her composure, and make a proper plan of escape.

When she arrived at the building and pushed her way inside, she instantly realised her mistake. The structure wasn't a quiet stable or shed. It was a warehouse, and its calm exterior had been very misleading. Inside, it was noisy and bustling with men and women running about on the warehouse floor, yelling loudly to one another as wooden crates were being stacked high, lining the walls.

Mila watched as a crate was hooked and lifted from the floor to the stacks by a giant piece of machinery, pulleys powered by a team of sweating draft horses and bare-chested, sweating men.

This was not the quiet escape she'd hoped it would be.

Mila tried to turn back the way she'd come, but as she spun around, a voice cut through the bustle and stopped her in her tracks.

"Good morning, little demon!" Culis called out.

She turned in horror towards the sound of his voice and flinched when he swiftly approached her. He didn't seem to notice her fear.

In fact, he smiled broadly down at her as he gestured proudly at the operation around them and said with pride, "What do you think?"

Unlike most of the other men, he still wore his shirt, but the sleeves were rolled up past his elbows, and sweat patches stained his collar. The thick bun of his hair still sat high, but the pieces that usually sat tousled around his temple now lay slick against his head. He had dust streaks on his forehead from where his hands had worked to keep the sweat from his eyes. The gold earring remained clean and glinting. He'd clearly been labouring, and he looked very pleased with himself.

Somehow, seeing him this way calmed her. Although the specifics of his energy remained a puzzle, his body language was open and carefree, and suddenly it seemed very hard to reconcile the unholy room in the manor with someone who seemed so happy to be getting his hands dirty with manual labour.

"We try to get the heavy lifting done before the real heat sets in," Culis was explaining. "These three crates –" he gestured, "– need to be on the road by midday if they're to reach Prious by tomorrow morning. They're full of lanterns for the upcoming evening harvest, and I have it on good authority that the Guild of Merchants had a similar shipment come into Traders Bay yesterday. I need our stock to reach Prious first."

Mila had been young when she'd lived in the large eastern region of Prious, but she still remembered the evening harvests that were held across every farming village and town, the way the lanterns had floated low, spilling light over the fields to allow work in the cool of the summer nights. It was essential work. Prious owned the vast Artor farming plains and was the veritable breadbasket of the nation. The people who lived there were renowned for their salt-of-the-earth attitudes and their pride in providing the country with most of its maize, grain and wheat products. As the night harvest only occurred for a limited time every year, Mila could understand why the lantern market was small and competitive.

Culis's sweaty face gleamed as he watched the crates that contained the lanterns being lowered onto carts. The muted energy rolling from him was suddenly slightly clearer to Mila as his shoulder inadvertently bumped against hers. It was only the tiniest moment of contact, but she enjoyed the unusual clarity. The energy of satisfaction and pleasure rolling from him was reassuring. It was the first time she'd been in his presence without feeling as though he was somehow tailoring himself for her perception. It also put her even more at ease about what she'd seen in the room of death. There had to be a reasonable explanation for it, she assured herself.

The moment didn't last long.

Once he was satisfied that the carts were loaded and moving onto the road, he abruptly moved away, and she was blind to him once more. He gestured for her to accompany him back to the manor and noticed when she baulked in fear.

"What's the matter?" he asked impatiently. "Come inside, before we steam to death out here."

"I found your room of death," she blurted out. "If your plan is to kill me, I'd rather it not be a surprise. Just tell me."

"What are you talking about?" he asked, no less impatient. "What room? Ohh..." A light of comprehension flickered on in his eyes. "Yes, I can see how that'd be a frightening thing to stumble across. Come on, I'll show you it properly. And, *no*, I'm not intending on killing you. Not unless you really piss me off," he said with a grin. "You're safe from me for a while at least. I've paid far too much money to not get my pound of flesh from you first."

His tone was jovial, as if he was thoroughly amused that she'd suspected he might kill her on the first day he'd acquired her. When she thought about it more, she supposed it was improbable. He *had* paid a lot of money for her, and he had plans he needed her help with. All things considered, she was probably safe for the moment.

So, she followed him back to the manor, and he took her directly back to the dreaded room.

Negotiations

"I'm a collector," Culis explained as he pushed the door open.

The wave of death energy rumbled out into the hallway again and hit Mila so hard it felt like trying to breathe while facing into a gale.

"I've visited many cultures during my time, and what has always fascinated me is their perception of death and whether or not they believe in an afterlife. This room is a...tribute to that."

"Quite the morbid tribute," said Mila.

Culis shrugged. "I suppose, to some, it may look that way. I see it differently. Death is as much a part of life as life itself is. In fact, it's an essential component. If something can't die, then it's probably not alive. How each of us choose to process this fact is fascinating to me. Within Artor, for example, we choose to believe in the concept of an afterlife, where there is consequence for your choices in life. We have the Rotting Muds that exist as a threat for disobedience, and Aluah, the Holy Place, that exists as a reward. Now that idea has only existed for the past forty-odd years, since the God-King arrived. Prior to that, what did we as a nation believe happened after death?"

He waited for her to answer.

"I'm not sure," she admitted.

"Never thought to ask?" he probed. Mila found it condescending, although she wasn't sure he'd intended it as such.

"More preoccupied with staying alive in my own reality." She bit back.

"Fair." Culis conceded with a nod. "Well, there are still many folk alive in Artor who remember it. You should ask them when you get the chance. It's interesting." He spoke with passion. This was genuinely a topic of real interest to him. "In other places, they have different beliefs. The Tuli believe that the blood of one who has lived seven decades must be shared at the moment of their seventieth birthday in order for their spirit to live on in the family collective." He gestured to the altar that was covered in dried blood. "No one in their society lives beyond this age unless they're being punished. To die a natural death of old age is the equivalent of being banished from the spiritual collective of ancestors."

The death symbology around the room suddenly began to make a lot more sense.

"And the animals?" Mila asked, gesturing to the grotesque display of corpses hanging from the ceiling.

"Those who live in the nation of Cabot believe the entrails of a person's familiar provides the map that will direct a dying person to their final resting place."

"A familiar?"

"A lifelong animal companion," Culis explained. "Another part of the culture there."

"I see," said Mila. She was still unwilling to enter the room and immerse herself further in the uncomfortable energy, but it suddenly seemed far less ominous than it had earlier.

"I keep it all in one room," Culis explained, as though reading her mind, "because they're quite confronting relics, and having them dotted around the house, mixed in with all my other knickknacks, could send the wrong message to someone who stumbles across one."

"But someone who stumbles across an entire *room* full of them will be fine?" Mila queried pointedly.

"Well, really, it serves you right for snooping around," Culis replied, but he did not seem angry. In fact, he smiled at her. "Now, come with me. I'm a busy man. If I'd wanted you dead, I would have simply left you with Jezebel. Understand?"

"I understand," she replied.

"Good," he said curtly. "Now follow me."

He led her up the grand staircase and into a large study. Bookshelves lined the walls, and a large oak desk sat in the middle, with a high-backed chair tucked in behind it. Mila imagined that downstairs was where Culis greeted travelling merchants, but this room was where they discussed business.

"We must get to work, if I'm to get my small ransom's worth out of you," he said as he unfurled a large map and laid it across his desk. "But first things first. Come here."

Mila obeyed slowly, letting her horns extend as she approached him, hoping to get a read of him again.

It didn't work.

Once she was close enough, he reached out and grasped her shoulders with both hands. She flinched at his touch and at the way his energy suddenly struck her.

Anticipation.

Despite his neutral face, he was very eager for what was about to occur. Knowing this made her more nervous somehow, and she stumbled a little as she arrived before him.

His eyes narrowed as he saw her fear.

"For the last time, I'm not going to hurt you," he said softly, then, more briskly, "not on purpose anyhow." He spun her around. "Don't move until I say so."

Through his touch, his energy suddenly sharpened to a clear beam. *Sincerity*. He was telling the truth. He wasn't going to hurt her.

She wanted to read deeper, more of him, but he released her shoulders, and the veil fell again. Mila stood still, fighting the impulse to look back over her shoulder at the fussing that was occurring at the desk behind her.

Finally, after what seemed like an age, Culis's hands came into view as he reached around her face and placed a thin black band around her neck, moving her short hair aside to clip it together at her nape. It was a necklace of some sort.

Mila made to turn back to him, but he held her still again.

"I didn't say so," he warned quietly.

His voice made her shiver. Then Mila heard a tiny *whoosh* beside her ear and felt the heat of a small flame beside her cheek. She stood as rigid as a statue, terrified of what was next to come.

Was he going to burn her? Brand her somehow?

Culis fidgeted with the clasp of the necklace, and Mila felt the flame come close, warm, but not uncomfortably so, to the back of her neck. For a few seconds, it seemed like nothing was happening.

Then, finally, Culis blew out the flame, his breath startling her.

"Okay, all done. You can move now."

Mila moved towards a mirror on the wall to inspect the necklace but was immediately distracted again, embarrassed by her overall reflection.

She hadn't noticed in her room the way her greasy hair was growing back in uneven clumps and hung awkwardly around her face, making her brown eyes look more narrow than usual. She hadn't noticed how her large, dark brows were now overgrown and untamed. They drew attention away from what were usually her best features – her strong jaw, high cheekbones and big lips. The blue shift she wore didn't hug a single curve where once it would have. She looked unbalanced, like an overgrown, gangly child, rather than the tall, strong woman she remembered herself to be. Beside Culis in his casual finery, she looked like a street urchin.

Her eyes were finally drawn to the black necklace that nestled into her throat. It sat like a thin noose against her tanned skin, a chain made of six thin, dark strands that were braided together to form a pretty, interlocking pattern. The material was something she'd never seen the likes of before. It felt as light as pumice but looked as smooth as glass.

As she continued to spin it around, she saw that what had once been the clasp was now a glob of melted black.

"It's a pretty piece of jewellery," she scoffed, "but not so pretty that I want to wear it forever."

Culis raised an eyebrow and grinned as he surveyed his work. "It's made of vasium. Ever heard of it?"

She hadn't.

"It's one of the most impressive metals of our time. This dainty looking thing cannot be cut by any metal or blade we have yet discovered."

"Wonderful," she said scathingly. "Why is it on me?"

"Because its weight varies, according to its distance from its sister." He held up a small, sparkling, silver and black rock in his left hand.

Mila reached for it, but Culis drew it away and placed it into his breast pocket.

"This is my insurance to keep you from running away and reneging on our contract. Stay close and your necklace will remain light as a bird's sneeze. You can go anywhere within this manor, and you'll only feel the pressure slightly increase around your neck. But go much further than, say, oh...a mile from this?" He patted the pocket gently. "The weight will increase significantly, eventually to the point where it will pin you by your neck to the ground. You'll be stuck there until someone from my staff comes to collect you."

Mila's eyes widened, and horror flowed through her.

"I hadn't been entertaining ideas of escape," she lied softly, realising that her frantic, failed escape attempt this morning had not gone unnoticed.

"And now you definitely won't," he said coolly.

"I made a deal with you," she argued. "I am here of my own free will. This is unnecessary."

"I am risking far too much on this venture to accept a demon's word as gospel. Besides, this will allow us to travel freely, without the requirement of a lead or shackles. I think, for both of us, that is the preferable option."

Mila glared at him, but Culis met her gaze evenly, showing no hint of remorse. He did, however, seem to soften slightly as he eyed her tattered hair.

"After this meeting, I will call one of the maids to fix you a bath and cut your hair, if you'd like?"

Mila turned back to the mirror and studied her reflection again. The necklace could not be ignored, but the rest of her truly did look awful.

"That would be...nice."

"Easily done." He waved away the gratitude. "I expect, after a few weeks, you'll have gained some of that weight back too. Hopefully, you'll feel healthy and comfortable here soon."

"Why bother with that?" she accused. "My comfort has never been your priority before."

"I was somewhat preoccupied with the small task of trying to keep you alive," he bit back.

"Ah, yes, forcing me to lick your feet to keep me alive. Truly a noble act."

"I improvised." He shrugged, unabashed, and took her insubordinate tone in stride. "It worked. You're alive, are you not?"

"For your own purposes, as I'm sure I'm about to discover."

"You're correct, little demon." He rapped with impatience, not shying away from her accusations, but not accepting them in their entirety either. "Having you alive is far more useful to me than having you dead."

He was mocking her. She did not take the bait.

"And what are these plans?"

"I'll tell you, " he leaned forward, "once you tell me what you sense from my energy."

"I can sense that you're an *arse*," she shot back immediately.

Culis threw back his head with genuine laughter. In the comfort of his own lair, he was the most relaxed she'd ever seen him.

"Okay, I set myself up for that one. How about this one? How exactly do demon powers work?"

"Why do you need to know?" Mila demanded.

"Because the more I know, the better I can tailor the product to the buyer."

"What product? What buyer?" Her blood ran cold.

"Little demon," he tutted condescendingly. "Do not play dumb now. You know I am a man of commerce. Surely, you've figured out by now that all of this – " he gestured up and down at her, " – is about product and buyer."

Mila felt as small and insignificant as a loaf of bread at market. "If you intend to treat me as nothing but a *product*, you may as well have left me with Jezebel," she seethed.

Culis held up a hand, losing patience. "Save your indignation for the end. It'll be far less annoying for the both of us."

Mila glowered at his words. His cocksure, superior attitude was infuriating but she really had no choice but to fall silent and wait for him to explain further.

"I bought you from Jezebel because I want you to help me find more demons," Culis said. He said it matter-of-factly, but leaned forward and could not hide his eagerness from his eyes entirely. "If I find more demons, I will convince them to sign their service over to me in a contract, as you have done. And then," he cocked an eyebrow, "I will sell them to other humans for vast amounts of money."

Mila blinked at him incredulously, unsure she'd understood correctly. "You want me to help you to *enslave* them?"

"Now, one could phrase it like that, or – " he quickly raised both his hands as though trying to halt her onslaught of venomous thoughts, " – you could choose to look at it from a more..." he gesticulated into the air, searching for the words he was after, "...*helpful* perspective." His voice was a purr, his eyes alight with anticipation. "Think about it like this. The Church condemns all seven Heretical Behaviours but only really punishes the First. You know better than I do the way humans view demons as a result. Your status in society is lower than that of a dog." He lifted his feet and placed them cross legged on the table. "But...I have a vision – an inspiration, a sincere desire, if you will – to change that."

She barely heard his words. The rage building within her made blood pound in her ears. What kind of man would wrest her from Jezebel's control and give her the illusion of safety, only to force her to start a slave trade of her own people? He was the essence of a snake in a human's body, sly and deceitful.

"What *vision*?" she demanded in a fury, the words barely making it from her mouth.

"My vision," he replied calmly, still leaning back infuriatingly, "is a world where the First is considered no worse than any other Heretical Behaviour and the burden of providing fodder for sacrifice to the God-King is split between humans and demons alike." He said it simply, as though he were suggesting something as innocuous as taking a stroll in the garden. "So, yes, one way to view it is that I am implementing a slave trade of demons. Another way to view it is that I am preventing the genocide of demons, all whilst making me the wealthiest man in the nation."

Mila was dumbstruck. "I don't believe that you care about that," she accused.

"About demon genocide?" His eyes gleamed and he sat upright again. "You're right. I don't. Not really, anyway. But *you* do." He said it slowly. A man closing a trap. "And I care immensely about my wealth. So, there's something for both of us, and the atmospherics are just right for a venture like this. There are enough religious zealots talking loudly in Traders Bay that such a shift is likely to happen in our lifetime. Anyone could capitalise on it. I'm just blessed with the brains and the means to do it first. And this is why I need you, I think."

He looked at her contemplatively. "It's certainly why I need to know how demon powers work – specifically your power. When you said at the dinner that you could sense the difference between demons and humans... A power like that would make my task of uncovering demons from their hidden lives a hell of a lot easier."

"You want me..." Mila spluttered, barely able to get the words out of her mouth.

"To help me develop a culture where demons have worth," Culis finished smoothly, giving her the words he wanted her to say.

"But only as objects," she accused, refusing to play along. "Only for our powers. And we'd be subjugated to humans in the process. I think many demons would choose sacrifice over such a life, such a humiliation."

"*You* did not," he pointed out simply, letting that statement echo in the space between them before speaking again. "Look," he said, using his tone to try calm her. "If the Church persecution continues as it has these past forty years, then, within the next...ten...twenty years? All demons will have been found and sacrificed, and your kind will be gone. What I'm proposing to you is, yes, servitude for your kind, but at least with servitude there's life and a chance we might actually be able to change the way the world works."

Mila was reminded of the mystery of the Church's persecution. Why did Abbott hate ikarei so much? Why had he chosen to do this to them? Perhaps working with Culis to change the status quo would expose a reason.

"And how...how do you plan to do that?" she asked cautiously.

"So glad you asked!" he said with genuine delight, deliberately choosing to interpret her question as her compliance. "Well, firstly, we'll need to ensure we select the right demons to recruit into the scheme. Demons with useful powers that can be monetised, not demons with...you know, the ability to hear the whispers of worms."

If Mila hadn't been so stressed, she might have laughed at that. Demons had started the rumour of useless powers years ago in an attempt reduce societal fear. She was surprised that someone like Culis would believe it.

"Then," Culis continued, "with the right advertisement and the well-considered allocation of demons to owners, we'll begin to see a shift. Mark my words, when the Sacrament of Contrition next comes upon us, I predict we'll see the elite prefer to offer up a disrespectful human servant, rather than offer up the demon whose power has earned them unprecedented status and wealth."

He was mad. She'd agreed to serve a mad man.

"This is heresy." She shook her head, unable to believe what she was hearing.

"The elite are always heretics when it suits them. Divine obedience is for the poor."

His disdainful tone caused Mila to think of Jahan again. Religiously devout Jahan. Jahan, who hated Culis, but also seemed to think that the persecution of demons by the Church was heavy-handed. She remembered the conversation she'd had with him only a few days earlier and realised that, perhaps, Culis's idea would be supported by Jahan and others like him. Perhaps it wasn't the most far-fetched, impossible idea that had ever been attempted.

"Look," he said in a more conciliatory tone, as if he knew where her thoughts were headed. "I've travelled enough to see what has happened in other nations around the world when a minority challenges the religious majority. There's usually a war, and religious wars are more corrosive and destructive than any other kind. There are no winners. You can never destroy a belief through force. You have to make it appealing for the belief itself to be changed. Otherwise, it only makes the zealots double down."

"But you're not proposing this because you hate war," she accused. "You want to be head of this demon trade and become even richer off the backs of the misery and suffering of my fellows."

He denied none of it, but smiled as he said, "Inflicting misery and suffering is such a tedious way to make money. How about this. We will write up contracts of employment, fair ones, ones that grant a demon freedom after, oh, say, ten years of servitude, amongst other rights."

It was too much to take in. Mila looked around the room, her eyes drawn to the soft leather chairs in the corner beside the fireplace.

"May I sit?" she asked.

Culis nodded, gesturing towards them. "Of course. And while it is a little early in the day, I don't think a nip of brandy would go amiss right at this moment."

He poured them each a small crystal goblet full of amber liquid and watched her intently as she drained the strong draught. He poured her another, and Mila sank back into the chair, rubbing her face into her hands, unable to believe the conversation she was having.

"What is your name?" he suddenly asked.

"Our horns amplify our power," she said by way of reply. "They make it clearer, stronger or more effective. But even without revealing them, a demon can still use a trace of power. For example, I can still sense you without revealing my horns, but the specificity of your energy is much less clear. And, in a crowded room, it would be impossible for me to focus on one person's energy without my horns up."

She deliberately used him in the example, hoping to reinforce his assumption that she could read him as clearly as she could read anyone else. She instinctively knew it would be dangerous for him to learn that he was uniquely difficult for her to sense.

"That is what I assumed. More or less. good to have it confirmed."

"And my name is Mila."

"Mila." He repeated the name and stared at her for a long moment, as though matching the new information to the face he knew. Then he nodded, stood, and returned to his desk, retrieving the map he'd brought out earlier and bringing it back over to their seats.

"Well, Mila. Now we're at the business side of things, inspect this map for me. We are here, the Highlands are here...and this is Traders Bay. Where do we start looking for our first demon?"

Mila inspected the map and felt bile rise in the back of her throat. This was all happening so fast. She still had no idea who she was signing her fellow demons over to, or what life she was subjecting them to.

"How will they be...collected?" she asked, shuddering at the term, but trying to buy herself time before giving a proper answer.

He studied her with a smirk on his face. "You and I, and a handful of others, will go together and find them. And when we do, you'll have to find the words to convince them to join us. They'll trust you far more than they will me."

She baulked at the idea of being so intimately involved. "They're unlikely to come willingly."

"There is no other choice. They must be convinced," Culis said with an infuriating shrug. "I have all but bound myself to Jezebel to give this idea a chance. It must be worth my while. If it turns out to be too hard, then I will simply exchange you back to her and take a long sea voyage to cool off my ties with the royal family for a while."

The cavalier way he delivered this threat made her freeze with the glass halfway to her lips. She hadn't known that returning her to Jezebel was a possibility he'd ever considered.

"You'd return me to her?" Her voice came out as a croak.

Culis's reply was firm. "I can't force you to cooperate with me, but if you don't, then I have no use for a sullen and difficult demon that does nothing but lurk around my house, frightening my staff."

"Well, I hardly knew what this venture was going to be when I accepted," Mila pushed back. "What am I supposed to even say to the other demons?"

"Now *that's* a wonderful question!" His eyes gleamed with delight. This had now become negotiation rather than an argument about her compliance. And he truly loved negotiating. "Let's determine that right now. The contracts will be ten years long, and the demons are obligated to serve their masters in whatever capacity required of them."

"With some exceptions, I should think," she interjected.

Culis's jovial demeanour turned quickly to icy professionalism. "Not *too* many exceptions," he corrected.

"A limitless contract may be the lot I'm subjected to," Mila said firmly, trying to keep the tremble from her voice. "But I will not help you subjugate my fellows to the same fate. If you want my help to discover the remaining demons and bind them into servitude, then you will allow exceptions I deem necessary."

"Is that so?" His eyes narrowed and something about that tiny movement suddenly brought an air of menace into the conversation.

Mila tried not to be cowed but took note of the shift as something she'd be wise to remember. Culis was naturally gifted with the ability to act and pretend to be something he was not, changing character as effortlessly and easily as one puts on a mask. She had no way to know if what he was saying was a lie. He was the most complicated individual she'd ever met; charming, greedy, narcissistic, ruthless...but what made him dangerous was his cunning, and he was using it against her now, dangling the tenuous hope of long-term change for the demons of Artor, against the threat of returning her to Jezebel if she defied him. It was the same skill that had driven Jezebel right into the palm of his hand and had put the Artor Trading Company at the forefront of procurement for the nation. She saw the game he was playing and hated it.

"We are living beings," Mila reminded him, quietly but firmly. "I am a living, feeling, thinking creature. No less than you."

"Probably *more* than me." His manner switched again as he offhandedly chuckled, then let out a sigh of resignation. "Fine. Here's how we'll do it. Today, you will draft the contracts that you think demons will agree to. I will review the conditions tonight and adjust them based on what I know the nobility will expect. From there, we will negotiate."

* * *

That night, she lay in the darkness on her pallet and, try as she might to frame and reframe her decision to work with Culis, she could not find a moment where her conscience truly felt comfortable with it.

The weight of what she'd agreed to do to her fellow ikarei was a shackle around her soul, despite the fact she'd done her best to negotiate the contracts and achieve an outcome that would, perhaps, be a better option for them than a life of being hunted for sacrifice. It had been an exhausting process, one which had reinforced just how few rights ikarei held as 'demons' in this world. She'd been left feeling drained and disillusioned.

There had been some real wins in the process and, truly, if human buyers could agree not to abuse their demons and provide medical treatment when required, then perhaps it would be a small step towards changing the wider psyche towards her people.

It had certainly not all been positive though. There were other negotiations she had lost, which seemed inexcusable. For example, Culis refused to include a guarantee that a demon would not be sacrificed after their period of servitude.

"To include that," he'd said, "we'd have to create an entirely separate contract for the God-King to sign, and considering that I'm already taking enormous liberties with his very vague permission to meddle with demons at all, we can't draw this to his attention if we want it to succeed."

"So, you're saying that a demon who's been successfully hiding for years could expose their existence, sign their life away for ten years, only to be sacrificed at the end of it?"

Culis rubbed his temples in frustration. "I can't change the law, Mila. We're just trying to change the status quo. Who knows what that will be in ten years' time for demons? And besides, if we don't do this, it seems like Jezebel will very likely take the idea into her own hands. And I assure you, whatever diabolical schemes you believe me capable of, I am nothing compared to her.

The conversation had sat uncomfortably with her for the rest of the day, like a stone in the throat, and it felt even larger now that she lay in the deep silence of her room, with no one and nothing around to distract her.

Was she being a traitor to her kind?

It could all go terribly wrong. But was Culis right about the religious shift starting in Traders Bay? Was it truly possible to change the status quo? It was an enormous gamble, not just with her own life, but the lives of all those she recruited into this scheme.

There was no real way to know what the future would hold.

There was still the other option. She could still refuse to help and accept that this would mean she'd be sent back to Jezebel.

That thought had barely formed in her mind when her hands began to tremble, and her mouth dried out. She pushed it away in a panic, battling for mental clarity. It took a few moments, but eventually, the tremors passed, and she was able to breathe again.

Logically, she knew this physical reaction was all part of some sort of come-down, a stress response born from the long duration she'd held tightly onto her emotions in Jezebel's presence. But knowing the logical reasons didn't prevent the fear from sucking at her until she didn't recognise herself anymore. It was in this moment that the harsh realisation struck her. She was too frightened to voluntarily return to Jezebel.

Coward. Traitor. Scum.

She was still caught in the clutches of creeping cowardice, the same one that had stayed her objections when Jahan had been dragged to his punishment. She was too frightened to say no.

Coward. Traitor. Scum.

The words burned into her like a hot knife, and she lay in a pit of self-loathing, ruminating on the words until sleep finally claimed her. But even then, nightmares plagued her, and scenes of hell unfolded within her mind.

In all of them, Mila herself was the devil.

The Demonstration

It wasn't the long trip inside the bouncing carriage that was causing Mila to feel sick. It was the way the landscape began to look hauntingly familiar, like something remembered from a waking dream. They were heading to Traders Bay.

She'd been fourteen when her family had cast her out, and during the following year of aimless wandering, she'd spent some time in the sprawling, notorious city that was Traders Bay. When she'd finally turned her back on it and headed for the Highlands, she'd hoped never to lay eyes on the port city again. Yet, as Jeralusah's thick, luscious, green fields began to turn into coastal cacti and tiny whitewashed cottages, it became increasingly obvious that this was their destination.

"Traders Bay?" she asked quietly.

Culis looked up from his book. "Yes. Have you been there before?"

"Unfortunately."

"What does that mean?"

She wished she hadn't spoken. Flashes of the life she'd endured there rose in her mind – the poverty, the squalid sharehouse, the killer who had stalked and butchered random women in her block of units, the blatant disregard of the City Watch. It'd been hell. She'd left as soon as she had been able to afford to do so.

"I've lived there before. It wasn't a pleasant experience."

"There's clearly more to that story," he said with a raised brow.

"There is."

He paused expectantly, but when Mila made it apparent that there was no further story forthcoming, he continued on. "I see, well, I hope you overcome your aversion. We'll be spending a lot of time there. It's a second home to me, and it's where I conduct almost all of my business."

"Is that what we're doing today? A business meeting?"

"No." Culis couldn't hide the smile from his face. "We're doing something far more important. That's why I had the maids attend to you this morning. You look beautiful, by the way."

The maids had indeed attended to Mila that morning, overcoming their fear of her and washing, plucking, styling and shaping her within an inch of her life. Her short hair had been parted to the side and elegantly slicked back into a modern style that somehow brought her femininity to the forefront and highlighted her cheekbones. She still wore the simple blue dress, but the finishing touches had been a pretty pink stain across her lips and a dark shadow dusted across her eyes. Mila had never experienced anything like it, and when she'd looked in the mirror again, she'd felt, for the first time in a long time, like she actually looked beautiful.

But that all came crashing down with his next words.

"I'm showing you at Central today."

Traders Bay was a merchant city at its core. Its many roads led like veins towards three large markets that were the beating hearts of the region. Buxton-Canal Market lay by the docks and was run by farmers and fishermen. It provided the main trade in daily essentials, fresh food and livestock. The stalls of the Porters Lane Market were stocked full of knickknacks, furniture, jewellery and decorations. Central Market, the smallest yet most notorious market, only ran once a week and was for the trade of exotic and rare goods.

"You're showing me at Central," she repeated slowly, in horror. "Like an exotic animal."

"You're not an animal, Mila," he corrected. "But you are exotic, and it's essential to display you and announce our venture to the world. Otherwise, what's the point?"

"So, this is your idea of an advertisement?" she said incredulously. "Whatever happened to pinning a notice on the town message board?"

"It's going to be a demonstration that will elicit envy and desire from the nobility and form the foundation of our future demon trade. You don't have to like it, but you're going to have to trust me," Culis replied. "I didn't get where I am by pinning notices to town message boards."

Mila swallowed her indignation. Whatever Culis had planned today was evidently very important to him, and if it didn't go the way he intended, then there was every chance he would simply sell her back to Jezebel, recoup his losses and turn his attention to other things.

He was right. She probably wouldn't like what was going to happen to her today. She simply had to endure it.

When they reached the city outskirts, Mila was accosted by all manner of smells, sounds and energies, as humanity in its most pungent form eked through the carriage windows. In comparison to the droll and demure population of Jeralusah, the folk of Traders Bay were an eclectic mix and far less conservative. The Heretical Behaviours were still avoided, but other, less serious vices abounded in broad daylight. Mila saw brothels, casinos and smoking houses as their carriage wound its way through the increasingly dense and serpent-like streets. Eventually, they came to a section where the street was so narrow they could go no further.

"This is us," Culis said.

He opened the door and stepped down from the carriage, holding out his hand for hers in an unexpected gesture of chivalry.

She took it – to read him – and was rewarded as his excitement and anticipation pounded through her. And thus, she descended into the cacophony of Central.

As its name implied, Central was located in the heart of the Traders Bay sprawl, which reached from the sparkling blue port on the western coast and ran for miles inland, dominating the entire southwest region of the country. While Jeralusah was the moral and religious centre of Artor, Traders Bay was its purse. By bringing Mila to Central, Culis was ensuring the announcement of his new business venture would be made on the biggest stage in the nation.

Mila was immediately assaulted by the energies of the many lives around her, and she raised her handkerchief, which was stuffed with the dried rubane, up to her nose, and inhaled deeply.

God, it was good.

She'd decided to bring it with her today, and as the nutty aroma filled her nostrils, and the numbing haze drifted over her brain, she sighed in relief and delight. Culis turned sharply, following the unusually loud sound of inhalation, and gave her a curious look, but said nothing and was quickly distracted elsewhere. This was the first time since she'd been captured that she'd used the weed, and the relief it brought her in such a human-dense environment was palpable. Today was a day where managing her own energy would be enough of a task, let alone receiving everyone else's.

Central was massive.

It was an oval arena filled with sand and ringed on all sides with tiered wooden seating. The ruthless sun beat down onto it, and while there were some shade sails provided for the elite boxes, most of the populace simply bore the brunt of the mid-summer ferocity.

Every few minutes, a new number would punctuate the din through a human loudspeaker system of twelve people that were rigged above the seating area. They would call out the next number, and this would prompt the next seller to take up his place on the sand and commence displaying and auctioning his wares.

Mila felt her stomach clench as she watched this routine unfold and realisation dawned on her. Culis expected her to be in the centre of that ring with him at some point today, to be displayed as property, as an anomaly, as something to be both reviled and desired.

She sniffed the rubane handkerchief again, willing it to be some kind of opiate instead.

Culis didn't appear to be in any rush. He still held her hand to ensure they did not get separated by the sweaty and fevered crowd of spectators, and she could sense his enjoyment of the spectacle around them. He navigated their way slowly through the crush until, eventually, they arrived at their allotted box, one specifically carved with the crest of the Artor Trading Company on the front panel.

Once seated, shaded and with a sweet, iced beverage in hand, Mila was able to turn her attention to the centre of the ring, and despite her apprehension, she was impressed by what she saw.

Only the most notable traders were invited to present their wares at Central, and everything Mila saw displayed made her jaw drop. Not only were the goods utterly decadent, but the way the traders each chose to use the gigantic space to showcase their wares was a spectacle in itself. Smaller and more delicate objects were not well suited to such a vast viewing platform, so traders had to get creative. One perfumer had a number of slaves, each adorned with a giant, purple, feather fan. The slaves scurried about the boundaries of the arena and wildly waved their fans as he strode by, puffing samples of the perfume into the generated breeze. It was very effective, and Mila was able to easily smell the enticing scent.

Another man had hired a number of devastatingly beautiful and exotic models from across the continent to walk the length of the arena, allowing glossy new fabrics, obtained from across the sea, to glide and shimmer across their immaculate bodies. The fabric reminded Mila of the scales of a freshwater fish that lived in the waterfalls near her home, sleek and everchanging in the sun's angles.

Other wares were far more easily showcased. A particularly beautiful and angry battle horse took her breath away as it galloped wildly around the arena, showing off its strength and prowess, before coming to a complete standstill at the snap of the trader's fingertips.

The entire scene felt more like a spectacle, a performance, rather than a market. She wondered again, with deepening apprehension, what Culis would expect her to do. She turned to ask him, but he was deep in conversation with someone to his left, so she settled instead for a scan of the crowd.

It had been a long time since she'd seen such a diverse population. In the Highlands, the villagers dressed simply and tended to hold themselves quietly. In such an isolated region of the world, everyone knew everyone, so it was always best to err on the side of politeness and caution, lest you accidentally offend someone important.

If one wasn't born in the village they lived in, then they had usually moved from the next one over to marry. Variation was found in the colourful clothes they wore, dyed with the abundance of berries and flowers from the rainforests, but the fabric was all the same, a simple fabric woven of local fibrous plants. Women generally wore loose-fitting, thin dresses, and men mostly went shirtless due to the extreme heat. The constant nudity of small children, right up until their years of blossoming, was not uncommon.

Traders Bay was different. It was located closer to the middle of the continent where the summer heat was not quite as oppressive. As it was closer to the sea and trading ports, the citizens of this region had access to a multitude of unusual fabrics and styles. As a result, their fashion still followed the typical summer traditional style, but was different somehow, more inventive and creative. Closer, Mila realised, to the extravagant style Jezebel favoured and probably inspired by her.

Almost every woman sported a fan of some sort, and some were fluttering them wildly in a vain attempt to generate a cool breeze. Others used theirs with more finesse to communicate with their envoy, directing them on when to bid and when to hold.

Culis finally finished his conversation with the man to his left and turned to her. At that moment, the number seventy-eight was called out over the loudspeaker.

He smiled and stood. "That's us. Hide your horns for the moment, if you can."

With that, he walked into the ring without so much as a glance rearward, clearly expecting her to follow him obediently.

Her stomach dropped, but she followed.

It was this or return to Jezebel.

She took a deep breath and tried to steady her raging nerves as she reached the bottom step of the tiered seating and made her way across the sandy arena to stand beside Culis in the centre.

"Ladies and gentlemen," Culis bellowed, throwing up his hands, demanding the attention of the space. He was the first after a long list of traders to have prepared no elaborate fanfare for his entrance, and it worked in his favour. The simplicity of his presentation, and probably his reputation, drew the curiosity of the crowd. For the first time all day, the constant background ruckus died down to a low hum.

"Today, I bring you a true rare gem. Something that has never before graced the floors of Central, and very few of which – I assure you – will ever grace it again."

Mila felt more than heard the murmur of curiosity ripple through the crowd. They wondered what the famed adventurer, the merchant lord, Christopher Culis of the notorious Artor Trading Company, had brought to Central today. She also knew that they were looking at her and trying to puzzle out what he meant by her being rare. Very few human slaves ever made it onto the floor of Central. Only the most exotic-looking or talented ones had ever been brought forward, and while Mila's hair had been fixed, and she was attractive, she was certainly not unique enough in her appearance to warrant the flourished herald that Culis was giving her.

"I present to you – " he paused for effect, " – my demon."

A rush of silence hit the stadium like a hammer, followed almost instantly by a burst of frenzied chatter.

"A demon?!"

"What does he mean by *my* demon?"

"This is heresy."

"She serves me under a binding contract as my servant. And her power," Culis continued, "is the ability to manipulate the age of anyone she touches."

Mila shot him a sharp glare, confused. But there was no way to confront him, especially not as a collective gasp of shock and intrigue rumbled through the crowd.

It was broken by a sharp cry. "Bullshit!"

The call came from somewhere within the stands and was loud enough for Mila to hear over the crowd.

It drew Culis's attention also. "Who was that?" he called in a deep voice, like a circus ringmaster announcing his next act. "A doubter? One who would publicly question my honour? Sounds to me like a perfect opportunity for a demonstration! Come on then, come down here. Don't be shy!"

"What are you doing?" Mila whispered frantically out of the corner of her mouth as the man who had jeered approached the centre of the arena.

Culis didn't deign to reply. Instead, he watched with a smug smile as the man from the crowd came near. He was tottering from side to side, evidently a little drunk from a morning of hot sun and heavy drink. He was also, Mila noticed, wearing the insignia of the Guild of Merchants. Even she, with her limited commercial knowledge, knew that this man worked for the rival of the Artor Trading Company, Culis's greatest competitor.

"Go on then!" the drunk man roared loudly before pulling down his pants and presenting his cock to Mila, much to the crowd's delight. "Lucky me to get touched by a pretty thing for free."

"Culis," she hissed.

Culis rolled his eyes a little at the man's behaviour, then said, "His face will suffice. Touch him," he ordered.

Mila couldn't believe what was happening, but to disobey at this point made no sense either. There was nowhere to hide. She had no option but to reach out and do as Culis commanded.

Her hand was inches away from the man's bare skin when she paused. Culis saw her moment of hesitation and pushed between her shoulder blades, forcing her hand abruptly onto the man's cheek.

Instantly, the man grabbed it with his own so she could not let go. At the same moment, he also let out a scream, as though he were in incredible pain and he began to wither away before her. Shrinking, wrinkling, hunching.

Mila tried to pull away in horror, but the man held her in place. The deep tenor of his voice morphed in time with the gnarling of his body, turning into a paltry, rusty croak.

He was ageing before their eyes. Ageing into an old, *old* man.

Mila stood watching, frozen in horror.

"Stop!" he begged, and she was finally able to move, wrenching her hand away.

The ageing immediately stopped, and the arena was silent and still as ice.

"Well?" Culis said calmly, not even needing to project his voice now. "Anyone else like to test my demon?"

Mila stared at her hand incredulously, her stomach as small as a raisin. *What had just happened?*

The old man stared down at his still exposed, now-shrivelled cock, and he cried out in despair, pulling his pants up, and then turning his gnarled hands over in front of his face. He let out a despairing sob.

Slowly, horrifically, he turned back the way he had come, shuffling grimly back towards his seat. He held the attention of the entire crowd for each tortuous step.

"Someone! Fetch that man a cane!" Culis joked lightly, bringing his eyes briefly over to Mila and her aghast face. "Oh, go on, demon, put everyone out of their misery. Touch him again."

Mila blinked at him in horror, but Culis just gave her a warning stare and offered no explanation. So, without any other option, she turned, easily catching up with the shuffling old man, and did as she was bid. She reached out to touch him between the shoulder blades. Something was afoot here, but now was certainly not the time for her to publicly question it.

The man screamed again at her touch and contorted, his hands ripping at his long hair in agony. But this time, it seemed as though time was moving backwards.

When Mila withdrew her hand, the ageing had reversed. In fact, now, the man looked slightly *younger* than he had been before the entire ordeal began.

She stared at him with wide, startled eyes as she suddenly sensed something in him that she hadn't sensed before.

Meanwhile, pandemonium erupted in the stands, and Culis had to bellow his next words in order to be heard.

"This demon is mine!" Culis cried. "Her power is mine to command! Eternal youth for me, and a swift, surreptitious death for my enemies! What wouldn't you give to have this in your possession, as I do? She serves me faithfully under an ironclad contract that binds her to me for the next ten years, and she uses her powers only under my express command, in accordance with my every whim."

Mila stared in fascination at the young man, who was now prancing gleefully around the arena, and then she was utterly overwhelmed as a maelstrom of energy and noise from the crowd erupted around her.

They were going ballistic at this announcement and the show they'd just witnessed.

Using demon powers for human benefit, as servants? Unheard of. Was it even allowed? Did their God-King Midas know? Had he given his consent?

The questions buzzed throughout the arena. Mila watched Culis survey the utter chaos he'd caused with deep pleasure. Mila could see what this meant to him, the attention, the envy, the drama of the big reveal.

It had all been so very clever.

The weak hit of rubane she'd sniffed before entering Central had stopped her from sensing the man's energy from afar, but as she'd touched him the second time, she'd been able catch a whiff of it. He had not been drunk or a gross fool.

In fact, the man was not a man at all.

He was an ikarei, and he'd been Culis's plant to impress the crowd. The display of pain, the tearing at his hair, had all been an elaborate distraction to hide his horns as he'd aged himself at will, which was probably the limit of his abilities.

For a moment, Mila wondered why Culis had wanted to trick the crowd rather than have her show her actual powers, but the answer quickly became obvious. Her own power was not visibly impactful, nor did Culis want others knowing it. It was infinitely more useful to him for her power to remain a secret.

As she studied Culis, she saw the look on his face and knew he was aware of the questions the crowd was now asking one another. He also knew that he'd lost all hope of being heard by the crowd in their current state of frenzy.

But he'd prepared for this. With a wave of his hand, a handful of servants ran out onto the arena holding white silk banners, which they unfurled and paraded around before the crowd.

Mila spun to read each of them.

Buy a demon from the Artor Trading Company, and improve all facets of your life: love, health, business, family...

How might your life change if you had a servant who could read minds?

Only ten available each year. Be one of the lucky few to buy and invest in our first procurement.

The Artor Trading Company holds exclusive rights to the demon trade. If you don't get one from us, you'll miss out.

Presumably it was this last one that caused the ripple of disturbance from the box that held the Guild of Merchants.

Mila's eyes were drawn by the movement, and she glanced over to see a fellow in his mid-fifties, face red with anger, using a pole to poke a loudspeaker in his nest and impart a message.

The loudspeaker nodded and then held his funnel to his mouth and screamed into it. "This is heresy!"

The cry was echoed by all the other loudspeakers, and the words settled the crowd for a moment, as everyone turned to Culis to gauge his response.

"Oh hush, Featherstone. Jealousy doesn't suit you." Culis dismissed him casually, and this approach worked on some of the crowd, who laughed, while others remained concerned that Featherstone had a point.

"The demons I will find for you will be *remarkable*," Culis continued to brag, "and will bring you untold power and status."

"I'm afraid not, Master Culis."

The icy tone of a priest entering the arena, accompanied by at least ten jesu, cut through Culis's moment of triumph. The crowd fell deathly silent when they appeared.

"As bothersome as it may seem to your commercial ambitions, Kurt Featherstone is correct. Your pronouncement is an act of heresy. Demons are not chattel, to be bought, sold or for us to negotiate contracts with. They are the living embodiment of heresy, condemned by the God-King for death alone."

It wasn't unusual for jesu to supervise these markets and ensure that the behaviours were not being committed. Culis must have expected at least some kind of challenge of this nature. Mila watched curiously to see what he would do.

"Did you not hear me earlier?" Culis said calmly. "I have the permission of our Almighty God-King himself to conduct this endeavour."

Mila blanched. *This* was his plan? She could not believe the bald-faced lie, and the ease with which it came from his mouth.

"Without consulting his Church? I think not." The young priest tutted, unconvinced. "Christopher Culis, you are a shrewd businessman, and you are famous for being many things. But, unfortunately for you, being a deeply religious man is not one of them, and to put it simply," he said with a raise of a thin eyebrow, "I do not believe you."

A thrill of excitement ran through the crowd. They had been entertained before, but that was nothing compared to the prospect of witnessing the forcible arrest of the darling of the Artor Trading Company.

"Surrender the demon to me now, without a fight," the priest snarled, "and I shall ask our God-King to be merciful with your punishment."

"You're the one who will make a fine pile of sand when the God-King loses patience with you for wasting his time with a matter he has already approved!" Culis bit back casually, refusing to be drawn into the increasing hostility of the situation.

It was an effective strategy. Mila saw the priest's confidence falter just a little. Regardless of which way this ended, Mila learned something important about Culis in that moment. The man could lie seamlessly under pressure, as easily as water heading downhill. That was a lesson she knew she could never let herself forget, not if she wanted to live.

And just when Mila thought the situation couldn't get any more convoluted, a sharp trumpet blast sounded at the entrance of Central, changing the atmosphere again.

Mila watched as, like a wave, the raucous crowd of observers became suddenly subdued. The tiered stands groaned as the collective weight of the audience suddenly dropped to their knees and bowed their heads. It happened so quickly, it felt more like instinct than obedience.

"Well, well." Another voice cut through the silence with a feminine pitch and scolding tone, as if concerned that the abrupt response of the enormous crowd hadn't been instantaneous enough for her liking.

Princess Jezebel was here.

They were doomed.

Jezebel the Unpredictable

Jezebel, wearing almost nothing, save a thick golden rope that covered just enough, stood at the entrance, surveying the scene before her.

For the first time all afternoon, Mila saw Culis's shoulders sag slightly, and that movement spoke volumes. Not only had he taken an inch on this venture and run a marathon with it, his demonstration had also revealed to Jezebel exactly why he'd wanted to obtain Mila from her. And it had nothing at all to do with the push-pull dynamic of their relationship, or deepening their bond, or whatever other bullshit he'd fed her.

Rather, it had everything to do with greed and furthering his own interests, and now Jezebel knew it too.

"Princess!" the priest called out, relieved to see her. "What an honour to have the God-King's daughter with us. Who else better placed to rectify this confusion. Does the heir to the Artor Trading Company speak the truth, or does he speak blasphemous lies?"

Jezebel turned her head and studied Culis and Mila silently for a moment before responding. Her face was not light and co-conspiratorial. It was clouded and sharp.

Mila's chest was so constricted with stress that her breath came in short gasps.

This was it. It was all about to fall apart.

Jezebel opened her mouth. "He speaks the truth," she said.

Mila's jaw dropped in shock.

"My father made it clear multiple times," the princess continued in a tone that now became somewhat scolding, "that there is *no* hierarchy to the Heretical Behaviours. This seems to be a fact that the Church continuously likes to conveniently forget!"

There was an excited muttering amongst the crowd. Mila wondered if there were dissidents among them and if they would seize this moment to further their cause. They would be foolish not to, for here was the princess, confirming their message; the Church could not be trusted to interpret the word of the God-King.

Mila remembered Jezebel's glee when Abbott had been corrected and silenced by Midas all those weeks ago. This priest's challenge today made it evident that the High Priest had ignored that correction and had not passed that message on to his priests, and this seemed to have made Jezebel furious. More furious even than recognising Culis's lie for what it was – at least for the moment.

"I shall remind you all now," she roared, "for the last time. One who commits *any* of the Eight is a suitable candidate for sacrifice. All heretic behaviour is condemned. All heretics will be sacrificed in time, and all those who are obedient and obey may be saved. This is the word of my father."

"Praise be," intoned the entire stadium obediently.

"Even in *ten years'* time," Culis interjected smoothly, seizing the moment. "A demon contracted to serve a human is not exempt from sacrifice. Their servitude merely...delays it, until the human master determines an appropriate time."

The delivery of this final pitch was the only misstep in an otherwise perfect performance. It sounded too much like a technicality, like desperate scrabbling. Even without full use of her power, Mila felt the energy of the crowd shift towards caution and hesitancy.

For a moment, she thought the cause lost. Even if they left here now without resistance from the priests, no one in the audience would have been convinced that a demon trade was a legitimate business enterprise. No one would invest enormous sums of money into it. The risk of reputation, loss of wealth, and perhaps even their lives, was too high.

And then, against all expectations, Jezebel spoke again. "Indeed."

And with that simple confirmation, she saved everything.

Suddenly, Culis had the royal house's public endorsement that this was a perfectly legitimate trade, and Culis had every right to sell a demon contract that expired after ten years.

From beside him, Mila felt Culis breathe again as the audience broke out into frenzied discussion. The priest signalled to his jesu to relax their ready stance before nodding respectfully to the princess and backing away. Culis used their departure to orchestrate his own, bowing a deep and sweeping bow of respect to the princess and shepherding Mila off the arena in the opposite direction, back to where their carriage waited.

"Best we depart immediately," he told her in a hushed voice, and for once, she was in complete agreement. The situation behind them had been a success, but still felt volatile somehow.

"Why was Jezebel here? And why did she support you?" she asked as they pushed their way from Central. "I thought it was all over when she appeared."

"I invited her," he admitted as he closed the door behind them and tapped the signal to the carriage driver. "I provided her with the opportunity she's always dreamed of, to publicly assert her authority over the Church. Although I'll admit, I didn't quite know if she was going to come, or if she was going to seize the moment when it appeared."

His audacity left Mila speechless.

Culis leaned back, savouring her expression. "I knew the accusation of blasphemy would be thrown around. Who better to challenge that than a princess who has been made to feel redundant by the Church? It was her opportunity to shout them down and claim her birthright. And she seized it. I'm proud of her."

"You're lucky," Mila scoffed. "I'd wager she was a heartbeat away from being done with the both of us. You'll have some mending to do if you still plan on being in her good graces."

"I know," he said gravely. "But, for now, let us take the win where it was offered. Don't worry. She'll come back around to me again in time. She always does."

"It's quite wrong the way you toy with her," Mila said, surprising both of them with her empathy for the princess.

"Don't delude yourself, little demon." Culis leaned forward, his eyes narrowing. "You know better than anyone that Jezebel loves to be toyed with."

Mila bit her tongue and sat back, wishing she'd said nothing. She did not want to be too outspoken or disagreeable, lest Culis tire of her quickly, and Jezebel certainly wasn't worth sticking her neck out for.

She sat in silence as they left Traders Bay behind them.

It wasn't until their journey back to Culis's manor was well and truly underway that he finally released a deep breath, cracked his knuckles, and engaged with her again.

"Well, I think, on the whole, that was a resounding success."

"A success!?" she spluttered. "Which part do you mean? The controversy? Outrage? Or the open threat of violence?"

Culis's smile broadened at her words. "All of it. Word of what occurred in Central today will be spread to every tavern in the country within a week. It was perfect."

The Worship Day Incident

Mila braced for the aftermath of the demonstration at Central. She expected to be poked and prodded over the course of the next few days, both by genuine customers and those who were simply morbidly curious. Culis, to his credit, surprised her by protecting her from all of that. Whilst there was certainly a distinct increase in the flurry of envoys and visitors who arrived at the manor, Mila found herself, gratefully, left alone.

It was a peaceful week. The servants of the manor still stared at her when they thought she wasn't looking, and swiftly avoided her gaze if she caught them at it, but the cook was kind enough and fed her as much as he did every other member of the household, so she never went hungry. She was given very few and infrequent chores and no one seemed to know if or how she was to be tasked, as Culis hadn't given any direction on the matter. As a result, Mila was largely left alone. She relished the freedom, particularly after spending so long under Jezebel's thumb. She knew her body and mind needed it, and she luxuriated in the long periods of calm and silence she was able to claim for herself, noticing with quiet pleasure that, with proper nutrition, her hair was starting to grow in thick again, and her nails were slowly becoming less brittle and breakable.

She tried to focus her efforts and mental energy on establishing a daily routine that consisted of all the small pleasures she'd once enjoyed in the Highlands. She found herself taking an early breakfast daily to avoid most of the servants, followed by a walk around the bounds of the large, forested property in the new air of the still morning.

She would walk as far from the manor as she comfortably could under the yoke of the vasium necklace, which was, unfortunately, quite effective in restricting her movements any further than about a mile from the main building where Culis slept. She'd tried to test the metal's potency by pushing through that initial sense of discomfort but hadn't managed more than a few steps before the weight became abruptly and utterly debilitating, driving her to her knees.

So, most days, she didn't push. She had nowhere to escape to anyway. She reminded herself that, even if she returned to the Highlands, she might find some peace initially, but all it would take was a single interaction with the wrong person, and the gossip would start.

In that small community, gossip could be as devastating and quick as a wildfire. Unless she intended to live a life of complete isolation, eventually word would spread about her return, and it'd only be a matter of time before the Church came for her again.

The Church.

She had plenty of time to ponder the mystery of Abbott's persecution of the ikarei. Was Jahan right when he'd said it all had to do with politics? Keeping relative peace in the nation by identifying a common enemy? It made sense in a sick way, and Mila was grateful then for these dissidents that existed in Traders Bay and supposedly wanted to challenge Abbott. Maybe one day they'd gain enough power and things would be different for ikarei. Maybe Culis wasn't just peddling snake oil to her and this venture of theirs could actually help challenge Abbott's doctrinal interpretations.

A pity Culis wasn't more trustworthy.

Her relationship with him fluctuated over the following days, and Mila could never quite tell where they stood with one another.

On some occasions, he asked her to join him in his office and use her power to help him. In these instances, she would observe his business negotiations and, afterwards, provide insights into whether the other trader had seemed amenable to his offer, or whether he could have pushed the bargain harder? In private, Culis treated her as a valued adviser, and Mila was happy to use her powers to assist him in this way. Sometimes she even found herself looking forward to those days.

Other times, especially when they were in public or certain members of the household were around, Culis treated her the same way he treated his most expensive horse – with a greeting, the occasional treat and a stern correction if she put a foot wrong. She didn't like it, or him, but all things considered, it was worlds better than the situation she'd endured under Jezebel, so she kept her mouth shut and her head down.

Worship Day sermons were unfortunately still part of the weekly routine however Mila was relieved to discover that, unlike the rest of the household, Culis had decreed that she was not required to attend.

"It would be wilful stupidity for me to pretend that you're devoutly worshipping the God-King once a week," he'd said. "Far better use to have you here, helping to maintain the manor in the absence of everyone else."

And it was true. The manor was largely empty on Worship Days, and Mila did end up with more chores in everyone's absence. Mostly ensuring the animals were fed and watered. She didn't mind in the slightest.

It was unusual for an entire wealthy household to make such a journey into the city once a week. She knew from her time with Jezabel that most of the nobility built private chapels on their own grounds to demonstrate their piety – if not their wealth. Culis had loudly declared that concept to be a waste of space and money, especially when they lived within a few short hours by carriage ride of the Grand Cathedral. So, instead, he allowed his staff to make a day of the trip and take the afternoons after the sermons for themselves to see their families. As a result, Worship Day was looked forward to with fervour by the staff, and the night before always carried a decidedly jolly air. Except for Culis, who always looked somewhat dour, and by that alone, Mila surmised that Worship Day must be the day he was obligated to spend with Jezebel.

It was on a Worship Day that the incident happened.

Culis was away as usual, evidently leaving the vasium sister-rock behind, hidden somewhere in the manor. Initially, Mila had considered trying to find it, but ultimately decided against it. Earning Culis's trust would pay off in the long term, and she had no doubt he was the kind of man who would certainly know if someone had been rifling through his study – even if she was meticulous about placing things back where she found them.

On this Worship Day, she rose in the morning as usual, and commenced her walk around the boundary of the property, watching the household procession head towards Jeralusah. Festive energy hovered around the group like a fog, and today, for some reason, she found herself particularly lonely and envious of the easy chatter and evident camaraderie among the manor staff. They seemed happy with their lives and enjoyed their service in Culis's employ. Perhaps she would one day be accepted among them?

For a moment, she found herself missing Jahan, the one person in Jezebel's household she'd shared any kind of bond with. Then she shook her head to clear the unhelpful thought. It would only lead to disappointment if she expected another open-minded soul like Jahan to exist in every household.

It was late morning when she finished her chores with the animals, and she was changing into fresh attire when the door of her tiny room unceremoniously burst open.

She jumped in shock at the unexpected intrusion and then instinctively tried to cover her naked torso in horror.

"Christopher!" the older man at her door exclaimed loudly, yelling over his shoulder as his eyes surveyed her. He looked utterly delighted that he'd caught her in this state of undress. "You didn't say anything about her being a succubus!" Then, with raised eyebrows and a predatory smirk, he added, "No wonder he's all but tethered you to the house."

Mila had been clutching at herself to hide from him, but at his words, and as the shock of his intrusion lifted, she made the decision to drop her arms and stand forthrightly naked before this man. She refused to be embarrassed by him and his crude entry, whoever he was. This was her room. He was in *her* space.

It didn't take Mila long – or any great skills of observation – to deduce his identity. Culis Senior looked very much like his son.

Long curls, blond – albeit slightly silvering – hung down to his cheekbones and were swept back lazily, giving him a casual, roguish sort of appearance. He and Christopher shared the same bright green eyes, but the father's jawline was slightly softer, with a more pointed chin. He stood tall, with broad shoulders. Looking at him was like being gifted a glimpse of the future and finding out how Christopher Culis would age in thirty-odd years. By all accounts, he would age like a fine wine.

Culis Senior was also dressed very well, but with a practicality that implied he was still a man of action, rather than one who had hung up his boots in later years for an easier life. He wore dark pants, knee-length brown leather boots, and a long-sleeved, white, flowing shirt tucked in neatly both front and back. Simple enough, but there was no disguising the rich, red dye of his cloak, that would have cost most farmers a few years' worth of wages. The fact he still wore it, despite being indoors, indicated that he had no qualms about anyone knowing he was obscenely rich.

She tried to reach out and sense him, to gauge why he was here and what he might want from her, but, like his son, his energy was frustratingly muffled – it must be a family trait.

The man's eyes caught the slight movement of her horns rising gently from beneath her hair, and his lips pursed with barely restrained glee.

"God, you're magnificent," he breathed.

Despite herself, Mila felt the intensity of his gaze force a slight blush to creep up onto her neck. She saw his eyes note that, too, with pleasure, and then her attention abruptly snapped to his son, whose shadow had finally caught up to that of his father and stood in the doorway beside him.

"You're completely right, Christopher. This is an untapped market. I can't believe I didn't think of it myself sooner. It's genius. The sooner we can put our prejudices aside, the sooner a lot of money is to be made here. Especially if they're all as easy on the eye as this one." He half turned back to Mila and gave her a small wink.

"Why have you come, Frank?" Culis asked softly. His shoulders were taut and his back straight. He didn't look at Mila, didn't acknowledge her defiantly naked torso.

"To congratulate you, of course, my son!" He slapped Culis on the back. The movement caused his cloak to slide back slightly, revealing a long, coiled whip holstered to his leather belt.

What an odd thing to carry, Mila registered but continued to say nothing.

"For your brilliant idea, and for the fact that you have the princess's support. It really is quite good that you offed Martin before his proposed fleece trade commenced. That could have really tied up our resources, but now we're fully able to bring the company around and support this endeavour."

Mila shot Culis a horrified look. He'd killed his brother?

Culis stiffened at these words, but his father ploughed on, either not seeing, or not caring, about his son's reaction.

"A monopoly on the demon trade? Ha! Although, you know the Guild of Merchants will come after you hard. They'll try to tax the shit out of the company fleet for this."

"You know I did nothing of the sort to Martin," was all Culis said, holding himself otherwise tightly in check.

"Have you bedded her yet?" the man changed tack abruptly.

Mila narrowed her eyes at him and placed her hands on her hips. "Excu – "

The backhanded slap came before she could finish the sentence, with a ferocity that knocked her to the floor.

"You'd best make sure they're trained better than that before you farm them out to nobility," the brute remarked coolly, surveying her. "Nobody wants a mouthy slave, demon powers or not."

"Father." Culis said the word from between gritted teeth. "Outside."

"Alright, alright. I've overstepped." His tone returned to congeniality. "But bed her sooner rather than later. You'll get all this tension out of the way, she'll know her place, and you'll be a better businessman for it. Trust me."

"Out," Culis snapped. He pushed his father out the door, closing it firmly behind them.

Slowly, Mila lifted her hand to her sore face, staring incredulously at the space just vacated by the men. She felt her anger rise.

That man – that vile creature – had raised Christopher Culis.

It explained...a lot.

Frightened and cowed, Mila stayed in her room the rest of the day. With no other servants in the manor, she imagined she'd attract the attention of Frank Culis wherever she went, and she had absolutely no desire for that to occur.

When the servants all returned that evening, Mila was surprised by a timid knock on her door. It was a red-headed woman named Tess, who Mila knew as one of the cook's helpers.

"Are...are you alright?" Tess asked nervously.

"I..." Mila hesitated before giving her answer. Was she alright? She'd been struck, and humiliated, and threatened. "I'm fine. Thank you," she said blandly.

"Mind if I pass that on to Master Culis?" she whispered. "He is quite concerned about you."

"Tell him whatever you need to," she said shortly before closing the door in the woman's face.

She didn't mean to be rude, but she was also not inclined to waste energy on trying to make Culis feel better about the actions of his father.

* * *

The following morning, Mila rose early to walk, but as she was leaving out the back door, she suddenly hesitated.

What if Frank was still here? She had no idea how long he would stay at the house, but she would do everything in her power to avoid another interaction with the man, especially being caught alone with him in the forest. So, she skipped her walk that morning and limited her movements to just the kitchens and the kitchen gardens for the day.

The cook quickly surmised the reason for her lingering presence but made no comment about it, and never implied that she was underfoot or being a nuisance. In fact, he briskly tasked her as though she were a kitchen hand, and Mila, gratefully, put herself to use.

Frank must have still been present in the manor, because she could sense an undercurrent of anxiety running through all the servants, which wasn't normally present. The unexpected sense of solidarity filled her with warmth. Despite the fact that the manor staff were still unsure about her, at least with Frank Culis in the house, she was now far from the worst thing wandering their hallways.

It was late into the evening when another knock came on her door. Despite the fact she'd been half expecting him, she was still startled to see Christopher Culis standing in the dark, empty kitchen. He looked exhausted, and his face was tight with tension.

"Good evening," he said softly. "He's finally gone."

"I see," she replied coolly.

"I knew he was coming," he said, wincing in discomfort. "I could have warned you what he was like."

"You could have," she agreed, then added, "I'm not sure I would have believed you."

"No," Culis agreed solemnly. "Perhaps that's why I didn't mention it in the first place. Sometimes the anticipation of such a visit only makes it worse." He spoke as though he were repeating a lesson he had long ago learned.

Despite herself and everything she knew about him, she felt pity for the tired man before her. He'd obviously endured far worse from his father, and for far longer, both as a child and an adult.

"How did he even know I was here?"

"Frank Culis is the head of the Artor Trading Company. I had to tell him about this demon venture. And, of course, he heard about what happened at Central. That's why he came."

"No, I mean this room. How did he know where exactly to find me?"

Culis sighed. "He has spies in my household, who report such details back to him."

"He spies on *you*? Your own father?"

Culis didn't reply, but simply ran his hands through his hair. It had evidently been a long few days for him.

"Do...do you want me to help find out who they are?" Mila offered.

At that, he looked up sharply, his eyes gleaming. "I knew your powers were good for something besides telling me what an arse I am."

Mila couldn't help but chuckle at that. "Well, I'll do my best. Most of the staff don't talk to me yet, but if I can get them talking, it shouldn't be too hard to figure out who isn't loyal."

"They'll come around. Give them a few weeks."

"It'd help if you didn't treat me like property in front of them," Mila accused softly.

Culis nodded wearily in acknowledgement. "That mustn't be pleasant, but it's necessary for the benefit of the spies," he explained. "I'm sure Featherstone has some of his own here too. As, too, probably does Jezebel. It wouldn't do for them to report back to her that I'm kind to you or treating you with anything other than disdain. I assumed you could read my energy and know that none of it was ever meant with sincerity."

Mila gulped, hoping she hadn't inadvertently exposed the gap in her power. Fortunately, Culis did not seem to notice.

"If you can sense the spies and help me to oust them, it would go a long way towards making this manor a far more comfortable place to live for both of us."

A house full of spies, Mila thought. *A dead brother he may or may not have murdered, a horrible father... What a life.*

As though he knew the direction of her thoughts, he met her eyes and shook his head firmly. "Don't do that," he said. "Don't pity me. Pitying one with power over you will only weaken you against them. Save your pity for those who can't hurt you."

"What an odd thing to say."

He shrugged. "It's true. And besides...I like your strength. The mental image of you facing down my father, bare-chested, without shame...it will give me years of enjoyment. Don't dilute that strength for anyone – especially not me."

With that odd compliment, and a wry smile, he bade her goodnight and left.

Mila went to her pallet, blew out her candle, and tried to sleep, but despite herself, the mental image that Culis had painted rose into her mind and it drew a wicked grin. She saw herself as Culis must have seen her – wild brown hair, defiant glare, naked torso facing down his father – and she liked it, liked the version of herself that she imagined he saw in his mind's eye. It made her feel as though she'd clawed back some power somehow.

Or perhaps she had never truly relinquished it – even though her time with Jezebel had made her feel as though it'd been stripped away.

She let the image linger in her mind, relishing it.

As she lay quietly in the darkness, she resolved that, from tomorrow, she would not forget her own strength again.

Hunting Demons

The demon hunt was always going to happen eventually.

The demonstration at Central and resulting meetings had delayed it for a few weeks, but Culis wouldn't wait forever. Regardless of whatever he thought about his father, there was no doubt that Frank's visit had reinvigorated Culis's barely restrained appetite to commence the venture. The very day after Frank left, Culis began to assemble his "hunting party".

Over the next few days, a number of strangers arrived at the manor, responding to summons that had been sent out by Culis's envoys. Within the week, Mila found herself setting out along the commercial road to the north with two travelling carts, eight horses, ten hand-picked Artor Trading Company members, and a very happy Christopher Culis.

They were heading to the Highlands.

Mila had been highly conflicted about starting their venture in her homeland, but her options had been limited. The ikarei kept their identities notoriously secret, even from one another, and ultimately, it was the only place where she knew for certain at least one demon lived. Her old mentor, Natalee.

In some ways, she was looking forward to seeing her, but mostly, Mila just felt fearful and conflicted about the decision she'd made to bring Culis and the hunting party directly to the doorstep of the woman she owed her life to.

She watched her fellow travellers warily as they trundled down the road, scrutinising each of them with her power, trying to determine whether they were good people or not.

One of them she recognised instantly as Baird, who, the minute they were out of the manor gates, pulled his horse up alongside the cart she sat in and swung himself inside, making himself comfortable amongst the rucksacks. He smiled at her with a familiarity she had not expected.

"Baird," he said, reintroducing himself with a thick hand extended in greeting.

"I recall," she replied, taking it in her own. Despite her discomfort with the situation, his steady and inoffensive energy put her immediately at ease, as did the way he spent the next few hours chatting to her about his background.

"I've been with the Artor Trading Company for nearly two decades but came under the arm of Master Culis here about ten years into that."

"How did that come about?"

Baird winced a little at the memory. "We stumbled across some islands unexpectedly."

"And?" Mila prompted when it became evident Baird wasn't about to freely offer more of the story.

"I'll just say this. Before we arrived, Artor had no name for them. After we left, they were forever referred to as 'The Cannibal Islands'."

Mila joined him in the wince. "I see."

"It was eventful," Culis contributed as he rode past them toward the front of the procession, his tall grey mare eager to lead.

Baird explained that he worked for Culis primarily as a mediator, negotiator and translator. He spoke over twenty languages and was readily accustomed to meeting people of all different backgrounds and customs. Mila could see why he'd be an effective mediator. He was both immediately likeable and naturally exuded a calming energy. She found herself sharing far more about her life with him during that journey than she'd ever intended to share with anyone from this household. The considered way he listened made her feel as though he was unlikely to report it all immediately back to Culis. Which, of course, was part of his charm. She knew he would.

The other recognisable member of the band was the self-ageing demon from the demonstration at Central, who had chosen to look distinctly middle-aged for this trip. After a few hours, he, too, came over to the cart and introduced himself, riding his roan mare alongside them.

"Arran Scarfone," he said with a slight nod. "An' I'm sorry for the uuhh...exposure. I 'ad to be revolting. It were the only thing I could think ter convince all o' Central that I weren't a plant."

"Well, it worked," Mila replied. "But I'm more surprised to find a demon already secretly working for Culis. How did you meet?"

"I weren't born in Artor," the broad-shouldered man replied with a thick accent that had not been present during the demonstration at Central. "T'was born in Keras. You've probably never 'eard of 'er. She's a cold 'n icy nation. Lies three seas south from Artor. Wouldn't recommend. Anyway...well, Midas's lot ain't spread to tha' part of the world yet, so those like us – " he gestured his hand between Mila and himself, " – y'know, with horns and powers, we're known as zoi.

Down there. An' there ain't many of us, so some brigh' spark a few hundred years ago decided tha' we were children of gods and should automatically reign in positions of nobility."

"Precisely what the Church warns us that demons want to achieve in Artor," Baird observed, but he said it without judgement...more like confirmation.

"Well, I reckon is all a load of crock," Arran objected. "I can change the appearance of my age at will. So what? Does tha' make me a wiser leader or a skilled commander? Nah. But plenty of the zoi reckon it does, and tha' 'as led to corruption and incompetence in every facet of society of Keras. I was a terrible general. I'm no leader, an' I'm certainly no fighter."

"No, you're a skulker, through and through," Baird interrupted again with a laugh. "If there's a shadow in a room, Scarfone will find it and lurk in it."

Arran tried to ignore him, but couldn't quite contain the wry, proud smile that spilled over at Baird's words. "When Culis's expedition arrived, 'e offered me a new job, doin' a different type of work for 'im. I accepted."

"Did you know you were coming to a country where you would be persecuted rather than worshipped?" Mila challenged, unable to quite believe it.

"Threat o' death is far more real in Artor, for sure. But I felt more persecuted in Keras, where I couldn' live the life I wanted. Persecution of a different kind, y'know? In this life, here, I can now do as I please."

"It would help me a lot if you could share that story with the ikarei we meet during this trip," Mila stated. "It would be compelling, I think, to see how satisfied you are working for a master you respect. It would help me convince them to relinquish their freedom."

Arran shook his head slowly at her words. "Nah. No can do. No one but these few souls in this group can know what I am. If word spreads, I'd lose every advantage I give Master Culis's work."

Mila was disappointed, but she understood. She was also fascinated that Arran Scarfone and the nation of Keras even existed. It had been just a few short weeks in Culis's house, and already her idea of the world had widened dramatically. She'd never known there were places one could go outside of Artor where it might be safe for ikarei. No one ever spoke of such lands, and the Church had certainly never encouraged it.

Her mind was opening...and a tiny whisper of hope had been planted inside her.

Before there had been no point trying to get this necklace off and escape. Where would she have gone? But now...now that she knew that she could flee to somewhere like Keras, away from Artor and the Church, there was actually a legitimate reason to try.

A tap on the side of the cart pulled Mila from her thoughts. She turned her head to find a muscular woman with a broad face and a thick blonde braid now riding alongside.

"Any chance the rest of us are going to get a chance to rest our horses, Bairdy? Or you just gonna hog the demon lady all day?"

Baird laughed and abandoned his place in the cart, riding off alongside Arran while the blonde woman made herself comfortable and began to accost Mila with a barrage of questions.

It was along this vein that the rest of the day unfolded. The hunting party took turns getting to know her, as though it were equally as important for them to understand their new travelling companion as it was for her.

The three women – Nemecca, Lyria and Philomena – were all very different to her, and quite different from one another. Nemecca was a tall blonde who moved with an unapologetic, forthright energy. Mila instantly liked her because her energy matched her presentation to the world almost exactly – a rare phenomenon in her experience.

Lyria, on the other hand, was short and dark-haired with the physique of a gymnast and emitted a very calm and controlled energy. Her questions to Mila had been about her family and upbringing more so than her adult life. When she left, Mila had the distinct feeling she'd just been interrogated and figured that Lyria and Arran probably worked closely with one another. She was also now certain that, for all his complaints about spies in his household, Culis definitely had his *own* spy network.

Philomena was the wife of Baird and had grown up in the Highlands before her devout father had moved them to Jeralusah to be closer to the God-King. She was the most religious of the three women, and while she managed to be friendly and make polite conversation, her visit to Mila's cart was decidedly shorter than the others' had been.

The remaining men – Bruce, Odin, Corbyn, Black Berran and Dabriel – each had their turn too. In their own ways they were all kind to her, although varied in their degrees of comfort and self-consciousness.

Mila noted with interest that, despite their differences, there were two common energies that existed between each member of the band. The first was a distinct sense of openness. It was obviously an asset as a professional adventurer to be curious and open about one's surroundings and, in this, Culis had recruited these people well. The other commonality she sensed was a hardness, a near-to-surface capacity for ruthlessness. The Artor Trading Company was an infamous brand, and it was not because they were all friendly faces and unending kindness. Mila knew that every person in this group was a lurking threat, deadly if required to be, and yet, despite identifying this, she found herself feeling far more at ease amongst them than she had amongst the rest of the manor staff. The entire hunting party bickered together with the good-natured ease of a group who worked together often and trusted one another implicitly. No spies in this group, she realised. That was the difference for Culis. None but his own.

Culis himself was the only one who spoke very little to her that day. He watched on with approval as his little band of demon hunters each took their turn sizing up Mila. He bantered with her occasionally from afar, but did not come and sit with her in the cart.

She didn't dwell on why and focused instead on how different her circumstances were now, compared to the last time she had been on this road. Just four months ago, she'd been chained in a windowless jail, being transported from her home to Jeralusah for sacrifice. Now, she sat freely in billowing traveller's robes, and from the bouncing cart, she was able to take in her surroundings. She noted with pleasure the way the grass in the fields changed shade and the flat land became hillier as they approached her homeland. By nightfall on the second day, it was apparent that they had truly entered the north. The last Jeralusan-style farmstead hadn't been seen since early that morning, and since then, they'd passed nothing that looked remotely occupied. The most notable change to their scenery, however, was the mountainous plateau of the Highlands. It had started off as a shadow in the distance, but as they drew closer, it loomed steeply above them, like an enormous fortification.

It was an enchanting and alien sight for most. The hot misty haze of the rainforest spilled from the top and over the edge of the rocky cliff face. It dribbled down towards the plains below like an eerie waterfall that never quite touched the bottom. As night fell, the cries of monkeys and other creatures could be heard echoing down unnervingly into their campsite.

The uncomfortable sensation of being watched by a million pairs of eyes from above was palpable.

Outwardly, the hunting party appeared to be unaffected by this, but Mila could sense their unease, and each of them, in their own way, solidified themselves against the new environment. To her surprise, they seemed particularly protective of her, although she was ostensibly the last member of the group who would be fearful of the Highland wilderness that lay ahead.

When they sat around the campfire on that second night, Black Berran ensured that Mila received the first cut of meat from the deer that Philomena had hunted, and when Nemecca pulled out her guitar to sing, she taught Mila the words to the chorus so that she could join in with the group.

She wasn't sure if the small kindnesses came from a recognition that she would be their guide through the imposing landscape ahead in the next few days, or perhaps a belief that she might truly be frightened by the sight of it. Either way, it lifted her spirits, and that night, when she readied her bedroll, she realised just how accustomed she'd become to loneliness in her life. These people weren't doing more for her than the bare minimum of kindness and decency, but it still made her feel lighter and happier than she'd felt in years.

The added joy came from the fact that they knew she was a demon and were still prepared to embrace her anyway. With every kindness and gesture of acceptance from the hunting party, the invisible yoke of fear of exposure that she'd carried since age fourteen had slowly begun to lift. She hadn't even noticed the departure of that weight until this moment.

She lay still in the wet, dewy grass and gazed up at the clear stars, enjoying them in a way she'd never been able to in the Highlands, due to the ever-present cover of the canopy.

It was peaceful. She *felt* at peace.

It was a new feeling for her, so she explored it a little, realising that something in what she was experiencing now might be the key to convincing other ikarei to submit to servitude.

What an interesting thought.

She dissected it further.

By being exposed like this, by openly serving Culis as his demon, there was no need to hide who she was anymore. She could be herself.

The Church already knew where she was and what she was. Everyone in Jeralusah knew. There was nothing left to hide. In Culis's employ, everyone she ever came across would know who and what she was, and they could accept or reject her according to their beliefs. She would never have to be anything other than herself ever again.

It was a life-changing realisation.

As she lay there in the grass, silent tears brimming in her eyes, for the first time since she'd agreed to help Culis, she felt truly as though she'd made the right decision.

The Highlands

On the hot midmorning of the third day, they reached the foot of the mountains. There was no gradual rise in gradient. The entry into the rainforest wilderlands was only accessible through a steep, narrow set of stairs that rose almost vertically up the high plateau to the whole different world that awaited them. The hunting party were required to leave their horses behind, guarded by Philomena and Bruce, as the rest of them began their ascent on foot.

The vertical climb lasted a full day, and it was nightfall when they finally reached the top. As they set up camp, Mila informed them the journey would be comparatively flat from then on and this drew an audible, collective sigh of relief from the group.

But their relief was short lived as the next few days were equally arduous, for different reasons. The humidity had been growing incrementally every day since they left Jeralusah, but now in the thick heat of the rainforest, they were also dealt wet, foggy mornings and thunderstorms that fell with clock-like precision every afternoon. Nothing they carried was ever truly dry again. Not their skin, shoes, clothes or bedding. Waterlogged food, such as their traveller's bread, was swiftly discarded, and their nights were now haunted by the unending wails of mosquitos and the accompanying slapping of hands on skin.

Despite all this, the Artor Trading Company uniform bore up well under the assaulting environment. It was a fit-for-purpose outfit that was also quite flattering, and for Mila, seeing the group of them all similarly dressed, pushing through the brutal undergrowth, was a striking sight. Their long-sleeved shirts were made of a thin, creamy fabric with a collar that could be buttoned high to protect the neck or left open to allow airflow onto the chest. Each person wore their shirt tucked neatly into light brown shorts that were looped with a leather utility belt. This belt allowed easy access to small essentials, such as knives, water flasks and rope. They each also wore protective leathers on their forearms and sturdy brown leather boots that rose to midcalf but came equipped with an interesting flap that allowed the ankle piece of the boot to be pulled and stretched all the way up to cover the knee if required. This had been a last-minute addition from the Culis Manor seamstress after Mila had advised them that, once they reached the mountain paths, they'd want the additional protection from leeches. The attire was all held together with a sophisticated yet sturdy buckle that had the Artor Trading Company crest etched upon it. This sat proudly on the front of the belt.

After just two days in the Highlands, despite the protection of their attire, Mila was the only member of the party not overcome with misery. In fact, she felt quite the opposite. Not only had she learned about Keras, a country where, if she could find it, she could finally live free from the Church. But also, she'd made friends with this group of humans and had found a sense of freedom *here,* in this world. Something that she never thought she'd feel.

The combination of these two revelations, coupled with drinking in the sweet, wet air of her homeland, filled her with so much energy and happiness that she often found herself quite literally bounding ahead with glee.

She spent the next few days running ahead through the undergrowth and then doubling back to encourage and tease the hunting party through a particularly difficult passage. She felt her strength and vitality coming back in waves and marvelled at the returning strength of her body. Sometimes, when the morale of the group seemed particularly low, she'd create ridiculous songs and use the rhythmic slapping of their hands against the barrage of bugs as her percussive accompaniment, trying to make them laugh. She felt overcome by mania. The happiness and overwhelming relief was all-consuming, and she willingly let herself soak in it, as if those feelings were a drug and she a long-denied addict.

Culis lost his patience with her unrelenting vibrancy on the fifth day after he accidentally dropped his last pair of dry socks in a leech-filled puddle of mud.

"Are you actually from hell, little demon?" he demanded. "Is this what hell is? Is that why you're so happy in this cesspit?"

She felt so untouchable that she just laughed at his words, truly finding them amusing.

"You've given me this," she replied with a broad smile, enjoying his look of confusion. It brought her even more glee, and feeling slightly hysterical, she leaned forward, seized his hand, and twirled herself beneath it, finishing with a flourishing curtsy.

Baird, who was nearby, packing his own rucksack, snorted with laughter at the exchange, but doubled over when he saw Culis's astonished face.

"What on earth do you mean?" Culis spluttered.

Mila noted with pleasure that he was flushing pink, and she considered it a profound victory to have unsettled him. Culis prided himself on never being caught socially unprepared.

"No more hiding!" she trilled, her arms thrown wide. "Thanks to you, everyone in the nation now knows I'm a demon. No more pretending for me, no more fear of exposure. I've carried a death sentence upon my shoulders for my whole life, and this week, it feels like it's been dissolved. You've no idea the weightlessness I feel."

With that, she spun off around the trees, feeling utterly childlike. When she came back, Culis had a broad grin on his face.

"What?" she asked.

"It's rare for him to see someone so happy in his presence," Baird chortled, pushing past them.

"It's rare," Culis corrected, "to see *you* so happy. I'm not sure I've ever seen you smile before." He paused for a moment, surveying her face intently before speaking again. "It's lovely. I hope it lasts."

The tenderness in the sentiment was unexpected, and Mila studied him back in return, wondering if he was being genuine. It appeared he was. A spark of warmth for the man rose inside her, and she turned away, unwilling to let him see it. Perhaps he wasn't entirely as self-centred as she'd presumed.

Unfortunately, as they drew closer to their destination, the joy began to wear off. If someone had asked under what circumstances she ever expected to be back in the Highlands, returning on a demon hunt would never have occurred to her. It wouldn't even have made the list of possibilities. And yet here she was, leading Culis and the Artor Trading Company militia through the thin, winding routes that led deeper and deeper into the rainforest. What would Natalee think of her? Would she even find any other demons?

She cursed Culis as her sombre mood slowly returned, and as they drew closer and closer to Natalee's village, Mila suddenly found herself sleepless with worry and doubt once again.

Brewich

While not well known throughout most of Artor, amongst Highlanders, the mountain town of Brewich was famous and considered one of the most beautiful and eclectic villages in the region. When Mila finally pushed through the last of the thick fronds and tangled vines to glimpse it, she took a great deal of satisfaction from hearing the amazed gasps of the group behind her, and even one from Culis as he surveyed what lay before them.

Rather than fighting against nature and the laws of the rainforest, the inhabitants of Brewich had used the natural design of the forest floor to dictate the layout of their town centre. Shop fronts were built in and around tall bayan tree roots. There were no streets wide enough for a horse and cart to pass through, and so the movement of bulk goods was either via pedalled tuk-tuks or delivered via an extensively complex network of wires that were bolted between the large trees, colour-coded to specify the destination of any parcel that was strapped onto one.

People walked everywhere, often alongside exceptionally tame forest animals, and it was commonplace to see large, multicoloured parrots flying from window to window, delivering mail. It was a lively, bustling and complicated sight to the uninitiated, and even Mila, after months spent in the sober and orderly Jeralusah, felt a little overwhelmed to be around so much movement again.

The hunting party stood out from the native Brewich folk, but to their credit, as seasoned adventurers, they did not disrupt the flow of human movement in the village. They were accustomed to the unexpected, and if they couldn't blend in, they at least knew how to portray themselves as inoffensive.

Mila led Culis down the main street and revelled in the feeling of being back in her element. She loved Brewich. The village was only a few miles south of Bori, and she'd spent so much time here that it was like a second home to her. Over the past few months, she'd been convinced many times that she'd never see any of the Highlands again. To now be back in Brewich, of all places, felt surreal. She felt a pang in her heart when she caught herself scanning the crowds for Cari.

She won't be here, Mila told herself. *Even if she was here, I shouldn't want to see her.*

She forced herself to push thoughts of the woman aside and instead led the group to a prominent taproom named Bronnies. There, she beckoned Culis to join her on a bench near the green stained-glass windows, which looked out onto the bustling street.

"You should let the others go explore, if they wish," she told him. "Our demon won't be around for a while yet. She comes out at dusk. We have a few hours."

Culis nodded and passed the hunting party a few quiet words before joining her at the bench. "This place is...like a lunatic's dream," he said in wonder. "It's been a while since I've seen infrastructure that is so innovative, so creative. They've genuinely tried to bring the rainforest into the design of every street and building." He gestured to a waitress to bring them two ales.

"No, no. We don't want ale," Mila interjected. "Not in a place like this." She waved the woman over to amend their order, requesting bungle juice.

"Well, well, look at you," Culis said with a grin. "Not ten minutes we've been back in your part of the world, and you're already calling the shots. What's bungle juice?"

"A local speciality. A drink made with fermented ginger and kamp-seed oil," Mila explained. "It's what you want to be drinking in these climates. And it doesn't export well, so you can't get it anywhere else but Brewich and the very near villages."

Culis's eyes brightened at the idea of this potential logistical challenge.

"How about you just focus on one procurement at a time?" Mila teased, but Culis determinedly ignored her.

"That's not the attitude that strikes fear into a rival's heart!" he bantered. "You never know who's cock Lady Luck will choose to kiss next!"

Mila snorted with laughter at the expression.

Culis continued to delightedly rant. "One must embrace every opportunity that presents itself, when it presents itself. There is no such thing as being inconvenienced by an opportunity!"

Their drinks arrived and, despite her uncertain regard for the man himself, Mila took great delight in watching Culis's first sip and his ensuing impressed expression.

"This is...delightful!"

"Isn't it?"

To her surprise, Culis seemed perfectly eager to spend a good part of the next hour discussing the complex notes and flavours of the beverage with her, and despite her apprehension for the task she was about to commence, Mila found herself enjoying the afternoon and not resenting his company. It was the first time the two of them were really able to talk in a way that had no undercurrent of tension.

When relaxed, Culis remained witty, but his demeanour seemed less combative. He was keen to learn about anything, and his eyes brightened in genuine interest as she spoke about her home and the Highlands. He was naturally charismatic and knew how to hold a good conversation, asking questions and contributing his own stories where they fit, but he never tried to dominate the conversation. He was happy to let her be the more interesting one and learn from what she had to say.

Mila found herself staring often at his lovely green eyes and the ever-present lock of blond hair that curled untidily on his forehead, and the glinting gold earring, wondering where this entirely pleasant version of him had sprung from and how much of it was real.

Finally, however, the topic of their conversation turned to the matter at hand – the demon they had come here for.

"She lives on the outskirts," Mila said. "And enters the village once dusk falls."

"And her power?"

"In low light, she can make herself look like anyone. A glance in her direction in a crowded place like this, and you would swear black and blue that you'd seen anyone she wished you to think, even the High Priest Abbott. Think how scandalous it would be if he was seen doing something of disrepute, such as escorting a barmaid upstairs to one of the private rooms."

"Interesting," Culis said softly. "I imagine that would be incredibly valuable to some of my more...nefarious customers. You could blackmail someone for something they hadn't even done."

"Exactly, or a spouse wanting a divorce could frame their partner, or she could be used to infiltrate guild meetings as a trusted spy..."

"But only at night?" he clarified.

"Only in low light," she corrected. "A brightly lit room would expose her, even if it were the witching hour."

"Interesting. So, she's quite useful, but only in circumstances we can control."

As dusk began to fall and their moment approached, Mila implored Culis to remain in his seat while she moved to the back of the taproom. She found a back door used by the kitchen staff and went out to wait in the alleyway beside the pile of kitchen garbage.

"You'd just scare her off," she'd told him. "I need to talk to her alone first. She's a flighty individual by nature, but she knows me, and she'll be less likely to flee if she thinks I'm alone. Don't approach us. If she agrees to the deal, I'll bring her to you."

Culis had nodded at this, and Mila left him, waiting for Natalee to show.

Although she vaguely knew what to look for, without her powers, she probably wouldn't have suspected the shambling old man who appeared to dig for scraps after the last beam of sunlight disappeared behind the dark canopy. Natalee might be able to change her appearance, but she couldn't change her energy, and Mila sensed the ikarei from the body beneath the brown cloak, which indicated some visual trickery was afoot.

"Natalee," she said softly.

The 'old man' froze. He appraised Mila slowly, and after registering her, decided to stay. He did, however, remain wary, and his voice was coated in suspicion when he replied.

"Mila. I heard you were taken by the Church."

"I was," she replied.

"How are you not dead?"

"I struck a bargain."

Natalee's eyes narrowed deeply. "A bargain with the God-King? I doubt it."

"Not with him specifically," Mila admitted. "It's a complicated story, and one I will readily share with you over a drink if you have the time tonight?"

"What do you want?" There were no pleasantries to be exchanged here. Demons did not expose one another like this; it went against a code that Natalee herself had taught Mila. The woman knew something was afoot.

"To talk," Mila admitted.

"Then talk. Here."

Mila sighed deeply and felt the tight spring of tension within her twist even tighter. This wasn't going to plan. And how did she even begin? Natalee's deep suspicion caused her to almost give up then and there, but the consequence of failure meant Culis returning her to the clutches of Jezebel. With that stony reality clenched around her heart, she knew she had to try.

"I have a proposition for you."

"Oh?"

"I work for someone who has devised a way to improve the lives of demons in Artor."

The old man's eyebrows raised again at this, but she said nothing, and Mila took that as permission to continue.

"The method is...controversial, and you're probably not going to like it. I'm not sure if I like it either, but I do believe that, in the long term, it will be effective. I only ask that you let me finish explaining before you dismiss me."

Natalee continued to say nothing, and so, with nothing else to work with, Mila explained, or tried her best to explain, the plan.

Telling Natalee's blank and unresponsive face that demons needed to sign contracts of servitude to humans was even harder than she'd anticipated it to be. She tried to skim lightly over those points and emphasise the outcomes that she was hoping for.

"If humans can be convinced that we're more valuable alive than dead, then in time, we can change the status quo around who gets picked for sacrifice and why."

"But to do so, we must subjugate ourselves and sign away our rights for ten years of our lives?" Natalee confirmed.

"Well...yes," Mila agreed, finishing with words that felt both weak and flat. She did not need her power to know that her attempt to sway Natalee had been ineffective.

"I'm sorry, Mila," Natalee replied. "I know you came to me about this because you suspected I could be tempted. You thought that I'd find something other than a life of skulking around and burrowing for scraps appealing in some way. But freedom is freedom, no matter how it is packaged. I appreciate that you've made this choice for yourself, and your idea is somewhat...aspirational. But the reality of servitude is not for me. I'd rather die free."

With that, she turned around and walked back down the alleyway from which she had come without even a farewell.

Mila sighed and held back tears. She'd tried. There was nothing more she could have done.

Suddenly, she heard an indignant cry in the dark at the end of the alleyway.

Natalee!

She raced towards the sound and gasped with horror at the sight around the corner. Nemecca and Odin held the old man firmly by his arms, as he thrashed uselessly against them.

"What are you doing!" Mila demanded of them in fury.

Culis appeared as though out of nowhere and stalked towards them, holding a torch up to the face of the captive. Incredibly, wherever the flame shone brightly, the true likeness of the demon woman was revealed. Natalee's true form was that of a middle-aged woman, strikingly beautiful, with raven hair and blue eyes. Eyes which now flashed furiously, first at Culis in defiance, and then at Mila in rage.

"This part of your operation then?" she spat. "Try the carrot first, and then the stick?"

"No!" Mila exclaimed and rounded on Culis. "What are you doing? I told you they must come willingly!"

"Oh, she will," Culis said without emotion.

In the darkness, Mila suddenly found herself unable to tell if it was Christopher Culis or his father who stood before her.

"Demon," he directed his words to Natalee, "you have two options. Sign a contract with me or submit to the Church's mercy."

"You *monster.*" Mila's rage surged, and she couldn't contain her tears.

She'd exposed the woman who had saved her life...for what? The naked hatred in Natalee's face, and the waves of venom pulsing directly at Mila, were too much to bear.

"I will *never* forgive you for this," Mila croaked at Culis, who didn't even seem to register her.

Instead, he procured a quill and contract as if from thin air and waved it before Natalee. "Make your choice. Submit to my plan or submit to the Church."

"I'd rather die!" Natalee spat at his feet.

Culis stared hard at her for a long moment and then nodded to the two who held her. "So be it. Put her in chains and gag her. We'll carry her out with us when we leave. That'll be a nice long time for her to really marinate in her decision."

"No!" Mila rushed at Nemecca in a last-ditch effort to help Natalee break free of the trap, but it was in vain. She was no fighter, and despite the camaraderie Nemecca had shared with Mila, the hardness Mila had seen in her earlier in the trip came through. She was still Culis's soldier through and through, and she swatted Mila's efforts away as if she were an insect.

Mila hit the ground hard, the breath knocked out of her.

As she lay there, watching the hunting party move back to their lodgings with Natalee in tow, she was seized by the urge to put as much distance between them and herself as possible. She turned the other direction and ran, aiming for the depths of the forest where she could lose herself, perhaps find a waterfall to cleanse the filth she suddenly felt all over her skin.

But she'd forgotten about the vasium.

She hadn't gone more than a few steps from the village boundary when she began to feel the pressure grow around her neck. The dead weight of the necklace forced her to the ground, subduing her.

Eventually, she was forced to crawl, and even then, she pushed further and further forward until movement became all but impossible and she lay scrabbling along the damp leaf litter of the dark forest.

Finally, exhausted, she stopped. With difficulty, she turned herself around and began dragging herself back through the grime of the rainforest floor towards Brewich. It felt good, like some kind of penance, to befoul herself in the dirt like this, as if this was the only thing she could do to prove to everyone, herself included, how unfair and wrong this all was.

When she returned to the lodgings, she found the hunting party all sitting at the dining table having a meal in what seemed to be an uncomfortable silence. Mila got the sense that she'd interrupted an argument.

Good. She hoped they were prepared to have another one.

She was filthy and sopping, but didn't hesitate as she stormed over to Culis, who wisely stood and moved away from earshot of the rest of the group to have the confrontation.

"You've made a mistake," she said in a soft, hard voice, fixing him with a gaze of death as they stood in the semi-dark of the street outside the guest house. "I was prepared to trust you, to work with you."

"You can still do both, but you must realise that she was never going to come willingly. We need demons to *join* us for this venture to work, Mila," he said, his voice equally as hard. It wasn't a concession or an apology. "I don't actually expect any of them to willingly join, but I do expect us to be able to convince them that this will be a better life for them once we've got them back at the manor."

"You *lied* to me."

"I did," he conceded. "But it was for everyone's benefit. You wouldn't have helped me if you'd known the truth, and I would have had to send you back to Jezebel."

"I will not help you anymore," she hissed.

"Oh, you will." His tone turned menacing, and Mila knew that the Jezebel threat remained real.

"I can't believe I bought all that sanctimonious horseshit about making life better for demons," she spat. "You're just trying to make yourself rich."

"Two things can be true at once."

"I will kill you if you force me to track another demon for you," she seethed, incensed by his nonchalance.

He seemed genuinely taken back. "A threat?" he said in surprise. "I didn't know you had that in you."

Red hot fury flashed through her again. "You know *nothing* about me. You know nothing about who I am and what I've had to do to survive in this *awful* society you humans have the gall to call 'civilised'. You think *we're* the heathens? The heretics? Well, take it from someone who can sense your energy...you are *scum*." She poked him hard in the chest. "All of you! Utter scum." She waved her hands furiously, breathing heavily. "Of every living creature on this great planet, it is humans that reek of rot and decay, not demons. *Humans.* And of all of them? You, Christopher Culis, are the most contemptible one I've ever met. I don't know why I'm disappointed. Shouldn't have expected anything more from the man who killed his own brother to get ahead."

As soon as the accusation left her lips, she regretted it. She didn't truly believe he'd killed Martin. His response to his father's comment about the matter had convinced her that he was innocent in that regard, but she was so angry that the words had just fallen out.

The chasm between them deepened.

Culis stared at her quietly for a long while before speaking again. "How lucky then for you," he said drily, "to owe a *murderer* your life."

Mila felt the fury leave her as quickly as it had arrived, replaced by a bone-deep exhaustion.

"Please," she begged him softly. "Don't do this. Give me time to try to talk her around. You saw what this freedom meant for me a few days ago. I can make her see it too. And if she won't do it, we can find another who will. I'll find someone. You'll have your demon trade. Just...don't do this to her. Don't turn me into a traitor to my own kind."

He surveyed her in silence for a long time, considering her words, before finally replying coolly, "It's as you said, demon. I'm just scum. Next time, save yourself the disappointment and don't expect me ever to be anything more than that."

He turned away and walked into the inn where they had acquired rooms for the evening, leaving Mila standing alone in the dark.

Fireside

Whatever illusion of civility had been forming between her and Culis was destroyed.

On his orders, she continued to use her power to scour crowds and determine who amongst them was a demon, but she executed the task with resentment and loathing. She'd tried to refuse it outright, but she'd been swiftly met with the choking weight of the vasium necklace when Culis had simply stalked off to try pursue the next one without her help. The power of that vile piece of jewellery was quickly becoming apparent. Culis could throw her into a river if he fancied, and she'd drown as he walked away from her.

So, against her will, she continued to lead the hunting party around the Highlands in search of demons, remaining sullen, and rejecting all gestures of friendship from Baird or any of the others. She'd learned that no matter the external warmth they showed her, they would each betray her to Culis in the blink of an eye.

For the next few days, despite being back in the familiarity of her homeland, she'd never felt more surrounded by enemies.

Things changed when the next demon came willingly. The demon Tarett was a young man with a round face, soft chin and bright brown eyes, who lived in the village of Lyndonberry. His family of humans loved him, and unlike Mila's, they had risked their own lives to keep him hidden and safe after his power appeared.

Mila sensed him as he was leaving the bakery and followed him until they reached a road on the outskirts of town that seemed empty and safe enough to talk. She was so nervous that she felt physically ill, acutely aware that Culis and the hunting party were watching the exchange from the forest, ready to fall upon them and seize Tarett as they'd done Natalee should this go wrong.

However, this time, her pitch fell onto receptive ears, and Tarett cautiously accepted. He loved his family and wished to spare them the life of secrecy they'd volunteered for, not to mention the heresy they were committing daily by lying about him to everyone they knew.

Culis was delighted. He accompanied them to Tarett's house with the contract in tow, transforming from angry kidnapper to kind benefactor in an instant. At the house, he shook Tarett's hand with warmth and smiled broadly during their discussions. He even embraced Tarett's mother when she began to cry.

Mila was disgusted by the act, but it worked. Tarett signed the contract within a day, although Mila noted that he looked both exhausted and determined when he stated quietly, "If this will truly change things for demons, how could I not help but try?"

Tarett's power was highly unusual. He could place large objects into far smaller objects, such as a loaf of bread into a coin purse. Culis was beyond delighted when it was revealed that he carried a black dog around with him, concealed completely (and apparently unharmed) inside his small breast pocket.

"This is...incredible. You're a thief's dream," Culis gasped.

"Well, there are a few limitations," Tarett cautioned. "The less compatible the sizes of two objects are, the more my horns extend as I'm carrying them. And the weight of both objects remains the same, so I could hardly steal a horse. But jewellery? Certainly."

"Incredibly useful for thieving." Culis nodded, impressed. "Or smuggling. You're worth an absolute fortune. Regardless of whatever price I ask of a buyer, they will surely believe they've won the better end of the bargain."

As he spoke, he threw a challenging glance towards Mila, as though daring her to accuse him of being secretive about his financial stake in this endeavour. She only scowled. She hated the way Tarett blushed at his words, as though he found the way Culis was talking about the financial viability of his powers to be a compliment. But, she supposed, in some twisted way, it was. No human had ever appreciated or admired demon powers before in the way Culis now openly did. And certainly no one had ever attached monetary value to them before.

The night before they departed Tarett's village, Mila sought Culis out to beg him again to free Natalee. She figured, surely, now that they had Tarett, the other woman's coercion wasn't required.

She found him sitting by the fire, listening to Arran and Baird discuss the latest politics from Traders Bay.

"They call 'emselves Children of Midas," Arran scoffed. "Not very original if you ask me."

"And they want...what?" Baird asked. "To overthrow the Church?"

"Wanna replace Abbott," Arran corrected. "But they're all cut from the same cloth as the Church. They'll try ter convince folks that they 'ave the true interpretations of the 'oly Texts, regardless of 'ow much bloodshed and up'eaval that causes, not cause they actually care, but cause they want the power tha' comes with being Midas's chosen. They all just want power."

"I'm sure they care – "

"They don't," Culis jumped in, firmly agreeing with Arran. "We've seen it over and over again in our travels, Baird. The ones who are truly spiritually enlightened don't give a rat's arse about enforcing that onto someone else. They lead by quiet example, content within their own knowledge that others will find their way to the correct path if that is what the god intends – like you, like Philomena."

"That's quite a self-righteous opinion," Mila said, "to be held by a man who's proven himself to be quite comfortable with kidnapping."

Culis's head snapped around at her approach, and he had the good grace to look extremely uncomfortable at her presence. Beside him, Baird looked solemn, but Arran turned his head away to hide a wide grin. Mila was angry with him too. He was a fellow ikarei, and he was enabling Natalee's imprisonment as much as Culis was.

"What can I do for you, Mila?"

"You can let her go," Mila said softly. "You have a willing demon now. Others will come. Please. Why must you keep Natalee?"

Culis kept his face neutral when he replied. "Even if I wanted to release her, I can't. I've sent her back to the manor with Nemecca. I didn't think the chains, gag and her thunderous, outraged presence would inspire other demons to believe we are here in good faith."

"Well, you aren't," she accused quietly.

To that, Culis had no response. He glared at her for a moment, and then his gaze seemed to soften. "This is good," he finally said, then turned back to Arran. "See?" he said to the other demon. "This is good! No one else challenges me like this." He turned to face Mila again and seemed sincere when he said, "Thank you, Mila."

Mila was confused. "For what?"

Culis paused before replying, as though weighing how much his response might inadvertently reveal, and then deciding to proceed anyway. “For helping slow the steady descent of me becoming my father.”

“It’s very convenient that you have such an unlikable father, upon whom you can lump the blame for your piss-poor morals,” Mila shot back.

“True.” Culis didn’t argue the point. He rose from the fire and stretched his arms above his head. “I think that’s my cue to retire. Goodnight, Arran, Baird...Mila.”

She watched as his back disappeared into the night.

“How can you willingly serve him?” She rounded on Arran as she sat down across the fire from them. “You’re one of us, and you’ve seen how he truly feels about our kind. You’ve seen what he did to Natalee, and you know the shackle he uses on me to keep me compliant. He’s despicable.”

“No, Christopher Culis is not a bad man,” Baird interjected quietly into the crackling fire, before Arran could answer. “I’ve known him a long, long time, and his father even longer. Now, while the decisions he’s made regarding that demon woman may not have been...his finest – ”

Arran huffed in agreement.

“ – to understand him and his actions,” Baird continued, “you have to understand how he was raised.”

“It’s true,” Arran agreed. “Once you know...it accounts for a lot.”

"Well," Mila said. "You'd better share it if you don't want your master stabbed in his sleep at some point over the next few nights."

Arran chuckled at that but when he turned to Baird he said. “I’m not sure 'ow much Master Culis would be comfortable for us to share with 'er.”

“I’m sure the gist will be fine. If she wants details, they can come from him.”

Arran nodded, satisfied with that response.

Baird picked up a stick and poked the fire as he began his story. "Christopher and his brother, Martin, were raised exclusively by Frank. I'm not sure who their mother was, or if they even had the same mother. Martin certainly had a darker complexion than either Christopher or Frank. Either way, when I met the man, he had these two little boys in tow, and there was no mother in sight. He raised them in a way I have never seen before or since. They were not taught to be men, but to be princes of his empire, and their values were anything but what one would consider normal."

"What do you mean?"

"Well, for example, from the time they could speak, they had to barter with their tutors for their food, always had to have something to trade, be it an acorn, or their unquestioning obedience. Nothing ever came without conditions. The boys weren't allowed friends. Even at their most tender ages, they could only have conquests. If Frank saw a connection happening between another child and one of his boys, he'd pull them aside and demand the child recite the ways in which that connection benefited the Artor Trading Company, and how it could be exploited if required. If Christopher or Martin could not provide a satisfactory answer, they were whipped."

Mila listened with her eyes wide and horrified, remembering the long whip Frank still carried at his side.

Baird continued. "Christopher received his father's special attentions in this instruction. I think Frank knew it was likely that Martin would die at thirty-five, due to the curse."

"Christopher didn't actually kill him, did he?" Mila asked softly.

Baird lowered his voice even more when he replied. "I truly don't know. They were raised to be bitter rivals their whole lives, but there were certainly some moments that I saw where they were close and confided in one another. But...Martin was an exceptional horseman who died from a fall from his horse. My gut tells me that was no accident, and Frank seems determined to blame his youngest son...or praise him for it, depending on the day."

Mila sat back, processing the information.

"So, you have to understand," Baird continued, "Christopher was raised to see the world around him, and the people in it, as only something to exploit. Personal connections were not valued, only wealth, power and intellect. Any concept he holds of honour or trust or friendship has come over the years from...well, from us." Baird gestured around at the sleeping members of the hunting party who lay around them. "And he has been an astute student. He truly loves us as his family. He enjoys us challenging his worldview."

"It's true," Arran agreed. "In the time I've known 'im, 'e loves talking about it and figuring 'imself out, separating 'imself from the teachings of 'is father. It's 'ard, though, cause he loves the lifestyle. You can see it in 'is eyes whenever we leave the manor walls. 'e desperately wants to travel, wants ter buy, sell and barter. Wants ter play tha' ancient game of opportunity versus risk versus reward. It lights a fire in 'im like nothing else...but 'e's still figuring out 'ow to 'ave one wit'out the other. 'e's never known a way to do it without being..."

"Evil," Mila finished the sentence for him.

"I was gonna say an arse." Arran laughed. "But I guess it must seem evil to you. Now I'm not trynna excuse the decision 'e made regarding tha' other demon woman."

"Natalee."

"Yeh. Natalee," Arran said. "The business with 'er? Tha' was messy. We can all agree on tha'. 'owever, an' I'll finish this conversation on one last note, you've gotta remember tha' Christopher was trained by his father ter act and react quickly under pressure. So, 'e'll often make harsh, snap decisions. It also means tha' when the dust settles, 'e's usually able ter see his mistakes, and he's not too proud ter change 'is mind if 'e can be convinced that a gentler way forward is the better path."

"Well, I hope he comes to his senses quickly," Mila said, staring into the fire. She tucked this new information deep inside her mind. Despite her fear and anger towards Culis, she now at least felt like she understood him a little, which was comforting. Mila knew that to defeat a shrewd enemy like Culis, understanding him would be key.

Rubane Secrets

Culis did indeed interact with the members of the hunting party in a way that seemed familial. His expressions were soft as he spoke to Black Berran while they shaved in the morning. His shoulders were low and his laugh came easily as he cooked bacon over a tiny crock pan alongside Arran and Lyria.

However, his walls came up again as soon as he noticed Mila or Tarett in the vicinity.

Interesting.

She tucked that information away. Knowing who he felt comfortable around and why was invaluable for plotting her escape. Earning their trust would help to earn his trust again. Then it would be easy to steal the sister stone and run.

Despite her anger and confusion towards Culis, Mila found it immensely reassuring to now have Tarett around. His belief in the plan gave it the legitimacy she'd been struggling to find and it made the rest of the trip far easier on her conscience – the Natalee predicament notwithstanding. She also enjoyed simply talking to him as they pushed through the rainforest towards other townships. It had been a long time since she'd spoken freely with another ikarei about ikarei affairs, and she both felt and saw that he, too, was enjoying it.

She noted Culis observing them with interest, and when they moved onto the town of Nettleton, Culis surprised Mila by making an announcement loudly and proudly in the village square.

"I am Christopher Culis, adventurer extraordinaire, and I openly share with you all that I have arrived in your fair town with demons in my employ. These demons are helping me in an endeavour sanctioned by the God-King himself. They are not to be harmed or arrested during my stay in your fine town."

The local acolyte's arms could not have crossed over his chest more swiftly, yet he made no move to impede their visit, despite the deep furrow that burned into his forehead.

The change in tactic turned out to be a masterstroke, for now that their presence had the local authority's begrudging acceptance, Mila and Tarett were free to roam the village. The additional formidable presence of Culis's hunting party provided a shield that effectively protected them from any petty harassment or persecution they might encounter.

For the first time in Mila's adult life, she was able to wander freely throughout the town, looking in shop windows, and buying wares without having to pretend to be human. Tarett also reveled in it, and his enthusiasm reinvigorated Mila's own feelings of lightness and joy. He moved through the street with his horns fully extended, a wide, bright smile etched onto his face. His exuberance could not be dimmed, and for the rest of the trip, Mila caught him playfully putting all manner of objects into the tiniest of containers just for the fun of it. To Mila's delight, he chose to pick on Baird, in particular, and the poor man always seemed to lose his boots or his pocketknife or water skin, finding them in all manner of peculiar places, such as his tiny, leather penny pouch.

With Tarett by her side, it was also far easier to convince other demons to join the venture, and it wasn't long before two more demons, Marie and then Flue, joined their ranks. Marie was a tiny, mousy little woman whose power was the ability to touch any written document and instantly know what it contained. Flue stood out from any crowd with their tall, slim legs, long silver hair and beautiful, androgynous features. Their power could make anyone remember them fondly, regardless of the nature of previous interactions between them. Flue informed the small group that, hypothetically, their power meant they could treat someone terribly, even cause physical harm, and the victim would only recall pleasant associations with them. In fact, enough repeated exposure to Flue's powers could cause a person to develop an outright obsession.

"I can't believe no one has ever thought of monetising these gifts before," Culis muttered in awe when Flue finished their explanation. "You're...divine."

Flue flinched at the terminology. "I am not Divine. I am mortal."

"I meant divine, as in exquisite," Culis amended. "Although, if we had some Testing Cats here, perhaps they'd be able to see you too."

Mila blinked incredulously at his words. Culis had always hinted at being irreverent, but since leaving behind Jeralusah, his strange and sacrilegious offhand comments had grown far more frequent and condemning. None of the hunting party seemed fazed by them, yet if a passing priest had heard his implication that Midas had somehow tricked the Testing Cats, he'd be next in line to be sacrificed, regardless of the fact he was human.

It made Mila wonder what they'd seen on their many travels to have caused such disillusionment, and she was reminded again of Keras and the land where ikarei were known as zoi and were worshiped. Midas and the Church only ruled the nation of Artor. Why should she stay here? Would the other ikarei want to come with her?

Mila dedicated the rest of the trip to befriending her new brethren and enjoyed the process of learning how to do it. She hadn't consciously tried to make friends with anyone since she was fourteen, and she felt in her bones that this experience was good for her. It was right that she should be around her own kind, and thankfully, they were all easy to get along with.

Once Tarett was comfortable amongst the group, he truly came out of his shell and revealed that he didn't have a serious bone in his body. His constant grin and sharp wit kept Mila from dwelling too fiercely on thoughts of escape, or the confrontation she knew she was going to have with Natalee on their return. And while Mila had befriended the members of the hunting party on their way up, it was Tarett who won over everyone's hearts and minds by the end. At times, she even found herself wondering if it was he, rather than Flue, who was possessed with the power of affection.

Flue kept mostly to themself, but was friendly when approached, and Marie was shy, but kind. To Mila's disapproval, she seemed to bond particularly well with Arran, and the two were often found walking and talking together, away from the others. Mila wondered if he was telling her about Keras, too, and what the other woman might make of the idea of escaping there.

There was hardly a chance to ask her, or any of them for that matter, for she dared not raise the topic while Arran was present. He was too loyal to Culis, and somehow, he always seemed to be around their little group. Mila wondered if it was because he was truly enjoying the company of his fellow ikarei, or if he was spying on them.

She suspected the latter.

One night, when the group of ikarei were the only ones seated by the fire, Mila asked Flue how they could know if any of their interactions or relationships in life were genuine.

"It's a good question." Flue replied. "A few years ago, quite accidentally, I discovered a herb, which I can distil into a scented oil that mutes my power," they swept their waist-length silver hair back from their neck before indicating a necklace at their breastbone.

It was a tiny silver ball on a chain, covered in pinholes. Flue shook it gently, and Mila smelled rubane essence waft from it.

"I wear it to protect others, and myself. I cannot have the villagers becoming obsessed with me. It is better to pass by innocuously where possible."

"What is the scent?" Marie asked in her high, quiet voice, but Flue shook their head and smiled gently.

"My secret, I'm afraid."

Mila chose not to divulge that she recognised it. She knew she was probably one of the few people in the entire nation who could name it. Rubane's power muting properties were not widely known. In fact, Mila had never met anyone else, other than Flue, who used it as she did.

She dwelt on this fact long after everyone else had gone to sleep.

* * *

Once the hunting party had collected Tarett, Flue and Marie, Culis declared the end of the expedition. He couldn't hide the delight he felt in having procured a small handful of demons, each with objectively rather useful powers, and Mila could tell he was itching to start advertising them.

The return journey seemed to go much faster than the initial foray into the rainforest, and when they all finally arrived back at the manor,

Mila caught herself feeling, for a fleeting moment, as if she were returning home, rather than having just left it.

Tarett, Marie and Flue were each given a small suite of their own, and like Mila, they were permitted to see the days out however they best saw fit. Each of them knew their stay here was temporary.

"After enough time has passed to ensure your notoriety has spread," Mila overheard Culis telling them, "I'll pair each of you off to a suitable master."

Mila was grateful that, although they were understandably a little nervous, for the most part, the small group seemed happy and content with their decision to trust her and come live at Culis Manor. None of them were forced to don a vasium necklace either, but then again, all of them thought they were here under their own free will.

They had no idea about Natalee.

When Mila arrived back at the manor, she quietly sought out Nemecca to inquire about Natalee's whereabouts and found out that she was being kept in a basement below the manor. She knew she needed to go visit her and try to entreat her to wilfully join the plan. But day after day passed, and still she was unable to force herself down those steps to have that conversation.

Still a coward, she realised as she lay in bed one night after yet another day of avoiding Natalee. Many things had changed since that morning when she'd first stood and wordlessly watched Jezebel condemn Jahan to his blinding, but not this. She'd been a coward then and was still a coward now.

Uneasy Truce

Mila could not shake off the shadow of Natalee's situation. Despite her desire to escape and the fact that she knew she needed to earn Culis's trust back enough for that to happen, it hung over her like a noose. As a result, she could not bring anything but a stony attitude to any interaction she had with him over the next week. He responded with his most suffocating air of disregard for it. Day to day, she avoided him as best she could, but that was no easy task. This was his manor, and Culis was everywhere and across everything.

If he wasn't receiving visitors and furthering the notoriety of the demon trade, he was walking and talking with Baird, or Arran or Nemecca in the hallways, laughing as they recalled stories from their travels, or listening as they passed on information from the outside world that Culis could incorporate into his schemes.

Mila was just as likely to stumble across him overseeing the warehouse as reading in the library, taking great delight in showing Marie his vast collection of books that she now had access to.

Once, Mila even caught him with his sleeves rolled up to his elbows in the kitchen just outside her room, trading secrets with the cook and concocting something that smelled of rosemary, garlic and burnt butter.

Mila made a point of leaving any room he entered, and Culis made a point of ignoring the behaviour and engaging with her as often as he could. They existed in this uncomfortable dance for the whole week, with Mila pulling away and Culis leaning in, both of them determined not to let the other win.

After Worship Day, Frank Culis made another appearance, which was the only thing that could make Mila's situation at the manor even worse. She braced for his impact on the household; however, to her shock, this time, he treated the three new demons with the utmost respect and civility, even organising an afternoon tea with them in the gardens, in order to get to know them better. Mila was excluded from this invite, for which she was grateful, but she still took up post at a library window and watched the entire affair from above, preparing to run down and intervene at the first sign that anything was amiss.

Thankfully, her concern was unwarranted. Frank chose, for some reason, to be perfectly congenial for this entire visit, and despite the fact that Mila breathed far easier once he departed, the other three ikarei didn't quite understand her concern. All in all, they were relaxed and at ease around the manor, and Mila was grateful they felt this way. She also enjoyed the fact that the humans of the household now had new faces to peer at with curiosity. Tarett, in particular, seemed to be in his element, and spent most of his days flirting easily with the maids. He could often be found hanging about in the kitchen, acting as more of a distraction than a helping hand, but he was so damned affable that even the cook tolerated his presence with a silent grin.

The day after Frank left, Mila resumed her morning walk and, along the way, gave herself a stern talking to about not yet visiting Natalee.

"You're going this afternoon," she scolded herself. "You've put this off for far too long. Your cowardice is humiliating."

"Mila!" someone in the distance called out to her and started jogging to catch up.

She squinted at the approaching figure in the haze of the rising morning heat, but once she realised who it was, she turned and continued to determinedly stroll.

"Good morning," Culis said with a smile when he caught up to her, his golden curls flopping lazily onto his forehead in time with his stride.

Mila did not reply. She was still not ready to trade pleasantries and pretend all was well between them.

"It *is* a good morning, Mila," he insisted. "Especially because you can stop quietly stewing in your hatred for me and start helping me again." He had a lightness to his step.

"Oh really?" she bit out.

"Yes," he said firmly. "Our Natalee stalemate is at an end."

"You've decided to set her free?" Mila stopped walking and turning to him incredulously.

"Not quite," he said. "But I thought you'd be pleased to hear that she's no longer locked under the house. I've decided to send her away, on a voyage with Baird. Let her experience what her life could look like under one of our contracts. Maybe she'll change her mind."

Mila stewed on this information for a long while and considered how she felt about it. While it wasn't granting Natalee freedom, it was certainly better for her than being locked in a basement indefinitely.

"What happens when she returns and still wants freedom?" she challenged, starting her walk again.

Culis followed. "Well, I suppose we'll deal with that if it happens. But take it from me...Baird can be pretty persuasive when he wants to be." He chuckled for a moment at his own private joke, then said, "for now at least, can you please accept this as a truce?"

"I'll accept it as a lull in the battle."

He sighed heavily. "Mila, mark this moment because it won't happen often." His tone became unusually serious as he said, "here and now, I will admit to you that what happened with Natalee up in the Highlands was a mistake, and the way I spoke to you about it was wrong. I...I am sorry."

She stopped walking again and turned to look at him in shock. Was this what Arran and Baird had meant that night by the fire? This kind of admittance, and an apology, was the last thing she'd ever expected from him.

He ran a hand through the wavy mess on his head. It was infuriating how handsome he could look while sweating and uncomfortable. "My pride and enthusiasm got the better of me." He continued. "I made the decision to detain her in that split second and it...it was wrong. I want you to know that it wasn't premeditated. I didn't – and I still don't – want to betray your trust."

"Why do it at all?" Mila said, determined not to let him off lightly. She'd seen him act out a range of emotions perfectly. What proof did she have that any of this was sincere?

"I suppose..." He took his time considering his answer. "I suppose I was fearful that I'd misjudged the situation, and that no demon would come willingly. That the entire venture would fail."

"You could have listened to me," Mila said. "You could have trusted me. I told you there would be others who would be willing."

"Mila, at the time, not even *you* seemed to believe that a demon would join us! I could see how conflicted you were about the hunt.

If you didn't even believe in the cause, why would any other demon? Why should I?"

"So, it seemed better to abduct the unwilling instead?" she snapped.

"Well, when you put it like that..."

She'd never seen such a deeply uncomfortable look on his face before and desperately wanted to touch him, to discover if it was real.

"Look. That wasn't my finest hour. I've admitted that. I've apologised. I've even tried to make amends. I don't have a better answer for you and I'm sorry if that's unsatisfactory. This is who I am." He tossed his arms into the air, resigned and frustrated. "You can hate me for being greedy and selfish. I am. I haven't tried to hide any of that from you. But, while I know it might not seem this way to you now. You should know that.... I am trying to be... less, like that."

Mila ate back a chuckle at the earnest discomfort in those words and she fought not to soften her gaze. He caught the glare and smiled at her. "It's good to have you around, Mila. New energy in my house, someone who isn't afraid of me."

They began walking again, their sandals crunching in unison on the gravel path.

"I am," she finally said to break the silence.

"Am what?"

"I am afraid of you."

"Really?" he asked with a small laugh. "Surely not still afraid you'll be sacrificed in my room of death?"

It was clearly intended as a joke, but Mila didn't lean into it. Instead, she rounded on him. "There's more than one way to hurt someone, Culis. You bought me from Jezebel as a way to *force* me into slavery and make you money. I am bound to your location by this necklace. You've threatened to sell me back to Jezebel if I'm not useful to you. You've betrayed your word to me and forced me to break mine to Natalee. If our history is anything to go by, you actually seem to find it very *easy* to hurt me!" she accused.

"What a list," he said uncomfortably. "If only it were all true. Then your hatred would truly be justified."

"It *is* true!" she snapped.

"Not all of it," he corrected. "The necklace? Yes. That binds you to me, but on the very first morning you were here, when I'd treated you with nothing but civility, you tried to escape and renege on our contract. You broke my trust first. And I *saved* you from Jezebel. I didn't need you for my trade. I could have started it another way. I've already had Arran working for me for years. It would have been harder without your power, but I would have found a way."

"And for that I should be eternally grateful, should I?"

"Yes...no! I just...dammit, Mila." He sighed in evident frustration and, despite herself, she felt a tiny sliver of flame alight in her gut at the sight of him. There was something about the way he seemed to be twisting himself into a knot, maybe revealing a smattering of shame that was so...endearing, vulnerable even.

"Look," he said eventually. "You...you don't need to do anything with the information I'm about to give you. It might not change your opinion of me at all. Which is fine, it's fair even. It shouldn't. It's far better for you to see me as dangerous and untrustworthy. That attitude will probably keep you safer in the long run. But if there's one thing I need you to know, it's this." He stopped walking again and ensured she was looking directly into his stern, earnest face before he spoke. "I didn't take you from Jezebel simply to have a demon I could use to make profit. I took you from her because something about you and your fierce will to live spoke to me, and the more I watched you, the more I realised that, if she'd hurt you again, I...would have regretted not acting to save you."

Mila considered his words in shocked silence, then said, "So...so you won't sell me back to her if I don't obey you?"

"No," Culis said, his voice almost returned to its usual balance. "I want you to join me because you believe in my ventures. I don't want to have to force you. Life should be fun, or at least entertaining. Otherwise, what's the point?"

Mila was still processing this when he spoke again.

"So," he said, collecting himself, "now that you know you won't be sent back to Jezebel...I'm headed to Traders Bay tomorrow and could use your help. Would you be willing to join me?"

"I am still your slave," she reminded him. "You could still simply order me to."

He rolled his eyes. "You are, and I could, but...do you *want* to come with me?"

Mila considered the question. Did she want to make the trip to Traders Bay? It would mean spending considerable time alone with Culis. Did she want to do that? It was certainly a good opportunity to continue to understand him a little better. She'd seen enough glimpses of his humanity peeking out from the merchant prince façade that she couldn't help but be curious and drawn to him, just a little. It was a very unsettling feeling, particularly as she also knew she could not trust a word that passed his sweet, honeyed lips. In fairness, they didn't look honeyed right now. They looked pursed with concern, waiting for her answer.

Mila held out her hand, wanting to read his energy before she fully committed. Culis reached out happily to shake it, not knowing her true intention. At their touch, his energy surged through her.

Happiness, earnest joy. He really wanted her to come, and it meant something to him that she wanted to come of her own volition.

"I'll come for the journey," she said finally, silently reminding herself that being in Traders Bay would be an ideal opportunity to research a way to get passage to Keras. "But I can't promise I'll use my power to help you with your business dealing. Sending Natalee away with Baird doesn't absolve you of that whole horrendous situation. I'm still figuring out how I feel about it all, and about you."

To her surprise, Culis's joyful energy did not diminish an inch at her words. Nor did he try to argue or convince her otherwise. He simply nodded.

"Deal."

She withdrew her hand first.

After he left, Mila considered what she'd learned from that brief touch. The great Christopher Culis, the selfish trader who loved nothing and no one but his own company, wanted her to join him for this trip. And it wasn't because he wanted something from her. His energy had revealed that he didn't care if she used her power for his benefit or not. He was genuinely happy to simply have her company for this trip.

Keras, she reminded herself, shaking her head free of the image of the windswept, golden bun of hair and green eyes that gleamed down at her with sheer delight.

Earning Culis's trust enough for him to let down his guard. Stealing the sister stone. Finding a ship heading to Keras and paying for passage that would take her far away from Artor and Christopher Culis. That's what she had to focus on.

If she'd hurt you again, I would have regretted not acting to save you.

The words echoed in her head, and a lick of flame sparked in her gut and would not go away.

Traders Bay

"Two weeks!" Mila exclaimed as she bounced along in the carriage. "You might have told me this yesterday. I don't have nearly enough clothes."

"We can buy you more clothes when we arrive," Culis said with a dismissive wave of his hand. "And I didn't tell you because I knew you wouldn't have agreed to come." He gave her a wry grin. "But, now you're here. And if you enjoy this trip and decide to accompany me on future ones, then you'll need more than just those few smocks in your room anyway. We'll be visiting numerous taverns, of both shining and dubious reputation, to conduct business and advertise the new demons. I need you to be able to blend in at both. Depending on the circumstance, I may even need you to play a role. You'll need clothes for everything."

"Working with you sounds intimidating."

"Yes, you are." He grinned again, and then returned his attention to the passing countryside.

She studied him intently, wondering how to take him and his words, but came away from that effort with no real clarity.

"You're staring at me, little demon."

"Just trying to figure out where you store all the arrogance. It can't be in your head. It's far too small to contain all that."

"There is one part of my body you can't see right now, that I assure you is large enough to store it all." Culis winked.

Mila choked on her laughter, annoyed that she'd rewarded him with it. "Ah yes. Juvenile humour. How apt."

"Well, what do you expect for someone with a head as small as mine?"

"True." She turned and faced the window to hide her grin.

When they finally arrived at Traders Bay, Culis wasted no time and took them straight to their first tavern, The Bonny Bosom. It was an eclectically designed taproom that featured a wall of wide, thick, glass cubes, each of which had been filled with water. These, when struck by the afternoon light from the street outside, created rainbows that danced across the tabletops in a very pleasing way.

"We'll stay here this afternoon," he said, settling into a seat. "And move on to another tomorrow."

"How do vendors know where to find you if you move to a new tavern each day you travel?" Mila asked, watching as Culis calmly thumbed through an old book of numbers and picked absently at the hot fried bread that was placed before them.

"They always end up figuring it out," he said cryptically, "and if they don't know how to keep an ear to the ground in a town like this, then I probably don't want them working with me in the first place."

Sure enough, it must have spread like wildfire that the legendary trader Christopher Culis was in this part of town, for it didn't take more than an hour or so before the bell on top of The Bonny Bosom's front door clanged, and a large, rooster of a man entered, identified Culis, and barrelled over to him with enthusiasm.

Thus began their week.

* * *

Mila's existing memories of Traders Bay were not pleasant.

As a young outcast from Prious, she'd lived on its formidable streets for a short, miserable time. Those had easily been the darkest few months of her life. Newly ostracised from her highly conservative family and community, with nothing but a young mind that had been trained to see sacrilege in even the most mundane interactions, she'd stumbled into the bustling city in a state of shock and had been promptly overwhelmed. Drowning under the weight of her new identity as a demon, trying to accept the reality of it, had sent her into a deep state of self-loathing. She'd done many things to survive in this place during those months, most of which only served to reinforce the vile thoughts she already felt for herself. It wasn't an exaggeration to say that Natalee had saved her life on the day she'd taken her in and educated her on the true history of the ikarei.

Her only other notable visit had been when she and Culis had come for the demonstration at Central just over a month ago, and that had been traumatising in its own way.

This visit was different to both. This time, Culis seemed to relish acting as a kind of vanguard, leading her with delight into the watering holes of both the upper and lower class. Demonstrating how he effortlessly blended into the society of each. It was fascinating to watch.

They moved from tavern to tavern each day, with Culis preferring to walk the connecting roads rather than to hail one of the many horse-drawn cabs. This allowed Mila to see more sides of the city than she'd ever seen before, but with Culis always at her side, it was impossible to sneak away and talk to someone about securing passage to Keras.

It was not all frustrating though.

With Culis's generous purse at her disposal, she was now able to shop and sample all sorts of unique and fashionable foods sold by small vendors on street corners they passed. Culis also funded her a new wardrobe, and when he noted her interest in the shop fronts, he indicated that she should purchase whatever she wished. She bought three items: a comb carved from a ram's horns, purported to carry the oils from the keratin that would smooth even the tightest knot; a small glass bead with a blue and white swirl inside that she threaded through a small, silver chain and strung about her neck; and a small bone-handled pocket knife that she tucked into her sock. It was the first time Mila had ever bought anything for herself simply because it pleased her.

She was particularly taken with the necklace, absentmindedly fiddling with the bead, rocking it back and forth across the chain with amusement, until she looked up from her drink at the next tavern to find Culis watching the action intently, as though hypnotised.

"Culis?" she asked.

He jumped at her voice, shaking himself free of wherever his mind had wandered. "It's pretty," he said with a small smile, and then his next client arrived, and with the speed of a released bowstring, his attention snapped back to the task at hand.

As the week progressed, Mila began to learn more about Culis's business acumen and techniques. Despite having no background in trading herself, she found herself fascinated by his work and the way he shaped each meeting with his steady stream of clientele. He conducted himself masterfully, sometimes haggling like a common fisherman over stock, other times acting so posh and conceited that he barely spoke a word and communicated almost solely through raised eyebrows and minute shakes of his head. Very occasionally, he looked genuinely happy to see someone, as if he wanted nothing more from their time than shared ale and a story.

He was generous with some folk, and brutally stingy with others. When it came to procurement, Mila noticed that he rarely traded in the ordinary and preferred the exotic. When it came to people, his preferences appeared to be similar.

"I generally prefer to let the Guild of Merchants worry about transporting the goods needed by common folk," he explained to Mila after placing an order with the captain of *The Reckless*, which would require the man to travel half the world in order to retrieve a shipment of crockery that was luminescent by night. "If it's not fun, or doesn't come with a grand tale to recount in my old age to my lap full of engrossed grandchildren, then why bother?"

He was utterly in his element when it came to negotiating, and Mila sensed equal amounts of respect and fear exuding from his associates. If he didn't already have an established rapport with a trader, then he could usually rely on his reputation to precede him. However, Mila noticed with interest that, on occasion, when this did not seem to be the case, he'd find a way to do something wholly unexpected, or occasionally downright cruel, always for the purpose of reinforcing his infamy.

She also noted that, regardless of the trade at hand, he never ceased dropping hints regarding the demons currently in his possession.

"I cannot tell you the specificity of their powers," he'd say cryptically to everyone. "Not without a deposit laid first. I'll only say that they're each immensely powerful in their own way. There truly is no comparison. The secrecy is half the reason for the exorbitant price. A demon's power should be known only to their master. That way, their powers can be used to their fullest extent and to their master's advantage."

He relied on the intrigue and conspiracy to advertise for him – and his instincts were correct. In their second week in Traders Bay, they had a number of envoys from rich, anonymous buyers approach them, inquiring about the demons and how to acquire one.

"This is all one big game to you, isn't it?" Mila noted aloud one evening, as the two of them retired to a small cabin on the upper floor of their evening accommodation, The Harried Hare. This particular establishment was situated conveniently beside the port, and the day's business dealings had mostly centred around long-haul freighting over the Windless Seas. All day, Mila had heard the soothing sounds of waves lapping against the western wall of the common room, accompanied by the sounds of the moored boats as they clunked arrhythmically.

It was here, staying so close to the dock, that she realised that, over the past few days, she'd been enjoying herself so much that she'd stopped thinking about ways to get passage to Keras.

The upstairs cabin she shared with Culis was quite small, but probably still one of the largest in the small establishment. It contained two separate sleeping cribs, a tiny fireplace, and a humble writing desk that was pressed against the far wall beneath a tiny round window. From there, one could see nothing but the blackness of the vast bay beyond them. It wasn't the first time this week they'd shared a room, but this was by far the cosiest.

As they entered, Culis moved swiftly to draw the curtain across the window, as though concerned someone might look in at them from one of the docked ships. Once satisfied of their privacy, he set about stoking the fire. The innkeeper had left them a small flask of wine and some salted herring as an evening snack, but Culis ignored it and withdrew from his traveller's satchel his own flask of rich port.

Mila accepted a glass and sat cross-legged on one of the cribs to drink it, while Culis took the seat by the fire.

"A game?" He repeated her words with a wry smile, leaning back on the chair and placing his hands behind his head. "What makes you say that?"

"It's just something I've noticed," Mila said. "Your enthusiasm is entirely authentic, but I can tell you enjoy playing the role of 'Trader Prince' a little too much."

Culis laughed heartily at that, but didn't deny her accusation. "Trader Prince? Is that what you read from me?" he probed.

She just shrugged, still not wanting to reveal that she found him impossible to read without his touch.

"Well, I do enjoy games, some more than others." He raised an eyebrow, and his quiet smirk suddenly made the response more flirtatious than perhaps the words themselves implied.

Mila instinctively reached out with her powers to try gauge his intentions, but again, she was met with what mentally felt like a thick garden hedge, one which allowed glimpses of the energy behind it, but prevented the formation of a full picture.

"What's the scowl for?" he teased lightly, sipping at his port. "Aren't you having fun?"

"It *has* been fun," she agreed. "And I'm not scowling."

He returned to stoking the fire. "I'm glad you're enjoying yourself. Are you glad you decided to come? At the start of this trip, your fear of the place, and dislike of me, was palpable. I was worried that I wouldn't be able to bring you here again."

"No," she admitted. "I've come to see a new side of it. It's not a terrible city, although it certainly has pockets I'd never want to venture down again. And you…" She halted, searching for the words. "You're…impressive to watch. It's been entertaining, to say the least."

"Good." Culis seemed very pleased by her observation. "It's a youthful city," he continued. "It's got an energy to it. That's why I like it."

"I think that's why I found it so overwhelming the first few times I was here," Mila replied. "Especially when I was younger. I didn't even really know what my powers were for a long time. I was picking up everything, with no way to filter my own energy from everyone else's around me."

"That sounds…awful." His happy mood shifted, and he studied her seriously.

She wondered if the sympathy was genuine. The firelight cast dancing orange shapes across his handsome face, and she hated that she couldn't tell. She found herself hoping it was.

"Yes," she agreed.

"Why did you come here, of all places?"

"I didn't really intend to. I grew up in Prious and knew nothing else of the world. On the morning my horns and power emerged, my father tried to lock me in the house while he went to fetch the local acolyte. I escaped through a window and knew I needed to flee, so I simply picked a direction that didn't seem too obvious, in case I was pursued. After a number of weeks of walking, I arrived in the Swilder's Quarter."

Culis's eyes widened in concern. "The Swilder's Quarter is the last part of the city I'd ever send a newcomer," he said softly. "You would have just been a child too."

Mila pursed her lips and nodded, looking away from him, unable to witness the pity in his eyes. "I nearly didn't make it out. It was thanks to Natalee that I survived."

"Natalee?" Culis looked uncomfortable at the mention of her name.

"Yes." She turned to face him again. "She was here too. We worked in the same factory. She realised what I was when she found me clutching at my head in horror as the man who preyed on the women in my sharehouse passed by my door. She took me under her wing, taught me the true history of my people, not the Church's lie. It helped me to process it all, to forgive myself for what I was."

"What is the true history?" Culis asked, leaning forward, earnest interest written across his face.

Mila considered the question, and the asker for a long moment. "I'm not sure you really want to know," she finally replied. "It's far easier to simply write us all off as demons."

"I *do* want to know! You forget that Arran has been a longtime friend and associate of mine. I am among the few who know that the zoi exist elsewhere in the world. It's never made sense to me that one would 'choose' to sell their soul for a...paltry mimicry of Midas's powers in their sleep. Never felt right to believe that every demon's existence is some deliberate heretical display of mockery, or challenge, or whatever it is the Church says it is. I'm good enough of a liar to generally know when I'm being lied to. So, tell me. What's the truth?"

Mila was careful to not let the shock show on her face, cautious even now that Culis might just be saying something he knew she'd find favourable in order to earn back her approval.

"You are truly interested?" she said slowly.

"Yes. Please share... Wait." He moved to the door of the room and flung it open. "Hendrichs!" he called out into the corridor. "I'd like some of that stew I saw cooking downstairs...two bowls, please. Yes, and both served with some of the thick bread that Orla makes. Surely, she's still got some from this morning. The thick kind, you know it.

Yes. And three, no...*four* peaches and – " he glanced over his shoulder at Mila and looked her up and down before adding to the hallway order, " – a few squares of chocolate. Dark, with a side of sea salt."

Mila's stomach rumbled at his words.

Once she'd eaten, the food sat warm in her belly. Despite the fact she knew the chocolate was an obvious bribe, she couldn't help but enjoy it.

"Now we're ready," Culis said eagerly. "Please, tell me the story, the history. Everything. I want to know it all."

Mila remembered how it had felt when she'd heard it from Natalee for the first time in that dingy room in her apartment.

She'd still been so far gone in the Church's teachings, still so caught up in her own self-loathing, that she'd initially shrunk away from the blasphemous words.

"You struck no bargain in your sleep with the devil," Natalee had said, holding her close, wiping her tears. "You did not fall from grace. You are not evil. That is all a lie. A wicked lie. The truth is that you are a being known as an ikarei, and we peacefully existed alongside humans long before Midas arrived and declared us all to be demons."

It had taken some time for Mila to eventually believe her. Of course an evil demon would say these things! She'd initially pulled away from Natalee's attempted comfort.

"Get away from me!" she'd cried out. "Demon! Heretic!"

"Neither of these," Natalee had replied calmly with a sad shake of her head, letting her go, but not letting her gaze drop. "When Midas arrived and announced himself, it was the ikarei who challenged his rule. Many believed that having powers did not make one a god – no matter how destructive those powers are. In response, the Church wrote the Heretical Behaviours, and created the mythology of Viah and the Rotting Muds. Creating a punishment for religious disobedience was a masterstroke. It meant that humans were so frightened and confused that it was easier to believe than to resist or question the message. But it is important that we ikarei remember this story, Mila. No Church should ever teach you to hate yourself or be fearful of questioning its doctrines. We are all uniquely and wonderfully made, no less or more than the animals and plants around us."

Mila looked up at Culis's shadowed, earnest face and took a deep breath as she opened her mouth and shared this story.

* * *

Later that night, as Mila lay back in her crib, she listened to the soft *thwucking* of bobbing boats below and wondered what Culis had made of it all. He'd sat and listened quietly for the whole story and had spent the rest of the night seemingly engrossed in his journal, writing furiously and silently until the candle burned low and he went to bed. It had felt good telling him. Felt good reminding herself that Midas and his Church were branding ikarei as demons for their own purposes.

She looked over at Culis's sleeping form and wished for the millionth time that she could sense his energy. She wondered if he inadvertently utilised rubane upon his person. Perhaps he used it in a soap and that somehow blocked her powers from sensing him from afar?

She mulled this over, and then sat bolt upright in the darkness as a new thought suddenly occurred to her.

Rubane.

She knew now that the weed affected more than just her own power. It also blocked Flue's. What if it blocked *all* demon powers?

She considered this revelation for a moment. It made sense, and when they returned to the other demons at Culis Manor, it would be a relatively easy theory to test out.

She lay back on her bed, excited, and for a moment, she delighted silently in the power and mystery of nature. Who would suspect such a small and humble weed could have such an impact? She thought for a moment about the tonics or oils she could distil with rubane to help other demons with more obvious powers stay hidden in society. It could change everything for them.

But it was the following thought that came later in the night that truly made her blood still.

Just as sleep was about to grip her, the most dangerous thought she'd ever had came to her: *what if Midas's gloves were made of rubane?*

She hadn't been able to sense anything from the God-King while she'd been in his grasp. At the time, she'd attributed that to both her own fear and his divinity, but in hindsight, she now identified the sensation as a muffling one.

Rubane.

If it was, indeed, in the gloves, then it had almost certainly dimmed her power, in the same way the gloves dimmed his and enabled him to touch things while he was wearing them.

It made sense. In fact, now that she had come to this realisation, no other explanation could satisfy the question of why the gloves did not disintegrate into sand at his touch. It had to be rubane.

The next logical thread of thought that flowed from this revelation came cautiously and was pulled from the mire of her mind, like a sticky strand of hair from a pot of thick honey. If this was true, if a simple weed such as rubane could mute a God-King's powers, then what did that say about his supposed divinity? His Divine authority over all? His invincibility? His immortality even? If he could be defeated by a weed, surely, he could be defeated by death itself? Had her ikarei ancestors been right? Was Midas not quite a god after all?

Perhaps, he was a demon.

An absurdly powerful demon, who had managed to implement, maintain and uphold the greatest lie in all of Artor's history.

No. She reined that insane thought back in carefully, her mind desperately seeking familiar purchase.

The cats, she reminded herself. The Testing Cats that could not see demons. The cats that loved Midas. They worshipped him, were devoted to him.

But the seed of doubt that had been planted had rooted quickly, and suddenly, even the behaviour of Midas's cats was starting to seem like poor proof of divinity. Cats as a species were impressive, intuitive and ethereal creatures. But their adoration alone did not make someone a god. What if, as Culis had jokingly inferred back in the Highlands, there was a way to trick the cats?

Mila blinked in the darkness, processing these thoughts, trying to make sense of them. What about the Church? The devotion of the priests? The entire way of life in Artor was built around the worship of Midas and avoiding the Heretical Behaviours, avoiding sacrifice.

Surely, if Midas was a demon, there would have been some sign of it over the decades. And where were his horns? Had he removed them somehow? Could they even *be* removed? She had once tried to cut hers off. Never again. It had been excruciating...and it hadn't worked. They'd grown back. She blinked that flashback away.

What if he'd found another way? A more permanent way to remove them?

The questions crashed like angry waves against Mila's mind and flooded the structure of everything she'd ever believed about her world. It was uncomfortable and frightening, but now that the door had been opened, she could not stop the barrage that seemed determined to surge in and overwhelm her.

Her breathing quickened and she began to sweat. She sat up in bed and clutched at the blanket, willing herself to be steady, to feel the fabric under her hands, to smell the air of the room – a smell of salt, incense and Culis. It grounded her. She took a long breath in and out, and slowly was able to gather an ounce of calm.

"They're just thoughts," she whispered to herself. "No one need know you've had them. You never have to act on them if you don't want to. They're just thoughts, and they can't harm you. They can't betray you. No one need ever know."

It stabilised her to hear the sound of her own voice, but found she couldn't quite believe the words, because the next thought that came to her was not just frightening, it was one that, if true, would demand that she take action.

If the rubane muted Midas's powers, then perhaps a demon doused in the herb could resist destruction at his hands.

Time seemed to stand still as she pondered this, and she realised in horror that, if she was the only person who knew about rubane's powers, then she was responsible for somehow testing this theory.

Suddenly, the world tilted.

Mila hit the floor with a sharp bang. She'd been accidentally holding her breath and had toppled out of her crib.

Culis roused immediately and struck a flint to light a lantern. "Mila, what...?"

He took one bleary look at her anguished expression and leapt from his own bed to be beside her in an instant.

"What's the matter?" he asked softly, brushing wet hair from her sweaty forehead. "What happened? A nightmare?"

Mila just shook her head, and to her horror, as she sucked in another breath, she began to shake uncontrollably.

"Hey...hey. It's okay." Culis asked no further questions. Instead, he sat on the floor behind her and pulled her up against him, at the same time taking the blanket from her bed and wrapping it around both of them.

With the heat of his chest against her back, and the pressure of his arms wrapped around her, his energy sank into her, uninhibited. It was so strong and powerful that, for a moment, every fear and horrid thought of the evening was utterly swept away.

Care, concern, attachment, fear.

It flowed into her with the heat of a raging furnace.

Are you alright? his energy silently implored. *Please be alright.*

Mila sent her power greedily hunting through his body, searching deeper, seeking any indication that this concern was born of selfish reasons, perhaps out of fear for the success of his demon trade.

It wasn't, she realised with relief, as she found not an ounce of selfishness inside of him at this moment. This wasn't the same fake pretence or care that he'd shown Jezebel. *This was genuine.*

The cold and hard thing that had been curled up defensively around her stomach began to relax its grip and unwind a little. Eventually, she was able to steady herself and felt her breathing return to normal. She pressed herself into the circle of his arms and allowed herself to enjoy it, closing her eyes and resting her head against his shoulder.

"Do you want to talk about it?" he asked softly against her ear after a little time had passed.

"Maybe one day," she whispered back and felt him nod above her.

"Do you want to get back into your bed?" He seemed hesitant, his energy thrumming through her with his true intent: *Don't go, don't move. I'm enjoying holding you*. His thumb slowly stroked the back of her hand in a wide circle. "Or do you want to stay here?" *With me,* his voiceless energy beseeched her.

Mila felt the stirring of heat in a place low in her belly as her body responded to an invitation she'd never expected to receive, or to want.

But she did want it.

Didn't she? She didn't know what she wanted. A large part of her wanted to lie here and investigate this new development, to luxuriate in the ease of her new access to him and enjoy his protective, caring energy. Perhaps explore the way it was transitioning into an appreciation for the smell of her hair and the feel of her body.

The other part of her knew that, despite her undeniable attraction to the man, she still had some ways to go before she could trust him, and when the vasium necklace reminded her of its presence by bumping gently against her neck, she made up her mind.

"I probably should get some sleep."

Even still, it was a slow extrication from his arms, and when she finally stood up, he seemed loath to remove his hands from her.

When he finally did break contact, the absence of his energy was a cool shock to her system. Mila regretfully rolled herself onto her own mattress, and Culis made a show of pulling up the blanket and tucking her in firmly, overdoing it to the point that Mila couldn't help but burst out laughing.

"Thank you," she said softly, watching as he finally returned to his own side of the room.

"You're not the only one haunted by the past," he said softly. "In my experience, sometimes it helps to have some human connection to help pull you through it."

She let him believe it was a flashback, grateful that she didn't have to explain that it had been more like a premonition – a horrifying mental image of her standing naked before Midas, her body drenched in rubane-infused oil, watching his hand descend towards her.

Reminisciary

Mila was exhausted the following day. She also found herself uncharacteristically emotional, as though her revelations of the previous evening had broken something within her.

Culis, watched her with concern in his eyes, but he didn't pester her with questions, for which she was grateful. Instead, he took care of her in his own quiet way, ensuring that her glass never ran dry and that her seat in the next tavern was not facing into the glare of the sun while he conducted his daily business. The quiet comfort of his attention was very welcome.

That evening, when the last negotiation finished, rather than retiring to their cabins at The Drunken Sailor, he led her out into the dark street and the hot evening air.

"Where are we going?" she asked.

"It's been a long couple of weeks. All work, no play. I figure a break in the usual routine might be just what we both need. Trust me." He added the last in response to her sceptical gaze.

They made their way down a number of well-lit streets and into Billiard, the education quarter of the city. Here, the buildings on either side of the street were tiny, white terraces that were used as sharehouses for students at the university. They stood in varying stages of neglect, having been rented out over decades by hordes of young men and women who were more preoccupied with their studies than household husbandry.

However, despite the unkempt appearance of the streets, Mila did not feel at risk there. The energy of this area was akin to what she felt in the Highlands. One of community. Perhaps because students were often poor, and good relationships with one's neighbours was a legitimate form of currency here.

They stopped at a corner to buy a small, student dinner, which consisted only of a thick sausage and a slice of doughy bread. It was simple, but delicious, and Mila used the bread to mop up every drop of hot grease that dripped from the meat as she ate. They were passed by crowds of drunken university students, who sought revelry in whatever ways they could within the confines of the law.

When the next wave of students threatened to separate them, Culis took her hand in his. It was warm and firm, with callouses along its ridges, both from ship ropes and frequent use of a pen. It was comforting that he'd reached for her to keep her safe and close in the crowd, and she was also overjoyed at the opportunity to read him again.

His energy tonight was as complicated as she'd expected it to be. He was feeling wary and cautious in their current surroundings, but also...jealousy? Something to do with the youth and exuberance of the students perhaps? Their zest for new experiences that Culis had long since grown bored of?

He was also still feeling protective of her. Interesting. It had certainly affected him to see her so distressed last night, and he'd been affected by her story.

When they finally arrived at the tavern Culis had been steering them towards, Mila couldn't see what was so different about it besides the fact that there seemed to be large crowds in front of it, and relatively few people actually inside.

Culis pushed through the line of people waiting, dragging Mila along behind him. A few people voiced their protestation, but most seemed to recognise him and let him pass without issue.

Inside, the tavern was drab, made up of just a few plain wooden tables and peeling wallpaper. An old man in the corner played a piano that was in sore need of a tune, or a new player. There were very few people actually sitting and drinking, and those who were seemed far older than the crowd outside, most sitting alone, large red noses hanging over warm mugs full of sour beer.

"Why are we here?" She turned to Culis, puzzled.

"I asked you to trust me," he said with a grin, clearly enjoying her confusion. "I ask it of you still."

"Trust is earned," she replied.

Culis let out a long-suffering sigh. "You're a hard taskmaster, little demon. Lord knows why I endeavour to earn it from you. But I do."

"Do you?" she challenged, genuinely surprised.

"Of course," he replied, equally surprised by her question. "I'm a little hurt that isn't obvious by now."

She wished she was still holding his hand to determine whether he was telling the truth or not. Regardless, she followed him out of the main room and down a staircase into a dingy-looking bathroom.

It stank.

"Culis..." she warned.

"Trust," was all he replied with a sly smile, and then gestured that she should enter a tiny, dirty stall on her left.

"What?"

"Please."

She glared at him but noted the rarity of his use of that word.

She took a deep breath and went into the appalling stall. Culis followed and closed the door behind them. It was a tiny space, and in an effort to avoid standing too close to the filthy latrine behind her, she pressed into his chest. He casually wrapped an arm around her shoulders as he leaned forward and pulled down on a small rusty lever behind her head.

His energy was far simpler now. *Pure joy.*

On the other side of the door, Mila heard a heavy grinding noise. She would have jumped if she hadn't been in his tight embrace, but she found it surprisingly grounding to be so close to him, especially with him feeling so happy. It was catching. Impossible to be frightened.

When the grinding noise stopped, Culis unlatched the door and walked out of the stall, tugging Mila behind him.

Incredibly, the dingy bathroom was gone, and in its place was a far cleaner, but still considerably bare, stone room. This room was occupied by a tall man, who looked like security, and a plump, jolly woman, who appeared in her late sixties and stood behind a table that had a book and a box on it.

"Master Christopher!" she exclaimed when she saw them. "How wonderful to have you in our fine establishment once again."

"Alita." He greeted her with a kiss to the cheeks. "You know the pleasure is all mine."

He introduced Mila, and Alita held out the book. "You'll both need to sign in."

Mila copied Culis as he placed his thumb onto an ink pad and pressed the black thumbprint beside his name in the book.

"It's insurance," Alita said in response to Mila's silent question. "If I find out that anyone from tonight gets reported, then this page of the book gets handed in, and everyone gets reported. One in, all in."

"This is Reminisciary," Culis explained. "A club you can only find if you know where it is, and a place where anyone can come and commit the Heretical Behaviours without fear of arrest and punishment. We wear these to stay anonymous inside." He handed her a fox mask and took a dark ram skull mask for himself. "But Alita here knows who everyone is, and what night they attended through the fingerprinting system. It helps to deter anyone who feels inclined to report anything that goes on inside to the Church."

"That's clever." Mila tied the mask in place and looked up at Culis, who had just placed his own.

"What do you think?" He gestured to the awful, dark mask that came complete with ram horns whirling out the side. "Now I have horns just like you!"

"Excuse me!" Mila was caught between laughter and indignation. "My horns are nothing like those monstrosities."

"No, to be fair, they're quite dainty. More like antlers than horns."

"*Antlers?*" She was outraged.

"Maybe that's how we change the public perception of demons," he continued to tease as he hustled her into the club, brushing aside layers of thick curtains. She heard faint music ahead. "Stop referring to them as horns and just tell everyone you're as sweet and innocent as a cute little woodland deer."

Mila opened her mouth to protest, but her words were washed away by the wall of music and energy that hit them when they pushed through the final thick curtain.

Dancing.

People were *dancing.*

Impossible.

She still remembered the scolding and sermon she'd received as a child from an acolyte of Prious when she'd been caught skipping with joy along the path home.

As a continued act of contrition for our blasphemous uprising against the Lord our God-King Midas, it is expressly forbidden to dance or frolic with joy in a public setting. All citizens of Artor – yes, Mila, even you – must, at all times, remain demure and restrained, weighed down with the heavy yoke of knowledge that our mundane and fallible eyes did not recognise the Master of our Souls when he emerged from the sea. It was an act of ignorance that will take the contrition of many generations before we may be forgiven.

Acts of dancing, revelry, festivals or celebrations were listed as the Second Heretical Behaviour, which, especially for those to whom the order was important, made the act of public dancing even more sacrilegious than other acts such as blaspheming, or harbouring a heretic.

And yet.

Time stood still as Mila surveyed the scene before her. The entire tavern floor was filled with the sweaty press of half-naked bodies, humans masked as animals, dancing decadently in sheer jubilation to a pounding drum beat and ecstatic duelling fiddles.

To the sides, the room was adorned with plush booths stuffed full of people talking animatedly, gesticulating wildly. Above them on the walls, and from the ceiling, hung all manner of idols: tree gods, goat gods, harvest gods, childbirth gods. It was unlikely anyone was using this space as a place of worship to any of the assorted deities peering down, but their presence was indicator enough. This was a place that celebrated heresy.

Mila looked up at Culis, who smiled broadly when he saw her open mouth. "How does a place like this exist?"

"Who cares?" he yelled back over the din. "Come have fun!" And with that, he grabbed her hands and whirled her into the swaying and stamping crush of the dance floor.

Mila had never felt anything like it. Her body and mind were seized by the energy of those around her, and for once, she didn't resist, losing herself utterly in it all, pulsing and pushing against the bodies around her. It was intoxicating, consuming, as though she had drunk lava and the heat of it had spread into the very fibres of her body.

A woman in a butterfly mask seized her and twirled her incessantly until she felt as though she might be sick. She stumbled when she was released and was caught up immediately in the arms of a lion man, whose muscles gleamed with sweat as he lifted her above his head. He deftly flipped her, catching her on the way down, as though she were nothing more than a rag doll.

Another man in the mask of a stag grabbed her, placed one hand around her waist, while the other caught her hand. The two of them galloped around the room, feet striking the boards in perfect time with the banging of the drums, sending sensations unlike anything Mila had ever felt before flooding through her.

Fun, she realised. This was what it meant to have *fun* and not feel guilty about it. This was something that had been denied and beaten out of the entire nation. No wonder pockets of rebellion like this existed. It was an intoxicating feeling, all-consuming. She felt as though she was high. She wasn't an individual anymore; she *was* the room, *was* the music, *was* the dance.

And then, the dark ram skull mask appeared before her. Culis reached out and drew her away from her partner, claiming her as his own, and they danced a different dance. Less vigorous, but no less energetic.

He caught her up with a hand behind her head, fingers tangling into her hair. His other hand found her waist, drawing her close, coaxing her to lean back into a dip as she'd seen other couples doing. She submitted, trusting him to catch her, and he did, holding her there for a moment, staring into her eyes.

Mila felt her stomach clench as she lay in his arms and stared back. That bubble of heat she'd felt the previous night now stoked, a new kind of fire awakened in her belly, something she hadn't felt since Cari. She felt it rise in him too – *heat, a need to claim, to touch.*

He hauled her back onto her feet abruptly, and together, they stood still amongst the swirling bodies. His eyes never left hers as he ran his hands over her arms, her neck, her jaw. His touch felt hot.

For a moment, the dark mask was so close to hers that she could feel the heat of his breath against her cheek, her lips. She wondered if he would kiss her – desperately hoped that he would – and then the music changed to an upbeat gypsy tune, and a fat, raucous woman and her tiny partner began to waltz violently around the room. They bumped heavily into Culis and Mila, apologising profusely, and though Culis's touch still seared as he reached out to steady Mila, the moment between them was gone.

He stepped back from her with a rueful grin, then took her hands and led her back into a dance. Mila twirled in his arms, submitting to his silent direction and the way he urged her body to whirl this way and that, but always, always caught up in his gaze whenever she returned to centre.

A shout behind them caused Culis to tear his eyes away from hers and peer towards the commotion. When he identified what it was, he looked back at Mila and mouthed over the music, "Come."

She followed him through the dancing bodies, past the crush of people standing amongst the booths, towards one booth in particular that was far more crowded than the others. A man and a woman sat in the middle, and they were talking animatedly, deliberately trying to draw more people over.

"The time is coming to push back! The Church is corrupt and power hungry."

"But it's Midas's word," a voice from the crowd called out. "We know what happens to us if we disobey."

"That's just the point," the woman said with a hiss of excitement. "It *is* Midas's word. And yet the Church picks and chooses how they implement it with astounding irregularity. My mother was there, at the Village of Truth. She knows what was said to us by the God-King, that all laws are to be observed in equal measure, and any who disobeys them should be sacrificed. We heard it again from the princess's own mouth just a few weeks ago."

Something about the name of the village rang a bell in Mila's head, but she couldn't place how she knew it. It also struck her as very odd that this type of discussion was happening in a place that was a literal den of iniquity. But perhaps it really was the only safe place for such speech.

"Abbott and the Church interpret the rules for themselves. The God-King's forgiveness for our nation will never be earned in this way."

Behind Mila, someone in a cat mask was running around and throwing Golden Sand up into the air as though it was glitter, twirling around beneath it as it showered down upon them. Whether it was actually Midas's sand or some kind of replica Mila didn't know, but the implication was obvious, and it made the hypocrisy of the conversation occurring to the other side of her even more pronounced.

She looked over at Culis to see if he was still eager to listen, or if he was ready to return to the dance floor. She'd had enough of religion to last a lifetime and was damned if she'd let it intrude into this night and ruin it for her.

Culis still seemed interested in the conversation but read the expression in her eyes and, with a nod, retreated and drew her back to the dancing.

Eventually, as all good things do, it had to end.

They danced until the early hours of morning, until Mila thought her feet would fall off, and even then, Culis did not hurry her but danced with her until she finally surrendered to the demands of her body to rest. When she finally gave the nod, he led her towards a back door that would lead them out onto the streets. There, they handed back their masks to Alita, who looked Mila over and smiled, glancing at the horns that Mila had not even realised were extended.

She swiftly withdrew them, embarrassed that she'd sought out the pleasure in the room so obviously.

"It's nice to have you here, dear," Alita said kindly. "My old neighbours, Tina and Creo, were ikarei. They were good neighbours. Always happy to look after my young Ferris whenever I needed to travel."

"You know about the ikarei?" Culis asked incredulously.

"Of course," Alita said with a gesture towards Mila. "But it's been a while since I've seen one in this place. It's a nice reminder for those of us who remember those times, to ensure they are not forgotten." She stood on her tiptoes and kissed Mila's sweaty forehead. "Thank you for coming."

Mila felt tears prick in the corners of her eyes. "Thank you," she replied, her voice thick with emotion.

Culis looked down at her with a newfound intensity and she reached out to grasp his arm, unafraid now to touch him. It was a mixed feeling of awe and shame that he felt as he processed Alita's words.

Mila withdrew her hand. "Time to leave," she said, and he nodded, following her out the door.

By the time they finally returned to their inn, the sun was already poking its head over the nearby horizon, and Culis informed her that the carriage to take them home would be arriving in an hour. So, instead of heading to bed, they went to the dining room and ate a greasy breakfast together while they waited.

Mila fell asleep in the carriage almost as soon as she sat down and woke only when it pulled up to the manor.

Groggy and disoriented, she muttered a farewell to Culis and stumbled with relief back to the comfort of her small, cosy room. Up until now, she hadn't realised how much the simple space had come to represent home, and other than Frank Culis's unexpected appearance all those weeks ago, no one had ever intruded into it. It was so good to come back to her own space and be with her own thoughts after weeks on the road, especially after the previous evening.

She snuggled into her own bed and stretched her feet out in it with joy, but before she fell asleep again, her last clear emotion was a deep, aching loneliness.

It felt strange and empty to be in a room that did not have Culis asleep in a bed on the other side of it.

Decisions

The following morning, the air was cool. Autumn had finally arrived.

Mila went out to the garden beside her room and stood in wonder for a long, long time with her bare feet in the cold dew. Back in the Highlands, it was hot year-round with the seasons alternating between wet and dry and the amount of humidity in the air being the main variable. Down here in Jeralusah, there was an actual winter season, albeit it was rather mild compared to the freezing temperatures experienced further south on the continent.

Still, the sensation of this cold air on her skin for the first time in fifteen years drew complicated memories up from the recesses of Mila's mind.

Her mother braiding her long hair and knitting her a warm woollen cap to keep her ears warm. Her father's bull beef stew warming them after a long, cold day in the field...

She pushed away the nostalgia and tried to focus instead on just the novelty of dry, chilled air against her tanned skin. She breathed it in deeply, letting it hit the back of her throat like soothing honey.

When she grew uncomfortable, she returned to her room and was delighted to find that the hot kitchen hearth on the other side of the stone wall, which usually made her room too hot to be in during summer days, was now the perfect accompaniment to the cool morning and warmed her room gently and invitingly.

There was a new menu in the kitchens now too. One that reflected the ongoing march of the seasons. In the peak summer heat, the food had focused on cool, light and flavoursome foods. Mila had grown used to eating cultured yoghurts with fruits and toasted nuts for most breakfasts, but now she found a thick and creamy porridge bubbling away in an enormous cast-iron cauldron, and the cook had insisted she add to her large bowl lashings of cinnamon and stewed rhubarb. It was delicious. As she ate, she pondered everything that had happened over the previous weeks, and realised she had a huge decision ahead of her.

With a full stomach and busy head, she went to the library. There, she found Culis with Flue, Tarett and Marie. The three ikarei had grown closer to one another in her absence, and they all greeted her cheerfully. Culis nodded at her when she entered but did not break from his deep conversation with Tarett, and her stomach jumped at the sight of him. He was wearing an emerald green overcoat that made his blond hair look gold. His face was alive and animated in conversation. He did not look like he'd just spent the past few weeks on the road. He looked joyful, energised and well-rested. Damn him.

"It went very well," he was saying. "There was a lot of interest, which is obviously a very good sign. The more offers we get, the more selective I can be with the master we accept for each of you." He caught Mila's gaze, grinning. "Ideally, I'd not have you stuck in Mila's position, contracted to a real bastard."

Mila smiled back.

"Oh, the misery of Culis Manor," Tarett lamented playfully, catching the softness in the exchange between them.

When Culis eventually left, Tarett immediately turned to her with a raised eyebrow. "Well?" he opened, with a knowing smile. "Looks like you two managed to hash out your differences." He gave her a cheeky wink. "I don't have your power, Mila, but even I can sense a lot less tension between you two than usual, or perhaps it's a lot more..."

"I don't know what you're talking about," Mila replied, but with horror, she felt heat rising on her neck.

"Travelling alone with the handsome Christopher Culis for two weeks? Come on, Mila." Marie joined the tease. "Don't tell me you didn't ease the loneliness on at least one of the nights?"

"Is that what you think we were doing?" Mila challenged.

Tarett held up his hands in mock submission. "All I know is that ever since I met you, you haven't looked at the man without scowling, but now something in your gaze has changed."

"You're making all of this up." Mila laughed, but urgently tried to change the subject. "I do suspect he may be looking at all of us a little differently now. While we were on the road, I taught him about the ikarei history."

"What's that mean?" Flue asked, and Mila sensed some embarrassment and shame rolling from them as Tarett and Marie exchanged looks of surprise.

"It's okay," she told Flue. "I didn't know about it either for the longest time. It's nothing to feel ashamed about. How is anyone supposed to know when we spend our whole lives surrounded by humans who are forbidden to talk about it?"

"Ahh. Don't you love it when you get a chance to share some important history? To really sink your teeth into the Eighth?" Tarett asked happily, rubbing his hands together.

The four of them spent the rest of the morning and the whole afternoon, with Marie leading the charge, educating Flue and researching everything about ikarei history that they could find in Culis's extensive libraries. Admittedly, there wasn't much, just the occasional reference or phrase here and there. Mila assumed most of the literature and true histories had been destroyed by the Church, but it was still a lovely day, one spent reminding one another of their worth and bonding the small group even closer.

Mila also wanted to use the opportunity to see if she could find any further information about Keras. She wanted to learn as much about that nation as she could, but unfortunately, with the others continually tossing Artor history books at her to thumb through, she quickly put that idea aside for another time.

Culis didn't disturb them, and Tarett mentioned in passing that he'd been summoned to the palace on business for the day.

To her own surprise, Mila felt her stomach clench angrily at that news, knowing that it probably meant that Jezebel had summoned him and the two were together right now. The hot feeling of rage she felt at that knowledge was startling.

Dangerous.

That evening after dinner, while the sun was setting and turning the sky into art, Mila went out into the garden alone.

She took a deep breath and closed her eyes as she listened to the soundtrack of dusk. Hounds bayed as they greeted the rising moon, the murmur behind her of sharp, but not unkind, directions being given in the kitchen, small birds whistling overhead as they prepared for sleep. A flock of bats flew from the forest and in the direction of a vineyard that Mila knew lay beyond the far hill.

The day had been wonderful. Finally home, with friends, spent reading and laughing, and a bubble of heat in her stomach that clenched painfully whenever she thought of Christopher Culis.

But days like today were not reality. Not really. And when she forced herself to consider what reality actually looked like, it really came down to three possible paths.

The first was to stick to the original plan. Flee to Keras at the first available opportunity, maybe take the other demons, including Natalee, with her. It had seemed like the best option for her when she'd first thought of it, but now, the more she dwelled on it, the more she realised that, not only was the plan fraught with danger, but its likelihood for success was very low. She'd have to steal the sister stone from Culis, escape the bustling and guarded manor somehow, trudge by foot to Traders Bay, find and free Natalee – who was somewhere on the sea with Baird – and then find a captain who either didn't know Culis (near impossible) or who didn't want to work with the Artor Trading Company.

Unless she somehow disguised herself, most traders would recognise her by description, if not sight, and she knew Culis wouldn't take kindly to anyone who helped his investment escape.

Culis.

If she escaped, she knew he'd come after her... wouldn't he? He was certainly no fool. He would easily deduce her destination, and he'd use his vast network of connections and spies to help him hunt her down. She wouldn't just be running from him. She'd be running from the entire Artor Trading Company. For a moment, she had a vision of arriving, bedraggled and sea-worn, to a port in Keras, only to see

Christopher Culis's grim expression as he stood, cross-armed, waiting for her at the end of the dock to bring her back.

It was not a pleasant vision, made even less pleasant by the resentful acknowledgement that maybe, just maybe, she didn't actually even want to escape from Culis anymore.

The second option was to stay here in Artor and try to blow open the great deception that had held the nation in a vice-like grip for half a century.

Midas was a fraud, she was almost certain of it now. He was an ikarei who was powerful beyond belief, not a god, and if she could prove it, then she could end the slaughter and suffering of...thousands. She could reshape the future of the entire nation. She cast a half-hearted glance around her to scan for more rubane and saw a couple new tiny, red flowers in the patch closest to the kitchen furnace. But there weren't many, and certainly not enough to distil them into anything useful. If this plan was to work, then she'd need to procure as much of the weed as possible in order to distil it into an effective, wearable ointment. Getting that amount of rubane and dousing the intended sacrifices in it to expose the God-King was no easier task than getting herself to Keras. Death and failure waited for her at every corner of that plan too.

The last option was to do nothing. To accept her fate as it currently stood. To help Culis achieve his goals and possibly change the status quo for demons as a result. Maybe life would get incrementally better for them. If Midas was truly just a demon, then inevitably, he would die one day...wouldn't he? Would that be enough to expose the Church for the farce that it was, or would they devise some kind of explanation for his mortality? Either way, there was a simplicity to this option that was comforting. And it did not require her to do anything brave or stupid; she simply needed to wait.

The third path was the obvious one. It was the way she had always done things – to wait and let the world around her play out as it might.

But tonight, the cool air made her restless, and that choice would not sit easy in her heart.

She'd been a coward too many times in these past months. Been a bystander when she should have taken action to stop a great wrong, and now here was another crossroads, a chance to choose differently. Would she be able to stand being in her own skin if she did nothing but watch, season after season, as another load of sacrifices – demon *or* human – were disintegrated before Midas? Knowing that he was a fraud and that she could have saved them if she'd just had the gumption to try?

How though?

It was too late to do anything about the autumn Sacrament, which she knew must have occurred while she was on the road with Culis, but perhaps she'd be able to get enough rubane to protect the ikarei condemned for the winter one.

She could try and convince Culis to return with her to the Highlands again. The constant heat in that part of the world saw rubane grow prolifically. In her mind's eye, she could picture her tiny house under the bayan trees and all the rubane that threatened to inundate it every year. There'd be more than enough rubane there to achieve this task. But she'd only be able to bring back what she could carry, and that would not be enough. Not for ten people.

Perhaps if Tarett was somehow allowed to come with her? Or perhaps she could infuse it in her home and then bring just the oil back here? Far more economical, but the infusion process could take weeks. How would she be able to do that without explaining everything to Culis?

Culis.

Everything always came back to him.

She hated that her stomach fluttered again as she considered him.

Could she trust him to help? Trust him with the secret of the rubane?

She weighed it up in her mind.

The risk wasn't that he'd be appalled by the idea, or that he'd be against the idea of challenging the Church. He'd proven he was clearly not a devout man, and all things considered, he'd probably find something like this rather fun. No, the risk was that he'd share the secret of the rubane with the humans he was selling demons to, giving them even more power over their slaves. It would prevent folk like Flue from being able to protect themselves, from using their power on their master to keep themselves safe if they needed to.

I'm just scum, he'd said to her in Brewich. *Next time, save yourself the disappointment and don't expect me to ever be anything more than that.*

It frightened her that he could make it so easy to forget that side of him. It was far easier to recall dancing with him in Reminisciary – and the hot thread of desire that had run between them – than to remember the look on his face when he'd ordered Natalee's capture, and the way he'd coldly ignored Mila's pleas for mercy.

Don't expect me ever to be anything more than that.

Despite what she'd felt of his energy, despite the connection that had sparked between them in Traders Bay, she needed to remember that this man was still a seasoned and professional liar, that up until now he'd been propelled through life by the driving energy of his own greed and ambition. Was it reasonable to expect that to have changed over the past few weeks?

No, she decided. He could not be trusted with this information, but she'd have to devise a good lie, because she needed his help. He was a professional merchant, wasn't he? He had the Artor Trading Company at his disposal. Surely, if he thought there was a need for it, he could sequester his entire fleet to obtain tons of rubane.

Yes. If she had Culis's support for this endeavour, then that would be the far more efficient option for obtaining enough of the stuff. All she needed to do was somehow convince the most commercially savvy businessman in the country that it was in his best interest to obtain tremendous amounts of a noxious weed that only grew in the most remote regions of the country. Without him needing to understand why.

Simple, she thought, and then realised she had made her choice.

A Case of Mistaken Identity

"We're going to Traders Bay, we're going to Traders Baaaaaaay!"

Mila sat on her stool by the bench and watched with a big smile as Tarett seized a squealing Tess by the wrists and spun her around the kitchen.

"Finally," Marie said with a quiet, happy sigh from beside Mila, ladling her porridge and hot rhubarb stew into her mouth. "I've always wanted to see it. And I'm excited to finally meet the candidates."

Mila was surprised and grateful that Culis had arranged this short-notice trip for them to meet those competing for the contracts, giving the demons the chance to "sift between the bastards" as he'd referred to it. She was about to reply to Marie when the door to the kitchen banged open and Philomena marched in brusquely.

"Well?" she demanded of them with a smile. "Are you all ready? We're leaving in the next half an hour."

"Argh!" Tess cried out as Tarett accidentally released his grip on her wrists in his excitement and flung her unceremoniously into a sack of flour.

"I'm sorry!" he gasped in mortification, running to help her.

"Get your demonic hides *out* of my kitchen," the cook bellowed, but could not completely hide his grin.

"To Traders Bay!" Tarett crowed as he helped Tess brush flour from her face.

Mila was so distracted with overseeing their departure that she completely missed the arrival of Frank Culis's carriage at the manor.

She didn't remain ignorant of it for long.

The aura of fear and unease that shadowed the serving members of the household exclusively when Frank was in the vicinity was notification enough that he had arrived. As soon as she sensed it, she made the decision to eat lunch in the stables, remaining there with the horses and enjoying their easy energy while she tried to plan her pitch to Culis.

When mid-afternoon hit, her plotting was disrupted by a commotion outside the stable. She heard raised voices, and distinctly made out Culis's sharp words of anger and another man replying in frustration. A few minutes later, she heard a horse being led in and unsaddled in the stall beside her.

The rider muttered and grumbled as he tended to his animal. "Not even my fault."

She stood up and peered over the divider. It was Baird.

She felt a thrill of excitement to see him. She liked Baird, but if he had returned, then it probably meant that Natalee was back, too, and Mila was both eager to finally face the woman and tell her about her new plan.

"Hello, Baird," she said cheerily. "Do you mind toning down the growls over there? The horses and I were having a very pleasant morning before you brought in your thundercloud."

Baird looked startled to see her but couldn't bring himself to even chuckle. His face was black with fury.

"I couldn't have done anything differently," he said bitterly, as though he expected her to already know why he was upset. "When it comes down to the letter of the law, I am a man of the Artor Trading Company, and Frank is the head, not Christopher."

"What are you talking about?" Mila asked, worried now.

"When Frank flags us down, flapping a Divine command in my face, and commands me to hand her over, what else am I supposed to do?"

"Hand *who* over?" she demanded, but she already knew.

Natalee.

"The worst part is that the plan was working. She was enjoying the journey," Baird said with genuine frustration. "I think she would have come around. She even used her powers one night to help me out of an uncomfortable situation on Malahawk Island with one of the local priestesses–"

"How did he find you?" Mila interrupted. "How did he even know she was with you?"

"Spies," was all Baird said, as he rubbed his eyes with both hands.

Mila absorbed this information for a moment. "What does he want with her?"

"He's acting on orders the God-King gave directly to the Artor Trading Company."

Horror shot through her. Why was Midas now suddenly getting involved? By all accounts, he'd been ambivalent about the demon trade, supportive even.

"I figure it's all come from the mind of Jezebel," Baird said to her unasked question. "But I don't know why they wanted Natalee specifically."

"I need to find out what's going on." Mila left Baird and returned to the house, knowing it was probably inevitable that by doing so she'd have to face Frank Culis. But her fury did wonders for reducing her fear.

She found father and son in Culis's study when she burst in without ceremony. Frank whirled around at the intrusion, dagger half unsheathed, but when he saw it was her, he put it back.

Mila felt slighted by the action. If he thought she wasn't angry enough to hurt him, he was sorely misguided.

"What's going on?" she demanded.

"Ah. Here she is." Frank shot an angry look at his son. "The one I was probably *supposed* to seize."

"What are you talking about?"

"Mila," Culis tried to regain control of the room, "please go."

"Tell me what has happened," she said through gritted teeth.

"My, how you allow them to address you, Christopher! When I have my own demon, rest assured, their manners will be – "

"I will be *dead* before I ever see a demon sold to you," Mila hissed.

"Now listen here – "

"*Enough!*" Culis's command silenced them both. "Mila, you may stay, but sit down. Frank, shut up."

For once, Mila and Frank were equally appalled, but in the end, they had no choice but to obey him.

"Now," Culis began once everyone was seated. "Mila. You're not going to like what has happened, but it's done now, and it was commanded by the God-King himself. The Artor Trading Company could not have refused."

"What has happened? Tell me," she demanded.

"The Dusk Ball approaches, and Midas demanded one of my demons as the official sacrifice for the event. In fact, the demand was very specific. He wanted the female demon who was currently on board a ship coming from Malahawk."

"Why her?" Mila asked quietly, letting this information wash over her.

"I suspect it's because," he said with a heavy sigh, "when Baird took Natalee from the manor to the ship, she used her power to look like you."

Mila's heart nearly stopped. "She *what?*"

"She was frightened. She didn't know what we were going to do to her. Perhaps she thought that we were taking her away to kill her and that we'd hesitate if she looked like you? I don't exactly know. But, as it happened, one of the spies must have seen her, and passed word to the palace about her destination...*your* destination."

"It was meant to be me then," she said, ice in her veins. This was Jezebel's punishment for her. "This order from Midas, it's come from Jezebel. She wanted it to be me...but she never learned my name. So, she couldn't ask for me specifically."

"Probably," Culis's father interjected, his hands interlinked behind his head as he leaned back in his chair and surveyed her in a way that made her shudder.

"What is this ball?" she asked Culis, ignoring Frank.

"The Dusk Ball. For one night a year, on the princess's birthday, her select few are permitted to dance and celebrate, but it comes at the cost of a life in sacrifice," Culis explained.

Mila felt as though she'd been punched in the stomach. "That's the most...hypocritical, appalling thing I've ever heard."

"Abbott would agree with you, but Midas himself oversees it, so there's little the High Priest can do," Culis said.

Mila barely heard him. For the rest of Artor, the prohibition against dancing and revelry had transformed many traditional celebrations into sombre events. Harvest festivals across the country were quiet affairs, where dancing had been replaced with much praying and chanting under the glow of elaborate lanterns. Village weddings were observed as long-winded Church services, which often included self-flagellation for the marital couple.

And yet, here in Jeralusah, the holiest place in the entire country, in just a few days, the God-King himself would be presiding over a ball where the elites would dance and celebrate Jezebel's birth, and the sacrifice demanded as payment for the evening of 'sin' would not come from amongst *their* ilk, but from a demon, from *Natalee*.

Mila was sickened.

"And...I assume your name is on the guest list," she accused. "When is it?"

"I have to go," Culis confirmed softly. "My absence would not be excusable. It's five days from now."

Five days? That was nothing. No time at all, and certainly not enough time to go to the Highlands and acquire the rubane she'd need to test her theory...and maybe save Natalee.

"Let it be me instead then," she said simply. "Set Natalee free, and I'll take her place as the sacrifice."

As the words left her mouth, her heart went cold with fear, but something else shifted within her. She was exhausted of being so fearful all the time, sick of looking in the mirror and seeing a coward. She knew she wouldn't be able to live with herself if Natalee was sacrificed in her place and this time she was determined that she would not let fear stop her from doing the right thing.

Culis seemed to think over what she offered, consider it, and then said, "No."

"Why not?" she demanded. "It's me Jezebel wants anyway. She's consumed with jealousy, and this won't end until I'm dead. Send *me* instead, Culis, I beg you."

Again, he surveyed her with his piercing eyes for a long moment and then brusquely turned back to his papers. "I don't know if you realise exactly how much I paid to buy you from Jezebel, but it was an astronomical sum. I obtained Natalee for free. This makes far more economic sense."

"Please don't do this." Her heart was in her mouth. "You know she doesn't deserve this fate. She's only here at all because of your pride. Don't punish her for that."

He continued firmly, as if she hadn't spoken. "I'm comfortable with following the order to the letter and giving them the demon they requested."

"Even you," she hissed, her breath heaving as her temper rose, "even you, *surely*, can see how wrong this is."

"Do not argue any further with me, Mila. This is my decision."

Desperate, she tried another angle. "This is not just a decision to toss a log of wood onto a fire. This is a *life* you are sacrificing. I *know* that means something to you...you are among the very few humans who have ever treated us with civility. Even kindness. You're curious, creative, progressive, intelligent..."

"Is she trying to flirt with you, Christopher?" Frank cut her off with a hearty laugh. "How pitiful."

"Culis, please," Mila pleaded with him.

"Stop – "

"Christopher – "

"Enough, Mila!" His sharp, angry tone shook the room. "No more of this. I'll remind you that your life is not your own; it is mine. I own you, and you are mine to do with as I see fit. And, in this instance, I do not see fit to rectify the princess's mistake!"

Mila stared at him, feeling though she'd been slapped.

Culis stared back at her without expression. His coldness brought tears to her eyes.

I own you. You are mine to do with as I see fit.

Fury rose inside her like a wave. She was furious at him, and furious with herself for feeling so betrayed.

"I...I didn't think it was actually possible to still be disappointed in you," she finally said, the words emerging through gritted teeth. "I think, at some point over the past few weeks, you had me convinced that you were not like this."

"Oh, is this a lovers' spat?" Frank leaned forward onto his elbows in an enthralled display. "How *intriguing*."

"No," Mila and Culis barked simultaneously, and Frank's eyes glistened.

"I'm leaving," Mila spat at them both with disgust. "This room reeks of rotten souls."

Frank Culis's laugh followed her out into the hallway as she slammed the door on them both.

Prison Break

That evening, Mila inspected the small amount of rubane she'd been infusing in the oil since she'd returned from Traders Bay. She tasted a tiny drop of it for potency and shook her head at the bitterness. It was only a very small bottle of oil, perhaps just enough to coat Natalee's face? Rubane was not a hugely potent weed, and when she'd smoked it back in her home in Bori, she'd required bushels of the stuff to really silence the outside world. For Natalee to have a chance at surviving direct skin contact with Midas's touch, it'd have to be an incredibly strong mix. This was a strong enough infusion, but only just.

Fates, this was all wrong. There had to be another way. Something else she could do to save Natalee. She weighed her options and realised there was one thing she hadn't thought of yet.

Breaking her out.

Her heart beat faster in her chest as she considered it.

Yes. It could be done. But only before Culis increased security, which he would almost certainly do now that he knew how angry she was about this plan.

She had no time to waste. If this was going to be successful, then she had to break Natalee out immediately.

Mila left her room and began her hunt for the imprisoned demon. It wasn't difficult to find her. She was being held in the only lock-up that existed in the basement of the manor, and when Mila arrived, she found her guarded only by Baird, who greeted her with a sorrowful, close-lipped smile.

She felt a twinge of guilt for what she was about to do to him. Of all the guards and staff of Culis's household, Baird was easily the friendliest, but at this point, she had run out of options, especially when he followed her inside and made no signs of leaving, denying her and Natalee any privacy.

The raven-haired Natalee did not look up from the parchment she had been painting on, and didn't miss a beat at the sound of approaching footsteps.

"Hello, Natalee, you stubborn cow," Mila said, spitting the words with vehemence as she approached the bars. She needed to start this fight quickly and she did not have a lot of time.

Natalee looked up, clearly shocked at Mila's presence and her unexpected tone.

Mila didn't hesitate. "Look at the mess you've made of this. If you had just trusted me at the start, then *all* of this could have been avoided. Now you'll be sacrificed at the Dusk Ball in a few days, and I'll have to start all over again, trudging through the Highlands, trying to find a new demon who's not as pigheaded as you."

Natalee's face went pale, and Mila realised she hadn't been told about her upcoming fate yet. She felt terrible that this was how the news was being broken to her, but it was too late to stop.

"Just as well that I won't have to waste any more time talking to Culis about your unappreciative – "

"Don't talk to me about being unappreciative." Natalee broke her staunch silence and threw herself against the bars, sneering at Mila, her face only inches away. "This is how you treat me? After all I've done for you – "

Mila scoffed with indignation. "I've been trying to *help* our people. If you weren't so blind, or so damn self-righteous – "

"Hey now!" Baird called out and started to walk over. He was completely ignored by both women.

Mila reached through the bars and snatched at Natalee's hair, yanking it forcefully.

Natalee yelped at the unexpected violence, and then her rage blossomed, and she reached for Mila's clothes, in the same instant Baird put his hand on Mila's shoulder, trying to break up the fight.

Mila did not hesitate. She released Natalee, and in the same breath, threw her hands over her right shoulder, grasping Baird's head from behind her. In one swift movement, she drew down her elbows and smashed his head forward into the bars, driving her right shoulder down into his abdomen. She heard the air fly out of him at the force of the simultaneous impact on both his head and stomach.

Despite the surprise of the assault, Baird was well-trained, and a huge man. He was stunned for only an instant, and it quickly became apparent that Mila's slight weight pulling his head into the bars, no matter her determination, wasn't forceful enough to knock him unconscious.

He reared back, trying to gain distance from her, when suddenly, Natalee's hands snaked through the bars, joining Mila's behind the unfortunate man's head and yanking it forward into the bars again.

She'd figured out what Mila was trying to do, and now she was helping, driving Baird's head forward and smashing it into the bars again and again. And again.

"I'm sure my son would rather you didn't kill his best man, if it's all the same to you." A bored drawl from behind them interrupted the beating.

Mila's heart instantly sank with recognition when she heard it, not even needing to look up to know the owner.

Frank.

Natalee paused and glanced up. Whatever she saw over Mila's shoulder was enough to make her release Baird's head and sigh with resignation.

Baird's limp body slid with a solid *thud* to the floor, and Mila winced in pity. She didn't want to turn around and look Frank in the eye.

Instead, she stared intently at Natalee and used the opportunity to whisper, "I promise I will fix this," then she stepped away from both Baird and the cage and threw her arms up to show she was unarmed.

She was seized roughly by a guard, who spun her around to face Frank, forcing her painfully onto her knees. Another guard pushed past her to check on Baird.

Culis also chose that moment to appear.

"What's going on?" he demanded, surveying the scene before him in confusion.

"He'll live," the guard pronounced from behind her, "just out cold."

Culis's eyes widened when he realised who the casualty was. He turned a hard glare onto Mila, as he put two and two together.

"Well, well," he said in a cool, disgusted voice. "Who'd have thought you'd have such a violent little streak in you, after all?" He knelt and inspected Baird's battered face. "After all I've done to try and keep you safe, this is what you do to a member of my household?"

"Guess you don't know your *property* as well as you thought you did," Mila shot back.

Culis stood up, looking at her in anger. "Take him to the infirmary, Gus. Quickly."

There was a bustle of movement as he was instantly obeyed by the other guards in the room. They propped Baird's limp body up between them, and Mila could sense their seething anger directed towards her.

She realised then, that in her panic to make haste and rescue Natalee, she'd made a real mistake. If she'd just taken a few more hours to plan this out a little better, then perhaps she could have come up with something more effective and less violent, a sleeping draught in Baird's cup perhaps? She liked Baird, and he was evidently held in high esteem by all other members of the household. This plan had failed, and it had earned her no allies.

Mila watched guiltily as they gently moved the unconscious man's body past her.

"Wait," Culis suddenly ordered.

The men carrying him paused.

Culis stalked over, reached into Baird's shirt, drawing out a key on a chain. The key to Natalee's cage – the object of Mila's failed rescue attempt.

Culis placed the chain over his own head, then nodded for the guards to continue on.

Finally, it was just the two Culis men, Mila and Natalee left in the basement. She wondered what would happen next. Would she be placed in a cell herself?

Culis seemed to be considering the same thing and came to that very conclusion. He opened the door to the other cell and gave her a mockingly low bow. "Your new chambers."

Mila went in without argument and flinched as the door clanged violently behind her. Culis was obviously deeply hurt by her actions, and she hated that it bothered her. She didn't want to waste another second of her life caring about a man who, an hour ago, had told her in no uncertain terms what she was to him.

His slave. Nothing more.

"So," Natalee said softly after everyone finally left. "I'm to be sacrificed at the Dusk Ball, is it? Not really the way I thought it would go, but at least it sounds like there might be some dancing involved."

Mila couldn't even bring herself to look at the woman. "I begged him," she said, hating that a small sob escaped her. "Begged him to let me take your place. It shouldn't be you."

"Shouldn't it?" Natalee asked unexpectedly.

"Of course not! It's my fault you're here at all! I exposed you in Brewich, and you were taken against your will. Without my interference, you'd still be safe."

"Perhaps. Still skulking in shadows and eating refuse from garbage piles to stay inconspicuous. Or perhaps I'd have been found anyway. Perhaps I'd be in a different dungeon, waiting for the Sacrament this winter."

"You can't know any of that for sure."

"Just as you couldn't have known that Culis was not going to keep his word when you came to find me," Natalee said firmly. "Look. I was furious with you when it happened, but going on that voyage with Baird was...the best thing that's ever happened to me. I was able to use my power to *help* people. I saw more of the world than I ever believed possible. It's huge, Mila! It's an enormous place, with endless seas, and many, many hundreds of different nations. My only regret is that I could only experience it for a few weeks before I was dragged rather unceremoniously back here by the Divine command. But my point is it made me realise that you were right to come find me and try to convince me to seek out something more, something different for demons. There's so much more for us out there than a life of hiding in Artor, trying to avoid detection. I am...grateful that I was able to experience it. Even if it led to this outcome."

Mila didn't know what to say. She was overwhelmed by the grace Natalee was showing her. She was about to reply, to tell Natalee about the rubane and her plan, when the main door of the basement swung open again, and Frank Culis re-entered.

He said nothing, but simply stalked over, unlocked Mila's cell, and drew her out roughly by the arm.

"Hey!" she cried out, fighting him. "What are you doing?"

"Where are you taking her?" Natalee demanded.

"Silence." Frank shook Mila as a dog shakes a rat. With his hand against her skin like this, she could clearly feel his energy. It was cold, proud and pragmatic, as though he believed that whatever was about to happen to her was long overdue.

She'd felt that same combination once before, in a villager determined to drown a sack full of kittens.

"Where are you taking me?" she cried out fearfully.

"You've attacked a member of the household. That has consequences."

Mila was not small, but despite the weight and muscle she'd been starting to recoup since living at Culis Manor, she was hardly a match for the tall and powerful Frank. Still, she fought against him every step of the way until the moment that they were out of the basement and back in the house.

The sun had started to rise, and in the dim, grey light that filtered through the windows, she could see some members of the household waiting, lined up in the corridors Frank was dragging her down. That was when she realised, this wasn't just Frank's punishment for her, it was a household punishment. She could read it in their eyes and feel the anger rising from them like steam as she passed between them.

I'm not a terrible person. She wished she could tell them. *I was trying to save Natalee.*

She scanned their faces as she passed through them, hunting for a sympathetic energy, for someone to help her.

Nothing.

When she saw the kitchen staff in the crowd and felt their fury, especially the cook's, all hope fled, and she felt real shame. She'd been protected and embraced by that particular group, and she'd repaid their trust and kindness by attacking a member of their family. She also balked when she saw Nemecca and Arran in the crowd. Their furious faces glared silently at her as she was dragged past them. Likewise, Corbyn and Black Berran, who stood further down the line, did not lift a finger to help.

She stopped fighting.

"Christopher Culis passes his judgement on you, demon." Frank spoke like a judge reading a sentence as he dragged her through the silent tunnel of people.

Culis himself was not present. Clearly, he couldn't bear to even look at her.

Finally, Frank dragged her out of the manor and away from the silent line of angry staff. He led her to the stables, gave a curt order, and a short minute later, the stable boy brought forward two large horses. Frank mounted one, and Mila did not resist as the stable boy pushed her up onto the other.

If this is what the household wanted, what Culis wanted, then maybe she deserved it.

Frank held her horse's reins tightly and kicked them both forward.

"Where are you taking me?" she asked fearfully.

He did not reply.

Mila's horse was in a light-hearted and curious mood and followed willingly in whatever direction Frank nudged him. They rode in uncomfortable silence for hours.

After a while, it occurred to Mila that Culis must have given his father the sister stone. Nothing else would explain the distance they were comfortably putting between themselves and the manor. That knowledge made her even more uncomfortable. Whatever was happening was obviously endorsed by Culis, but why had he not come to enact this punishment himself? Had her actions truly broken any semblance of a relationship between them?

They passed through a bustling town that Mila did not recognise and eventually rode into a field of crops.

This is where Frank finally halted the huffing horses, commanding Mila to dismount hers. Trembling, she obeyed.

"The manor is that direction," he said coldly, pointing back the way they had come. "Christopher will be travelling to Jeralusah to attend the Dusk Ball in a few days. If you don't make it back to the manor by then, he won't wait."

Mila blinked at him, not understanding.

Frank smiled down at her from his horse, like an vulture looking down at a hare. "It gives me a great deal of satisfaction to know that you'll spend the majority of your next few days crawling on your hands and knees. And I wouldn't dally if I were you. I'm not entirely sure what will happen to you if you don't get back to the manor before Christopher departs but...from here to the Holy City? That's quite an enormous amount of distance for the vasium. Best not find out."

Without another word, he kicked his horse and turned it around, riding back the way he had come. Mila's horse followed without her, and soon they were all out of sight.

She blinked in confusion for a moment, as she stared after them. What was happening?

Then she felt a tug around her neck and realised, with horror, that Frank had the sister stone on him, and he was riding far, far away from her.

Vasium

Fear stabbed through Mila like a knife as she began to sprint after him. She tried to keep up, to match his horse's brisk pace, but with each second of distance that grew between them, she felt the despicable tug of the necklace, pulling her toward the ground.

It was no use. The horse bore Frank swiftly away, and eventually, the pressure around her neck forced Mila to bow her head and resort to moving on her hands and knees, her legs alone unable to withstand the increasing weight.

Frank's parting words, *I'm not entirely sure what will happen to you,* echoed mockingly in her head as she crawled. She scrabbled along desperately, crying in panic, heaving for breath that wouldn't come.

No, no, no. Not like this.

She knew what would happen to her if she got too far away from the sister stone, remembering the power of the necklace she'd felt back in the Highlands.

She'd die out here if she couldn't keep moving, if no one came for her.

Her palms and knees turned bloody as she frantically crawled in the direction Frank had gone. But, despite her fight, inevitably, the weight grew too intense. It made its way from her neck and seeped down into her arms, legs, and spine.

Eventually, exhausted, Mila simply collapsed. And once she was down, there was no hope of her getting back up again.

She lay crushed against the farmed soil in the midday sun and cried in frustration and fear.

She couldn't move.

It was impossible not to panic.

She lay there for hours, weeping and heaving ragged, frenzied breaths of dirt, with her mouth pressed firmly against the ground. Eventually, she tried to prop herself up onto her elbows, so she could wiggle forward, but it was useless. The vasium made it feel as though someone had placed a horse on top of her.

Finally, it was only her extreme thirst and the cool promise of the falling night that prompted her to try something new.

Rather than focusing on what she could not move, she focused on what she still *could* move. She could move her fingers, yes, and her hands. In fact, she could move her arms, so long as she slid them forward through the soil, and didn't try to lift them from the ground. She could do the same with her legs, and she could move her feet back and forth. These realisations strengthened her.

She wasn't trapped. She would be able to move – it just wouldn't be very efficient...or graceful.

Thus, she began the excruciating process of trying to propel herself forward. She drew her arms through the dirt and pushed them above her head, tucking her toes up under her feet, and then, in somewhat of a swimming motion, pushed down with her toes and pulled herself forward with her arms. It only yielded her about ten inches at a time, but she forced herself to focus on the small victory. Ten pulls like that, and she'd be half a body-length closer to the manor.

And every body-length closer would marginally lighten the invisible weights that rode her bones. This was a task that would get less arduous over time, she tried to reassure herself.

She was desperately thirsty, but to dwell on that was to waste precious energy. It was either lie in that field and die, or keep moving, and Mila wanted to live.

* * *

More than once, she thought she might die that night; however, when she found herself still alive as the sun began to rise and tenderly pool its light across the morning sky, she felt a renewed sense of hope.

It had been the loneliest and longest night of her life, with the bugs and some curious hares being the only witnesses to her misery. She'd pulled herself inch by painful inch through the field, with the only break in the monotony being when she found a running irrigation creek at the end of the paddock, where she could drink her desperate fill.

She tried to reassure herself that Frank would surely leave the sister stone at the manor for Culis now that the punishment had been implemented. It appeared that she was right, for by the time the sun began to rise, she'd closed the distance in that direction enough for her to lift her head up off the dirt and pull herself up onto her elbows. This was a huge victory, as it made movement significantly easier.

Mila found herself making half-decent progress for a few hours. At midmorning, she eventually reached the shade of a tree, where she decided to finally rest.

Full exposure to the sun in the heat of the day, despite the autumn cool air, would still be punishing, and she had no water. Also, she was afraid of humans at the best of times, but in her current state, she was terrified of someone finding her. Ahead, she could see the fuzzy outline of the town. She figured if she started pulling herself from this tree in the early afternoon, she'd reach town by nightfall, giving her the cover of darkness to disguise her condition as she navigated it.

She slept soundly under the tree, exhausted by her efforts, and cursed herself when she finally awoke, having accidentally slept far longer than she'd intended. Dusk was now well upon her.

She sighed and recommenced the frustratingly slow movement towards town, muscles aching after her sleep, protesting the repetitive, unnatural and punishing actions. She tore the sleeves off her shirt to wrap around her elbows, which were fast transitioning from hot, red grazes into open wounds. Despite her agony, she continued, steeling her mind against the pain. With every pull, the town came slightly closer, and she focused all her energy on cursing Culis.

Her instincts had been right. He couldn't be trusted. She was so glad she'd not told him about the rubane, hadn't let that glimpse into his energy soften her towards him too much.

She felt so betrayed. The fact that Frank had both the key to her cell and the sister stone was evidence enough that Culis had told his father to do this to her, or had at least agreed with Frank that this torture was a suitable punishment for her attack on Baird. To know he could feel that deep, protective energy that she'd sensed from him in Traders Bay, and could still do this to her? It was terrifying. He was indeed the monster she'd once thought him to be.

When she reached the edge of the town, it was blissfully dark. She still wasn't quite able to move on hands and knees yet, but the weight upon her body had lightened enough that she could alternate between reaching forward on her injured forearms, and occasionally using the palms of her hands. The ability to vary her technique and rest one part of her body at a time was a small blessing.

The town roads were another challenge. Initially, she almost cried with relief when she transitioned from the brutal soil with its small rocks and thorns, to the smooth cobbles of the road. It felt like velvet in comparison.

For a moment, she lay on her back and breathed heavily, luxuriating in the success of having made it this far, but it didn't take long for her to realise that the roads would bring a new issue.

The streets ran through the town like tunnels in a rabbit warren, and picking her way through the winding, nonsensical layout was a whole new different kind of torture. Too many times, she fought her way down a long street, only to find that it was a cul-de-sac, and she could go no further. It was both utterly infuriating and also drove deeper the dagger of hopeless despair.

She'd never be out of the town before sunrise, and what would happen to her when the people of the town saw her in this condition? What if she was detained and couldn't complete her task?

She was just about to give up when, somehow, she stumbled onto the main street of the town – a completely straight road that ran north as far as the eye could see.

This was it. She might have cried with relief if her body had any water to spare.

Mila pulled herself eagerly along it, anxious to have the town far behind her before sunbreak.

Her hopes were rewarded by the incremental lightening of the necklace around her neck. It was with great joy that she found after a short while that she could finally push herself completely up onto her hands and knees to crawl properly.

Finally, an efficient method of movement.

She didn't care for a moment if she looked ungainly. She crawled as swiftly along the street as a rat scarpers through a sewer pipe, and with relief, it occurred to her that, once she was out of this town, the worst would probably be behind her.

She was going to make it. She was going to survive this!

And then she heard a voice.

"Enough! Get out of here, Kevin!" It was a young woman's shrill tone, followed by the slam of a door that echoed down the road.

Mila froze. A young man tumbled out onto the street, wiping his mouth, as though recovering from a slap. He staggered a little, and Mila didn't need her power to discern that he was spectacularly drunk.

"You whoreeee," he yelled out, facing the window of the house he'd just been ejected from. "We all know you'll get it on with any man who so much as winks at ya...so why not meeee? You whoooooreeee." He turned away from the house, muttering to himself furiously. "Why not me?"

Then he spotted Mila.

"And what do we 'ave here?"

Her blood froze. Even if he hadn't been a jilted drunk, she still would have been wary around him. His energy was cocksure, arrogant and mean.

"Why ya crawling around over here, miss?" He sauntered over to her like a stalking hyena. "Ya dropped something?" He came closer and saw her bloody forearms. "Ya crippled or somethin'?"

Mila ignored him, hoping her lack of attention would make him go away. But she could sense his sly curiosity, and also his eagerness for some entertainment.

She trembled when he walked up beside her and placed his cold hand on her back.

"Reckon you might stand up now, if yer able to."

"Don't touch me," she said sternly, with as much authority as she could muster.

This was a nightmare. She couldn't run away. She'd barely be able to fight him. She was more helpless than she'd ever been in her life.

"Not able to then, eh? Ya stuck like this?" He laughed.

"I'm playing a game," she lied bravely. "With my brothers. And if they find you harassing me, you'll be sorry."

For half a second, she felt his resolve falter, but then he looked around the dead-silent street and gave a little chuckle before unzipping his trousers.

"Nah, I reckon yer lying. An' if yer not? Well, all the more reason for us ter get this over with quickly, eh?"

His stinking hand came over her mouth in an attempt to cut off her scream. She bit it hard, drawing blood. He smacked her in the face in retaliation, and she struck her head hard on the cobbles.

He swore loudly and shook his hand, as if to shake away the pain. "Come 'ere!" he roared, reaching for her again.

Mila tried to scream, but he kicked her soundly in the gut, winding her so fiercely that she saw black spots appear before her eyes.

Fighting for breath, she was vaguely aware of his hands ripping away the last of the fabric of her ruined trousers. She heard a high-pitched keening sound, but she couldn't orientate to where it was coming from. The crack of her head against the cobbles, following the day of fear, pain and exhaustion, was too much.

Blearily, slowly, she realised that the keening sound was coming from her own mouth, and she managed to make it stop.

At about the same time, she became aware that something else was now going on above her.

The drunk man had stopped touching her, and someone else was talking.

"I think that's quite enough, even for such a foul excuse of a man," came the hard, angry voice.

"Aye, yer her brother, eh? She said ya'd be around. I didna mean no – "

"Leave. Now."

"I didna mean – Aaargh!"

Mila saw a flash and realised it was a sword. The drunk man screamed and fled, clearly injured.

Her saviour bent down. "Mila...Mila are you alright?"

She blinked the fuzziness away from her eyes, and for an instant thought she must be hallucinating.

It was Culis, kneeling next to her with grave concern written all over his face.

She groaned and tried to sit up but couldn't with the crushing pressure of the necklace around her throat, despite his closeness.

"How?" she croaked, touching her throat. Shouldn't he have the sister stone with him?"

"I'm sorry. I don't have it," Culis's voice was flat and low with barely restrained fury. "Frank knew I'd come for you when I found out, so he's hidden it somewhere in the manor. Mila, I'm so sorry. This – " he surveyed her, " – this is horrific."

"I hate you," she managed to choke out.

He nodded seriously. "That's okay. When you're safely home, you can hate me all you need, unobstructed. But, for the moment, let me help you. The vasium only affects your sense of your own weight. It won't affect my strength."

He bent down, reached for her, and before she could resist, he carefully picked her up and carried her towards his horse, a bay gelding standing patiently to the side. His determined energy assaulted her senses with his sudden contact.

"Culis!" she shrieked in mortification, beginning to cry, her shame and exhaustion overtaking her. "I have no trousers."

"Oh, Mila. Oh no, I'm so sorry." He put her down and without hesitation, swiftly stripped off his own. He stood before her in the street, in just his underwear, and handed them to her. "Here. Put these on."

"What a gentleman." She tried not to sneer, still crying as she pulled them on, feeling hysterical.

"Now come, let me get you up onto Orion."

"Don't touch me."

"Please, Mila, let me help."

"Don't touch me!" she screamed at him, overwhelmed.

How dare he be here now, with concern written all over his face? How dare he be distressed about this punishment he'd ordered? She felt so betrayed, so foolish, so terrified of him and the way he could feel one thing for her and still do something so awful.

"I trusted you," she said, hating the fact that she couldn't stop crying.

"I came for you the moment I heard what he'd done," Culis said softly, kneeling beside her but not daring to touch her, even though it looked like he desperately wanted to. "I've been searching for you all night, as soon as I got it out of Nemecca."

It took a long while for his words to make sense to her brain.

"So this wasn't...you didn't...you didn't order this?" she garbled.

"Mila," Culis said, "this is sadistic. I would never have demanded this. I intended to keep you locked in the cell for a few days. That's it, I swear. Please, read me. You know what I'm saying is true."

"I can't," she growled softly, hating that this was how this secret was coming out.

"You can't what?"

She let a long breath out. "I can't read you. I don't know if you're lying or telling the truth."

His eyes widened. "You can't sense my energy?"

"I can. But...only when I'm touching you. You and your father are exceptions to my power. I'm not sure why. A unique trait of a horrid, deceitful family, I assume."

Culis closed his eyes and then, to her utter surprise, began to laugh.

"What's so funny?" she demanded.

"Are you telling me that, for months, I've been assuming we were having something akin to a silent, one-way conversation? That while I've thought you were reading my energy and understanding my true intentions, in reality, I've been doing the equivalent of talking to a brick wall?"

"I...yes. I guess I am."

Culis's deep belly laugh rolled through the quiet street. Mila just stared at him as though he'd gone mad.

"Oh my," he finally heaved. "This explains so much." He held out his hand and looked imploringly at her. "Mila, please. For the love of all things good, please take my hand."

As soon as her skin touched his, the flood gates opened, and his powerful energy bombarded her again. She marvelled at the way her power didn't need to scan or hunt through him for answers as it did with others. With him, when they touched, it was as though she could simply absorb him.

And right now, his energy was thick with *awe*, *appreciation*, and *respect*. He liked her...liked her a *lot*, and he certainly hadn't ordered this punishment. He was horrified and furious, his heart literally aching to see her in this state. His concern and depth of emotion were nearly overriding his good sense. It was taking every inch of his self-control to not reach for her and pull her into his arms.

But he didn't. He didn't want to scare her, didn't want to force her into an embrace she did not want, would surely reject...

"You see?" he said gently. "I might be an accomplished liar, but...I'm not lying about this."

She chuckled wearily and withdrew her hand. "I believe that you didn't know."

"Can I please...can I help? Let me put you on the horse."

Mila finally nodded and let him lift her.

He walked beside them in silence for a few minutes, still touching her thigh with his hand to both steady her and ensure she could read him. Mila did not have the strength to fight the vasium and sit up on Orion, so she lay forward, and the weight of his supporting hand to help her balance was welcome.

After a while, he said, "I underestimated the staff's anger toward you. Not even Nemecca wanted to help me find you. You really couldn't have picked a nicer person to bludgeon than Baird."

"I am sorry for that," Mila murmured. "Not for trying to save Natalee, but for thinking I had to hurt someone else to do it. I panicked."

"I understand," Culis said gravely. "It's Baird and the rest of the household you'll have to convince when we return." There were a few more quiet steps, and then he said, "Actually, the more I think about it, the more it seems possible that my father did this to you because he was trying to help me...maybe help you too."

"What in hell do you mean?" Mila's anger began to rise again. "Culis...I was nearly raped. I've nearly died countless times since he left me in that field. I am wounded and exhausted and starving and thirsty."

"I know, I know," he said quickly. "But you attacked a well-loved member of my household, and I was never going to punish you in a manner that the staff, especially his friends, would accept as satisfactory." He mulled this over for a moment, then said, "Now that I think about it, they almost certainly would have sought retribution on you.

Father realised this." And then said, even more quietly, "He devised this brutal, and very public, scenario to punish you in a manner that would appease them."

"He credited you," Mila realised. "In front of all the staff, he said this was *your* judgement."

Culis was silent as he processed this, and Mila felt his energy respond with a pang of sadness.

"He could have undermined me in my own household," he said slowly. "Could have proclaimed my judgement was clouded by you, or called me weak. But he didn't. He took it upon himself to do this to you in my name, to reinforce my notoriety."

Mila felt the aching pain within him as he spoke, the long-abandoned hope of a boy that his father might love him without conditions, without playing games to make him earn it, or decipher it.

"He's a...complicated man," she finally said. It was the most gracious descriptor she could manage just then.

"He is," Culis agreed, and for a few long minutes, they were silent.

When they passed a tavern, Culis left her for a moment as he ducked in and came out holding a few pints of water for her to drink.

Nothing had ever tasted sweeter.

He waited until she had drunk her fill and then they resumed their trudge again.

"Mila," he eventually said, cautiously. "When we get back to the manor..."

"Your brain is always ticking, isn't it?"

"Never still," he agreed. "And if I've surmised my father's intent correctly, then it'd be a crying shame for my staff to see me bringing you home and have all your suffering account for nothing. So, forgive my ceaselessly scheming brain for just one moment and listen. Once you've recovered some strength and can stand again, what if I was to leave you outside the manor grounds and ride back alone? That way, a few hours later, you can bring yourself home and present yourself to me, ensuring you look suitably bedraggled and contrite. You'll tell your story. Baird's friends will be appeased by the hardship you endured. The staff will gossip about you. There'll be good and bad stories. Mostly, you'll be pitied, but there may even be some admiration. Importantly, no one will feel as though you got off lightly. They may even eventually forgive you."

Mila pondered the idea. "Why can't you just punish me by sending me to the ball in Natalee's stead?" she asked eventually.

"You know why," he replied, his energy shifting from contemplative to something far softer as he gripped her leg more firmly and his thoughts focused on her.

"I don't actually," Mila said. "Not really."

"Fates, Mila." He ran his free hand through his hair in exasperation. "For a demon whose power supposedly makes her the most intuitive, empathetic being on this continent, you're sure being deliberately obtuse. Apparently, you want me to spell it out? Okay." He reached up and Mila let herself be pulled from Orion and back to the ground. Culis knelt with her, looking into her face with determination.

"Look me in the eye, because I don't want you to miss this." He did not take his hands away from her shoulders, needing her to feel the truth of his words. His face was taut. "I am...*so* drawn to you, Mila." His voice was low, but the words were firm and clear. "I have been from the second I met you in that crypt. Like the horizon to a sunset, your pull on me is...frighteningly relentless."

Mila's heart pounded hard in her chest at his words. Was this really happening? Was he really saying this to her with sincerity?

She could sense his energy clearly.

He was.

"I admired your quiet strength in Jezebel's court. The way you never seemed to panic, no matter what was demanded of you. The way you held yourself in the face of your rapidly approaching death. I...I just couldn't look away, and I couldn't bear to see your light extinguished. I told you before we left for Traders Bay that I'd felt compelled to save you from Jezebel for the sake of my conscience. What I didn't tell you was that I knew in my heart that if she hurt you again, I wouldn't be able to stop myself hurting her in return. So, I devised this...insane plan to rescue you and bring you to come live with me at my manor, and although you didn't like me and didn't trust me, you agreed. I told myself that this was good. That I'd use you to start this demon trade and then I'd leave you alone and let you live out your life in peace.

"But the more I learned about you, the less I could keep away. When I saw you all dressed up to come with me to Central, no longer looking like the starved and abused waif, your beauty finally starting to shine through...it took my breath away. And when we went to the Highlands, when you let your protective shell lower and I began to see *you,* it was all over. I was just...lost, enraptured, watching the way you frolicked through that hellscape in sheer delight, the look on your face when you saw Brewich and realised you were home.

"I ruined it all with that terrible decision about Natalee, and even though you hated me and made my life miserable in response, I still couldn't stop thinking about you. I needed to fix things somehow. So, I sent Natalee away with Baird, hoping against all hope that this would mend some of the wrong I'd done by you both. And when you agreed to come to Traders Bay with me...I..."

The intensity of his beautiful eyes was burning. Mila couldn't pull away. The tidal wave of his emotion washed into her, encompassing her.

“I don’t know what it is about you,” he said, “but being in your presence makes me... it doesn’t feel arduous to want to live up to your expectations of me. It feels liberating. So please, please, don’t ask me to let you be the sacrifice at the ball again. There’s not a bone in my body that would obey that command. I’d let them take my entire household, myself included, before I’d let them take you.”

“Culis...” she whispered, running her fingers through his hair, something she’d wanted to do since she met him. Her heart felt so full, but still so unsure of how to respond to such an unexpected declaration. She was indeed drawn to him, but she also had months of deep-rooted distrust weighing her down. Opening herself up to the idea of something deeper would take a level of bravery that she did not have the energy to muster within herself at the moment.

“It’s okay,” he said quietly. “You don’t need to say anything. I understand, more than you know, how difficult it is to trust someone like me. I just needed you to know, you’re perfect for me. And I...I want to put in the work to be the same for you. I want you to read me and know the truth, over and over.” He smiled at her, and it was a beautiful, open, sad smile.

“Perfect?” she teased with a little smile in response. “So, I’m not just a pain in your arse?”

“Speaking of arses...” Culis’s tone lightened as he stood up and hauled her up onto Orion again. “Have you ever seen what you look like from behind? Look, Mila, I could go on about how much I like your humour and your intelligence, and how your sparkling company is worth a room full of gold. But it also doesn’t hurt that you look like a priceless sculpture when you’re bending down, even when you’re shovelling horse shit.”

Mila burst out laughing at that image.

"I'm serious!" Culis said, laughing too. "It's an arse that could be carved from marble."

"Stop," she wheezed.

"I'm not kidding!"

"Okay, okay. Enough."

"No, no," he insisted. "You wanted to hear it, so now you must."

And so it went on like this for hours. With Culis flattering every ridiculous angle he'd ever seen of her since he first met her, and Mila protesting and laughing until breath became painful and she literally had to beg him to stop.

She knew he was doing it, in part, to help her forget the horror of her past day, and damn him, it worked. But knowing this didn't diminish the huge ball of light that had grown inside her at his words.

You're perfect for me.

When the sun finally rose fully and Culis left her again to go steal some trousers from a nearby clothesline, Mila found herself feeling, despite everything, happy.

Playing the Game

Orion carried Mila all the way to relative safety of Culis Manor's woodland property. There, she dismounted, and Culis left her as planned, returning to the manor to wait for her.

When Mila was about a mile from the front gates of the manor, she was finally able to stand completely upright, and as she approached the guardhouse, they quickly identified her and sent a messenger running to their master to notify him of her return. They grinned at her as she stumbled past them but did not challenge or stop her. She sensed a deep energy of satisfaction emanating from them, and also a little bit of awe.

It seemed Frank Culis might have been right. How infuriating.

As she entered the house, the grand staircase was filled was gawkers, who whispered loudly as she painstakingly ascended, every step agony, despite the fact she was able to stand upright again. She knew they pressed their ears against the door to Culis's study after she closed it behind her.

He raised his head from a thick book as she entered. Beside him on the desk sat the sister stone.

"Welcome back. I trust you've learned your lesson?" he said loudly, ensuring he'd be overheard by those outside.

"I have," she croaked. "I'm...sorry. Sorry to you, sorry to Baird. It won't...won't happen again."

"Good. Then you are dismissed." Culis called for Nemecca to enter the room. She arrived startlingly quickly. Eavesdropper.

"Take Mila to the infirmary immediately."

Mila leaned heavily on Nemecca's arm, needing the support more than she wanted to admit. To her surprise, as they walked into the hallway, she was accosted by a cloud of energy from the household staff that was the equivalent of a silent round of applause.

She knew she'd never forgive Frank Culis for what he'd put her through, but she could not deny that the energies of the manor staff were all positive towards herself and Culis. They were impressed that she'd made it back in one piece, they approved of her current dishevelled state, and they were glad she'd apologised to their master, who they respected and liked. They, Nemecca included, felt affirmed that she'd been rightfully punished.

And now they could all get on with their lives.

She felt a grin rise unbidden to her face as she headed to the infirmary, where she had her wounds bound and tended to. From there, Nemecca took her to the kitchen. The cook, Petrie – who introduced himself by name for the first time – had a hot meal ready and waiting. She sat in the sun and found herself surrounded by curious onlookers, who insisted she regale them with her story. She tried her best, but she was too exhausted, and eventually, Nemecca stepped in and escorted her to bed, where she fell into a deep sleep that lasted the rest of the day.

* * *

When she finally awoke, it was late the following afternoon. Mila couldn't believe she'd slept so long, but as she leapt from her bed, the violent ache of her body was evidence that she'd needed it. She had no time to waste now, and despite the pain, she headed immediately to Natalee's cell with the small vial of rubane oil from under her bed. She inspected it again as she walked, sighing in frustration at its size.

When she arrived at Natalee's cell, she was relieved to find that, despite the fact that the guard was hesitant and suspicious of her, he had not been given orders to prevent her from visiting.

Natalee leapt to her feet at the sound of Mila's voice and came over to the bars. "You're alive? I'm surprised he didn't kill you."

"We have no time to waste. This guard is not going to let us talk for long," Mila interrupted. "I'm going to try and get the key tonight. If I fail, place this oil over your forehead and face before the sacrifice." Mila pressed the tiny vial into Natalee's hand. "Do not let anyone see you do it."

"What is it?" Natalee asked, palming the bottle.

"Maybe nothing," Mila admitted. "But anything at this point is worth a shot."

"That's enough," the guard called out, suspicious and alert enough to know there was more than a simple goodbye occurring.

Mila drew away reluctantly. "I'll see you soon," she said.

She refused to say goodbye. There was still a chance for Natalee, and she would see it attempted.

As night fell, Mila lay awake on her bed, waiting until the dark cape of night fully cloaked the manor, persuading even the most wakeful and conscientious servants to accept the call of their beds.

Finally, when she was certain only the guards at the far front gate were still awake, she rose and moved towards the stairs, as silently as a dead man's breath, climbing them slowly until she reached the floor where Culis slept.

When she entered the large room, her eye was immediately drawn to his sprawled-out figure lying across his four-poster bed, atop the blankets, as though he had collapsed there with exhaustion and been unable to drag himself beneath them. The green curtains that hung from the wooden beams were only partially drawn, and as she approached, she noted the hilt of a dagger peeking out from beneath his pillow. The sight of it almost caused her to turn back. Despite his lack of guard, or perhaps because of it, she knew Culis would be a man who would strike first and ask questions later if startled from his sleep.

But, after a moment or two of contemplation, she continued to inch forward. She could do this.

Within a few quiet paces, she was standing beside him. She noted the gentle rise and fall of his chest as he slept and paused for a moment, admiring the peaceful expression on his face. He was definitely a handsome man. One who turned heads, even without the magnetic aura he brought into every room with him.

She could see the glint of the chain and the key to Natalee's cell poking through the cut of his collar and reached a hand towards him, intending to simply part his shirt and identify the key more fully.

Without warning, his hand shot out and seized her wrist, yanking her over his body in a flurry of limbs.

Within a second, she found herself pinned beneath him, his hand at her throat.

"I knew it," he said grimly. "And you must think me a fool if you thought I didn't suspect an attempt like this tonight."

He'd been awake all night.

It had all been an act. He'd never even been asleep, just lying in wait for her.

“I had to try,” she gasped and tried to wriggle free from under him.

For a moment, her struggle caused him to shift his weight in an effort to pin her. The movement brought her attention directly to the positioning of their bodies, the way he lay between her open legs, pushing up slightly against her hips, his face hovering inches above her own.

The heat of her body suddenly found his bare skin and seeped eagerly into it, like the flame of a candle slowly heating its waxen case. It took her breath away to have him so close.

Desire, heat, determination to possess...

It was intoxicating.

She made a small, involuntary noise, and the flame in her stomach roared to life as she saw in his eyes a similar disarming occur. Her body was a furnace. It was consuming and urgent, this sudden, undeniable need for him, for Culis. His masculine energy and scent pounded into her, and suddenly, she wanted his touch, his undivided attention, and his desire for her more than anything in the world.

She allowed herself to relax and her body to soften under his, shifting again, this time drawing her knees up a little to pull his hips in closer to hers.

His eyes widened as he felt her shift. His hand left her throat, moving to cup her face. He held her body steady as he ground against her, his thigh pressed firmly high between her legs, drawing from her an unexpected “oh!”.

“Did you come here to rob me, or seduce me, little demon?” he whispered against her ear as he rolled his thigh against her hot core again. “Even after everything I shared with you today. You’d still try make me look the fool at the ball tomorrow?”

She could barely catch her breath, let alone respond.

He reached up with his free hand and took a fistful of her hair, drawing her head back and exposing her throat. He kissed the soft skin there, ensuring the rest of her remained pinned beneath him. His lips burned like a brand.

"Perhaps I was too hasty in giving you free roam of the house on your return," he whispered, his voice suddenly husky. "Perhaps a little restriction tonight would be good for you."

He ground his thigh up against her again, and she tried to gasp, but no sound came out. She could feel his amusement, and his hot arousal.

"Do you want me to stop?" he asked, "or do you want me to continue? Tell me, Mila," he demanded, knowing full well she could not reply, not with his hand bunched like this in her hair, holding her throat bared at this angle. It was restricting, but not painful, not unless she struggled. And she could still breathe, but making sound was impossible.

"I'll keep going until you tell me to stop," he whispered, and he did. Repeating the movement again and again against the place between her legs that already felt aflame.

She soundlessly cried out and writhed desperately under him, until frustration nearly brought tears to her eyes.

Finally, he released her hair.

She lowered her chin, finally able to speak, beg. "*Please,*" she gasped.

"Mmm." He surveyed her briefly, then smiled and took her hands, holding them above her head, tying them together with the curtain that draped from the frame. "I'd have considered it, if I believed that's why you were here. But I don't need your power to know that you actually came here tonight to rob me, and frankly, little demon, I'm a bit hurt."

He didn't look hurt. In fact, the glint in his eye spoke of nothing but mischief as he sat up, tugged the curtain he'd knotted around her wrists to ensure they were held tight, and then moved away, back to his side of the bed, radiating smugness as he waited for her to realise what was happening.

Or rather, what wasn't.

"Hey!" she protested, indignantly. "Untie me!"

His smile widened. "Maybe in the morning. In the meantime, get some sleep."

With that he rolled over, turning his back to her.

When Mila realised he wasn't going to do anything more with her tonight, she let out an exasperated, and somewhat embarrassed, huff.

"You deserve it," he responded to her wordless complaint.

It wasn't until the early hours of the morning that she was woken by the warmth of him leaning over her to untie her from the curtain.

Once freed, she didn't linger. She fled back to her own room – equal parts mortified and frustrated.

In her own bed, she was unable to fall back asleep, tossing and turning with her mind full of Culis and her body full of desire, until the morning sun was high and it was time to get up.

Today was the day of the Dusk Ball.

Today was the day of Natalee's sacrifice.

The Dusk Ball

It was early afternoon when Mila saw Culis again. By that time, the stress she felt about Natalee's upcoming sacrifice had replaced any mortification she'd experienced in his room earlier that morning.

"I want to attend the ball tonight," she demanded as she confronted him in the hallway after lunch.

"Mila...no."

"In *secret*," she added, and he fell silent, listening. "No one will ever know I was there...but I have to be, Culis. This is my fault. I wouldn't be able to live with myself if I let Natalee go through this alone."

"I...can't. I don't want you to die," he said, reaching out to touch the back of her hand with his fingertips, wanting to share himself with her. The energy was painful. His concern and fear were undeniable.

"Culis," Mila said gently. "If you do truly want to make amends with me, if I am not a pet or a slave, but someone you respect, then you'll know that you have to let me do this. This is my choice. I want to accept the risks that I know exist."

And Culis, despite his anguish, knew she was right, and this was a true chance for him to prove to her that he'd meant what he'd said.

"I'll only accept it on the condition that you follow my instructions to the letter about the method of getting you in and out."

"Agreed."

That was how, a few hours later, Mila found herself passing through the black gates of the palace in the carriage with him, and although she knew that this was the only decision she could have possibly made, it still felt like deliberately returning to a cage.

A cold shiver passed over her as the shadows around them deepened, and she nearly lost her nerve entirely when she saw the spires of the Grand Cathedral rising high and imposing against the deep orange sunset.

"It's not too late to turn back," Culis said softly, as though reading her mind, and something about being offered the choice to leave strengthened her resolve to see this through.

"You know I will not."

"Well, whatever you're planning to do tonight, don't let it get you killed. And remember, Jezebel *cannot* be permitted to know you are present."

"I know, and I'm not planning to do anything."

"So, your intention is truly just to watch?" Doubt laced through his every word, and his beautiful eyes narrowed in suspicion.

"How could I not want to see you present yourself to society in that hideous shade of orange?" she joked, trying to lighten the mood.

"This?" Culis plucked at his tangerine overcoat, looking a little hurt. "I like it!"

"You like to make a statement," Mila corrected. "But it's not nice. And it's certainly not your colour."

"It's the Dusk Ball!" Culis protested. "And I'll have you note that this coat was made by some of the finest artisans in Traders Bay. It's the colour of the dying leaf of a bone tree! Correct to the exact shade!"

"Well, they certainly captured the 'dying' part," Mila teased.

"Jealousy!" Culis harrumphed. "And insulting my magnificent coat won't distract me like you think it will. Mila, if you have something planned for tonight, tell me. I could help." His eyes were earnest as he reached towards her – placing a warm hand on her knee, so she could feel his energy again.

She appreciated his desire to be open with her, and she desperately wished she could reciprocate, but the rubane secret was too destructive in the wrong hands.

"There's nothing. There's no plan." She sighed and placed her head in her hands. "The God-King will touch Natalee tonight and that will be the end of it."

Culis knew her too well by now to be satisfied with this answer, but he drew back and decided to let it go. "Okay," he said briskly, changing the subject. "Here's how the evening is going to pan out. We're nearly at Jezebel's apartments. You're going to hide in the compartment under the seat. Do not come out. I'll greet the princess and dazzle her with my magnificent coat. She will join me in the carriage, then we'll go to the Grand Cathedral. Only once we've departed and the carriage has been taken around the rear should you emerge and find a good vantage point from which to watch. There are plenty of windows. I would suggest you climb a tall tree...I'm sure you'll figure it out, but...promise me you'll stay well away from the building."

Mila nodded but did not promise.

The evasion was noted by Culis, who let out a huge sigh, but continued to give his directions. "I will attempt to leave soon after the sacrifice. You must ensure you are back in the hidden compartment well before that. It is entirely possible that Jezebel will want to return to my manor with me. If I tap my heel upon the floor sharply, three times, it is my signal to you to stay hidden. If you hear it, stay put until either myself or Arran comes to let you out. You could be hidden in there for over six hours. Understand?"

"I do." She nodded gravely. "Thank you for bringing me with you, and for trusting me."

"Don't butcher that trust, please."

Mila gulped at his words, and Culis's sharp eyes noted the movement.

He rolled his own in resignation. "Ahh. So, you *are* going to butcher it. Well, at least now I have a heads up."

"I..."

"Mila. You don't have to tell me, but don't lie to me please. Just get into the compartment. We're nearly there."

She felt a little ashamed, but nodded, kneeled down, and clambered past his ankles into a tiny secret cabin that sat behind a false wall under his seat of the carriage.

I can't tell you everything right now, she thought regretfully as she lay in the small dark space and Culis closed the small door behind her, *but someday I will explain it all.*

She'd never really minded the dark, or small spaces, but this compartment felt eerily like a coffin once the door was closed behind her. It was pitch black and was not high enough for her to lift her head from the floor more than an inch. She did not have enough room to roll over.

"Are you okay?" Culis asked with concern from outside, his voice only a little muffled.

"Mmhmm," she responded. "Am I going to be able to breathe in here for six hours?" she asked, suddenly concerned.

"Of course," he replied. "All my carriages have these installed, and you're far from the first to do a long stint in one. They're essential for smuggling."

"Of course, silly me."

The carriage slowed. From this position, Mila could hear the clopping of the horses' hooves incredibly clearly, like they were right next to her head.

"We've arrived," Culis said in a low whisper. "Remember my instructions. I'll see you here, in one piece, in a few hours."

Mila did not reply. She heard the carriage door open, accompanied by Jezebel's excited gasp of joy and the rush of her footsteps. Mila felt her stomach clench, imagining the princess throwing herself at Culis, and him drawing her into an embrace.

"You look...breathtaking. Happy birthday, Princess." Culis's voice was low and filled with wonder.

"Take me to my party," Jezebel said with a joyful laugh.

Mila could feel the power of her happiness bombarding the carriage.

"Your will is my command." His reply was teasing and light-hearted.

Mila caught the sound of a kiss, and then the carriage rocked as Culis and Jezebel found their seats.

"Come to me," Mila heard Culis purr.

Mila forced herself to steady her breathing, thrusting aside the glass shards of jealousy that were forming in her throat.

This is all an act, she reminded herself as the sickly sounds of kissing commenced above her. *I know how he truly feels about her...and me.*

It was one thing to know it and quite another to accept that Culis was currently here, with Jezebel, pretending to be her besotted lover.

"And my birthday present?" Mila heard Jezebel suddenly demand.

"The demon you requested is in the carriage following us," Culis replied. "She can be taken and prepared by the acolytes once we arrive."

"The demon sacrifice is my father's requirement," she said in a pouty voice. "Where's *my* present?"

For a moment, Mila thought Culis was in danger, for she hadn't seen a present for Jezebel in the carriage, and he'd never mentioned procuring one for her.

But a chuckle from above told her that she should have known him better than that.

"Ahhh, I was hoping to wait until the end of the night to give it to you, but seeing as you're such an impatient little thing– "

Jezebel giggled. Mila wanted to retch.

" – I suppose you can have it now."

A tinkle of metal sounded in the air, and Jezebel's gasp accompanied the outpouring of delighted energy. "It's quite exotic."

"What else do you get the woman who can have anyone and anything she wants?"

Mila felt herself shrivelling up as she listened to their chatter. Despite everything that had so recently come to light about Culis's real feelings, everything she heard above her seemed so real, and it was undeniable that he had clearly invested considerable time thinking about how best to woo Jezebel. Mila knew she had no real claim over him, and that trying to stake such a claim while he still had ownership rights to her life was downright foolish.

And yet...

No, she chided herself. There were bigger things at stake tonight than her inconvenient crush on Christopher Culis. If the rubane worked as she suspected it would, then there was a chance that the entire Church establishment would come crumbling down. That was what she should be thinking about right now. Not the way Culis was holding Jezebel and buying her exotic gifts.

Thankfully, Mila's torture was coming to an end, and the muffled, echoing sound of drums from the Grand Cathedral grew louder as the carriage approached. She didn't have to wait much longer for Culis and Jezebel to dismount and make their way into the hall.

Their absence brought Mila palpable relief.

The horses were clucked forward by the driver, and the carriage moved again. This time it went only a short distance before it stopped, and Mila heard the door open.

It was Arran's voice she clearly heard this time.

He whispered into darkness, "A'ight, there's nobody around bu' a few footmen. I reckon you'd be right to spear off when it suits you."

Mila cautiously pushed the hinged door of the secret compartment open and rolled out onto the floor of the carriage. It was dark, but her night vision was now well-adjusted, and the light of the Grand Cathedral came streaming in from the left like a flood of gold.

Mila turned her head away from it and slipped from the carriage into the darkness on the other side, cautiously working her way around the other carriages and their bored drivers, who were all milling around with their horses. It was easy to reach the edge of the hard standing unnoticed and slip away into the nearby gardens.

From here, she released a big breath and took stock of the next step in her plan.

She eyed the towering monolith that stood beside her and took a moment to appreciate the sight.

Great raised braziers had been erected at the entrance, and the firelight threw hot orange light at the golden walls, turning the entrance into a glittering beacon for revellers to approach like entranced moths. The women were all dressed in gowns inspired by elements of late autumn: hues of deep purple and orange, spiderwebs and cool, starry skies. From her position, Mila could also hear the most gorgeous, ethereal music emitting from the heart of the building: deep drums, low flutes, a woman singing – her deep velvety, reverberating alto catching on the wind – a lone fiddle playing a slow, lonely, heart-wrenching solo. The combination of the lights, music, costumes and unshakable sense of danger made Mila feel as though she'd been transported out of Artor and into a dream. She tried to steady her pulse and catch her breath, but it was near impossible.

That was, until a firm male hand grabbed her forearm sharply and wrenched her around.

"Servants were explicitly ordered to stay away this eve – Oh!"

A familiar face glared down at her, an eyepatch illuminated by the gleam coming from the building.

"Mila," Jahan said incredulously. "What are you *doing* here?"

Moment of Truth

Jahan's energy was one part fury, one part worry, and one part...relief. "I-I thought..." he stuttered. "You're meant to be..."

"Hello, Jahan," Mila said with a smile, both relieved to see him and concerned about what his next move might be. She'd been a fool not to anticipate extra security, but of all the guards to catch her tonight, Jahan was the least likely to report her...maybe.

"It's good to see you again," she said.

"What are you doing here?" he asked again in shock.

"I've come to watch the sacrifice."

"*You're* meant to be the sacrifice."

"I am?" she said in mock surprise. "But the order specifically demanded the demon on the ship?"

"That was evidently, not you," Jahan surmised grimly. "Huh. Well, I know one person who is going to be furious when that small error becomes glaringly evident in a few hours."

"Not you, I hope," she said cautiously, risking a smile.

He stared at her in silence for a short moment, then couldn't help but smile back. "No. Not me. For reasons that are beyond my better judgement...I'm glad you live to see another day. But you're really poking the rattlesnake by being here at all. Why have you come?"

"I told you," Mila replied honestly. "I'm here to watch the sacrifice."

"I don't believe you. You're up to something."

She sighed. "Jahan, you can stay by my side all evening if you wish and shadow my every move, but I promise you, if I can find a good vantage point, I'll be sitting tight and doing nothing but watching."

Jahan eyed her dubiously, then looked her up and down and seemed to notice the bandages wrapped around her forearms for the first time. "Mila..." He reached for her hand again and inspected them closely, his face darkening. "What happened to you?"

"It's nothing." She snatched her hand back. "A...miscommunication."

"Culis did this to you?" Jahan was enraged. His energy murderous. Its intensity caught Mila off guard. "He's hurting you?"

"No!" she assured him swiftly. "Not Christopher Culis, anyhow. His father is another story but...I can look out for myself. Don't worry about me."

Jahan seemed conflicted, reluctant to let the topic go without a more thorough explanation.

"One way that I *could* use your help," Mila said, trying to redirect his anger, "is if you could recommend a good vantage point for me."

"You're kidding."

"I'm not," she assured him. "And I meant what I said when I told you that you could supervise me for the evening too. I'm not here to make mischief tonight, promise."

Jahan cracked a smile that told her he thought she was bluffing, and he was prepared to call it. "Alright then. Well, come with me. I'll take you to the best vantage point there is."

"That's not a secret name for the dungeon, is it?" she said, suddenly cautious about his good humour.

He laughed. "No, but we might both end up there if I'm spotted away from my post, scurrying around with you. So, follow me quietly and exactly. Step for step."

His energy was now full of amusement and excitement. She hadn't expected this from him at all, but he seemed truly buoyed to discover that she was alive. There was no malice in him, or deceit. She could trust him, Mila realised, and he was helping her tonight for the simple reason that he liked her.

He led her to the back wall of the Grand Cathedral, where he knelt and lifted a trapdoor that revealed a set of stairs going down into the ground. "It's a servants' entrance," he explained quietly. "Hurry up. If we're going to get caught, then this is the place it will happen."

Mila scurried down after him, reassured by the lack of any other human energy down in the hole. The narrow stairwell opened into a small kitchen, from which a number of other doorways and tunnels led in different directions.

"What is it with this place and tunnels?" she asked herself, but Jahan answered.

"Well, the architects didn't want to ruin the magnificence of the tower by having all these small servants' quarters huddled around the base of it. So, the servants get to scurry around underground instead. Now follow me." He picked one tunnel and grabbed her hand, pulling her along behind him. This tunnel turned into a winding stairwell that rose up and up and up. "We're in the actual wall of the Grand Cathedral now," Jahan said softly, as though afraid they'd be heard by those in the hall itself, and while it might have been possible on a regular evening, tonight the pulsing music from within was so loud that it hummed through the sandstone bricks that surrounded them.

"How much further?" she asked.

"We're nearly there."

He lied. It was a long ascent, and by the time they got to the top Mila was panting and a little dizzy, but when she looked around, she immediately saw that it had been worth it. They were in a small wooden room that had been built high into the domed roof of the Grand Cathedral itself, above even where the stained-glass windows reached. It was an oddly shaped space, with one long, curved wall and three straight ones. It was also tiny, with only room for a single mattress in one corner and a small desk with an old piece of parchment and an empty ink bottle in the other. Behind where Jahan stood, there was a small rectangular opening, more peephole than window, and when Mila looked out of it she could see the entire expanse of the hall below.

"This is incredible," she said, drawing back and looking at him in wonder. "What is this place?"

"Originally it was an acolyte's nest, a place for junior acolytes to observe ceremonies and learn the etiquette before participating themselves. But it hasn't been used like that for years. Not since it was my childhood bedroom."

"It was what?" Mila looked around the tiny, bare space again. "This was your bedroom?" For a moment, she imagined a young Jahan sitting up here, alone and lonely, with the chanting of priests echoing up from below as he tried to sleep. It was a disturbing image. "Why?"

"I was taken from my mother when I was young and raised as an acolyte in the Church," Jahan replied, turning away from her and now taking his turn to look out the peephole.

"So...then why aren't you an acolyte?" she asked.

She felt his energy shift. *Discomfort, shame, anger.*

"I never wanted to be an acolyte," was all he offered.

"But...your parents wanted you to do it?" she pressed.

"No. Not at all. My mother hated the Church."

"But...I don't understand. You were brought here to be an acolyte anyway? By who?"

"Abbott came to the Village of Truth one day and selected me. He said I had potential. That's all I really remember. I was quite young. Maybe five summers?"

Mila stared at him, and Jahan determinedly avoided her gaze and continued to stare out the peephole.

Finally, he sighed and relented. "Look, it's a long story. I'd rather not go into it. Suffice to say, I made a terrible acolyte, and they appointed me into Princess Jezebel's service instead when I was ten, to be her companion and guard. They figured she'd be more likely to tell someone her own age if she was plotting trouble. I've served her since then."

"I see," Mila said gently. "Well, thank you for sharing that with me. It's nice getting to know you a little more every time I see you."

He smiled at her, then gestured to the peephole. "Well, go on. You wanted a good vantage place to observe from...so you'd better observe."

Mila nodded and moved forward, pressing her eyes to the space and looking down at the flurry of light and colour of the dancers and revellers below her.

It was beautiful.

"It's disgusting," she said. "It just goes to show that some things are only a sin if you're poor and common."

"That's not true. According to Abbott, this entire evening is the definition of heresy," he said from behind her. "If the High Priest had his way, this wouldn't be occurring."

"But you don't agree with him," she challenged, sensing the dislike for Abbott rolling off him, but not taking her eyes from those dancing below.

"Correct," he said. "Both my mother and I serve the God-King and not the Church, and I know that, tonight, while it may seem like hypocrisy to you, it isn't about revelling in sin for the sake of it. It's not even truly about celebrating Jezebel. It's actually the night the God-King reminds the Church that he is not beholden to any earthly restriction. He is Divine. He is the final authority on what is and isn't acceptable in his presence, and he can change his mind whenever it pleases him."

"Jahan?" Mila turned to face him, extending her horns as far as they would go and watching in delight as his eyes barely concealed his horror and shock.

"I'm already a demon, so there's really no need to try to convert me. 'Midas is God, he can do whatever he likes' would have sufficed."

Outraged laughter burst from the guard, and Mila appreciated his willingness to see humour when there was some to be found. She smiled at him, and he smiled back. His energy beamed at her.

"Stay here," he said suddenly. "I'll be back."

He disappeared down the winding staircase and returned sooner than she expected with a flask of wine that he'd evidently swiped from the kitchen below.

"Really?" she asked incredulously. It was the last thing she expected to see the consummate professional partaking in. He was already bending the rules by escorting her up here while he was supposed to be on duty, patrolling the grounds somewhere below them.

"Why not? If you're planning on being here until the ceremony, then we'll be waiting a while. And if anyone finds us, I'll just say that I have the demon who was trespassing on the grounds in my custody and am escorting her to the dungeon." His energy was playful and happy. Quite impossible to turn down.

"Well, you're all covered then." She accepted the flask from his hand and took a swig from the bottle. It was good. A deep, rich purple – just the kind she liked.

Jahan also took a swig, and then took his turn peering down onto the scene below.

When Mila next looked, she looked for Culis.

He was easy to find. His bun looked relatively neat from above, and the gold shoulder panels of his ugly, dark orange jacket glinted up to the ceiling. He and Jezebel carved their way through the dancefloor elegantly. It was clearly neither one's first time dancing, and the way they cut shapes and moved to the music was utterly mesmerising. Mila realised with some embarrassment, that this was not at all how she must have looked when she was dancing at Reminisciary. She suddenly found herself feeling awkward that Culis had said nothing about her obvious inexperience, particularly when he knew how to dance like this.

"Have you ever done it?" she asked Jahan, feeling a little sick watching them together and pulling away from the window.

"Done what?"

"Danced."

"Never."

"Well, shall we try it?"

"What, here? Now?"

"When else?" She laughed and tried to lighten her mood. "It's the only night it's ever permitted. Why should we not indulge?"

"I...I..." he stuttered a little, then thought about it and smiled. "I guess there's no reason why we can't!"

"Exactly!"

He looked astonished by her apparent enthusiasm. "And you want to dance with me?"

"No, I want to dance with the other person in the room with me... Yes, you dolt. *You*."

"Well then! Let's do it." He held his palm out to her, and she took it gently. He pulled her in close, as they'd seen the couples doing below, and then paused. "What next?" he asked softly.

Mila went to reply, but as she did so, she caught a deep whiff of his scent and was deeply distracted. He smelled of a rich, spicy cologne combined with the musk of pipe tobacco and the earthy scent of soil from the garden. It was a heady mix, not to mention the wine was also starting to hit her.

"I...uh...err."

"Haven't you done this before?" he asked, leaning down to her and bringing his face close.

A brief flash of memory from the time they'd kissed at the dinner passed her eyes, and suddenly her stomach twisted with a sharp thrill of desire.

Well, this is unexpected.

"Only once," she managed to splutter out, caught off guard by this unexpected feeling. "I don't really know what I'm doing."

"So, we'll invent our own way to do it." He stood straight up again and began to coax her into rocking back and forth with him, spinning her gently to the beat of the drums from below.

One, two, three. One, two, three...

It was a very simple movement, but effective, and with every turn, she was coaxed by the angle and his hand on her waist to lean further and further into him, until she was all but pressed against his hot chest. She did not resist. His energy was amazing – calm happiness mixed with a small zing of exhilaration – but whether this was from finally doing something he'd always been forbidden to do, or because of her presence, she was unsure. Either way, she relished the way her body easily melded against his and their breathing automatically synchronised, just as it had at the dinner party all those months ago.

This felt easy, natural, wonderful.

One, two, three. One, two, three...

An image of Culis suddenly rose, unbidden in her mind. His offer to help tonight, his earnest face, his laugh... *Don't butcher that trust, please.*

She felt a pang of uncertainty and guilt about having this moment with Jahan, but was saved when the music below suddenly shifted to something much faster and their slow, timely rocking was no longer quite right.

Mila broke away and looked up into Jahan's handsome, scarred face. "That was lovely, thank you."

"Look at you, enjoying a little hypocrisy." He intended it as a joke, but it struck a nerve with Mila.

"A demon is being sacrificed tonight," she solemnly reminded him, pulling away further. "Her death is demanded because this *entire night* is directly in contravention of the Second Heretical Behaviour. I don't understand how you're okay with Midas ordering yet another death, purely so that the elite may dance and flirt and feel good about themselves for one evening. It's sickening."

"Mila." Jahan's energy had transformed quickly and was now cold and forthright.

But she couldn't stop, the words – the truth – tumbling from her mouth in fury. "Are the poor and common folk given similar concessions tonight? Gifted the same licence for one night of celebration of the God-King's power? You know they are not. This entire event is nothing but the hypocritical indulgence of a maniac to pacify his elite."

"Enough." The speed with which the change came over Jahan was utterly terrifying. His voice took a hard, flat edge and became a warrior's voice, a man prepared to do violence in defence of his beliefs. Her words had crossed a line. In the magic of the dance and the softness of his happiness, she'd forgotten what a zealot he was.

"It is one thing for me to tolerate your continued existence at our God-King's pleasure, but quite another for you to directly blaspheme him to my face."

"Is that what you were just doing? Tolerating my existence?"

"He is Divine, Mila," Jahan snapped, ignoring her barb. But a red flush began to creep up his neck. The friendly, flirtatious dance partner from moments earlier was completely washed away by this new, fearsome, harsh wall of a man. "He is a god. He is not beholden to the rules. They're for *us*, our punishment. They are not for him."

His anger was absolute, and Mila knew that speaking again would probably gain her nothing but his further ire. And yet, the words came out of her before she could stop them.

"If you watch the sacrifice tonight with me, you'll see proof that he is not a god." She winced as Jahan's furious energy struck her like a battering ram, and she braced for the physical blow she expected to follow.

A strike never came, but when she unclenched her eyes, she saw Jahan's upper lip curled into a snarl. He looked at her as though she were infected with the plague.

"Get away from me," he whispered hoarsely, backing towards the door they'd come from. "Don't come near me with that kind of talk ever again. To even think it is a death sentence, let alone to say it out loud."

"Please..." she begged. "Just...listen to what I have to say." The words were out in the open now. She might as well try. She spoke quickly, knowing she probably only had seconds before he stormed out of the room. "King Midas...I've met him, I've been within an inch of him. Jahan. I'm telling you the truth when I say, I could not sense him *at all*. His energy was blocked."

Jahan's hard face didn't waver, but he hadn't left yet either.

"Initially, I attributed the cause of the block to be something to do with the fact that he is Divine. But the more I dwelt on it, the more I realised that there's something else at play, something blocking his *power*. And if a god's power can be blocked...is he all powerful? Is he truly a god? Think about it, Jahan. The red gloves he wears...they don't disintegrate at his touch."

"Because they are holy," he snapped.

"Holy or not, they're made out of something that resists his power," she bit back, trying to keep herself calm. "And I have found something that blocks and resists demon powers. It is a weed."

"A...what?" Jahan shook his head, trying to keep up.

"A weed," she repeated. "A weed that grows in the Highlands. It can block demon powers. I use it, other demons use it. Now, wouldn't it make sense that those gloves can block and resist his power because they have this weed woven into them? Why else would they be resistant to Midas's touch?"

She was surprised that Jahan still stood before her. When did logic override the sticky mire of belief? At what point did devotion and faith bow to moral courage? Jahan was intelligent, but he was also part of the system that had never truly been a threat to him. He gained nothing if his God was exposed as false. His whole life in devotion to his service could be proved a waste. And yet, to his credit, he still stood in the room with her, listening.

"Jahan, I promise that I don't need you to play any part in this that would expose or threaten you. I don't even need you to believe or support me, but just...please watch the sacrifice tonight. I have given the demon an oil infused with the weed to put on her forehead. If Midas is truly a god, then it will have no effect on his power, and the sacrifice will proceed as planned. If he is a demon, then she will survive his touch. That's the test. That's it. Nothing more."

Jahan breathed deeply through his nose and closed his eye.

Mila kept her voice low and stepped toward him, gently touching his forearm with her fingers, trying to ground and reassure him. "If I'm wrong, then no one will be any the wiser that something was different about the sacrifice tonight. But...no true god should fear being tested. Not unless they have something to hide."

Jahan's eye flew open at her touch. He held her gaze with a look she could not draw back from.

"I will allow you to witness your friend's death," he finally croaked out. "But then I will arrest you, and hand you over to Abbott."

Mila swiftly pulled her hand away and stepped back. "Okay," she said calmly, coldly.

And then she went back to the peephole, turning her back on him.

* * *

Natalee was naked when they brought her in, save for golden chains around her neck and hands, and shimmering gold powder that had been blown onto her skin and stuck to her sweat.

She was accompanied on all sides by jesu in their ceremonial armour, all chanting their hypnotic baritone prayer. High Priest Abbott led the procession, and Mila watched from above as the revellers drew back to either side of the hall, many with bowed heads. They would have been the epitome of contrition if some weren't still swaying with the effects of strong drink.

Mila also caught a glimpse of Jezebel's face when she realised the demon being presented wasn't Mila. Her fury was palpable, even from this distance, but there was nothing she could do or say about it now.

"It's happening," Mila whispered to Jahan, who had stood, silent and resolute by the door for the past hour. "Please come watch. It's the most important thing you'll ever witness in your whole life."

He ignored her initially, but then curiosity got the better of him and he slowly moved over to where she stood. Mila shuffled to the side to make room for him at the peephole.

"For this night of sin," Midas proclaimed below, his deep voice reverberating through the Grand Cathedral. "For the revelry you indulge in, despite the blindness and heresy of your ancestors, I accept this sacrifice as your penance."

"I am contrite." The murmur spread throughout the gathering.

Jahan muttered it fervently from beside Mila, as though begging forgiveness for ever entertaining Mila's idea. She risked a glance over at him and saw his eye tightly closed, his hands clasped together in earnest prayer.

Natalee was brought before Midas and forced to her knees. Mila caught her breath when she saw the woman and, for a moment, was seized by a terrible, aching fear.

What if this didn't work? What if this was the end? What if Midas was truly a god and she'd been wrong this entire time? Jahan would arrest her. She'd be responsible for Natalee's death, and she'd be sacrificed next...

Below her, Natalee cried out in fear and rage, fighting against those who held her down, but with little effect. Midas stood above her with one hand raised, pulling off his glove, finger by finger, drawing out the pageantry of the action.

After a pregnant pause, he slowly stretched his freed hand before his face and observed it with interest, as though he were unused to seeing the nakedness of his own palm. Finally, he slowly lowered it, extending his thumb towards the sacrifice.

Mila watched with wide eyes and held breath as, with an air of finality, the God-King Midas pressed his thumb against Natalee's forehead.

The Aftermath

Nothing happened.

Mila saw Natalee's eyes go wide and heard Abbott's monotonous intonation hitch a moment. There was a heartbeat of silence, and the world seemed to pause before two huge bangs abruptly sounded from within the braziers on either side of Midas's dais.

And then an enormous explosion rocked the Grand Cathedral and blew Mila's world apart.

The tiny acolytes nook where she and Jahan crouched was violently blasted by a wall of air and fire that easily punched a hole into the wall right between them, bringing the whole room and everything in it crumbling down, and sending debris plummeting towards the crowd below.

The only thing that saved Mila and Jahan from becoming little more than splattered memories on the hard floor below was a large swath of thick fabric that had been hanging as decoration from the ceiling. Mila was all but catapulted into it by the force of the explosion. Instinctively she grabbed out and clung to the thick velvet.

Panting in panic as her brain caught up to her body, she tried to make sense of what had just happened. As she did so, chaos erupted below.

The explosions had upended at least ten giant pillars, crushing several revellers and spilling glass and sand throughout the hall. One enormous stained-glass window had been completely blown out, another two were damaged, with huge holes made by chunks of flying debris ruining the painstakingly crafted images. From Mila's vantage point, the people below looked like a disturbed ants' nest. Screaming and scurrying about in every direction. The archway to the exit was still clear, but a pillar had fallen on a woman who'd been trying to get out that way. The dead body was covered in sand and blood and was blocking the stairs. For the moment, this seemed to deter anyone else from wanting to get near.

Mila's ears were ringing. She knew she had to get down from this curtain soon, before she, or it, fell, so she started carefully inching her way down the fabric, watching Jahan doing the same just below her. They were about ten feet from the ground when they were spotted, simultaneously it seemed, by Culis, Jezebel, and Abbott.

Culis had his arm around Jezebel's shoulders and was drawing her close to protect her from anything else that might decide to fall from the roof. He had a bloody graze on his left cheek and dust all through his hair, but otherwise seemed unharmed. His eyes lit up in panic when he saw Mila.

I'm sorry, she thought when she saw him, but there was no way to convey it.

Jezebel looked enraged. She opened her mouth to say something but was interrupted when Abbott took it upon himself to grab Mila. He lunched for her dress and tore her off the last bit of curtain, throwing her to the floor, and kicking her hard in the head with his boot.

"Demon!" he seethed. "We've been attacked by this demon!"

"No!" Mila cried out, throwing her hands out to protect her head from his blows. "It wasn't me."

"Stop!" Culis's voice cut through the pain and Abbott was pulled away. "This is my property you're defacing, High Priest," she heard him say from above her.

She risked a peek to see Culis standing protectively above her, his hideous orange overcoat gleaming in the remaining firelight as he stared down Abbott.

"Explain yourself."

"Explain *myself*?" The outrage emitting from Abbott was volcanic. "We...the God-King has just been attacked by *your property*."

"No!" Mila cried out again. "I swear it wasn't me."

The God-King himself watched the hubbub from a little distance away, surrounded by jesu who stood with shields and swords at the ready, braced for the next threat. He did not intercede. Rather, he seemed interested in watching Abbott alone.

Natalee was nowhere to be seen.

"Why would she blow *herself* up?" Culis challenged cuttingly. "I'd look a little closer to home for the culprit, High Priest. Maybe those Children of Midas had some say." He turned to Mila. "Come, demon." He picked her up from the ground and began hustling her towards the exit. His grip was firm, his energy frayed and stressed. He was terrified that she'd been caught like this and had no idea if he was going to be able to get her out alive.

"Wait," Jezebel cut in and Mila's heart sank. "I demand an explanation. What is she doing here?"

"She came as a servant," Culis replied coolly. "She's good with the horses, but she was meant to stay outside with the carriage." He shook Mila for dramatic effect. "You disobedient little rat."

"I mean, why was it not *her*?" Jezebel snarled, pointed a perfect, manicured finger directly at Mila's heart.

Culis looked over at the princess and pulled off the most immaculate bit of acting Mila had ever witnessed. His expression was nothing but a perfect balance of confusion and indignation.

"The Divine command asked for the demon on the ship, Princess. It was quite specific."

Jezebel's eyes flashed, realising that something in her plan had gone wrong, and it was too late to fix it. Then she rounded on Jahan. "And why were *you* with her?"

Culis didn't wait around to hear him answer. He continued to push Mila away from the group, grabbing her hand and striding with confidence towards the exit. Mila followed, trying to match his pace, trying desperately not to behave as though she were prey fleeing the roving eye of the hunter. She knew Abbott, at least, was still watching her.

Together, she and Culis stepped over the dead body of the woman by the archway and walked briskly out of the hall and towards their carriage, which sat clear of the traffic.

Standing around it were six guards.

For a moment, Mila's heart plummeted, certain they were about to be arrested, but then she recognised their faces. Nemecca was grinning at her broadly, a streak of black soot across her brow. Corbyn and Arran also gave her a nod of welcome as she approached. Black Berran stood to the rear, and Baird was there too.

What were they all doing here?

When they reached the door of the carriage, Culis all but threw her inside and was halfway in behind her when an enraged cry from the top of the stairs was heard.

"Halt!"

Culis froze, then turned and looked over his shoulder.

Mila saw Abbott through the carriage window, his black robe flowing around him, buffeted by the wind. His old face was stern and unyielding, and the shadows caused by a flickering nearby torch gave him an altogether skull-like visage. He was surrounded by four jesu. Their swords were drawn.

"He's not going to let this go." Culis sighed into the carriage in an exhausted fashion. Then he turned to the High Priest and called back congenially, "High Priest, what can we do for you?" As he stepped back down from the carriage, he shut the door behind him, enclosing Mila within.

"Tell me what is going on, Culis," Mila heard Abbott demand. "It looks to me as though you are fleeing the scene of the crime and taking the culprit with you."

"Fleeing the scene of the... High Priest, in case you hadn't noticed –" Through the window, Mila saw Culis gesture to the archway behind them, which was now swamped by a flood of panicked people who had become brave enough to finally use it. A cloud of golden dust spilled into the air around them, blowing from one of the huge, broken pillars and illuminating the night. It was pandemonium. "The Grand Cathedral has just been attacked. I'm leaving for my own personal safety and taking my asset with me."

"Your asset," the High Priest hissed, "is precisely what I'm here for."

He pointed as he descended the stairs. His jesu went ahead of him and surrounded the carriage on all four sides. Mila shrank down and dropped to the floor, hoping to hide as much of herself as possible so as not to antagonise the situation any further.

She could still hear Abbott through the thin walls of the carriage.

"Hand her over," he demanded in a calm voice that was not accustomed to refusal.

"Why?" Culis challenged plainly, his confidence unshaken.

Abbott's cold fury was palpable. "I am the God-King's own High Priest!"

"And, I note, *not* the God-King himself," Culis replied calmly. "And while I hold great respect for you and your station, High Priest, I am not required to obey you, nor are you entitled to rob me."

"Rob you?!" spluttered Abbott, his calm tone slipping. "Your supposed ownership of the spawn of hell is blatant heresy!"

"My spawn of hell has just appeared before our Almighty God-King, who was not perturbed in the slightest at her presence at his ball, or of my ownership of her. Do you presume to know better than our God-King Midas? Shall I go tell him as such after you slaughter my property, in my own carriage, without cause?"

"She had something to do with that explosion in there. I know it," the priest seethed, his voice a thick, syrupy poison.

"Did she?" Culis's tone was perfectly pitched to mild curiosity. "What did she do?"

There was a long moment of silence. It stretched for an age and made Mila itch with the agony of anticipation.

She still dared not raise her head to see what was occurring outside.

Eventually, she heard the crunch of footsteps on gravel and realised that the jesu had been recalled.

After another few moments of tension, Culis opened the carriage door, looked around for her, nodding grimly when he saw her lying on the floor.

"Stay down," he said quietly, as Arran clucked at the skittish horses.

Mila remained crouched on the floor until the carriage had passed through the gates of the palace, and only then did Culis reach forward and grab her forearm, helping her up to her seat.

"What the hell did you do to that man?" he asked with a small shake of his head.

"Nothing," she said shakily. "Honestly, I had nothing to do with that explosion. I have no idea what happened in there." She was rambling, desperate for him to believe her. "I was in a little hidden room, watching the ceremony like we agreed, and then everything just...exploded!"

"Mila...Mila!" Culis placed his hands on her shoulders to steady her. "It's okay. I know you weren't responsible for that."

"You do?" she asked incredulously. "How?"

"Because – " he looked out the window where they could see the shadows of the six guards sitting on the outside of the rumbling carriage, " – it was us." He tried to give her a controlled smile but couldn't hide the pride he felt entirely.

Mila gaped at him, unable to believe what she was hearing.

He continued. "If that wasn't enough of a distraction for Natalee to slink out of there, then I don't know what would be. Not a perfect plan, by any stretch of the imagination, but it was the best we could do at short notice, and it's unattributable. I'm not sure why Abbott thinks you masterminded it."

"Everything is my fault. My continued existence is an affront to him."

"You're an affront alright." He sighed and ran his hand through his hair, looking at her with a gleam in his eye.

"Why didn't you tell me about your plan?" she demanded.

"I honestly thought you had your own trick up your sleeve!" he replied incredulously. "I truly didn't believe you came along to just watch. We waited until the very last possible second... waiting for *you* to act first." He sighed, rubbed his chin, then chuckled. "I can't believe I let you guilt me into staging a demon rescue and nearly blowing up God."

At that Mila, overcome by adrenaline and hysteria, burst out laughing.

"And," Culis continued, "I can't believe we waited so long to act that we nearly failed!"

Mila howled with laughter, feeling the stress of the night ebbing from her body with each hiccup. It felt amazing and must have been contagious, because she was soon joined by Culis, who wiped tears from his own eyes as the carriage took them back to the manor.

* * *

Over the next few hours that passed quietly in the carriage, Mila mulled over the events of the evening.

She felt both intense hope and a hollow sadness when she thought of Natalee. She desperately hoped the woman had escaped but had no way to know for sure, and she remained horrified that she'd put her friend through this ordeal in the first place.

She also felt a deep sense of satisfaction and victory that she'd been able to convince Culis to recant on his position regarding Natalee's sacrifice. The risks he'd taken tonight to save the demon woman confirmed something he'd apparently been trying to show Mila for a while now – that he indeed had a conscience and a sense of right and wrong.

More than that – he had a heart.

Culis wasn't simply a mould of his abhorrent father. Planning that explosion would have required the careful coordination of many moving parts and people. He'd risked much in executing it. And he'd done it for her.

She studied him as he sat across from her. He was looking out at the stars, his bun had fallen loose in the chaos, and his long curls now sat dishevelled around his high cheekbones and taut jaw. She felt a deep pull towards him but pushed away the strong urge to reach out and trail a hand down the side of his face.

Now is not the time. Think of something else, Mila.

She was elated that the rubane had worked.

Unbeknownst to him, Culis's plan *had* failed, and the explosion had actually occurred a second too late. Natalee should be dead, and Mila, Abbott and Midas himself knew it. And Jahan, she remembered. Jahan now knew too.

Midas's power was vulnerable to rubane, just like the powers of *all* demons. Which meant...Midas was not a god. He was just an extraordinarily powerful demon.

The Church was a lie. The behaviours, their whole society, *everything* was a lie. She'd been shunned by her family for *a lie*.

It was huge. It was overwhelming. It was too much.

Mila promised herself that, tomorrow, after a long sleep, she would carefully consider what her next steps needed to be.

She thought of Jahan.

Dancing with him tonight had felt...wonderful. When he wasn't bogged down in his religious horseshit, there seemed to be something very kindred between the two of them, an energy that felt familiar and strong.

Had he seen the way Midas's power had faltered for that split second? Would that be enough to free him from the clutches of his beliefs? The concept of freeing him and nurturing the person beneath his religious veneer was thrilling, and she smiled as she considered it.

“What are you smiling about?” Culis asked her softly, leaning forward a little.

“I’m so grateful that everything tonight happened as it did,” she replied truthfully. “Thank you for what you did for Natalee.”

“Well, my heart is still racing a little, and I’m sure there'll be an aftermath for us to weather. Our abrupt departure certainly raised at least a few eyebrows. But, for now...you’re welcome. And also...that reminds me. I have something for you.”

Mila looked on in confusion as Culis unexpectedly reached into his breast pocket and drew out a small leather pouch, tied at the top with a thin gold ribbon.

“Finding the perfect bit of jewellery for you has taken some time, and I’m still not sure this one is...quite right. I promise I’ll be more creative with future pieces, but, considering the last piece of jewellery I gave you was that awful necklace...well, this can only be an improvement.”

Mila took the pouch and opened it. Inside it was a small, thin, solid gold hoop. One that matched the hoop glinting in his own ear.

“For you,” he said, tucking her hair behind her left ear so that he could see it properly and inspect the available real estate.

“We’ll match!” she said with a laugh, turning the pretty piece over in her palm, her heart singing. “Thank you. It’s beautiful.” She looked up at him, and he smiled when he saw how earnestly she meant it.

“I was...quite put out when I heard you giving Jezebel a gift tonight,” she admitted reluctantly.

"Really?" he gave a little smile and put his hand back on her knee as he stared at her intently. “You know exactly how I feel about you, and about her. And that was an ugly necklace I found in a pawn shop when we were in Traders Bay. I was actually looking for something for you when I saw that. It reminded me that Jezebel would expect something for her birthday. Thank fates I remembered."

She laughed at that and he leaned in a little closer, still smiling at her, then sniffed and pulled back slightly in confusion. "Did you have wine tonight?"

"I had some wine," she admitted.

"When? In your hidey hole? With the guard?" His tone was teasing initially, but then grew more serious. "Come to think of it, what was that guard doing up there with you? I saw you both come flying out of that ceiling nook."

"Jahan? He...he found me while I was sneaking around in the garden."

"And he didn't arrest you?"

"No, he helped me. He...we...he was something akin to a friend when I lived at the palace."

"Ah." Culis's sharp brain did not take long to put two and two together and he leaned back, smiling a little sourly. "The guard from the dinner party. I understand." He paused for a minute and then let out a long breath. "What a hard life, to be such a striking woman."

Mila rolled her eyes.

"I mean it." Culis leaned forward again and touched her knee so she would feel the truth of his words. "Any lucky sod can be beautiful, but striking is more important, and damn you, but you have both and don't even seem to realise it. The way you hold yourself, your self-assurance, your eyes... It's utterly enchanting. You command a second look every time you enter a room. Or in my case, a third, fourth, a fifth..."

Mila flushed at the intensity of his words and his gaze. There was no joke written in them this time.

"And clearly, Jahan is not immune either."

She sensed a bite of jealously fly through him and she flushed. Culis realised he'd inadvertently shown more of himself than he'd intended, but to his credit he did not pull his hand away.

Mila went to respond, but Arran suddenly opened the door, and the moment was interrupted. They'd arrived. Mila had been so caught up that she hadn't even noticed the carriage had stopped.

Culis stepped out first, holding out his hand to assist her. His touch was warm. His desire running hot. His pride, rough and dangerous. The jealousy had stoked something in him.

They walked up towards the manor side by side, and her mind reached for something to say to him. It was starting to rain. She didn't want Jahan to be the last topic of conversation they shared before they retired.

"Culis?" she said softly as he closed the front door behind them and finally let go of her hand.

"Mmm?" he asked.

"Was it...uncomfortable dancing with me at Reminisciary?"

"What?" He shot her a look of pure confusion, as though this was the last thing he'd been expecting her to say.

"I saw how you danced tonight with Jezebel and...well, it was perfect, and looked fun and fast. That's not how it looked when we danced."

"Mila." Culis shook his head slowly and then abruptly stalked towards her, forcing her to walk backwards with him until her back was pressed firmly against the wall below the staircase. "From what I recall of our dancing," he whispered, his lips an inch away from hers, his hands bundled tightly into her hair, the hard planes of his body pressed fully against her, "it was practically sex. And there's not a moment of that memory I would trade for a single second of any dance, with any other woman in the world."

The energy of his desire mingled with hers and made her gasp for air. Almost without meaning to, she ran her hands up the backs of his shoulders, wanting to pull him down and into her, wanting to feel his bare skin, to push his lips finally, *finally* against her own. She desperately needed to know what they felt like.

Just as she leaned in to close the gap between them, he released her and slipped away, just out of reach.

"No?" she asked in confusion, trying not to let hurt engulf her.

"Not while that necklace remains on your neck," he corrected gently, running his fingers along the object that sat in the hollow of her throat. "I do not kiss my slaves. First thing tomorrow, I will have it removed. And then..." He touched her lips with the tip of his finger. "Then I will be sure you are coming to me freely."

"Oh." She gaped at him. "You'll release me?"

"I hope you'll stay," he said with a nervous smile. "But...I'll understand if you choose to leave."

There was a moment of silence that hung between them, and for half a second, Mila did not know what she would choose.

Culis saw the indecision on her face and stepped away. "Good night, Mila," he said softly.

"Yes...okay... Good night. Sleep well." She backed away from him slowly and then moved towards the corridor, towards her bedroom.

"Yes. Sleep well," he repeated, but he made no move to go further up the stairs. Instead, he watched her with flames in his eyes, burning for her to return to him.

Fates, she wanted to return.

"Good night!" she said again, more loudly than she meant to, forcing herself to turn away, and feeling as she walked, as though every cell in her body was suddenly alight with white, laughing fire.

When she reached her room, Mila changed into a short, comfortable, cotton nightgown and laid down on her bed pallet, eager for sleep to take her.

Infuriatingly, she found that she could only toss and turn uncomfortably. She burned.

Culis.

He wanted to remove the necklace, to free her.

That in itself was amazing. She'd never expected anything like this to transpire for her. Freedom. She would have her life back...and yet, right now, through the haze of lust, it all seemed secondary. The temptation to go up the stairs and follow him into his chambers was too real.

She rolled over in bed, maddened. She was undeniably drawn to him, and despite having had many legitimate reasons to dislike him over the past few months, she knew now that she didn't.

In fact, she liked him a lot.

She liked his humour and his intellect and the way he treated his staff. She liked his ambition, and the creativity with which he conducted his business. And she liked the fact that he liked her, the way he wanted to see her, to know her and understand her. She trusted the energy she felt from him. It felt good. Too good.

No.

Not now. Not tonight. Tonight, she needed to sleep. There'd be time to investigate these feelings and desires she felt for Culis tomorrow.

She breathed through that elation, that anticipation, that nervousness...and let it go. Culis would still be here in the morning, and dwelling on any of her emotions right this minute would not help her sleep.

She closed her eyes again, but her efforts to sleep were thwarted once more by a startling wave of yet more intense emotions: anger, hatred, humiliation. She hated Jezebel. Hated the woman with an intensity that surprised her, unrivalled by anything she'd ever felt before for another living creature. Previously her dislike and fear had been mingled with pity for the princess, but tonight, all pity vanished. If Midas was truly just a demon, then Jezebel had to have known this, or at least suspected it. She would have never felt "half Divine", as she'd always proclaimed. She had enabled her father's lie for her own comfort and status.

The more Mila thought about how the fearsome woman controlled the lives of both Culis and Jahan, the more enraged she became, and she allowed herself to feel all of it, to let it seethe inside her with an intensity she'd never experienced before.

Eventually, though, like all feelings that are allowed to be realised, it slowly began to pass. Mila breathed and let it go. She'd come back to it another time, but for now, she'd done enough processing. She needed to sleep.

She closed her eyes again and tried to clear her mind of all thought. This time, she sought to distract herself from her emotions by attempting a meditation exercise, spreading her awareness away from her body and throughout the manor instead. She hadn't done this exercise in the months since her capture, as the number of people continually bustling around made it difficult to perform. Now, however, in the witching hour of night, with everyone asleep, it was safe for her to let her horns grow, expand her powers, and try to sense as many living things in the giant house as possible.

She caught many things in her mental feelers. Rodents living inside the walls, a useless cat that usually roamed the kitchen pretending to be hard at work during daylight hours. She sensed the sleeping souls of every servant and employee of the manor. Petrie would be up in about an hour to commence preparation for the morning meal, but currently was so deeply asleep he might as well have been dead.

She expanded her powers up to the next level of the house, where she sensed Culis, still a muted energy to her power, but she could register that he was at least there in his room, and she was comforted by that knowledge.

And then, just as she was turning her mind from his room to another, she sensed something entirely odd and alarming.

Someone *else* was in Culis's room.

And whoever it was, was wide awake, and pulsing with murderous intent.

Assassins

Mila ran.

She instinctively seized a small iron saucepan as she passed through the kitchen and sprinted up the corridor. The presence, whoever it was, was burning brightly in her mind, like a bonfire in the woods. She kept her power fixated tightly upon it as she ran and watched in horror as the flame in her mind split into two.

There were *two* of them. Two people moving slowly toward Culis. Predators about to pounce.

Hurry, hurry, hurry.

Her chest and stomach clenched in pain as she flew through the enormous house. Her feet had wings, and adrenaline streaked through her, but it was not going to be enough. She would not be fast enough.

The two fires in her mind moved to either side of where Culis's still presence lay. He did not so much as twitch. He was sound asleep, completely unaware.

She bounded up the flight of stairs, taking them three at a time. The assassins were fixated. They had their target in their sights. They moved with smooth efficiency.

Hurry, for the love of fate.

I'm going to be too late.

She felt the moment the figure on the left strengthened its resolve and lifted a blade above its head.

It was in that moment – screaming like a banshee – that Mila burst into Culis's room, propelling herself through the air, landing atop the giant assassin's head, and smashing the saucepan frantically into his face.

"Assassins!" she screeched as she beat the weight directly into the man's nose. The appendage snapped loudly.

Out the corner of her eye, she saw the second figure make a slicing movement down over the bed.

Culis bellowed in pain, and Mila's heart shattered.

A moment later, two swords clashed against another. Culis had somehow managed to arm himself and was fighting back.

That confirmation was the only attention she was able to give to him as her current predicament grew swiftly more dire. The giant she was atop reached up with the hand that held his knife, the point, fortunately, facing down.

She kicked at it, sending the knife clattering across the floor, then coiled around his neck like a determined snake. She smashed the pan into his face again and again with all her strength, resisting the hand that tried to grab her hair and pull her off, forcing him to release her as he clutched his nose when she aimed for it again.

He tried to punch her, but the angle was awkward, and his blow thudded weakly against her thigh. She slammed the heavy pan into his nose again.

It hit true for a third time, making a wet squelching sound of blood and mangled flesh where a proud nose had once perched.

Clearly in agony, and desperate to dislodge his unexpected passenger, the giant man suddenly backed up and threw himself into the wall, smacking Mila into it headfirst.

Oof.

The air burst violently free from her lungs, and she lost her grip on his head, sliding with a cry to the floor.

The man swiftly turned and kicked her, the blow so intense that she slid across the sleek wooden floor, smacking hard against the floor-to-ceiling window.

Winded, her eyes rolled back in her head. Behind her, she heard a loud crack and became vaguely aware of the glass spider-webbing around her.

She somehow managed to lift her head to dodge a second kick, which had been aimed at her face. The boot overshot its mark and shattered the weakened glass behind her completely.

Instinct more than anything drove Mila to roll backwards, out the newly open window. She landed hard onto the roof below amid broken glass and tiles, but managed to finally regain her breath and scramble to her feet.

The would-be assassin followed, much to her dismay.

The man was huge and bleeding profusely from his face.

He was also very, *very* unhappy with her.

She could feel his murderous rage pulsing, blinded to any thoughts other than those that involved putting her in the ground. The rain that had gently started earlier in the evening was coming down hard now, soaking them both, but also wetting the sloping tiles upon which they stood.

As he advanced towards her, Mila took a few steps backwards, but realised quickly that she was going to have to jump from this roof if she stood even the smallest chance of surviving this encounter. She'd lost the advantage that surprise and the small saucepan in her hand had given her, and Culis wasn't coming to save her. For all she knew, he was already dead.

"You're the demon," the assassin said with a growl.

Mila took the advantage and turned to leap off the roof, committing to a fall that almost certainly would result in broken bones, at a minimum.

But the giant was fast, as well as huge. He lunged forward, catching hold of her arm in a burst of fire and pain that radiated up her shoulder.

"Oh no, you don't," he snarled. "Not that easily."

He hauled her back up onto the roof as though she were a kitten.

When he punched her directly in the face, Mila's world spun and went momentarily black.

When she came to, he was on top of her. Knee on her chest, hands around her neck, choking the life from her.

This is it.

Her hands scrabbled uselessly against his huge mitts. He was so big and strong, he was about to snap her neck in the process of wringing it. She had mere seconds left.

Her desperate hands clawed at his, feebly trying to pull them away.

Suddenly, her power flared and flowed through her skin, into him, touching him, feeling his rage.

Less, her dying, oxygen-starved brain commanded his rage.

Less.

It obeyed.

The strangling pressure around her throat relented, and Mila heaved in air with a hoarse, painful rasp.

The man looked at his hands in confusion, as if unsure what he was doing with them and why.

Mila could feel, incredulously, that his pulsing rage had lessened somehow. The lethal energy had drained out of him, dampened...*by her command.*

Impossible.

Suddenly, she was filled by a surge of ecstasy as the assassin's stolen energy entered *her* body. She gasped with the sheer force of it, the power, the *life force* of someone else being ripped away and stuffed into her own body. It was intoxicating.

Mila felt as though she was glowing, consumed by more light and power than she'd ever known was possible to feel. Her body was so full, she feared it might float off the rooftop and into the sky...

Bang!

Her ecstasy was interrupted by a bloodied and exhausted-looking Culis jumping from the window.

He landed hard on the tiles of the rooftop, brandishing a heavy, lead candlestick in his hands.

The giant heard him land and spun around warily, but too late. The candlestick was already swinging. It caught him square across the face, snapping his neck to the side and spinning him off the roof to his death below.

It all happened in a matter of seconds. Mila stood dumbfounded in the rain, blinking stupidly at the body with the broken neck that lay on the cobbles two storeys below her.

"Mila." Culis's voice broke through her reverie.

When she turned to him, he was reaching a hand out towards her.

She took it, feeling numb. Her brain resisted her attempts to make sense of what had just happened.

The sensation of weightlessness, fearlessness, divinity, ebbed achingly away and left her with little but a body covered in cuts and tiny shards of glass. And the pain of these wounds was nothing compared to her aching throat and hands.

Culis's hand was bloody, but warm. It steadied her. Brought her brain back to ground. He wrapped his other arm around her back and helped her into the room.

Mila clung to him, to the human contact, which brought relief, comfort, and in some small way, disappointment. Whatever that ethereal feeling had been earlier, it'd been the most intense high she'd ever experienced. But it was gone now, just a shadow ebbing in the corner of her mind. She wanted to process everything that had just happened, but she couldn't yet.

The noise from their fight had drawn Culis's guards to his room. When they re-entered the bedroom, Baird was staring at them and the destroyed room in amazement.

"What happened?" he demanded.

Culis pulled Baird aside, but refused to relinquish Mila's hand as he did so, wrapping his fingers tightly around hers. She couldn't hear his exact words to Baird but could make out the curt tone. Baird nodded with a severe expression on his face and then turned and barked orders at the other guards, who had joined them.

They took the body of the dead assassin with them and hurriedly left. All but the healer.

Culis turned back to Mila. "Are you injured?" he asked with obvious concern.

She shook her head, despite the cuts and glass all over her. He was the one who needed urgent medical attention, not her. He was clearly sporting a wound on his right side. There was a lot of blood, and he was grimacing.

The healer scuttled forward to treat him, but Culis still refused to release Mila's hand, forcing the healer to cut away his bloody nightshirt in order to commence tending to the wound.

Concern, protection...love.

"Mila. How did you know they were here?" Culis asked gently, tucking a loose strand of hair behind her ear, staring at her with a wide-eyed look of relief.

"I sensed them," she replied, still trying to catch her breath.

"You can sense from that distance?" His eyes narrowed in confusion, focused only on her, as though his side weren't being scraped clean and sewn back together. "I didn't know that was possible. You're amazing."

"I don't do it often," she admitted. "When too many people are awake, it's draining. But I can scan a room my powers. Which is what I did tonight. I sensed you in bed, asleep. And then I sensed them – " she gestured to the broken window, " – and their intent."

"And you ran to save me," he said gravely. "You *did* save me. If you hadn't leapt on one, I wouldn't have stood a chance. Cowards. Two men against one asleep in his bed. They didn't expect to encounter a demon though." He smiled at her, and Mila couldn't help but return it, although her throat and face hurt when she did so.

Once Culis had been stitched up, she finally allowed the healer to turn his attention to her cuts. Culis only agreed to release her hand when he saw the healer needed to conduct a full inspection of Mila's injuries and ensure all the glass shards had been removed. There wasn't much he could do about the swelling bruises on her face or neck.

Finally, he finished, and Mila turned to look at Culis.

"What now?" he asked.

"I...I think I'd just like to go back to bed," she said softly, through a throat that was becoming sorer by the minute.

"Leave us." Culis dismissed the healer, then approached Mila again, reaching for her slowly, as though afraid to startle her. He was so close she could feel the heat of his body, and the gingery smell of the healer's ointments.

He reached a hand up to her cheek and tilted her face towards his, running a hand gently over her neck, tracing the injury there with fury written all over his face. Mila wanted his gentle touch to continue, so she leaned into it.

"I'm going to find out who did this," he promised. "But for tonight, let me look after you, please."

He waited for her small nod before he took her hand and slowly walked her back down to her small room.

Once there, he became rather businesslike. He stoked the fire until the room became hot again, while she sat shivering on the edge of her bed.

Satisfied with that, in the brisk manner of a nurse, and without ceremony, he stripped her out of her sopping wet nightgown that now clung to her.

He didn't stare or flush at her nakedness, but simply helped place a fresh gown over her head. He then took a towel and ran it over her hair, wringing out the water.

Finally, he herded her over to her small pallet. Once she laid down, he clambered in after her.

"Move over," he whispered.

She obeyed without protest or resistance. Culis slid in close behind her back and pressed his warmth against her, wrapping an arm tightly around her middle and pulling her deeply into his chest.

Despite the heat of his body, Mila began to tremble in earnest, as the shock of her near death hit her. Culis had anticipated this. He tucked her still-damp hair behind her ears and whispered to her as she shook violently inside the circle of his arms.

"You're safe," he repeated over and over. "I have you, you're safe."

Finally, once the intensity of the shaking lessened, Mila rolled to face him, her nose pressed closely into his. "You seem okay?" she queried quietly.

"This isn't the first time I've survived something I shouldn't have."

"I couldn't let you die," she whispered.

"I'm a little surprised that you came to save me," he replied with a small grin.

"Are you really?" she asked incredulously.

"No," he chuckled, "not at all. I intrigue you too much for you to let me die." He bit back a tiny smile that was trying to escape, as if unsure she'd appreciate the humour at a time like this. "Here." He pulled her flush against his warm, hard body, all humour now leaving his face. "I want you to read it all."

Mila had never been so close to him before, and it was intoxicating. She pressed her face closer, into the crook of his neck, where she could feel his pounding pulse against her lips.

Culis cupped his palm behind her head, drawing her close. His energy poured out of him and finally, finally, she was able to reach his depths.

She drank it all in, all of him, his desperation to connect to her, to be truly seen by her. There was no false pretence or plotting found inside him, only a deep need to be seen and loved, a desire, she realised, matched firmly by her own.

She tilted her head up. Their lips were now so close that she felt as though she were breathing him in, could feel every thud of his heart in his chest, beating into her skin, the ragged rhythm of his breathing...

"Mila," he whispered, his voice catching on her name. "I know the necklace, but...tomorrow. I promise. Just. Please. May I?"

"For the love of all things... Just shut up and kiss me, Culis."

And then he finally, *finally* broke whatever semblance of distance remained between them with a slow, long, utterly consuming kiss.

Desperate Measures

Mila woke the following morning curled deeply in Culis's embrace, still encased by his energy, his desire to protect and touch her.

She stirred gently, and when he realised she was awake, he pulled her even closer.

"Good morning, gorgeous," he murmured against her skin.

When he placed a gentle kiss on her lips, Mila felt her body respond instantly. She pulled him in, deepening the kiss and clutching at his shirt, desperately wanting to feel the bare skin underneath. He groaned with delight at her response and pressed himself even more firmly against her, fingers tangling in her hair.

His hands ran down the length of her, brushing over her jaw, her neck, down to her breasts, running his hand gently over one and over her stomach.

Mila arched and her breath hitched. His touch was fire to her skin, setting each nerve alight. She couldn't get enough of him. She wanted to breathe him in.

"Let's go get this accursed necklace off you," Culis whispered hungrily against her ear.

Bang, bang, bang!

A loud knocking at her door startled them both, and Baird's voice made Culis groan with frustration.

"Master Culis, Marcina LaVencia has arrived."

Culis stared down at Mila, and she felt the sharp energy of his regret and disappointment flow through him.

"Ahhh." He kissed her again. "Mila. I'm so sorry, but we have to go meet her. She's here for Flue."

Mila sat up quickly. "For Flue? Can I meet her first?"

"Yes, of course." Culis kissed her again, then regretfully pulled away and left the bed. "To be continued," he said in a low voice, his eyes smouldering. "And we're getting that necklace off. Today."

* * *

Marcina LaVencia was a beautiful woman of indeterminate age, who Culis greeted with a level of familiarity that rankled Mila a little.

"Well, Christopher." She rubbed her hands with anticipation. "I have taken an extraordinary gamble on you and your demons. Paying for one without even knowing who it might be or what their powers are. Tell me. Who and what have I purchased?"

"*Nearly* purchased," Culis corrected. "The demon who has chosen you as their master is Flue," he said with a wave of his hand.

Despite everything she now knew about Culis, Mila's stomach still lurched as Flue was brought into the room on command.

"Flue can cause anyone to become infatuated with them."

Marcina's eyes grew wide. "At will?"

"The opposite, actually. Flue appears to have to make a concerted effort for it *not* to happen."

Marcina stood and walked towards Flue, wonder written all over her face. "Is it happening now?" she asked, half joking, half afraid. "Or am I just overcome with excitement at this prospect?"

"How do you hope to use Flue?" Mila asked curiously, disliking the way the woman was appraising them as though they were cattle at a market.

Marcina glanced at her sharply, and then piercingly at Culis, as though waiting for him to silence his slave.

Culis merely shrugged and gave a little smile. "Convincing Mila is the final step of the sale," he said, astonishing everyone in the room, including Mila.

"Ahh." Marcina's tone became conciliatory. Her voice was deep, eyebrows dark and arched, and her eyes were a brilliant green. Too green to be natural. She must have added some kind of enhancer to them. "You've been a most...influential ambassador for your kind," she purred.

"How do you intend to use Flue?" Mila repeated.

"My dear." Marcina seemed offended that Mila did not know her legacy by sight alone. "I am the head of The Harem. We train and house exclusive courtesans."

In horror, Mila rounded on Culis. "Flue cannot go into a whore house."

"Demon!" Marcina suddenly barked in a scolding tone, then collected herself. "Mila. Do you even know what a courtesan is? Do not denigrate me and my business into the equivalent of a dark dockside rumble." She turned to Flue, with an entirely different, far kinder tone. "My employees are all artists. You will be too. Companions of The Harem are all highly skilled flirts, trained in the art of conversation, the keeping of secrets, and provision of entertainment. Sex is but a very small part of what we offer our clientele. And not only will you be a most invaluable addition...I do believe you'll enjoy yourself. Most of my employees do."

Mila looked at Flue. "You chose this? Was there no better option?"

Flue gazed back at her for a long moment before giving a small shrug. "I...it doesn't sound like the worst way to spend the next ten years. Better perhaps than being golden dust."

"But, Flue..." Mila whispered, feeling the familiar agony of her own guilt.

"Up until I met you, Mila, my life was one of fear and hiding. This...this at least offers something different. It might...it might be okay."

"Precisely!" Marcina gleamed with a clasp of her hands in a somewhat extravagant gesture. "Shall we sign the contracts then?"

Mila still wasn't quite convinced, but Flue's agreement and the fact this had been their choice over other options seemed to be enough for everyone else. So, contracts were signed, and Mila hugged Flue fiercely.

"You're only just over in Traders Bay," she whispered. "It's not that far, and we are there often with Culis's business. I will ensure we see one another as often as business permits. You're not alone."

Flue nodded, looking nervous but determined, and then they were gone.

Culis stood alone with Mila in the room, glowing with pleasure. "It's happening," he breathed. "It's working."

"Was a courtesan really the best offer for Flue?" she challenged. "Surely, there were others. I sense your hand in this decision."

"Flue will be fine," Culis assured her. "Marcina is not a cruel woman, and Flue's power will ensure that they're never pushed beyond the boundaries of what they wish to do. I will take you there to visit them in a month, and if Flue is desperately unhappy, then I promise I will invoke one of the loopholes in the contract and refund

Marcina for their return. But Flue won't be unhappy, I guarantee it. I would not have sold them into a situation they weren't well equipped to handle – and believe me, there were a number of unsuitable purchasers who offered quite a bit more than Marcina did. Flue got to meet them all, and we had robust discussions on who would and wouldn't be suitable for them."

Mila wasn't sure how she felt about the other demons being referred to as "our" demons, but it did give her some relief to know that Culis had been discretionary about who he offered Flue's contract to, and that he'd given Flue the power to make the final decision on the matter.

"Once again, you just have to trust that I know what I'm doing," Culis said, watching her face as she processed the information. "Even though I know I'm just a piece of scum..." He let that float between them.

"Hmm," Mila said softly, but couldn't hide her smile.

"Mila." Culis's gaze grew deeply intense, and he walked over to her, catching her shoulders with both hands.

His closeness reminded her immediately of where they'd left things that morning, and it made her stomach draw in tightly in anticipation.

"I know it's not a traditional way of improving the conditions for anyone. But I truly believe this will work. We'll look back in time on this day as a momentous one."

The earnestness and openness of his energy matched his expression completely. He believed in what he was saying, in what they were doing. He looked at her in a way she'd never seen him look at anyone or anything before. It was as though he'd thrown away the cloak of what it meant to be the infamous Christopher Culis of the Artor Trading Company and stood before her now, simply as a man, wanting to be believed, trusted and understood. He seemed vulnerable somehow, as though he was opening to her a part of himself that he barely even recognised.

It was beautiful, she realised. Beautiful to witness.

Suddenly, all she wanted was to kiss him again, to be reminded of what he tasted like. She leaned forward –

"Why is this day momentous?" A sharp, feminine voice from the doorway broke the spell.

Culis and Mila whirled in shock at the intrusion.

Jezebel.

Culis released Mila and stepped away quickly. It was the worst thing he could have done.

The abrupt movement was not missed, and the princess's eyebrows narrowed in suspicion and rage. "I. Knew. It." Jealousy permeated her every word. "I *knew* that something was amiss. Someone open a window, because it *reeks* of betrayal in here."

"Jezebel, there's nothing – " Culis tried, but he was swiftly silenced.

"Enough! To think I came all the way here to apologise, to degenerate myself," Jezebel shrilled. "I thought I'd made a mistake when I woke this morning, hoping the men I'd sent to kill you had failed. But now I see this – " she gestured at the space between the two of them, " – and regret that the thought of your death gave me pause for even a second! My instincts were correct!"

She sent the assassins, Mila realised, and saw Culis stiffen as he came to the same conclusion.

It became fully apparent then, the full extent of the danger they were in. Jezebel's emotions were so frayed that her behaviour was bordering on lunacy. She'd been so hurt by his abrupt departure from the ball that she'd sent *assassins* after him.

They were all teetering on the edge of her insanity, and Culis's long game with her was almost entirely to blame.

"I just sold a demon," Culis interjected as quickly as he could. "That is why it's a momentous day, princess, nothing more."

Mila registered with a chill that he'd returned to using her formal title. Culis hardly ever used her royal title when they were alone together. Using it now revealed more than anything else that he was frightened, and that knowledge frightened Mila even more.

"I walked in on you *holding her*!" Jezebel screeched, her voice pitched higher than usual in her blind, hurt rage. "And last night, you left me alone at my *own ball* after we'd been attacked because you wanted to save your *precious* demon. Everyone saw, including my father. I was *humiliated!*" She screamed out the last word, letting it echo through the room and out into the corridor.

Culis's sudden backhand against Mila's already battered face came out of nowhere. She cried out as she fell to the floor. It hadn't been the painful action, so much as that the unexpected violence had been shocking.

She hated that tears rose unbidden to her eyes. She blinked through them, looking up in shock to see Culis moving to Jezebel, who was also gaping at what had just happened.

Culis's desired outcome had been achieved. His slap had momentarily driven the wind out of Jezebel's tantrum. She allowed Culis to reach for her, pulling her hips against him.

But when he tried to kiss her, she held her shoulders away.

"My love," he pressed. "You know better than anyone that I am a selfish man, driven by greed. You knew this when you brought me into your bed and your life. You did not turn away then in fear or insecurity but embraced me for my nature. Now...I am not proud of the fact that the need to protect my asset came ahead of my feelings for you last night; however, you cannot expect my nature to change overnight into a...considerate and devoted partner. I don't know if it's possible for me to truly love another...but so much as I am able, I love you."

Culis turned the angle of embrace slightly so he could glance behind Jezebel and see Mila on the floor from the corner of his eye. She saw the panicked query flash across his face for a split second.

Is it enough? he was asking. *Are we safe?*

In response, she instinctively scanned Jezebel's energy. The princess's rage had softened at his words, but there was still a fierce hardness bubbling inside her.

Mila shook her head. He needed to do more.

Culis understood and ploughed on in honeyed tones. "You're a woman unlike any other I have ever met. You understand my nature because yours matches mine perfectly. I had hoped that, because of this, you might turn out to be the only woman in the world who could possibly understand when my self-absorption overrides my ability to act in your best interests. Much in the same way I understand your need to express your unhappiness towards me in...unusual and frightening ways. I don't hate you for sending the assassins. I... I love you for that."

Jezebel hiccoughed a laugh through tears at that last part, and from the floor Mila could barely believe what she was witnessing. This silver-tongued man was talking his way out of Jezebel's wrath and back into her favour.

Mila felt Jezebel's intent to destroy them begin to melt away as she ingested his words. She also sensed that Jezebel was particularly pleased by the fact that Mila was on the floor crying, so Mila made an effort to sob freely and loudly.

But it was not quite enough.

Mila had spent months honing her ability to read Jezebel into an acute beam. She knew every minuscule nuance about the woman.

And right now, she knew, despite the fact that she had been mollified, Jezebel's next words would be devastatingly flippant, with catastrophic consequences. It would be a demand of some kind, an assurance of Culis's love for her, a way for him to prove it once and for all. Probably a demand that he commit some form of violence on Mila, disfigure her somehow. They weren't safe yet.

Culis still needed to do more.

She urgently inclined her head upward again. Culis grimaced for half a second in acknowledgement of her message, before he dropped to his knee.

To the complete shock of everyone in the room, he placed his hand on his heart. "Jezebel, my love is not a perfect love, but I offer it, and myself, to you without reservation. Will you marry me?"

Mila's mouth dropped open, and her blood turned cold.

Jezebel's eyes bulged, then narrowed with suspicion. "You want to be a prince," she accused.

"I want nothing more than to run my company and have you by my side as my wife. I will swear off my claim to any royal title."

Mila felt realisation slowly fill Jezebel's body. Her face began to illuminate with joy. An open happiness radiated from her, so pure and strong that even in the midst of Mila's anguish, she couldn't help but feel terrible for her.

Despite the turmoil of the moment, she was once again struck by the sad truth of Jezebel's life. The woman had no friends, and whether Midas was a god or not, it was undeniable that Jezebel had been raised in a world with no one to love and no one who loved her back. She had grown up feared, adored, reviled, worshipped and, ultimately, alone and miserable. Culis's proposal meant something to her that had never been offered before – unconditional love, from someone who purported to see her flaws and love her anyway.

With her power focused on Jezebel, Mila felt the very moment that Culis's gesture hit home. Something hard broke inside Jezebel. Her cold heart opened a crack and warmth spilled out.

She flung herself onto him, arms wrapped passionately around his neck, her beautiful face awash with emotion.

"I will marry you," she whispered hoarsely, then poured herself into their kiss.

Epilogue

Abbott was not happy.

He stood beside Midas in the Grand Cathedral, quietly surveying the destruction from the dais. Golden Sand blew throughout the hall, around their sandals, into their hair. Fifty acolytes worked furiously, trying desperately to collect it all and stop it from twirling around in the small gusts that billowed throughout the great space.

The broken glass pillars would need to be replaced, as would the flooring of the dais. The expensive mosaic would have to be redone.

"Come," Midas said softly.

Abbott obediently followed the God-King away from the chaotic scene and back to his personal apartments, where they could finally talk, alone.

"Who do you think is responsible?" Midas demanded as he reached for a tall, thin pitcher and poured himself a flask of wine.

"I don't know yet." Abbott sat down on a plush settee and put his head in his hands. He was exhausted. "But, publicly, we should blame those separatists, the Children of Midas. That'll take the wind out of their sails for a while."

It grated deeply at Abbott that Midas had been quiet about the dissidents ever since they'd reared their heads. He could have shut them and their entire infernal doctrine down with a single word, and yet, for reasons known only to himself, he continually ignored Abbott's requests to do so.

"I disagree. That would only derail the effort to find the real culprits," the God-King said with a dismissive wave of his hand.

Abbott bristled. He watched as Midas settled himself comfortably in another seat and gazed out the window.

Abbott wondered if they were going to discuss the mishap that had occurred at the sacrifice, just prior to the explosion, or if Midas would simply ignore it and pretend it never happened.

He could barely believe it himself. Had Midas's powers truly not worked on the demon?

The more Abbott thought about it, the more he realised that the explosion had actually been a blessing in disguise. He had no idea what he would have done – what *Midas* would have done – if the entire crowd at the ball had seen the demon standing defiant to his touch. It would have brought everything tumbling down. Such an occurrence had never happened before...and could not be allowed to happen again.

Midas seemed to be thinking about it too. "Did we apprehend the sacrifice?" he finally asked.

"Unfortunately, not," Abbott replied through gritted teeth, rankled by the failure. "She escaped in the chaos."

"How did she resist my touch?" Midas mused aloud, looking at his hands in fascination. "It was as though her very skin was made of these gloves."

Not for the first time, Abbott desperately wished that Midas had not killed the man who'd kindly made him the gloves all those years ago, at least not before finding out what they were made of, but he said nothing. Midas already knew his feelings about the matter.

What he said instead was, "It's imperative that we find and interrogate her. I have jesu on the hunt as we speak. We need to know if she is simply an anomaly with a protective power, or if her ability to resist your touch was a more deliberate act. If it's the former, then we have very little to worry about, but if it's the latter, that's a far bigger problem."

Abbott couldn't unsee the look of hope and relief he'd seen on the face of that other demon, Culis's demon. He wanted to tell Midas about it, but her continued existence was already such a sore topic between them that he hesitated. Allowing his daughter to torture the creature for her own entertainment had been one thing, but allowing her continued survival in the employ of that trader? Permitting her to leave the ball after the explosion? Abbott didn't understand these decisions at all. It went against everything he thought they'd tried to accomplish over the past four decades.

Why Midas had suddenly decided this particular demon was permitted to live and breathe so openly in their midst was a mystery, and even more infuriating was the fact that he would suffer no questions about it.

"If that female is resistant to my magic, you will bring her to me alive."

Abbott noted the hunger on Midas's face and barely restrained himself from rolling his eyes. They might uncover someone who could destroy the fabric of the Church they'd created, and all Midas could think about was finally bedding a woman he could touch with his bare hands. It would have been comical if it wasn't so stupid.

"I will do my best to find her. Never fear, little brother." Abbott stood up and walked to the door. "You know I'll always do whatever it takes to protect you."

Midas nodded and then groaned as he leaned back with a sigh of exhaustion that seemed to carry the weight of the world. He closed his eyes and drained his flask.

Abbott spared his limp form a parting glance as he pushed open the heavy wooden door. "The Church must be protected at all costs," he muttered, closing the door behind him.

Acknowledgements

This book certainly didn't find its final form in isolation.

A huge thank you to all my original and beta readers: Katherine, Trevor, Corinna, Raven, Rosie, Danielle, Sara, other Sara, Vindhya and Rhearne. The detail and thought you put into your reviews were enormously helpful and well above what I expected to receive.

An enormous thank you to the literary power couple Oscar and Emma, who always had time to dissect in detail and be as invested in my plot as I was. I genuinely could not have done this without you. And to Scott, who cracked open the heart of Heretic Behaviour in order to help me give it more soul.

To Ricky, not just for your highly entertaining theatrical readings, but for providing me with such a safe, easy and supportive environment to knuckle down and actually get this done. I love you.

To my mum, who read every draft with more relish and vigour than I could have ever believed possible.

Thank you to my editor Shannon Cave for your thoughtful reviews and comments, and my illustrator Kelley Guthauser for the beautiful work you did on the cover.

Finally, thank you to the community of friends, family and coworkers who have supported me on this journey with unprecedented enthusiasm. I am beyond honoured to count you all in my circle and have you along for the journey with me.

About the author

Elyse Catherine Glynn lives in Australia and has been writing fantasy since she was ten years old. She decided to finally pursue the passion seriously in 2024 and left her full-time work as a captain in the Australian Army to dedicate herself fully to publishing her debut novel, *Heretic Behaviour*.

As a teenager she went to a conservative religious school, and as a result, has spent much of her adult life deconstructing religion and its influences. She has lived in the Netherlands, Wales, the USA and all around Australia, but now lives with her partner and cat in the beautiful Scenic Rim of Queensland. She loves nature and has spent many days waltzing around the Australian outback, seeking inspiration and magic. Elements from all of the above can be found in this work.

When she's not writing or reading, she can generally be found busking, watching hours of 'Fundie Snark' on YouTube, freaking herself out by listening to too many true crime podcasts, or applying to go on *Australian Survivor*.

She can be contacted on social media on the following handles:

TikTok: @ecglynn

Threads/Instagram: @elyse.glynn

Facebook: E.C. Glynn - Author

www.ingramcontent.com/pod-product-compliance
Lightning Source LLC
Chambersburg PA
CBHW030341310726
48979CB00001B/131
* 9 7 8 1 7 6 3 6 7 6 4 3 5 *